CASSILDA'S SONG

TALES INSPIRED BY ROBERT W. CHAMBERS' KING IN YELLOW MYTHOS

Also from Chaosium

Lovecraftian Fiction

The Antarktos Cycle
Arkham Tales
Atomic Age Cthulhu (Coming Soon)
The Book of Eibon
Cthulhu's Dark Cults
Eldritch Chrome
Frontier Cthulhu
The Hastur Cycle
The Innsmouth Cycle
The Ithaqua Cycle
The Klarkash-Ton Cycle
Madness on the Orient Express (New)
The Necronomicon
The Nyarlathotep Cycle
Steampunk Cthulhu
The Strange Cases of Rudolph Pearson by William Jones
Tales out of Innsmouth
The Tsathoggua Cycle
Twice Upon an Apocalypse (Coming Soon)
The Xothic Legend Cycle
The Yith Cycle

Weird Fiction Collections

The Complete Pegana by Lord Dunsany
Eldritch Evolutions by Lois Gresh
Mysteries of the Worm by Robert Bloch
The Terror & Other Stories by Arthur Machen
The Three Impostors & Other Stories by Arthur Machen
The White People & Other Stories by Arthur Machen
The Yellow Sign and Other Stories by Robert W. Chambers

Science Fiction

A Long Way Home
Extreme Planets

Horror

Edge of Sundown (Coming Soon)
Once Upon an Apocalypse
Undead & Unbound

Occult Texts

The Book of Dyzan

CASSILDA'S SONG

TALES INSPIRED BY ROBERT W. CHAMBERS' KING IN YELLOW MYTHOS

BY

MOLLY TANZER, DAMIEN ANGELICA WALTERS, HELEN MARSHALL,
MAURA MCHUGH, CHESYA BURKE, S.P. MISKOWSKI,
ANN K. SCHWADER, LYNDA E. RUCKER, LUCY A. SNYDER,
AND OTHERS

Cassilda's Song
Edited by Joseph S. Pulver, Sr.
Cover Illustration © 2015 Steve Santiago.
Cover model photographed by Marcus J. Ranum.
The Yellow Sign created by Kevin Ross.
Cover and Interior Design by Nicholas Nacario.
Cassilda's Song is published by Chaosium Inc.
This book is copyright © 2015 by Chaosium Inc.; all rights reserved
All stories are original to this collection.
All material © 2015 by Chaosium Inc. and the authors.
Similarities between characters in this book and persons living or
dead are strictly coincidental.
www.chaosium.com.

CONTENTS

Introduction *by Joseph S. Pulver, Sr.* 7

Black Stars on Canvas, a Reproduction in Acrylic
by Damien Angelica Walters 11

She Will Be Raised a Queen *by E. Catherine Tobler*............ 25

Yella *by Nicole Cushing*...................................... 37

Yellow Bird *by Lynda E. Rucker* 45

Exposure *by Helen Marshall* 55

Just Beyond Her Dreaming *by Mercedes M. Yardley* 69

In the Quad of Project 327 *by Chesya Burke* 85

Stones, Maybe *by Ursula Pflug*................................ 97

Les Fleurs du Mal *by Allyson Bird* 109

While The Black Stars Burn *by Lucy A. Snyder* 119

Old Tsah-Hov *by Anya Martin* 129

The Neurastheniac *by Selena Chambers* 143

Dancing the Mask *by Ann K. Schwader* 161

Family *by Maura McHugh*...................................... 169

Pro Patria! *by Nadia Bulkin*................................. 181

Her Beginning is Her End is Her Beginning
by E. Catherine Tobler and Damien Angelica Walters.......... 195

Grave-Worms *by Molly Tanzer* 221

Strange is the Night *by S.P. Miskowski* 237

Author Biographies 255

UNMASKED FIRE
BY JOSEPH S. PULVER, SR.

Along the shore the cloud waves break,
The twin suns sink beneath the lake,
The shadows lengthen
    In Carcosa.

Strange is the night where black stars rise,
And strange moons circle through the skies
But stranger still is
    Lost Carcosa.

Songs that the Hyades shall sing,
Where flap the tatters of the King,
Must die unheard in
    Dim Carcosa.

Song of my soul, my voice is dead;
Die thou, unsung, as tears unshed
Shall dry and die in
    Lost Carcosa.

Cassilda's Song in "The King in Yellow"
Act 1, Scene 2.

The black stars are up.
Upon the shore of madness, the cloud waves break.
The thunder of her song rises.
Cassilda is an avalanche.
From the breast of experience, from the shadows and tatters of the mind wounded, come the laughter and the tears now grasped by the fallen leaves of Trakl's autumn. Cassilda's complicated sisters, unwill-

ing to be hidden away and boarded up, sound the thunder. Hot and colorful, in full view and shaded by the aroma of discord, they stand before you unmasked.

No mere *True Detective* fans, they have gone back to (fallen literary titan) Robert W. Chambers' 1895 weird fiction collection, *The King in Yellow* ('*…a series of vaguely connected short stories having as a background a monstrous and suppressed book whose perusal brings fright, madness and spectral tragedy, really achieves notable heights of cosmic fear.*'—H. P. Lovecraft), in search of heart and soul, device and detail, and returned transformed by the cosmic horrors lurking behind the Yellow Sign. Within the four core *King in Yellow* tales, "The Repairer of Reputations", "The Mask", "The Court of the Dragon", and "The Yellow Sign", Cassilda's daughters found spectral tragedy, dread, madness, and 'dark hints' into the *anti-prudence* yearnings of the Other Victorians, and steeped in and empowered by Chambers' timeless renderings, they allowed the unsettling, dark menace of his decadence to soar.

The 1895 release of Chambers' best-remembered work of *weird fiction* was salted with nihilism and ennui, and ripe with *derangement*, haunting beauty, and eerie torments. Poe's influence was present in the core tales and one could easily argue Chambers may have been influenced by the French Decadents and the disquieting transfigurations of the Symbolists. All this and more can be said of the works collected in this anthology. Carcosa, accursed and ancient, and cloud-misted Lake of Hali are here. The Hyades sing and the cloud waves break in these tales. The authority of Bierce's cosmic horror is here. The talismantic Yellow Sign, and the titular 'hidden' King, and The Imperial Dynasty of America, will influence and alter you, as they have the accounts by these writers. Cassilda and other unreliable narrators, government-sponsored Lethal Chambers, and the *many* mysteries of the *mythical* Play, are boldly represented in these tributes to Chambers.

Of Chambers' female characters, Frederic Tabor Cooper said, "They are all of them what men like to think women to be, rather than the actual women themselves." Not so here, for the Sisters of the Yellow Sign have brought their talents (and important, dynamic talents they are—*many* women are at the heart of the *Weird Renaissance* we are currently delighting in) and visions to center stage. Come. Delight! Not content to be seamstresses and cleaning ladies and set dressers, the contributors to *Cassilda's Song* have claimed the canon and are now the lead actors; they have created the sets and stages and written the dialogue. They control the productions.

There are no pretenders here. The Daughters of the Yellow Sign, each a titan of unmasked fire in their own right, have parted the curtains. From Hali's deeps and Carcosa's gloomy balconies and Styx-black towers, come their lamentations and rage and the consequences of intrigues and follies born in Oblivion. Run into their embrace. Their carriages wait to take you from shadowed rooms and cobblestones to The Place Where the Black Stars Hang.

Have you seen the Yellow Sign? The Daughters of Carcosa know its message, every wound and poison, and are about to reveal its gravity to you.

Have your covert desires ridden the currents of the River of Night's Dreaming? They are about to.

Cassilda is burning, threatening… The knots and scars of her plans and schemes, her choices, the path to the doorsteps cracked by the clock and the rain, are full of memories and fear. She cries your name. Come, the thunder rises. There is a song of beauty, of power—a cascade of heartthrobbing passions, in the air.

Upon the shore of madness, Cassilda walks—*UNMASKED*!

Joe Pulver
Berlin
May 2015

Black Stars on Canvas, a Reproduction in Acrylic
by Damien Angelica Walters

This is how it begins: a rumor, a whisper, a story. The stuff of urban legends, a tale told between glasses of absinthe, fragrant curls of smoke from clove cigarettes, tangled legs; the words never spoken too loud or too sure.

Neveah doesn't remember the first time she heard it, which probably says more about her state of intoxication at the time rather than her memory. She only knows that she's heard it enough to decree it nothing more than wishful thinking, even if it is a good story.

What artist hasn't dreamed of a patron's notice? A patron who can change the shape of your life from one shitty bartending job after another, from galleries of splintered wood floors and the smell of mildew not quite concealed by the heavy aromas of patchouli and body odor, to long days spent in front of an easel with no worry that the electricity will cut off, to bright spotlights, champagne in crystal flutes, pearl necklaces, and fat checkbooks carried by those who need art for their summer houses, their mistresses' cottages, their ski chalets.

But a patron who requires an audition, the details of which are never spoken, only alluded to with vague mentions of stars, suns, and masks, is a fairy tale of impossibility. Still, or because of it, the tale is told, and told, and told.

Some of the rumors add that the audition is not just for a patron, but for perfection. Walk through a good artist, come out a great; enter a great, exit a genius.

Neveah finds that even harder to believe, thinks the whole thing is like the game she played as a child—telephone—where the final message ends up bearing no resemblance to the one at the beginning.

This is also how it begins: an invitation slipped beneath the door, heavy card stock, a blank envelope containing neither name nor address, an embossed symbol at the center of the enclosed card, a symbol done in brush strokes of yellow—a hideous, bilious yellow that inexplicably sets Neveah's teeth on the verge of grinding molars into enameled dust. A yellow that hurts her eyes if she focuses on it too long, which is ridiculous because it's just a color, but it's a color full of wrong. Her fingers tremble and her heart flutters bird-quick in the bone cage of her ribs.

One word on the back of card, in small, simple lettering: *unmask*.

The air rushes from Neveah's lungs with a whoosh and she presses the flat of her palm against the wall to stay upright. She traces the symbol with her thumb, reads the word again, sinks to the floor with her back against the wall.

An invitation with no address, no indication of when or how or what isn't an invitation at all, but she knows it is. Knows in her gut it isn't a joke, but a cipher. Something to be untangled. Fitting, albeit frustrating. The most appreciated successes are the most hard won.

She closes her eyes, tries to remember everything she's heard, but when you hear something enough, you stop listening. The only thing she remembers for certain is that everyone calls the patron the Yellow King, but she's never heard his real name mentioned. Not surprising, though, that a patron would hide their identity to keep every artist in town from knocking at their door, playing sycophant and darling in hope of notice. Once or twice she thinks she heard that the auditions are held in Carcosa, which she assumes is the name of his house or more likely, since it has a name, his *estate*, but how can she count on any of it to be true when up until now she's thought it all a pretty bedtime story?

A false beginning: a glass of wine, a sketch pad, a sharpened pencil, the invitation. A symbol, a color, and a word aren't much to go on, but the answer to the puzzle has to be buried somewhere inside, has to be part of the audition.

Neveah first holds the card up to her brightest light, looking through the symbol, hoping to see words perhaps hidden within. She sees nothing, which doesn't surprise her; it wouldn't possibly be that easy, and she's embarrassed that she even tried.

She forces herself to stare at the symbol, fighting a strange instinct to turn away and a slippery, squirming sensation in her belly. Tries to commit the curves and lines to memory, but when she looks away the image escapes. Yet she feels it there, pricking at the back of her mind but refusing to come forward.

Strange, this.

Strange, this entire process.

She takes up her pencil and begins to sketch while casting frequent glances from card to paper. When she finishes, the symbol on her sketch pad is not the same as that on the card, not even close, which doesn't make sense. She tries again on a fresh sheet of paper, and again, the same result, as if the symbol itself resists replication.

Her head aching, she tosses her pencil aside. How in the hell do you begin when you don't know where to start or with what? It's illogical and cruel and setting her up for failure.

Another beginning: a blank canvas, a palette, tubes of yellow paint, her studio—the spare bedroom in her tiny rented townhouse in a neighborhood occupied by other starving artists of varying talents and successes, struggling actors, models with achingly long, thin limbs; a steady rush of bodies always on the move, but with that curious bonhomie created by a common drive, desire, and often a touch of madness, sweet like honey on the tongue.

Neveah mixes Cadmium Yellow, Yellow Ochre, Naples Yellow, a touch of Burnt Sienna, a tiny speck of Olive Green. She blends, holds the palette next to the invitation, adds more Yellow Ochre. Blends again. Winces at the color. The ugliness, the sense of wrongness. It calls to mind hospital hallways, bile, subcutaneous fat, bilirubin, gonorrhea discharge, Pantone 379.

When finally she's lost count of how many colors she's added or how much, the color on her palette appears a near perfect match, but on the canvas, not so.

She scrapes the palette clean, mixes again. The same resulting mismatch which is absurd because she's always had an eye for color. Give her any painting by any artist and she can replicate the colors or come so close that the naked eye sees no deviation.

Here though, the mismatch is obvious. Her canvas doesn't have that same effect on her gaze, doesn't make her cringe. It's ugly, to be sure, but the wrong kind of ugly. She hurls a tube of paint across the room and stands with her hands on her hips and her lower lip held tight between her teeth.

In the beginning was the word: six letters, two syllables. Unmask, the word like a totem on her tongue. And what is unmasking? Peeling off a façade, revealing the real. Isn't that what art is, though, when it comes down to it? A version of real that lives within the artist.

And how does an artist unmask, but by painting. She grins, rubs her palms together, but it seems like a far too easy solution, and it doesn't give her any indication of the specifics of the audition. Then again, she's never met the Yellow King. Maybe this is the audition: will she focus her efforts on the card or will she simply paint?

Clever, maddening, or an obvious and wrong path? She pulls her hair into a loose ponytail. Only one way to find out.

She prepares her favorite colors: Rose Madder for passion, Manganese Violet mixed with Flake White for longing, Viridian with veins of Mars Black for tangled thoughts, Payne's Grey for despair, a touch of Cerulean for hope. With a blank canvas in front of her, her palette tucked in the crook of her arm, and a brush in hand, she closes her eyes, finds the piece in her mind that wants to be made real.

The studio fills with the sound of bristles on canvas as Neveah slips into that curious fog of paint and brush, the emotions bubbling up and taking shape. After a time, she scrapes away the Cerulean and the Violet on her palette, squeezes more Grey, Black, and Viridian.

The painting is unlike anything she's done before. It's a landscape, but one in ruin, with crumbling buildings, cobblestone streets, and improbably, a hazy sky filled with black stars and a sun. It's ugly and gives a sensation of desolation, but it feels right.

As she turns to set aside her palette, she catches movement from the corner of her eye. There, near the edge of the canvas, a hint of yellow. One glance at the palette assures her she didn't use any yellow, but it's there, the same ugly shade as on the invitation.

The studio fills with the sound of fabric rustling over cobbles. Neveah's brush clatters to the floor; she turns her hands palms up. A sense of dislocation rushes over her and her ears go thick and muffled. In that strange baffling, the rustling noise is louder and moving closer. Inside her, deep inside, she feels something opening, a doorway leading out? In? To?

She feels silk brush against her skin, pulling her in (where?), wrapping her in warmth like the afterglow of a perfect orgasm. An exquisite sensation of spiraling into perfection. Her back arches, her lips part. Time bifurcates—she is standing in her studio, she is floating weightless elsewhere—and then fades. She drifts, sinking down and down and—

The door slams shut, sound turns back to right, and she staggers back, panting. Although the room isn't cold, she shivers, and beads of sweat dot her brow, the small of her back, between her breasts.

"Hello?" she says, her voice a thready whisper, but if someone else was near, they're gone now.

She touches a hand to her clammy chest, but the sensation of opening is long gone, too, replaced with a hard knot of hollow. She tries to summon the doorway, the sensation, back, but it refuses, yet she feels as if she's made progress and it feels like a beginning at least. She hopes it's the right one.

Interlude I, the tattered edges of a beginning: Neveah overheard a name once in a snippet of conversation at a party, and she wasn't eavesdropping, merely on her way to the restroom; she paused only for a moment when she heard the word audition and a name.

Maybe she misheard, but she remembers the eyes widened in alarm and the silence when they realized she was listening so she doesn't think so.

※

This, too, is a beginning: a blank canvas propped against an easel, a palette with tiny mounds and craters of paint—an alien landscape of nascency, a selection of brushes, a tin of solvent, ambient music taking shape in the air.

Neveah tips her head from side to side, rolls her shoulders. She props the painting of the strange landscape on an easel next to the blank canvas and double-checks the colors on her palette. In spite of the yellow in the painting, since she didn't use the color when she created the landscape, she's not using any this time either. She isn't sure if that's the right choice to make or not; she's going by instinct alone and has to trust that it knows what it's doing. And anyway, she already knows she can't mix its match.

She selects a brush and begins. Two hours later, she stands in front of the easel with her brow creased and her mouth downturned. There's no sensation of a doorway opening, of slipping away. She touches her chest, grimacing at the spot of emptiness within.

The proportions of her replica are all wrong. From a distance, they seem fine, but a closer view reveals that the stars are slightly out of shape, the sun not perfectly round, the haze in the sky too subdued, the cobbles out of place, and there's no hint of yellow anywhere. She steps backward and forward several times to be sure.

She runs a hand across her forehead, pulls both paintings from their easels and sets them against the wall. Side by side, the differences remain the same: not noticeable when standing halfway across the room; glaringly obvious when two feet away. It reminds her of trying and failing to replicate the symbol and the specific yellow color and she's terrified that she had one chance and blew it completely.

※

Interlude II, finding a thread to a beginning: a party, artists Neveah knows, artists she doesn't, coolers filled with beer, a table crowded with bowls of potato chips, plates of sliced veggies, store-bought hummus.

She moves through the room, engaging in conversations and laughter. Drops the overheard and remembered name into a few. No one recognizes it, but later, shoved into her hand by someone who vanishes into the crowd—a scrap of paper with the name and a phone number.

※

Of such beginnings: Three canvases, three replicas, not one a match to her original, and the doorway remains closed.

※

Interlude III, a beginning that is not: a phone call, the space between rings that feels like taffy pulled out of shape, the hitch in the breath when a ring cuts off and a husky voice says, "Hello."

"Is this Ivy Milland?" Neveah asks with one hand fisted between her breasts.

"Yes."

"I'm Neveah Scott, a friend of Simon's. Simon Phillips? You don't know me but I was given your name by another friend, and I was hoping you'd be able to tell me about the, the audition. I got an invitation but I'm not sure what I'm supposed to do. I'm not trying to cheat, but if you have any advice…"

There's a harsh intake of breath. Neveah gnaws on a cuticle. Should she have said who the audition was with? Does Ivy even know what she's talking about?

"Don't do it," Ivy finally says, her voice gone even deeper.

"But I—"

"That's my advice, my only advice. Don't fucking do it. Throw out the invitation and forget you ever had it."

Then silence on the line.

"Dammit." Neveah tosses her phone aside. Steeples her fingers beneath her chin. Glares at the paintings resting against the studio wall.

The next beginning: paint, brush, and canvas. Neveah paces back and forth in front of her original painting, studying the details in sidelong glances. Madness is repeating the same thing over and over, expecting a new result. She taps the brush handle against her lips and steps close to the original. Runs her hand along the edge; feels a faint vibration in her chest.

She crouches down and eyes the details at the edge—half of a building, a mix of whole and split cobbles, the left side of a star. Maybe…

She slides the blank canvas next to the original, begins with the other half of the star, and spreads out from there, extending, not replicating, the landscape. Time slips as she gives herself over to the steady rhythm of her brush and the pauses to add and mix the paint—a symphony of creation, of beginning.

When she finishes, the world muffles its sound and the doorway begins to open. As it does, details of the new painting stand out in stark relief—a blade of dying grass pushing up from the dirt between two cobbles, the jagged edge of a broken pane of glass, the shadowed branches of a stunted tree. The noise of fabric moving across cobblestone breaks through the muffling and on the first painting, the bit of yellow is larger, large enough to see that it's the hem of a robe or a similar garment and for a split second, she sees the fabric ripple.

Then she slips down and into nothing, into everything. Silk on skin, an embrace of warmth—pleasure, perfection, transcendence. Whispers touch her arms, as if tasting her flesh with incomprehensible words, and then draw away. Time slides, stretches as she rides an unseen current, her limbs buoyant, her mouth open, and then there *is* no time, only a sublime infinity.

Until the doorway closes, cutting her off, cutting her loose. She silences a groan behind trembling hands, but when the groan ends, she's smiling.

And the next beginning, and the next: two more paintings continuing the landscape, two more sensations of opening, of a perfect state of being, two more spots of yellow on the original painting.

Lined side by side, the paintings are a perfect symmetry; the buildings, the sky, flow from one canvas to the other as if they were painted as one then split apart. The full image is still in the making—the latest piece shows the edge of a new building, a second sun, the hint of a dark lake.

The weight of the air in her studio has changed, grown denser, and there's a scent of rich earth and old brick, a lingering dampness on her skin, and occasionally, the soft susurration of water caressing a shore.

The paintings no longer speak of desolation, but of possibility; the work is a glimpse into a secret world, a world into which she's been invited. She trails her fingers across the surfaces, moving delicately across the ridges of paint. Feels an ache, a longing, an emptiness desperate to be filled, but she knows it's only a matter of time before she falls again and that knowledge makes it tolerable.

The ringing of the phone pulls her from her thoughts, but her gaze is still locked on her creation as she answers. A husky voice says, "Meet me at The Lamplight in an hour and I'll tell you what you need to know." Then the call disconnects.

Neveah glares at her phone. Contemplates ignoring the summons, for that's what it is. She doesn't need anything from Ivy; the answers are in front of her, but a strand of doubt coils in her abdomen nonetheless. Maybe there's a piece of the puzzle she can't see. Better to spare a few moments of her time than to wonder.

☙

Interlude IV, someone else's beginning: a small dive bar, cheap drinks, the thick scent of greasy hamburgers and beer battered fries, a few patrons sitting at the bar watching a Ravens game on the flat screen.

Inside The Lamplight, Neveah orders a beer and takes a booth with a bird's eye view of the front door.

Ivy isn't at all what Neveah expected. If she's five feet tall, it's barely, and beneath her baggy jeans and oversized sweater, her limbs are stick-thin. She slips into the booth with a wince, as if the act is painful.

Her pupils are dilated, sharp commas frame the corners of her mouth, deep lines groove her forehead, and her nails are bitten to the quick.

She opens not with a greeting or even an inquiry as to Neveah's identity, only a low, "When did you get the invitation?"

"About a month ago," Neveah says.

"Have you found the doorway yet?"

Neveah twists her fingers together. Doesn't answer. The intensity of Ivy's gaze and the anger within it is startling.

"Did you find Carcosa?" Ivy hisses the last word. "Did you paint it?"

"I'm not sure. I've been painting a place with a lake and stars and two suns."

Ivy nods, plucking at her sleeve. Offers a sly smile. "Did he show you what it's like?"

Neveah touches the center of her chest with her fingertips, feels the hollow, thinks of floating.

Ivy leans over the table, leans kissing close. "He did, didn't he? He gave you a taste, I can tell. You're marked—I see it in your eye—but understand this: you'll never get there. *Never.* There's no way in. Artists have been trying for years. Quit while you still have enough of you left, burn your painting, burn the invitation, and forget about Carcosa. You won't be able to, but you can try."

"I don't understand."

Ivy scratches her arm; her sleeve rides up, revealing scars and scabs and a constellation of crude stars tattooed on her skin. She yanks the fabric down and her mouth twists into cruelty. "I don't understand," she mocks.

"Did he let *you* in?"

Ivy slams her hand on the table hard enough to draw glances from the customers at the bar, but if she notices she doesn't care. "Do you really think he'll pick you? There's nothing special about you. He'll never let you in." She makes a sound, half-sob, half-laugh. "All he'll leave when he's through, when he's used you up and tossed you aside, is a black hole that you can't ever fill, no matter how fucking hard you try. The mark in your eye doesn't mean a damn thing. He can take it away like that." Ivy snaps her fingers.

Neveah slides from the booth fast enough to jam her hip against the table, and as she reaches the front door, Ivy's mocking voice rings out once more. "Call me when he locks you out and let me know how you feel then."

The mark of a beginning: a face leaning close to a mirror, a dark mote in the brown of an iris, the echo of a voice: *you'll never get there.*

Bullshit, Neveah thinks. She hasn't been marked—she's been chosen.

Endless beginnings: late nights, the sound of a brush on canvas, of a forearm wiping sweat from a brow, sharp inhales pinpointing when the doorway opens and she falls into perfect, when she hears water touching the shore, footsteps, the robe whisking across cobblestones, harsh sighs when the doorway closes and normal sound returns.

When she finishes the eleventh painting, after the doorway shuts, Neveah realizes the edges match both the tenth and the first. In a frenzy, she arranges the pieces in a circle, stands in the center.

"Carcosa." She breathes the word and knows it to be both truth and beginning.

A flicker of yellow passes from painting to painting, the movement too quick to see directly. She holds her breath, stands as still as possible with her arms at her sides. Sweat trickles a cold snake along the length of her spine. A fleeting glimpse of a robed figure with broad shoulders and a hooded visage; the weighted sensation of eyes upon her, of a gaze hidden behind brick and broken glass. Is he judging her work, judging *her*?

The doorway opens. She exhales. Waits. But there's no warmth, no time slipping away, only the hollow, and then the door slams shut with a force strong enough to send her to her knees. The movement of the yellow ceases and with dismay, she sees it's no longer visible in any of the paintings, not even the first.

No, please, no.

She hears Ivy's words—*there's no way in*—and clamps her hands over her ears. No, Ivy wasn't right. She couldn't possibly be right.

"I don't understand," Neveah cries. "I painted it. I painted all of it. What more do you want?"

An impossible beginning: the paintings still arranged in a circle, the palette waiting atop an upside down plastic crate, sketch books stacked haphazardly in the corner atop another crate, a box overflowing with tubes of paint, brushes sitting in a tin of solvent, paint-streaked rags and twists of paper like deformed origami scattered on the floor, the tang of acrylic in the air. Everything in its place, waiting like a faithful dog while its master is away.

Waiting. But not for her. Not anymore.

Every night for weeks, she's returned to the studio, and the sensation of place has faded a little more with each visit. Carcosa has become nothing more than paint on canvas, and the dark mote in her eye has begun to fade even as the emptiness has swollen, grown fat and pregnant.

She knows there are only two possibilities: either she failed the audition or Ivy was right. Both leave the taste of ashes in her mouth, but Neveah doesn't want to accept that this is the end. She can't. Not when she worked so hard. (Not when she tasted perfection.)

"Damn you," she shrieks, but her voice dissolves into tears.

She scrambles for her box of paints. Squeezes tubes into anorectic commas, fills her palms with any—every—color. With sorrow coursing down her cheeks, she smears the paint across the paintings, obscuring the lake, the stars, the suns, the windows, the cobbles, concealing her failure.

Then she walks out of her studio, slamming the door shut behind her.

Interlude V, the absence of a beginning: Neveah works, sleeps, eats, pisses, shits. She fucks beautiful men and women, traces suns and stars on their flesh, leaves behind the impression of her teeth and if they insist they want to see her again, a false phone number. Her fingers ache to hold a brush, the crook of her arm yearns for the shape and the weight of her palette, but she quells the hurt with glasses of red wine.

She doesn't have the skill. She's never had the skill.

Sometimes she catches glimpses of the man in the tattered robe, his face concealed, in half-open doorways, in glimmers of wine, in plate glass windows, in dreams, and each time she turns away, shaking with need and anger. If he's judged her and found her lacking, why then must he rub salt in the open wound? Why won't he let her forget?

No narcotic, no orgasm, no fantasy, can fill the hollow he's left behind.

The end of a beginning: Neveah opens the door to her studio, takes a deep breath, turns on the light. Cups her elbows in her palms. The weight of the emptiness is a heavy burden, one she's tired of carrying, and she's been dreaming of taking a razor to her skin to see if the hollow will run out—a rat to desert the shipwreck she's become. Maybe if she throws everything away and forgets, the ache will fade. She won't end up like Ivy. She refuses. She's better than that. She's stronger. (She hopes.)

She gently takes down the first painting and sets it against the wall. Takes down the second. Flakes of paint spiral to the floor and expose what's underneath—Carcosa, the real Carcosa, not of paint and brush but of brick and stone and earth. Still there, still waiting.

Laughter, high and thin and sharp, slips from her lips. She races across the studio, digs through her brushes and tools, finds a palette knife. Places the paintings back where they belong and stands in the center, breathing hard. Carefully, she scrapes away the paint, beginning with the first piece, revealing—unpainting—the real. The architecture expands, stretches, filling and replacing her studio.

The doorway blooms like a shadowy rose. Sobbing in relief, in wonder, she holds out her arms, trails her fingertips across brick and mortar. Smells the water of the lake, the rich loam of the shore, feels the cobblestones rough beneath her bare feet. She's floating, falling, in silk and nothing.

The rustle of fabric fills the air and he emerges, the darkness of his hidden eyes boring into hers, from between two building. The Yellow King—not lie or myth, but real and here. Here for *her*.

And then the doorway begins to close, leaving only a whip-thin trace of the sweetness, and Carcosa begins to bleed back into the paintings.

"No," she says. "Please, no."

A voice intones, "Unmask."

And finally, she understands. Laughing, she disrobes, opens a tube of paint, and squeezes it into her palm. She covers her breasts, belly, arms, legs, and face; covers herself completely.

Carcosa returns. The King—*her* King—waits.

With the palette knife, she begins to remove the paint, already impossibly dry, from her skin, and as she peels away the false to bare the real, black stars take shape in her veins and twin suns burn in her eyes. A little like dying; a little like lust and barbed wire entwined. She is everywhere and nowhere, everything and nothing, undone and remade and undone again.

A robed arm lifts, a hand extends. As Neveah slips her own into his, she trembles, unsure if this is the correct ending, but it is *an* ending, and all endings are also beginnings.

"Unmask," she whispers with a smile and the last traces of paint flake from her cheeks and seesaw like confetti to the floor.

⁂

This is how it begins: a rumor, a whisper, a story.

SHE WILL BE RAISED A QUEEN
BY E. CATHERINE TOBLER

I dream of water.

When the men found me in the sulfur-yellow waters of the nameless lake, some thought I was a mermaid. Ridiculous, Ambrose Kowal declared with a twitch of his impeccable mustache, for mermaids did not vacillate in sulfur, did not draw succor from the volcanic stench of the plague-ridden air.

Indeed, my skin was not scaled and I possessed no tail; the men touched my legs, hands encircling my ankles before spreading me wide for study until I kicked out in protest and sent Nicholas to the crusted ground, the salt staining his otherwise fine suit for the rest of his days. Likewise, my hair was not crusted with precious jewels and did not drape my breasts as a second skin. It was only drenched with sulfur and salts, tangled with weeds, reeking of Hell's depths, Frederick said in a voice gone rough and hollow both, and wouldn't he know, for had they not listened to his own story of the black stars in the black sky just nine days before? They had, within Ambrose's own comfortable rooms. She was a *queen*, a queen of Carcosa, and would do, Frederick whispered and reached a hand for me.

Enough preposterous stories, Ambrose demurred though his voice shook, as if he understood more than Frederick had spoken. Ambrose pushed Frederick's trembling hands away and said perhaps I was a selkie, for they shed one skin for another as easily as people did clothes, appropriating delectable shapes of women as components of their mischief, even though they remained beastly beneath and would do anything to once again inhabit their natural skins. It could be a skin might yet be discarded upon these crusted shores, but long as we looked no skins rested upon the ragged sulfur shores or within the foul waters. I thought I found one, torn and sodden and clinging to the edge of a steaming sulfur pool, but in the end it was only seaweed between my fingers, rotting and slick.

By the time our search concluded, I in my tattered shift was shivering as icy rain streamed from the clouded pewter sky. The men guided me out of the sickened world and into the heart of the city they sought to rebuild. Within the city's salt-streaked walls, there beat the heart of a virtuous civilization yet; despite the ruin that battered its doors nightly, here the people made to recover and return to the world they had once known. Women and men and children like I had never seen, each with business somewhere, most paying me no mind as I was taken deeper into the city. This was a city of cobble, pieces that often had no rhyme or reason pushed into something attempting to be new and glorious. The stones that made the houses had been blackened by fire, but the people did scrub them with brush and soap, even if the black could not be stripped. The black stones gleamed strangely as we walked past and through them. Within the mayor's house—Ambrose himself, the house as tidy as his mustache—warm drawing rooms with even warmer cakes and cooler ales awaited; small bedrooms with salvaged iron tubs and clean-swept fireplaces; soft linens strange to my hands, even as I found them familiar once I curled within.

I did not, however, spend much time within the bed or its linens, usually discovered by displeased servants curled into the bottom of the iron tub beside the fireplace. There, I listened to the echo of the world beyond the walls of this room, distant voices trying to unknot the problem of me, me who did not even have a name. (Of course I had a name (and beyond a name had a song), but they had not asked, for knowing the name of a thing, even of a person, makes it genuine and true and whole.)

Whatever might we call her, Ambrose wondered to his men over precious drinks and cigars, other than a Distinct and Terrible Problem.

Such a Distinct and Terrible Problem would I delight to explore at great lengths—and depths, Frederick said. (For much worse, I would cut him from thigh to throat , but it was always those first words I remembered, the way his rough hand branded my knee, the way his soft flesh gave way beneath the hard heel of my sulfur-crusted foot.)

When these conversations became tiresome, and they quickly did—how could they mean to determine the fate of a person upon whom they had no claim?—I opened the faucet to unleash the stream of water hidden within the old pipes, but not even this was wholly satisfying. The water held the tang of brass and did not taste as sweet as waters I remembered. What waters I remembered, I could not yet say, but opening my mouth to the flood of faucet water earned me only a deeper longing and the disapproval of the maid assigned to me. Ladies did not behave thus, she told me; was I a lady, then? Not mermaid, not selkie, not lady. And what had Frederick said—a queen of Carcosa and I would do.

Even though my origins were unknown, the Kowals allowed me to roam. The house was as unfamiliar and strange to me as I was to the Kowals. Ambrose watched me when he thought me unaware, his wisp of a wife afraid to come within arm's reach of me. She drapes herself in blue, for the Mother, she says, and makes a strange sign with her trembling and pale hands whenever I pass. I cannot decide if it is pleasure or pain I experience at the sight of such things; it delights me in a way I think it should not.

For what is to be made of a woman found in a sulfur lake near the edge of the world where none do wander? And why *did* those men wander, in that place upon that very day where I so happened to be. Why did those men wander into the ruined world, I asked Lady Kowal even as she backed away. She shook her head, her teeth worrying her bottom lip as her fingers traced strange patterns into her blue skirts. She was certain she did not know and could not say—but not *knowing* and not *saying* were two wholly different things, and when I told her such, she gave me a look that might have sent others running. Her eyes ran with venom, her throat drawn in tight lines that would allow no words passage. She fled me then, a skittering bug, her skirts frantic across the polished floors.

The house with its straight walls and narrow entries holds no consolation for me; everything closes a person away from the world, and no matter how ruined and desolate since the plagues that carried everything away, I miss the skies and the crumble of ground between my toes. This house the Kowals have so carefully constructed is terrible in its geometries—until I wander to its tapering apex and discover the yellow room. It is not a room, cousin Angelica makes sure to explain, as if I am a child and simply do not know.

Angelica says it is only a space allotted for leftovers, where boxes and crates may be stacked into piles to molder and die in the shadows, where the discards of the household are placed so no one must look upon them. So that none must admit the ageless and transcendent portrait of the woman called The Violet, whom Pascal so loved he filled (and here Angelica blushed so fiercely that even within the yellow room's shadows, I could see the way it flooded her thin cheeks)— Whom Pascal so loved, he filled her with a child even as he withheld one from his proper ladywife. A space created so none within proper rooms would be faced with the evidence of years having passed at all.

Everything was coated in dust, the exact opposite of the water I dream. Powder beneath my fingers, it was unbearable, as dry as the shell of the past it lives within. But the paper—

Once, this not-room was papered in yellow; now, only fragments cling to the walls, as if they have also attempted to shed their pasts. In the darkened corners, where wall meets wall in a soft kiss, the paper holds fast, refusing the idea of going. Time has come? Time does not matter, the paper says, and glows distinctly gold in the dim light.

Within its yellow expanse, there are roads and rivers and people and places not yet travelled. My fingers trace them from afar, but know every curve and dip, and though the paper has flaked completely away from the edge of the door, my fingers remember an undulation of hip and waist and breast held within. I can close my eyes and picture that form, woman and river both, and I can travel.

When night comes, I unbutton my skin and leave.

Beyond the flaking yellow paper, I am what I have always been. I have no need of skin, of features that eyes can caress; here, none will feel the need to regard me as anything other than what I am. Not mermaid, not selkie, not even woman in this place. I reach beyond every word, something wholly other and pure. Beyond definition, even if I have a name.

There are no pathways I may describe so that any might understand, and yet my feet know the way. Every step brings words to my lips, words long known and forgotten both. Beyond the clouds, where the waters of the lake of Hali suck the sulfur from my feet, beyond the diming light of Aldebaran, where misted air curls as hands around my bare flesh, I find another who is much like me.

This Other stands in arched and twilight shadows and has no face within the hollow of its tattered cloak. Even as my fingers slip over cheekbones and lips, there is no face beneath them. I know every ridge and valley and they are not there. I can taste the sulfur in the mouth, but there is no mouth. I open my mouth and the nothingness floods me, cold and sharp as it glides over tongue, down throat.

Much shall be done, it is said, and there is no voice, but for the vibration in my bones. This voice has tasted me, even as there is nothing to taste. It has found me cold and sharp in return, black and silted like the bottom of the clouded lake.

Thy will *be* done, I promised, no matter that there is no will. It shall be done, and when I return to the yellow room that is not a room, I finger my skin back into place. A line of small black stars like buttons bleed up through my skin to mark the inside line of my arm, and I breathe as if I have never breathed before. The breath of the Other moves within my body. I sink into evening-cool sheets, black stars reel overhead, and Ambrose wonders over another cup of brandy what he might do with me. To me.

Come morning, in the east dining room with its slanting sunlight, cousin Angelica opens every raspberry as though she is looking for something. She pulls the scarlet fruit from its stem, and slides her thumbs into the hole left behind. She pries the tender berries apart, spreading the flesh flat between her fingers before consumption. Her fingers are sticky wet and red, fragrant in the otherwise sterile sitting room. Her mouth puckers.

The longing to tell her about the yellow room overwhelms me. I want to tell her of the paths, but find every word stolen before I may speak. I swallow the desire as she does the berries and my own mouth purses. I drown the truth of my journey in bergamot and lavender tea. It never happened, I tell myself. I never left that bed, that iron tub. Never unbuttoned my skin.

Beneath the table's edge, I ruck my skirt up my thighs; I press every finger into my exposed flesh, and there is no evidence of buttons or buttonholes but for the stars which line the inside of my arm. One does not require evidence to have a truth be known, of course, but I look, and see the dark line across my wrist, where I may be opened.

My flesh has been unbuttoned and touched and rebuttoned and covered.

Angelica tells me how terrible it is to live here. She cannot bear the narrow hallways and the low sky and the way life never changes. Even as life does change here—for they are building an Empire! Ambrose tells her—she says it never changes. Nights hang endless above her bed and she wakes feeling as though she has never slept, as if she has spent the whole night wandering. Her eyes meet my own.

This is a doorway, but I do not cross the threshold. I do not tell her of the yellow paper, because—

The yellow *lake*, she says. (In those days, the lake's designation was under continued discussion and debate, a vote being brought to bear upon the citizens of this new settlement as they hastened to create what could not be destroyed as all that had been before, even though the waters had a name, possessed and singular, wholly its own even if unspoken.)

She wants to go, having only heard of the way I was found. Ambrose won't tell her a thing about me and she hates him. Hates him. The yellow lake, she presses.

I don't have to close my eyes to picture its ragged shape; the taste of sulfur still rests within the corner of my mouth, despite the tea. I cannot take her there, I tell her. She would be devoured, I do not say. *The lake, sucking my feet clean. Sucking my skin off.*

Angelica presses herself more deeply into her chair and stares at me, as if she can compel me to terrible acts. Her eyes are the color of the black stars that flood in a river between my legs every night and within the hollow of her throat, I see another echo of the black stars, something just beneath the skin that moves—

Ambrose enters the room and Angelica sits as straight as a board, as if she has been skewered beneath the table with a knife. All color bleeds from her skin, and she is a shadow, if a shadow could be thin enough to allow sunlight through its black body, illuminating the rags and bones of her heart. When she flees the room, I'm surprised she doesn't trail blood from a wound. I can smell it, even though it does not exist.

My tea grows cold as Ambrose sits across from me. His own tea steams warm between us, his hands loosely cupped around the china. I wish you to come to me, he tells me; I wish you to tell no one, for there are matters between you and me and these things must be laid plain. Bare. If you are such a queen, he says.

But he cannot seemingly say more than this; he looks ill at the very idea he has questioned it. I spread my hands flat upon the table and beneath my fingers, the ivory lace of the cloth runs black. It is stars that bleed into the lacework, stars that creep their way toward

Ambrose who wants to withdraw, but cannot. I watch as if from a distance as this blackness lifts itself in a gentle cloud and swallows him. His mouth notches open in a silent horror and the stars rush in and down and I envy his mouth, I envy his lungs, at the way the darkness expands him, makes him more than he just was, as it fills every lacking part of him.

I wish the darkness to tear Ambrose open the way Angelica does her raspberries—who knows such sweet things in the midst of ruin and rebuilding—but the darkness knows patience and knows when the time will be right for such things. For now, the darkness withdraws and Ambrose shudders and slumps to the table with a sodden, broken sound. I leave the table and encounter his ladywife in the narrow hallway—taken by surprise, she stands so close to me I can feel the chill that rolls from her; it is not yet winter, yet she carries it on her skin, much as Angelica. She gasps softly, as if she means to draw away from me, but her attention is beyond our close encounter; I glance behind, to find Ambrose righting the teacup he has overturned and broken, the tea spreading a sepia stain into the lace cloth. Lady Kowal rushes to his side, to make all things better.

The stains scatter like stars and I take my leave of the Kowals, wandering as I will, always and ever upward, to the yellow room that commands my interest. Today its flaking walls are not vacant; Nicholas kneels upon the floor in his salt-stained suit, his tie already undone. His head is thrown back, arms limp at his sides, palms staring at the low ceiling. The boxes are thrown about as if some great beast were only just romping among them. He does not move when I approach, but for his fingers curling inward to kiss palms.

I circle him, slow but sure, and when I look upon his face—his eyes yet closed, his lips parted—he speaks without having to look upon me. *In this place, none will feel the need to regard me as anything other than what I am.* His tongue wets his lips and he speaks my name, and the world falls apart. There are no paths we may speak of, yet we travel them by the four winds, the clouded waters of lake Hali sucking us free of our skins as we go. Nicholas screams, for some part of him yet doubted I was the thing he sought; there was only ever a king, part of his mind says, a king aging and tattered, and all have gone mad. All have gone—

Nicholas grows silent under the touch of my hands. Through the woods, where the trees are tall and strong, rising from the dark floor of the world, I take him in hand and guide him to that place from which he cannot return. And he goes willingly, calling me nymph, daring me to bring the rain, and so it rains in hot sheets that obscure the twin suns. Beneath us, stones rise from the ground, broken and round as if they were once bodies and not stones at all. Moss riots over them, soft and dark between each stone; Nicholas rakes his fingers through the green and is covered, pulled into the ground, and devoured. The seeds of him scatter in the dark, burst, and grow, and it is my king who at last enfolds me from behind, in vaporous arms as he shows me the hole within the world, the place where everything turns to sand and spirals inward, as if down a drain. Everything falls to black stars, I have only to bring him, bring him to the shore. Nicholas was but the seed.

Come morning, in the east dining room with the windows now covered, darkened, cousin Angelica opens every raspberry as though she is looking for something. Her hands shake and she cannot dislodge the berry from its stem. She allows me to help, but as my hands enfold her own, we are drawn somewhere else entirely.

The yellow lake, a handful of years ago. A slim and pale body spread in the waters, clinging to the ragged edge. This could be me, but it is another; it is Angelica drawn from the sulfuric water by three pairs of hands that have never worked a hard day in their life despite the longing for a rebuilt empire. They are already rebuilding an empire—just one none shall know exists, an empire existing to serve and fulfill their needs above all others. They draw Angelica from the sulfur, her skin burned and ragged, but Ambrose knows ways to make her whole again, he promises. He knows how to mend a sick body, enough so that one might once again carry a child, a creature born of this broken world, from a body others discarded; a creature that might reach across worlds, might draw down the light of Hyades and make it shine once more.

But oh my King we never ceased shining—what do they mean to do?

Angelica tries to pull her hand free, but time only stutters and carries us into the yellow room, toward the thing Angelica does not want me to see. There are no boxes, nor dust, only a small and tidy room with a golden draped couch in its center. The walls are perfectly papered, every river and body hidden within intact. With her eyes, Angelica follows one long line around the room as the shadow falls over her, as her body is parted by three sets of hands like a raspberry. She begins in the northwest corner, an innocuous curl that looks like a leaf, but this leaf becomes a hand that she slides her own into. This hand is cool and not warm like those working her; this hand lifts her from the couch, from the terrible yellow room, straight into the color itself where all is good and glorious. Here, Angelica consumes lemonade and yellow apples until she feels she might burst. She pockets each and every apple seed, saying that one day, she might need their special poison. One day. And Frederick's seed stirs within her now, burrowed into her womb—

—whom he so loved, he filled her with a child even as he withheld one from his proper ladywife—

Angelica wrenches from my touch, the raspberry between us gone to blood on my fingers, bright and startling in the shadows of the room. Angelica staggers backward, and I think that it was not Frederick I was meant to bring and there is a pain within me sharp as the look on Angelica's face. She shakes as do autumn leaves, wishing me to keep my distance, and I want to tell her I know and now understand, but I realize then that to know the name of a thing is not always to know what it is. Speak his name, I tell her, but she has no need. I know down to my bones. It was not Frederick alone, nor Ambrose or Nicholas, but these three in collusion; these three who held my legs, who called me mermaid and selkie and knew all the while what I was, what they hoped to tame.

When night deepens, I climb to the yellow room and find Ambrose kneeling before a sofa draped in gold. Candles ring the sofa, boxes carted away, floors swept to gleaming. The portrait of The Violet alone leans against a wall, her eyes as pools of candlelight. She regards me as I enter, as does Ambrose, both mouths tilted with a secret. The same secret, I think.

Ambrose extends a hand to me, but I do not take it; I walk unassisted, unlacing the borrowed gown I wear before I unbutton my skin. The black stars part beneath my fingers and Ambrose's mouth opens in silent wonder as he watches. Beneath the heat of the candles, the paper on the walls curls up, a dozen hands asking to be taken, and so we take them, and I pull Ambrose where he believes he longs to go.

Through the paper, the world becomes what Ambrose cannot ever explain; he will try, confined to his chair as he will be while his ladywife walks free, but he will not be able to speak the words to convey all he has seen, all he has come to know in the deepest marrow of him. In this realm, he is stripped of what he carries elsewhere, down to his bones, because that's all anyone is here. Bone and blood and sometimes breath if the king gifts you with such. Ambrose lifts his hands, looking through the transparent web of his fingers, shrieking when he finds them only bones.

My feet move bare and soundless over the mossy ground and Ambrose follows as a weighted shadow, down paths we never name, but intimately know, the world around us upside down and backwards, but familiar even so. Through the bare branches of the ivory trees that hang like flawless curtains, black stars cascade, flooding into rivers upon the ground, flowing ever toward a central point, a golden and ocher hollow in the world where stands the king. The king Ambrose has so wished to know, that he tried to hollow out bodies and build an entry for him. But you cannot give entry to what has always and ever been and Ambrose falls to his knees at the sight of such glory, his mouth gaping in wordless horror. He has wanted to see the king's face and now that he sees the face that is not a face, it is me his gaze returns to.

He thinks to find solace in my arms with their black stars; he thinks this starlight will be like that of his childhood, before the world fell to pieces and plagues, before every single thing he ever loved was lost. Ambrose reaches a trembling hand for me, but his fingers do not unravel me. Anger etches his face then and his hold turns violent. The way of men.

I unbutton my skin, parting my wrist at the mark of every black star as if my skin is but a long glove up my arm. I am not certain what transfixes Ambrose more, the sight of the stars or the sight of me beyond their streaming light, but he cannot move. With my unbuttoned hand, I mark him in black stars, flooding him the way I did in the dining room, but this time there is no mercy, and he is utterly lost beneath the waves, unable to swallow all that flows into him. Ambrose shudders and vomits stars into the heavens as he collapses at the feet of my king.

It is exceedingly late when I find Frederick, pacing within Ambrose's sitting room; it is a room made for men, of hard lines and hot fires, so when I stride barefoot and naked across the carpets, Frederick cannot help but stop his pacing and stare. What *are* you, he asks, but within his question is the answer; he doesn't not care what I am, so long as he might partake of whatever it is. He looks to the door, as if expecting the mistress of the house, but the ladies are tucked safely away; they have already seen these horrors, haven't they? I have come for them, I tell Frederick, and placed them beyond reach, where they may no longer be defiled. Where Angelica's belly can safely swell and she will deliver unto this world a child, a child who will wear no mask.

Remove your own, Frederick implores me, and follows when I walk way. He follows as Ambrose followed, easily swayed by bare flesh, perhaps because it is ephemeral, perhaps because they can never quite possess it the way they long to. He wonders at the line of black stars that mark my spine and does not dare touch them until we reach the yellow room. His fingers, like Ambrose's, do not open my skin; I allow him to feel the heat of me, the promise of an unbuttoning, but he gets nowhere, even as he can feel there is more. What *are* you, he wonders again, and I tell him that he does not want to know, because he does not care. His mouth is a cruel twist and within his eyes, the horrors Angelica knew simmer; I see Lady Kowal pressed to the couch in her turn, each woman seeking support within the portrait-eyes of The Violet. It does not matter if she was also pressed to the couch; I do not care. Whatever these men have done, it is enough.

I put Frederick on his knees in the thick moss of the ground, yellow papered room becoming an unending ivory wood, everything upside down and backwards and delicious as black stars flow over his broad and bare shoulders before scattering away into the moss and trees. They pile like snow as the tatters of my king begin to flow around me and with my legs wrapping Frederick tight—mermaid, he calls me, mermaid—I cut Frederick from thigh to throat and fill him with the awful truth he has always known. He is unbuttoned in ways never dreamed until now. He stares and begs to know, what am I, what am I, show me *who*—

In black stars I mark him, a sign he and Ambrose will both carry, a burden they shall know for the rest of their days. Men who once dreamed themselves so important to the success of an Empire; men who once dared to look upon the face of a thing they never should have. Men who dared take rein of bodies that were not, and could never be, their own.

Show me, Frederick begs as the stars take from him the last bits of what make him *him*. When I show Frederick, when he sees the truth—that such things have no beginning and no end and simply are—he looks beyond me, seeking the eyes of The Violet, reaching for some ease, though there is none he may ever find. Show me, he whispers. Show me, he whispers for all his days, and I show him, constantly and always.

He dreams of water, the black-star ocean, and mermaid he calls the child when she flits into view. Mermaid, he says, but no—she will be raised a queen.

YELLA
BY NICOLE CUSHING

The empty man's in his tiny, cluttered livin room, stubbin out the butt of his cigarette and sippin cheap bourbon out of a Kentucky Derby shot glass. Just sittin there, lookin at the ceramic rabbits and pigs on the coffee table. Lookin out the window at the dead, dark houses across the street. Sittin there, strainin to hear his wife.

She's down in the cellar and refuses to come back upstairs. Been down there fer almost five days, now. She ain't got a word to say about *why* she's doin all this, neither. She ain't even bothered to call out sick to her supervisor at the plant. Might already be fired.

What does a man do in a situation like this? *Who* does a man *call* in a situation like this? If he got her boss on the phone, what would he tell him? If he called up her doctor, what would he tell her? That she's havin a nervous breakdown? Do ya just up and *say* that to people?

It's almost enough to make *him* have a nervous breakdown. His brain's like a pot of spaghetti on the stove, boilin-n-stirrin, boilin-n-stirrin...

He takes another sippa bourbon to turn down the heat in his head. To put a stop to the stirrin. Then another sip—no, *more* than a sip, this time. A gulp. Winces a little as it goes down. It's almost midnight and he's only on his fifth glass. He'll need to drink quicker if he hopes to pass out into a nice cozy, carefree sleep.

He's been through some shit in his life, but it's been a long time since he's felt this worked up, confused and (let's face it) embarrassed. It don't make no sense that he's embarrassed. He's the only one who knows she's actin like this. But he reckons he's embarrassed at the thought that someone *might find out* how bad she is and yell at him fer not doin somethin sooner. But it gets all *complicated*, yanno? He can't just up and have her committed.

Oh yeah, and that makes him think of another thing: he's spooked, too. Spooked that she's had herself a nervous breakdown, sure, but more spooked that she'll be pissed at him if he tries to have her committed. Things ain't exactly been smooth sailin between em. Ain't been smooth sailin fer almost a year, now. She's been actin weird. Talkin dirty in her sleep and grindin her hips in bed like she's fuckin another guy, in her dreams. Slippin outside at all hours of the night, sayin she's watchin the stars (even on nights when the clouds make it so there ain't no fuckin stars). He thinks that there's probably another man. That she's plannin on leavin.

If he had her put away fer a few weeks, then that would be just the excuse she'd need to leave. She'd come home from the hospital, scream at him, pack her things, and make a beeline fer the door. Run off with this other fella. And this is wife number three and he don't need the heartache of another divorce and—even more—he don't need to go down to the fuckin courthouse and deal with all the asshole judges and lawyer-leeches and nosy clerks again, so he does...

Nothin.

(No, it ain't like that at all...He's *doin* shit...Hell, yeah, he's *doin shit*. He's bringin sandwiches down to her each night, cereal each mornin. And it ain't just that, he's also *plannin*. He's comin up with strategies, so he can solve this on his own, so they won't have a big fat hospital bill, that's what he's doin! He ain't bein *careless*. No, he ain't. He ain't... he....)

Yesterday, the mailman delivered a thick envelope from her company's H.R. department. The empty man don't have the courage to open it, so he uses it as a coaster fer his shot glass.

Sometimes, late at night, when there ain't no cars passin through their little piece-a-shit subdivision, he can hear her down there (shufflin around on the concrete, talkin to herself). He pays particular attention to her when she talks to herself, cause he thinks that might give him a much-needed clue about all this shit. She won't *tell* him what this is all about, but he hopes that maybe *she'll let it slip* in her mutterin. Her voice is muffled down there, so he can never make out the words all that good. As best he can tell, she talks about a fairy tale. (Or maybe a Bible story?) Somethin about a king, and a king's death, and his resurrection—transformed—and the kingdom bein equally divided "amongst em all". *What the fuck is a forty year old woman doin, sayin that kinda shit? To herself? In the fuckin cellar?* That's some fucked up shit, right there. A little creepy, too.

But tonight, so far, he ain't been able to hear her say nothin. And, fucked up or not (creepy or not) her voice has been a comfort and he misses it. Even batshit chatter's better than silence. It gets real lonely, late at night in a house with no sound. Yeah, there's the whir of heat flowin through vents, the buzz of energy coursin through bulbs. There's the hummin, whinin sound the house seems to make late at night—ya might call it a *noise of no noise*, yanno? But it ain't the same. It ain't *human*.

It'd be different if they had kids. At least then, there'd be the pitter-patter of little feet—as they say—gallopin around late at night to use the bathroom. They'd be stirrin in the middle of the night to get a glass of water or whine about monsters under their beds. Yeah, they'd be a pain in the ass a lotta the time but at least they'd be company. "It's so alone without babies," she'd always said. "Let's start a family." And they tried. And they tried. And they...

He thinks about turnin on the TV just to have somethin to remind him of a normal life, of a normal family where the woman don't hide out in the cellar and they have two kids and all their problems are shit ya can laugh at. Or maybe he'll turn on some late night rerun of Sports Center, and hope they show highlights from the Louisville game. And he's got his hand on the remote and he's clickin over to ESPN and he sees they're playin highlights of the Maryland game, instead, but they got a good team this year so he pays attention and then...

Ugly, hoarse screams. Like she's wounded in her belly and the flaps of the wound are screamin lips. Like her heart and guts have little mouths of their own and they're screamin too. She ain't ever made noises like these before!

And he can't help himself. He lets out a little, sissy-like wail and flinches at the noise. Takes another sippa bourbon. Shakes his head.

And the fella on ESPN is oblivious to it all, talkin about how the game went to double overtime and how Maryland has backbone and they just wanted it more than Michigan State. "These are the kinda games that separate the men from the boys. It was justa battle of wills and Maryland had more mental toughness".

And he shakes his head. Shakes it again. Slaps himself.

Then more screams. Like her whole body is nothin but row after row of mouths...

And he decides that he's gonna fix this, once and fer all. He has a fuckin backbone. His will is gonna be stronger than hers. He's John Fuckin Wayne, the cavalry to the rescue. Off to the cellar he stumbles. Door creaks as he opens it. But now she's not screamin no more. Now he just hears that buzz, a kinda ringin in his ears. That noise of *no noise*. He don't see her, neither. Don't see nothin but blackness.

Don't hear her, don't see her. But, Christ Almighty, he can *smell* her.

As he stands at the top of the stairs he catches a whiff of...somethin nasty—a buncha odors that have come together in recent weeks to become her new perfume. The sour smell of unwashed clothes and b.o., the hot, ammonia-like smell of piss-soaked pants, and the stench of fresh shit. Even this far away, he can smell her. Even the mustiness of the place is overwhelmed by *her* smell. He's tried to make her take a shower. He has...He has...He...

Gags. "Patti?"

Nothin, so he yells louder. "PATTI?"

And he turns on the light and runs down the wooden stairs. *Boom-squeak, boom-squeak*...And along the way the steps fuckin bite him. And the splinter's a bigass motherfucker, right up close to his toes. He calls himself a dumbass fer goin around barefoot but them steel-toed work shoes hurt to wear all the time.

But he's a tough son of a bitch and ain't gonna let a little thing like a splinter stop him. He'll just limp a little, that's all. And he gets to the bottom and sees all her clothes thrown across the floor. Her bigass bra's at one end of the line. Then her panties, with a fuckin pile of shit slathered all over em. The shit has gotten on just about everthin. On the jeans. On the T-shirt. On the sweatshirt she'd worn over the T-shirt. On the little pink socks. And he dry heaves. Stumbles. Braces himself against the wall, feelin thick dust and grime cling to his fingers. Feelin spider webs. Feelin cinder blocks.

And then he kinda hears somethin—somethin off in a far corner of the cellar—that he thinks might be her. Like, maybe she's whisperin. No, not whisperin, *breathin heavy*—all fast-like. Kinda like hissin. Kinda like her breath is blowin through a mouth full of slobber.

He follows the sound. Finds her. Jesus Christ, he wishes he didn't.

She's nekkid. Nekkid, on the cellar floor, legs spread wide. She's got shit-stains around her hips and even some on her belly. Looks like there's even dried shit crusted in her pubes. And she's sweatin round her forehead (and a little down her face). Her hair's soaked, like she took a shower. But she ain't taken a shower in days.

Then there's the blotches. That's the best he can describe em, *blotches*. He ain't seen em before. They weren't there at dinner time. He's tryin to noodle through what they are.

Bruises?

Ink stains?

Sores?

They're startin on her forehead and runnin all the way down to her toes. They're dark and they're throbbin. *Squirmin*. Like somethin's just *underneath* her skin. Like somethin's *tryin to get out* from underneath her skin, from underneath the blotches.

It's enough to make any man prissy-prance his way outta there, but he ain't gonna be scared off. He's gonna do what he shoulda done days ago. Gonna be a fuckin *man*. He walks right up to her and points at em. Stammers fer a moment, but gets the words out. "W-what are they? What the fuck are they?!"

And she raises her eyes up to meet his, and gives him this look of disgust. Like he's the lowest, most weakass piece-a-shit in the world. "They're His. Yeahhh, boy. Not yers, *His*. Fuckin miracles. MIRA-CLES!"

Some men might just go back upstairs after hearin somethin that nutty. Some men might just take that as the sign that it's time to call an ambulance to have her taken away, cause she's nekkid and talkin outta her head. But not him. Nosirree, he's gonna get this straightened out here and now. Gets down on the cellar floor next to her. Can barely hold his puke back in his throat as he gets an even closer whiff of her. Then, with one quick movement, he's grabbin a handful of her hair. Twistin it. Shakes her like a rag doll.

"Now stoppit! Stoppit! Stop actin like yer crazy. *Y'ain't* crazy! Y'hear me?"

And she starts beggin and whimperin. "Lemme go, Billy. Lemme go! Ya don't know what yer doin, here. Lemme go…"

And he thinks: *Who's weakass now?*

And he says: "See…the way yer talkin now…that's the most sense ya made all this time. I'll letcha go, but ya *better* keep on makin sense. None of this weird shit about miracles, y'hear me?"

And then…she *shrieks*.

Shrieks that grab onta his ears and gnaw on em. Shrieks that give him a headache and, somehow, make him sick to his stomach. And then she's jabberin somethin, all fast-like. Like a surge of power just went through her system, speedin everthin up. "Dese bays anyers! Anyers!"

He can't understand it, at first. She's sayin it too fast. Only after hearin it four or five times does it start to make sense.

"These babies ain't yers. Ain't yers!"

And his grip on her hair loosens.

She's slowin down now. Like she knows she's taken the wind outta his sails. Like she wants to make sure he hears ever last word of this. "That's the truth. They ain't yers. The Yella Angel came down."

And his grip loosens some more.

She's lookin at him with a sick smile "Fucked me real good. Yeahhh, boy. Fucked me better than y'ever did." Then she pats one of the blotches on her belly. "Don't shoot blanks, the way ya did, neither."

And his grip is gone.

"Yella Angel says 'The age of kings and of dynasties has ceased', that now *everone* gets a share of the kingdom. Even folks like us, who work in factories. From the lowest of the low to the highest of the high, we *all* get our fair share of it. And the Angel left part of the kingdom in me, alright." Then she pats the blotch on her belly again. Giggles (sick, child-like giggles). "Fucked me realll good. Yeahhh, boy. Fucked me better than y'ever did. Yella Angel says Carcosa's the birthright of every man, woman, and child. Says Carcosa's fuckin *everwhere*! Says it ain't 'lost'...not no more. Says it's now hidden in plain sight and He's gonna show it to *everone*—one at a time. Yeahhh, boy...We fucked under a thousand black stars. We fucked in the cloud waves. He fucked me better than y'ever could. Don't shoot blanks, neither. Yer jizz's just...empty. But Him, His is fuckin full of all kinda good stuff. I ain't gonna lie, He was rough. But after I got used to it, it felt so damned good...the way His jizz shot up my cunt and up my ass and down my throat and in all the *other holes* He made in me. Yeahhh, boy, we fucked in the long shadows where ya couldn't see us—even though we were right there, in plain sight! Even managed to hide the pregnancy from ya!" Then she laughs. "Fuckin idjit! Been a long labor but it's almost through. Can't hide it no more, so I'm spillin the beans. Spillin the beans cause He says that's what I should do now. He says it's important for you to know about Him, now. But I don't wantchu to get jealous! Hell, no! Yanno why ya shouldn't be jealous? He'll be comin fer ya, soon, too! Gonna come-n-poke ya. Yer gonna turn sissy fer Him, ain'tcha? Ya turn sissy fer Him, He'll give ya babies, too. Don't make no difference if y'ain't gotta pussy or a womb. He'll *make* some fer ya, *claw* some into ya! At first I only had one womb, muhself, but now I got over a dozen. Yeahhh, boy."

More giggles.

And he's shakin and feels sick and wants to puke but don't wanna do it here. Anywhere but here. And he walks away, backwards, and steps on her shit-stained panties.

And she lets loose with a belly laugh.

And he wants to scream at her, wants to slap her and punch her and get a kitchen knife and fuckin stab a little respect into her. But, even more than that, he wants to be free of her. So he does the only thing left to do – he turns and runs up the stairs. *Boom-squeak, boom-squeak...*

And he can still hear her down there, braggin about how she got away with all this right under his nose.

Boom-squeak, boom-squeak...

Shuts the door.

And the fella on ESPN is oblivious to it all, chatterin away back in the livin room, talkin about the AFC playoff picture, and how weather won't be no factor in any of these games. Says that even if it's twenty-fuckin-below, they'll be out there playin, because they want it, yanno? Says it's simply a case of mind over matter...

And he walks through the kitchen and he's trackin shit all over the floor, but he don't care no more. He'll clean it up, later. He's gotta have a drink. Gotta have a drink. Gotta have a...

Grabs the whole bottle of bourbon. Don't care how nasty the taste in his mouth is. There's somethin nastier than that in his head, and he needs to get rid of it. And he's trackin more shit through the house, into the livin room, and he's drinkin straight from the bottle, and when that bottle's empty he fetches another, and he's watchin ESPN, and whenever they talk about mental toughness, or playin injured, or "showin so much heart", he lets out a "Whoooo!" and a "Fuck, yeah!". And with each glug of bourbon he's able to ferget a little more of what happened in the cellar.

And, durin a commercial break, he looks up at the ceilin fan and sees that *it's* still and the *whole room* is spinnin. And a weird thought crosses his mind: what if the room really *is* spinnin? What if bein drunk makes ya see things the way they really are? And he's about to take another glug from the jug, so to speak, when there's a feelin like there's somethin in his belly that's gonna punch its way out. Like, it's in his belly and it's punchin its way up into his throat. And then it's in his throat and punchin at his teeth and gums. And he's gaggin, he's dry heavin, and nothin's comin out yet, but he knows it's just a matter of time.

And he's runnin round the house, stumblin his way to the bathroom. But he stubs his toes against a kitchen stool and falls and pukes on himself and the floor. It's yella and brown and lumpy with black stringy stuff inside it. And the smell of it—like store brand Parmesan cheese—combined with the scent of the shit on the floor (on his feet) makes him upchuck even more.

And thoughts are like screams inside his head:
I'm the world's biggest piece-a-shit and...
I should just blow my fuckin brains out, or maybe...
I should go to A.A. or somethin and...
The thoughts, they're all pourin down over him, like rocks in a collapsin cave. And there's no more resistin em. There's no more fight in him. There's just surrender (to sleep, to dreams).

And the dreams are like dogs, rippin him apart.

The Yella Angel...in a tattered robe – stretchin His arms out wide, so that He's all he can see.

The Yella Angel...pinnin him down, makin gentle clicks and trills and purrin sounds, as if to comfort him, just before He rams him hard in the ass with somethin that ain't flesh-n-blood, but that's...heat? That's... energy? It's tearin his insides apart. Burnin em. Remakin em. It's coursin through him, like electricity through a light bulb.

The Yella Angel...somehow...drillin holes?...into his back, his arms, his legs and fuckin those, too.

The Yella Angel...whisperin truths, afterwards. Fucked-up, brain-bendin truths too awful to ever ferget ."The age of kings has ceased. All the earth shall equally inherit a piece of the kingdom. The sun, itself, is the yellow sign – shining on one and all. As long as it hangs in the sky, you shall have no will of your own!"

And he wakes up, covered in puke, shakin with the DTs. Paces around the house. Looks out the livin room window at the neighborhood—alive with mornin busyness. Looks out at the bright, cloudless sky. Screams at the beautiful day.

YELLOW BIRD
BY LYNDA E. RUCKER

On great grey plains the dead stones lie
Here time itself will someday die
So strange the tales of
        Lost Carcosa.

My mother comes to me in my dreams. She smells of star anise and lilies with something underneath I cannot quite identify, something old and strange and not quite wholesome. She is the most beautiful woman I have ever seen. When she wraps me in her arms I want to die. I tell her that; I press myself against her and I say, "I would die for you," and she never answers me. When the dream starts to fragment I clutch for pieces of her: a bit of hair or flesh to carry over into my waking life, to remember her by. She leaves me with nothing. She departs with the dawn every time. And every day without her is duller than the last, but someday I will find her again and we will never leave one another's sides.

I am only a little afraid of her. Sometimes in the dream I imagine she wears a mask; that beneath it lies something terrible, but only sometimes.

It was the hottest day of July, smack in the middle of a long Georgia summer, and I was reading books in the ruins of my great-granddaddy's house when they came back. I heard them long before I saw them, because they drove an old pickup truck with a loud exhaust that kept backfiring, and they were whooping and hollering like crazy things. I didn't think they *would* come back, because after they took the iron frame of my great-granddaddy's old bed, what else was there to steal? I knew I had to make myself scarce all the same though. The last thing I wanted was to deal with a bunch of meth-heads, even though I was just a kid, only twelve and no threat to them.

My great-granddaddy's house was really just a shack in the woods, and he'd been dead a long time by then, since way before I was born, and was gone from his shack well before he died. They put him in a nursing home for his dementia a real long time ago, in the early 1980s. Ever since, nobody had lived there and the place had just been falling apart. Part of the kitchen wall was just gone, a big old hole like a monster had come along and torn it open. And you couldn't really go in the bedroom at the other end of the shack at all because half the ceiling had collapsed. Unless, of course, you were a drug addict trying to steal the last piece of metal left in the whole damn place so you could sell it for scrap.

But the living room, in the middle, was sounder than the rooms on either side of it, and it had one long wall lined with books. Most of them were even older than my great-granddaddy, from the early 1900s and before. I don't know where he got all these books or whether he read them or anything. I live with my grandma. My great-granddaddy's family never liked her because she was my granddaddy's second wife, which I guess was bad or something, and now they're all dead anyway, so we never talk about them.

I'd never heard of any of the books. They weren't the kind of classics they make you read at school. Some were dull, and lots of them were ruined, so many pages stuck together from mold and mildew you couldn't open them. Some weren't in English. Some were novels, others histories. There was a travelogue from Africa, a history of railroads, an entire book about church bells. A book of home remedies (I tried some; turns out, washing your hands in stumpwater by the light of a full moon doesn't cure a wart), a handbook for minister's wives, a nineteenth century French novel I'd been painstakingly trying to translate word for word into a notebook with the help of a dictionary from the library.

But one book was the best, because it was different from all the others. The cover was a worn, fading gold. There was no title, just a single symbol on the front of it. I am not going to draw it here or tell you what it looked like because it is a secret. On the inside, there weren't any pages with authors' names or publication dates. There was just a play that began on the first page. But as you read it, it changed; first it was a poem, and then like an old illuminated manuscript, and then handwritten, dark ink on its yellow cracking pages. Parts of it were in languages and alphabets I could not identify. You could tell it was very old. Reading it was like dreaming, in that it was the most vivid thing in the world while it was happening but when I was done, it scattered to the edges of my memory, and if I so much as tried to recollect anything about it, put it into some waking sense, it dissipated. I did dream about it as well. I still do. I wake up from those dreams feeling angry and agitated, like I have lost or forgotten the most important thing in the world. Sometimes in the morning I try so hard to hold onto the tatters of the night but it's all swept away so callously by daylight.

At my granddaddy's house I'd made a little nest for myself in that living room. I'd brought blankets from my grandma's, and I'd pulled the rotting chairs and sofa round to make a kind of fortress and thrown blankets over them as well. I had some snacks, cans of Coke and a bag of Cheetos and a pack of Chips Ahoy. It felt like the safest place in the world when I was all tucked up in there even if I was in a old falling-down shack in the woods that meth-heads liked to steal stuff from.

I didn't think they'd come back though. I mean, surely there was nothing left for them.

When I heard them, I acted faster than I could think. My heart felt like it was going to explode, and I scrambled over the sofa and out the hole in the kitchen wall and into the woods.

I never told my grandma I was going over there. It's just a five minute walk up the road from where we live, but she wouldn't have liked it. She would have said it was dangerous but the real reason was that I felt like she didn't like me having much to do with that side of the family.

My grandma raised me, but when I was little I used to have daydreams about my mother coming back to take care of me. I didn't know much about her. Her name is Cassie and mine's Camie which is short for Camilla but nobody ever calls me that. I don't like it, it sounds like an old lady's name.

Cassie used to come visit sometimes. She was so beautiful I was afraid to look at her. I couldn't believe she was my mother. When I look at myself in a mirror I just look ordinary, but she was like a princess in a book. She had long hair to her waist and smooth dark skin and violet eyes.

My grandma didn't like it when she would come visit. Cassie would never say she was coming, she would just turn up. She always brought me presents my grandma wouldn't let me keep. Usually it was some kind of fine cloth, or scarves, or wraps. Because I was just a kid I thought they were boring presents even though I was excited about them in general because it was my mother who had given them to me. One night I heard them arguing and my grandma was telling her she shouldn't come around and she shouldn't give me things. My grandma said, "It's confusing for her." I guess she was talking about me, but I didn't feel confused. I felt a lot of things when Cassie turned up like she did, but confused wasn't one of them.

I can't remember if that's the last time I saw her or not. She was never around for long; at first she'd dote on me and call me her baby and then after about a day or so it was like she got fed up with me and I was just a pain. And she always seemed sad. Then she'd go away again without saying anything to anybody. We'd just get up in the morning and she'd be gone.

By the time I was twelve, I hadn't seen her for a few years, and my grandma never mentioned her. I was afraid to ever ask about her because I thought she might be dead.

You know, my grandma was so funny about her I've thought maybe Cassie wasn't even her daughter, which meant maybe I'm not really her granddaughter either. But like I said, nobody ever tells me anything.

My father, I only have one memory of him, and I must have been really little. He had been cutting wood all day for my grandma to burn in her wood stove, and I remember he came in afterward and he smelled like wood and sweat and he let me sit in his lap. He had a cigarette and a beer, and his voice was low and made me feel calm and safe. I don't know what happened to him after that. I don't even know his name. We don't talk about him either.

So there I was, out in the woods, and I could hear them yelling at each other and knew they were up to something but I didn't know what. My curiosity got the better of me, and I crept closer till I was right outside the hole in the kitchen wall.

As best I could tell from two rooms away, it seemed like there were three of them, a girl and two guys. I heard a lot of banging and swearing, and the old shack was shaking like something heavy kept getting slammed around. But that's not the reason I went back inside. I went back inside because I remembered I'd left my book, the book with the gold cover, lying right out in plain sight, and I was suddenly so scared they'd take it or do something to it.

So I went back through that hole in the kitchen wall, and I peeked round into the living room from the kitchen and saw they weren't in the living room but in the bedroom, and I was trying to gauge if I had time to run toward my little nest and snatch that book when I realized why they were making such an almighty racket.

I had been wrong; there *was* something else to steal. They had gone into the rotting bathroom at the back of the falling-down bedroom and they were trying to drag the clawfoot bathtub across the floor. Of course; it was made of cast iron too.

I crossed the living room and peeked round the door of the bedroom. They weren't doing a very good job. The tub's back end, the part the girl was supposed to be moving, had fallen through the rotten floor. Plus it was just too damn heavy for three skinny addicts to move across the room and out of the house, let alone lift into the back of a pickup truck.

They were all vaguely familiar to me, older brothers and sister to kids I knew at school. The girl's face was thin and sad, and she had a name I could almost remember, one of those names that's not a name like Star or Treasure or something.

One of the guys said, "Shit. We got to break this up before we can get it out of here. Need a big hammer or something."

The girl said, "Fuuuuck."

I backed up as quietly as I could. But the girl said, "What's that?" and one of the guys said, "Nothing," and she said, "No, I heard something," and the guys laughed and one of them said, "Yeah, right," but they were headed toward the doorway now and I sprang backward. I scrambled past my little nest with one hand outstretched to grab my book but I missed and knocked it off the sofa instead. It clattered to the floor and I just ran. Why didn't I bend down and snatch it up first? I'll never forgive myself for being such a coward.

"I told you there was somebody!" the girl called after me, and one of the guys said, "Naw, that ain't nobody, just Camie Huff, that crazy old lady's granddaughter." I sprang out the hole in the kitchen wall but as I headed for the woods I heard the other one say, "We better get out of here, she's probably going to tell somebody we're here," and the first guy went, "Who, her crazy grandma?" and then they all started laughing and my face and ears burned with anger as I ran from them, away from their laughter and back into the woods.

How do you know when something's real and when it isn't? I mean that as a serious question. How can you know? You can't ever go outside of your own head and your own thoughts. What if everything you see and hear around you isn't real?

There's no way you can ever know, is there?

I think maybe none of us are as real as we think we are.

It was that anger that stopped me, the anger that kept me from running off through the woods till my lungs felt like they were going to burst. I was so mad at them, and so mad at myself. I don't know what I thought I was going to do, but I only ran a little ways, and then I waited for what felt like a long while. There was just the sound of my breathing and the cicadas that never stopped whirring all summer long, the sweat slicking my back, and the long distant drone of a plane overhead. I counted my breathing to get a sense of how long I waited; I hit the thousands and kept going. I felt like I was counting myself into a trance, but I couldn't just go home. Not without retrieving my book and making sure it was safe. A few thousands breaths in, I headed back.

I was sure they must have left by then. Maybe they'd gone off to get that hammer. I crept back, but as I got closer to the big hole in the kitchen again, I could hear them inside, still talking and laughing.

And then the next thing I knew I was knocked off my feet. In my memory, what happened was not an explosion the way that you see it in movies, or imagine it might be. I don't remember whether there was a loud noise. I just remember a sense of shock, falling over, and something more like a roar that engulfed me. Then somebody was screaming for what seemed like a long time.

The sky and the air around me had turned grey, and ash swirled about us like I was in a burning snowstorm. I tried to get to my feet, but they kept slipping out from under me because the ash was so thick you couldn't see the ground, and it seemed like the sun was blotted out. The girl was still screaming. I wanted to get to her even though I was so scared. I didn't care who I was with. I just didn't want to be alone.

My great-granddaddy's cabin was on fire, I could figure out that much. It was so hot, and the fire was *roaring* like a living thing. Surely somebody would see the smoke rising up from the woods and call 911. I started crawling in the ash and I got around the front of the house and that's where the girl was, and as soon as she saw me she stopped screaming. I guess she was in shock. Her face and arms were covered in raw, angry welts that must have been burns, but she wasn't hurt as badly as she'd sounded.

I tried to ask her what happened to the guys, but I couldn't make my voice work. My whole body felt like it was full of smoke and when I tried to speak I couldn't stop coughing. Then a chill wind blew across us and just like that we weren't *there* any longer.

The girl grabbed my hand and I held onto hers tighter than I ever held onto anybody. We had been on the verge of getting burned up alive and suddenly we were not; instead, we were on a great grey bleak plain under a dim relentless sky. The fire, the shack, the woods, the hot summer day, were all gone.

The plain was broken only by enormous stalagmite structures twisting up toward that twilight sky. They were made of stone, and somehow I knew that they were made—they had not just formed that way—but whatever made them had been dead a long time, maybe for millions of years.

And then I heard my mother's voice. She was whispering to me, but I can't remember most of the things she said. Seven words are all I have ever remembered. She was close enough to touch, and I reached for her, but then the wind on the plains was furious, a roar that became the roar of the fire again and I was on my back on a stretcher and they were trying to jam something plastic in my mouth and saying it would help me breathe and I didn't want anything in my mouth and I didn't want to breathe if it meant I couldn't go back to that place and hear my mother's voice again.

I knew I was losing consciousness, but I also knew I needed to say the words she had said to me. If I spoke them, I would remember them forever. As I writhed and gasped for breath with smoke-wracked lungs the words were all but torn from my mouth:

"Come back to me in lost Carcosa..."

That was five years and a lifetime ago.

Nobody knew what happened to the guys. People do blow themselves up and die trying to make meth in plastic Coke bottles like they were doing, but they never found any bodies, so they guessed the guys must not have been hurt too bad, and must have run off. A couple years ago I heard they found one of them in Memphis but it turned out to be a false alarm.

I also heard the girl went crazy, but you hear a lot of stuff.

What did I care about any of that, though? I only ever went back to my granddaddy's again one more time, to see if I could find my book. Of course there was nothing left.

So I started looking online. Plugging words into search engines, coming up against dead ends, or finding weird old pages abandoned in the nineties, or forums that seemed promising but turned out to be populated by cranks.

I kept searching. I learned about the places far below the surface of the internet, beyond the reach of search engines and surveillance tools, where all the real exchanges of information, and much darker things, take place. I got a job flipping burgers at McDonald's after school and I saved up for a laptop. I learned how to access places on the deep web I can't tell you about. Places where they know about the yellow symbol that was on my book. Shadowy cyber corners where you pay in darkcoin for information from people who have gone so far underground they might as well not exist.

I write letters, too, and I have a post office box in town that people use to send me photocopies of old books and ancient manuscripts they have hidden away, although I have yet to find another book like the one I lost. I've learned not to say too much about that, either. It excites the attention of the kind of people you don't want attention from.

In a year I'll be eighteen. My grandma is getting older and her health is failing. I think she thinks I am going to stay at home forever and take care of her. But the minute I am old enough I am going away, just like my mother did.

I know I will find my way back to her again if I have to spend my life searching. I have what I need most, the last words my mother ever spoke to me as the cold winds of lost Carcosa swept over us both, the words that I have never dared to speak again. They sit on my lips like fire. And I dream of that place every night now, with its blackened suns and stars and its stark and ancient landscape of dead things left by lost races.

But *I* am not dead, and I am only a little lost. I wish I had some piece of her, the fabrics my grandma destroyed, but then I remember that I am myself a piece of her.

The place frightens me. There was a wrongness about it, and so maybe there is a wrongness about her, and a wrongness about me. Or maybe the wrongness is the wrongness of an ordinary girl, a girl who was so lost and so unhappy she made up a story saying that her mother went away to be a queen in some blighted land. Like a sick fairy tale with no happily ever after.

Which story is real? Which story is true? How do I see past my own eyes? How do I hear what a god hears so I know what is false?

Well, even a god may be deluded or insane. So may I, by virtue of the company I keep if nothing else. My correspondents and informants speak in riddles; they believe in purity by way of corruption, of madness on the road to enlightenment. I pretend like I care about their crazed and glorious ideals but I don't. I only care about *her*, and finding her again.

One other question troubles me: if she is the queen, mustn't there be a king?

When I ask this question, my informants fall silent. They retreat. Sometimes they never respond to me again at all. But I know he is out there as well, because sometimes I can feel him pressing at the borders of my dreams about her. I do not know whether I am afraid of her, but I know I am afraid of him; yet do I not mean what I say to her with *I would die for you*?

This is what I tell myself when I wake sweating and sobbing from the dreams; when she has held me close and I have tasted her contaminated skin; when I have tried to burrow back inside of her and I feel her wretchedness consuming me: that I will sacrifice myself for her willingly, gladly, unceasingly. *I will die for you, Mother. I will.*

My greatest fear, and my unspeakable conviction, is not that she will reject this offering.

It is that she will embrace it.

EXPOSURE
BY HELEN MARSHALL

"Did you bring the sunscreen?"

The boat was unsteady, hurled up the height of the enormous waves cast off in the wake of the cruise ships heading to more popular destination, sliding down with a lurch that made Serena feel like fucking hurling. Not her mother, though, no, Serena's mother had a smile like a clenched fist.

"The sunscreen, Serena. Did you bring it? It's important, I told you it's important."

Nothing.

"Serena, I asked you a question: did you bring the sunscreen?"

"Yes, Mom—jesus!—I brought the sunscreen!"

A long pause. Serena squinted. The glare of the ocean was bleak and blinding. It should have been beautiful, being out on the ocean like this, it should have been glorious—but then, Serena should have been on one of the cruise ships, she should have been wearing a neat little black bikini, should have been sunbathing on the deck, should have been staking out the side of the pool and working on her tan.

Should have been.

"That's it, it must be, in the distance, Serena, don't you think that must be it?"

"I guess."

"You guess? You guess? Ha, she guesses."

Serena rolled her eyes, and her mother ignored it for once, too fucking happy to be here, too fucking happy to be part of the crowd of tourists. Not that there were all that many of them—there wouldn't be, would there? Really, only a handful, German, Italian, English, American—all middle-aged men with bald patches, bulbous sunburnt noses—fucking gross. Some of them clutched at guidebooks and cameras. Her mother didn't have a camera. Her mother didn't want anything as crass as a camera. Whatever she wanted, she wanted to see on her own.

Serena didn't understand it. This had never been *her* thing, this had always been her mother's thing. When Serena was twelve her mother had dragged her to Athens. Last year it had been Istanbul. And, okay, maybe those places had a certain charm. Maybe there had been something to the Acropolis, watching the marble changing from gold to rose to white to pale blue as it reflected the last glow of the twilight—maybe that had been just a little bit nice—but then it got back to the way things always were between them, her mother screaming at her for forgetting the sunscreen, her mother freaking out when she talked to anyone for even ten seconds. Like the hotel concierge was some pedophile. And he wasn't, of course he wasn't! It was just cultural, right? It was just how they were in Greece!

Fucking Carcosa.

She could have gone to Venice.

She could have gone to Barcelona. Or Paris.

Carcosa was nothing but rocks, ruins—no one went to Carcosa, not now, not anymore. A few outcroppings, a few standing pillars. Once, Serena had read, the place had been beautiful. Once they had written about the towers. They had written about the Lake of Hali.

Dim Carcosa. Lost Carcosa. Strange the night where the black stars rise. That's what the guidebook had said.

But what was left of it now? Rubble. An ancient junkyard. No looming towers. No Aldebaran. No Hyades. No Alar. No Hastur. No Hali. A hundred years ago the French team of archaeologists had drained the fucking thing, and why? Malaria! The Lake of Hali had been breeding fucking malaria-infested mosquitoes!

"The sunscreen," her mother reminded her, this time her voice was sharp, cutting.

Serena looked over her shoulder at the cruise ships heading for Mykonos—the white sand beaches she'd been staring at for months in the brochures—and tried desperately to discover the secret of self-teleportation, to will herself onboard *that* ship and not this one, not this dinky little boat fighting the waves, the sailors all dark-haired and dark-skinned, speaking whatever fucking language they spoke, and the tourists with their cameras primed and ready—like Carcosa really meant something to them, like this was it, this was *it*, this was fucking Carcosa!

Fucking losers, Serena thought.

⸸

Quiet now.

Blessed, fucking peace.

Serena walked along the shoreline. Her mother was somewhere—anywhere—not here, and thank God for that. Their split had been predictable: the spilled sunscreen, her mother scrubbing away at the oil-slick sand to find something usable, rubbing gravel and who knows what else into her arms until they glistened and blistered at the same time. She was mad, absolutely mad! Serena had been ecstatic to see her storm off, arms and legs crusted like a panko chicken breast, with a trio of tourists from Germany.

Five hours, she had been told. That was all.

Five hours to kill.

Serena kicked a rock. It rolled lazily for a moment, crushing the tiny shells that littered the beach. Serena had examined them earlier, strange spiralled things, flat, gleaming shards in the shape of fans, and amongst them the petrified husks of insects. It sent a shiver up her spine, the thought of what might be wriggling in the waters.

Serena did not like the waters. They were not blue waters as they should have been, but purplish like a fed tick. The algae she had read. Something like that. And the light here was different. Too bright, but somehow thick, like mist, substantial—you could never see too far. The black stars, a trick of that same light, because they weren't black, not really, not stars really—something to do with the atmosphere, some sort of dust in the air, like how the northern lights could make the sky seem alive and crawling, the black stars were like that, except they made the sky seem dead, they made the sky seem like a giant bloated corpse crawling with flies…

How the black stars seemed to move.

Serena didn't like it.

She remembered the bus ride they had taken to the harbour city. Bouncing along on broken vinyl-covered seats, padding spilling out, her mother ignoring her, staring at the guidebook, not letting her see.

"You don't care, Serena," she had said, "so just fucking sit there, would you?"

So Serena had been staring out the window, watching the lights of the villages they passed. They were high up. The island was mostly mountainous, mostly volcanic rock, she remembered being thrilled by the heights when there had been daylight, looking out at the red rock beneath them, the tiny houses clustered together on sharp, improbable plateaus.

But then the storm blew in—sudden, furious—and it frightened her how high up they were. How the roads had gone slick and Serena could feel the back of the bus beginning to fishtail as they took the curves. She experimented with news headlines in her head: Two Americans Dead or No Survivors in Tragic Crash. Began to see if she could make them feel real to her, if she could envisage that future—but it all sounded too senseless. Prosaic in a way that made it ridiculous. Those kinds of stories didn't involve Americans. It was always people from somewhere else—India, perhaps, or China. It couldn't happen to her. She watched the lights of the villages like constellations below her. If they were there, she knew she would find her way home.

And then abruptly, terrifyingly, the lights were gone.

For a moment Serena fumbled for her mother's hand—a moment, that was all it was, a single moment of desperation, a single moment of wanting her mother to hold her and tell it would be okay.

"Jesus, Serena," her mother had said at last, rolling her eyes, "the drivers do this all the time. They know the way."

Whatever.

She fucking hated it here.

The sun was lower now. The pillars cut jagged lines into it, brightness spilling out all around.

Boarding time, thank god. Serena waited by the boat. It bobbed up and down lazily. The sailors were moving around cargo containers. Two of them leaned against the rail, smoking a single cigarette between them that stank something fierce.

"Hey," Serena called. That one looked up—the one that, maybe, no promises, she would like to fuck. He had the cigarette between his fingers. "Hey—can I?"

He shrugged. He smiled at her, and held up the cigarette.

"That's right. Yes, a smoke. I can—good, okay."

She walked up the ramp, and he caught her around the waist when she stumbled in the unstable rhythm. His grip was strong. It lingered. She didn't shake herself free but instead casually plucked the cigarette out of his hand. The smell of it made her choke, but she liked the way the smoke curled in the air like a cat's tail. She liked the way the sailor had held her around the waist.

"Well, Nameless," she said, passing the cigarette back with a smile. "You seem alright."

"Alright," he intoned.

"Some English then?"

He shrugged, and smiled around a second cigarette.

"This is such a crock, isn't it? Carcosa. Fuck."

He sucked on the cigarette casually.

"They say the island is haunted."

"Ah," he said, "the island." He shrugged. "Haunted?" Then gave a lazy wink.

"But you don't believe that, do you? Ha, if you do."

"Ha," he said. The cigarette dangled precariously off his lower lip.

Just beyond them now a small crowd was forming on the pier. They all wore a look of irritable disappointment—not at leaving, but having ever have arrived in the first place. In Athens, they had that look, in Venice, in Barcelona. In Paris, they had it too but they were all too afraid to show their true feelings: instead, everyone had exclaimed over the buttered croissants, the quality of the wine all the while doing their best to pretend the Seine hadn't stunk with urine. They had snapped pictures. God, they loved taking pictures, even though they hated whatever they were looking at, even though it disappointed them so hugely. What were they snapping pictures of? A bunch of broken rocks? Whatever they thought they had captured, someone else had been there first. If there was anything Serena had learned, it was the endless disappointment of the already discovered. The great glories of the past—gods and poets, conquerors, angels, artists, all the filthy, dangerous *romance* of the world—had drained away like water through a sink hole.

The crowd grumbled. Weary men, sunburnt and angry, their flab a glistening mound under their cotton shirts. Women fanned themselves with brochures, their faces still twisted into unnatural shapes from smiling into the sun.

Serena sniffed delicately, plugged away at the cigarette, as Nameless the sailor and the others began shuffling these cows onboard. They huddled together in little clots.

Where was her mother?

Nameless clicked a little tally with every tourist who stepped on board. Click, went the tally. Click, click, click. Each numbered and accounted for.

But where was her mother?

There was the German trio with their fingers thick as Bratwursts and their Kommandant scowls glowing in the guttering light.

"Hey," Serena called to them. "You there."

They bristled as a unit, and Serena flinched away.

"Hey," Serena tried again—this time to Nameless. He was grinning happily at his tally as the others began to close the gate. "My mother's still out there."

"Mother?"

"Yes. She hasn't come back yet onto the boat yet."

"No," he grinned. He pointed at the tally.

"We can't leave yet."

"We leave." He pointed at the tally again.

"Jesus, I'm trying to tell you, she's still out there. She hasn't come on board yet."

Serena hated his uncomprehending stare.

"We leave," he insisted, "*now*."

"You said—" she gritted her teeth "—no one stays on the island. My mother is on the island."

It was ridiculous. Fully ridiculous. Of course, they couldn't leave. She looked around for allies, but they had all turned against her. They had reservations for dinner, appointments, there were cocktails waiting for them in quiet cafes, and the afternoon's exertions were over—they should be abandoned as quickly and efficiently as possible.

She felt a coldness slither down her spine, a sense of how alone she was at that moment and how utterly unprepared she was for it. Her mother kept their passports in her purse, had only given her enough cash for tips...

Nameless shrugged his shoulders comically, waggled his eyebrows at her, and for a moment Serena thought it had all been a joke. She smiled. The tight knot at the centre of her belly began to lose, and her relief was such thought she felt a sudden urge to throw her arms around the Germans and kiss them on their sweaty, schnitzel faces.

Then Nameless pulled her in close again, so close she could smell the smoke on him and the salt and the sweat and something else, rancid, sweet as rotten meat. In that moment she was afraid, suddenly, that he was going to kiss her. Instead, he whispered into her ear—and the smell of him was so much worse, it was like smelling a dead animal—"I come back," Nameless said, "an hour or two. No more. No one stays on the island, but you stay, for now, and I come back."

And he gave her a small but deliberate push. Serena stumbled forward onto the gangway, her sandal catching awkwardly in the planking and nearly sending her for a nasty spill. She turned and stared at the sailor, all doe eyes and hurt, but he merely took his cigarette from his mouth with a flourish. Casually, he flicked the edge of it into the water.

The tourists smiled. It would be easier this way, for them, and she would be fine. Of course she was fine. After all, whatever the city was, it was in a guidebook now, and they all damn well knew that for a place such as this a guidebook was as good as a eulogy.

They left her on the shore, standing in the wavering sunlight, feeling naked and exposed as they watched her, each of them smiling, each of them with their fucking cameras, each of them grasping after one final, fatal shot of the shoreline.

Serena stumbled through the columns, calling, but she could not think where to look. Her mother had always wanted to go to Carcosa but that was it. There was no special part of Carcosa she had always wanted to see, as far as Serena could remember. It was just Carcosa. The entirety of it. It was a thing that could not be divided up. No piece would be enough.

Serena's mother was not one to miss appointments. She had a pocketbook in which she kept everything in order. That pocketbook ruled her life: every hour perfectly accounted for, traffic snarls anticipated, emergency phone numbers recorded. Whatever was happening was clearly impossible.

That meant only one thing. Serena's mother was dead.

Once the thought slipped around her like a noose she could not escape it. It was logical. It fit the facts. Serena seized up with shivers. She could not breathe.

Her mother was dead.

Her mother was dead.

Serena had never been one for sustained momentum. She was fickle, and she liked being fickle. Now she was tired. The rocks felt hot to the touch. It felt like she was running over fucking coals. Her skin was starting to burn even though evening had swept in already, she could feel it itching, that telltale sign she'd been out too long. She was thirsty. She was hungry. She was crying and that was a fucking waste of water, wasn't it?

Serena sat on the shore and she stared up the sky. Hours had passed, how many she didn't know. Her fear was like amnesia, but even that was starting to wear off. She dug her fingers into the sand. There were shells there. They had been left behind too, like she had been left behind. Something had crawled out of them, naked, and decided that life would be better without any protection. The shells shattered against her fingertips. They would have made bad protection anyway.

The sky was black. The stars were black. It made the water black too, black and slick as blood in an unlit room. She was watching for lights now because she couldn't watch for shapes anymore. She imagined the Germans wherever they were guzzling beer and staring up at the moon. She imagined them drunkenly stumbling back to their rooms to fuck. The wife would be too tired. She'd spent the day exploring Carcosa after all. It was too much to ask of one person: Carcosa and fucking.

Serena thought about the husband, sad and still horny. She thought about him standing in front of the toilet, his thick sausage fingers wrapped around his thick sausage penis.

But then Serena stopped thinking those things because the first body had drifted onto the shore.

It wasn't one of the Germans, she would have recognized the Germans anywhere. But she was sure he had been with them, this fucking guy now with his hair tangled up in the seaweed, his face still fresh but his cheeks starting to bloat as if he'd been holding his breath. He bobbed gently in the water. There were air pockets hiking up the armpits of his brightly coloured shirt. A camera tugged at his neck. It was an anchor now that he had found the sandy ridge of the beach. It held him in place.

There were two more not far behind him. A woman. She had a wedding ring, big and gaudy. She had bridal eyes, but they were frozen up, staring up at the black sky. Then a much fatter walrus of a woman just behind her.

Serena stepped into the water. Her feet slouched into the mud. There were more of them coming, bloated shapes that broke the pale gleam of the waves apart. She couldn't see them properly, not in the darkness, but she knew they were out there, slowly drifting toward her. She rummaged through the pockets of the closest one for money, documentation, anything, then she realized what she was doing, rummaging through the slick and heavy pockets of dead people, and she stumbled away. Fell over backwards. Now she was lying half in the water, half out, damp cut-off jeans and the salt licking the sunscreen from her thighs.

Her toes bounced gently off the toes of the dead man.

Her revulsion was immediate. Serena scrabbled back onto the sand. Every part of her dripped, even the parts that hadn't been in the water. She was sweating heavily. Shaking. She got to her feet and started to run. Her sandals weren't very well-equipped for this sort of business, so eventually she tossed them aside and ran on her bare feet the way she had when she was twelve years old. The rocks cut her feet to ribbons but she kept running.

"Mom," she screamed, "Mom!"

No one answered her.

"Mom!"

Still no one. She squeezed her eyes shut.

"They're all dead! You can come out now!"

But for one brief second she thought she heard something in reply, something like heavy breathing, and she almost wept in relief. That was it then. Her mother had just been waiting for them to die, and now that they were gone she would reveal herself and take Serena home.

"Mom!" she screamed again.

In the silence that came after her screaming she realized it wasn't heavy breathing at all. It was the sound of the waves beating against the shoreline, and it wasn't even that sound. It was the sound of the silence between the beats. The sound of the great lung of the ocean inhaling.

Her own lungs were heavy now. The black air was too thick to breathe properly. She couldn't get enough oxygen and so, slowly, her frantic pace stumbled to a crawl. She wandered directionless, completely adrift.

Then there were lights in the distance—like a constellation, some sort of hope in the darkness. She tried to remember what else she had read in the guidebook about Carcosa. Who else lived on the island? What language did they speak? She couldn't remember. She hadn't cared at the time. She hadn't even wanted to come here, not to fucking Carcosa, dead Carcosa, lost Carcosa...

She knew she was leaving a bloody set of footprints behind her, but she didn't care. There were lights ahead. That was something.

Lights and then sounds. A series of dense bass notes that reverberated through the rock, shook her ankles, shook her knees, sent her pelvis swinging.

She hadn't expected to find a party here. In fact, it was just about the last thing she had expected to find, but even from a distance, she could recognize the pattern of the flashing lights, the way the earth shook and jived.

Something about it all—the loss of her mother, the horror of the dead bodies, those dark, insectoid stars—began to crack her up, and between the cracks the single word "PARTY!" rose out of her subconscious. Instinct kicked in. Even though she was soaked from the waist down and barefoot, there was a subtle but electric transformation taking place. She knew it. This was where she was supposed to be. This was always the place she was supposed to be. Maybe it was fucking Carcosa, but it was also *fucking* Carcosa, baby, or it could be—she thought—it could be, just like Mykonos, just like Paris, everywhere had a nightlife, right?

The music was loud, and she couldn't understand the language of the people around her. That didn't matter. What mattered was the way she smiled, that glow she had, how she could make soaked cut-offs seem like that's the way they were supposed to be worn. She glinted and glimmered in the darkness. She was like a gem.

"Hey," she said to the dark-haired man at the bar. He had long hair and teeth white like bleached bone. His arms were ripped and bulging, and for one brief moment the shape his muscles reminded her of the pockets coming out of the dead man's pants, filled up with air, bulbous. She didn't care though. She let her finger touch his finger. She paid with the dead man's money, which turned out to be hundred dollar bills. That didn't matter because the bartender said she didn't need to pay anyway.

"Fuck it," she said, flashing a smile at him. "It's a tip."

She went out onto the dance floor, trailing blood-stained footprints behind her. Her feet slid, and she made that seem cool too. Pretty soon there were men all around her, exactly the way she wanted there to be. One of them was pressing up against her from behind. She could feel his erection pressing against her ass. His hands touched her wrist. His hands touched her neck.

"See, I come back," he said, and Serena recognized the voice, the slight hiss of it. Nameless the Sailor. He had come back for her after all. Fucking perfect. Everything would be all right. This was all as it was supposed to be.

"What happened to everyone?" she asked him.

"Threw them overboard," he said and started laughing. She couldn't tell if he was serious or not. She liked the feel of him against her, and she pressed herself hard against his crotch. He smelled like cigarettes. He looked dirty, but dirty in a kind of hot way.

"Why did you do that?" Serena asked him over her shoulder. She was trying hard to concentrate, but inside something inside her was heating up like a pot with the lid clamped down, first steam frothing at the edges, then the hissing as it hit the metal plate and vaporized instantly. That's how she felt. She was the pot. She was the boiling water. She was changing inside.

"The cameras," he said, still smiling, "you know, *click click*." His teeth bit together as he made the noises.

"They were doing it wrong, huh?" she whispered, and she knew she was onto something there. Them with their stupid cameras. Their fat, sausage fingers, their eyes wanting to devour Carcosa, their disappointment…

"Wrong." He brought his mouth close to her ear and the way he said it made it seem sexy. He was sliding his hands down her hips, underneath the belt of her jeans. "Ha."

Serena arched her hips against him. It seemed as if he was everywhere now and the feel of his hands against her made her wet. She wanted to fuck him. She wanted to fuck him oh so badly but whenever she turned he turned too and so they were dancing like that, movement for movement as if they were already fucking and she just hadn't noticed when they started.

"And my mother?" she managed to ask him, the breath coming like liquid out of her mouth.

"Not her," he said. "Not your mother. Come."

Suddenly his arms were like cabling and he was leading her off the dance floor. She stumbled, big smears of blood painted the tiles, but no one else seemed to notice. When she looked behind herself she could see every place she had been. She could see the pattern of her dancing, and where Nameless had stood behind her. The sight was shocking. It pulled her back into herself. She grew afraid of him, his gargantuan presence, larger than life. It was as if he slipped out of his body and into something more suited to himself. Reverse evolution. He looked as if he had only recently crawled his way out of the ocean.

But it was not only him. It was everyone. They were massive, towering creatures with slablike faces and jutting jaws, composed of a soft jelly that shook and quivered to the music. Their bodies glistened. They left their own trail as they moved, thin threads of silk that crisscrossed the stonework. They were beautiful in the way that strangers are beautiful, soft-shelled creatures.

Here it was, the filthy romance of the world. Here was everything. Everything.

For a brief instant she wanted to touch them: wanted it painfully, wanted it more deeply than she had ever wanted anything before in her life. They had stripped her down to pure craving. The air was hot in her lungs, everything was hot, and she knew how easy it would be to strip off her shorts, her soaked top, to move naked amongst them. To feel their bodies pushed up against her, the raw, manic energy of it.

Their bodies were so soft, softer even than the bodies of the tourists floating in the water. Serena did not know where they had come from, but she knew, instinctively, that they were weak. She knew this because she was good at sensing weakness. She knew it the way her mother knew it. She knew they were reaching for her the way she had reached for her mother's hand, fumbling around in the darkness, wanting someone to hold. And knowing that made her powerful. It made her disdainful. It made her hate them a little bit for being so fucking weak that they would want her. They were as soft damageable as a newborn's skull.

Nameless tugged her forward.

To see her mother.

To see her mother now.

This was what her mother had wanted. This. Carcosa. This was what she had been looking for all this time.

She loved these fucking *things*.

"Your mother?" said Nameless, but Serena could feel that his grip had grown spongy. She brushed it off without any problem at all. "Please?" he looked hurt. Bewildered. A kicked puppy.

"Just fuck right off, would you?" Serena said. "My mother's fucking dead."

Serena followed the trail of her blood away from the party.

Eventually the noises grew quiet around her. The lights grew dim. As midnight devoured the rocks and pillars, the crumbling foundations, Serena came to the shore. The bodies were still there. A whole crowd of them had gathered. They made her feel worshipped, the way they clustered around her. She decided she liked them better like that. She liked them better than she had liked them while they had been alive. What a fucking drag they had been then.

She gathered up the cameras one by one. Most of the cameras were busted or drenched. A few shed sparks when she clicked the power buttons. Only one worked, it was practically antique, mechanical. There were canisters of film, little plastic waterproof jars, tucked away. Serena had never used a camera like this, but it felt right, somehow, holding this ancient thing, spilling its guts out. She wanted to know what it was *they* had seen. What had drawn them to this place. She peered at the frames one by one. She expected to see the crumbling rocks. Stupid German faces smiling blandly into the camera, dumb piggy eyes, not knowing how close they were to death, how it would be such a small push to send them overboard...

She laughed at what she saw. Just fucking laughed.

Night washed in. The darkness was nearly complete. Serena sat down heavily amidst the stones and the shells, and, making a necklace of the film, one long winding ribbon of pure black, she settled down to wait for the light to find her.

JUST BEYOND HER DREAMING

BY MERCEDES M. YARDLEY

She had a lover nobody could see.
There was nothing strange in this. In fact, it was better this way.

She had a husband, or at least a man she was married to. And this invisible lover that nobody could see or hear or smell or taste (he really was very delicious) was what kept her contented and sane for a while. Until, at last, he didn't.

But nobody likes to talk about that. Not really.

It's disturbing.

Unsavory.

But oh, it was so *glorious*.

※

She had wished for a name of beauty, but that wasn't what was given to her. Perhaps her mother was in poor humor or ignorant or simply mad in the throes of childbirth, but she called her "Hester" before she died.

Hester spent years pretending that she had said, "Heather," as the flowers, or "Ether," as the phantasmagoric, or even "Esther," who had been a great and beautiful queen.

But Hester it was and Hester it had always been, and after she curled up outside in the meadow with bare feet and a dirty shift reading

The Scarlet Letter, she burned with shame for days. Every time anyone called her by name, she heard the obscene way their teeth closed as they hissed it out.

"I won't be that," she said once to nobody in particular, and naturally they didn't care.

But several years down the road when her lover spoke to her? He called her sweet things. Pretty things. "My darling" and "little bird" and her favorite, simply "lover." He never spoke her name, not once in all the time they were together, and that was one of her favorite things about him.

But that was in the future. Now she was a child, now an awkward adolescent. Now it was all about rules and society and making sure her ankles didn't show. Now it was about being a lady and having a governess and looking for a father where she really didn't have one. He was a paper doll in a finely cut blue suit. He was a sea captain on an ocean without stars. He was a million different things, just as she had been everyone but Hester, and none of them were correct.

He died, and it really was a relief. She went under the care of a relative, and life didn't change so much. She still looked at the moving wallpaper and heard the whisper of dead things. Perhaps they were her parents. Perhaps it was her soul.

Things like that didn't matter so very much to a young woman with coltish knees and hair that didn't know how to settle under a bonnet.

But what did matter? Paint. Her art. Pictures. Dreams.

Ladies didn't paint, but Hester did. Real women sat near the window and sewed intricate little swatches of embroidery. They didn't pull their hair loose and lean into the room's sunlight with a hunger that was absolutely indecent. They didn't close their eyes and smell the deep, dark scent of the paints and powders and brushes as Hester did.

"What a degenerate," a woman whispered to Hester's aunt. This woman's face was lined and caked and had more paints and powders and brushes on it than any of Hester's canvases ever would.

"Poor thing lost both parents," her aunt sighed. "I really try to do the best I can."

"You're a saint," the Puritan Harlot said, and patted the aunt's hand. "Nobody could expect any more. You've done all you could."

They burbled and cooed about Hester's inevitable future as a spinster, but Hester had already kicked her shoes off and slipped out the back door. The sun fell on her hair as she unlaced the top of her dress, breathing in the good air as she ran for the fields.

Wild things run, and Hester knew she belonged to the grasses and skies.

"I did my best," she whispered to the bees and birds. Her skirt was hiked up far too high. Feral flowers and thistles bit at her pale legs.

"I know," she heard, and she spun around.

Nobody was there.

That was the first time she and her lover never met.

Hester was shameful but her hair was rich and her lips full. She caught the eye of a solid older man whose previous two wives had died young. Young, but hard. They had both been desert girls, their eyes green and squinted against the too-bright sun. Here, the rivers drowned them. The grasses choked them. Like snakes, they had shriveled and died when dragged out of their burrows and left somewhere strange and foreign. Children expelled from their wombs and life expelled from their lips. That was all.

William, for that was this man's name, had watched with helpless horror as both wives had passed on. Ineffectual man that he was, he had rung doctors and wrung his hands, but that didn't stop their chests from heaving, their lungs from expanding, their blood from flowing.

He began with a wife. He ended up with a corpse.

Wife two was also lovely although a bit swivel-eyed. She made an even spindlier corpse.

Wife three? She would be young and lush. She'd be able to survive the fields and greenery. Half wood-sprite, half fawn, and she and William would be stolidly and deliriously happy. Within dignified reason, of course.

He watched Hester's bonnet slip from her head as she tore through the field. Something moved in his chest. Perhaps it was resignation. Perhaps it was joy.

He called upon Hester's aunt that very day. Hester was improper, yes. Impetuous, certainly. But he was a man of fine reputation. He could provide for her. Train her up in the way she should go. He could do all of these things, certainly, and what's more, he was perfectly willing to. He had a satisfactory estate and his children needed a mother. He would be willing to overlook her more girlish nature and raise her into the fine young woman he, and Hester's aunt, knew she could be.

The aunt was grateful. Hester, not so much. But her opinion meant nothing in this matter, and she knew it.

The wedding was stiff and fine. She wore a dress too constricting and too good for her. It was trimmed in lace and pearls fetched by the sea.

"You look wonderful, darling," William said. He calculated net worth with his eyes. He found an errant stray of her hair and pushed it back with a thick finger. "As beautiful as any of my other wives were."

"Thank you," she said demurely, but her eyes were full of lions and forget-me-nots and the sea.

William smiled at her.

"Love isn't really so important. You'll see. Standing is. Reputation and luxuries. All of this will be agreeable by and by."

"That comforts me," Hester lied, but it was a lie of kindness, and so she was forgiven.

After the wedding, which was simply ordinary, she moved into William's home.

"Good afternoon, children. This is your new mother."

They looked at her and she looked at them. William nodded and a servant took Hester's only bag.

"I'll just run this up to the master bedroom," he said, and disappeared. A puff of smoke. A breath. A black cat in the moonlight.

"Does he always move as stealthy as that?" she asked the children, and they nodded.

"I think he is a ghost," one of them whispered. Hester thought perhaps it was a boy, but they were all dressed in such frills and with ringlets spun so tightly that she really couldn't be sure.

"I wouldn't be surprised," she said, and the girl/boy child grinned, showing missing teeth, and Hester smiled back. Perhaps this could be bearable after all.

Hope deceived her. Three years went by and it was hardly bearable at all.

"Wear your hair up, darling. You don't want to look unkempt."

"If Sister Allistair invites you for tea, you simply must go. There's no other way to look at it."

"You have new standing, Hester. Mold yourself into the part. This is who you are now."

William's words showered on her skin as falling stars, and they burned just as badly. She twisted her hair into rolls and stabbed it with pins. She crushed her ribs with boned corsets. She pressed her feet into tiny, pointed shoes, tied her bows far too tightly, and always blackened her lashes immediately after her early-morning cry.

"Our other mothers were sad, too," the girl/boy children would tell her. Hester would smile and put her arms around them, nuzzling them as one wild bird does to another.

"I'm not sad, darling ones. Don't you ever think so."

Sadness was feeling and Hester didn't feel. At least not like she used to. She helped her newish children with their letters and their singing. She supervised the cook in the kitchen, which mostly amounted to saying, "That was lovely, Hilda. Would you please do the beef again soon?" and when William was away, which was often, she sat at the window and stared out.

"You aren't meant to be here," her invisible lover said next to her elbow. She heard him more and more now, but they were not lovers yet, you see. They were still voices caught in the ether. Ephemeral beings that had yet to touch.

"Here is as well as anywhere else, I suppose," she sighed, and the exhalation from her breath fogged the window. Somehow, this made her ache.

"My little bird," he said, and something about the crystalline flavor of his voice made her ache more, in the most decadent of ways.

"I want to tell you a story," he said, "but only after you've lived."

She knew he was gone before she turned to look, so she didn't bother. But she put her hand against the glass and wondered.

The Bible said that Mary, Holy Mother of God pondered sacred things in her heart. Hester did the same. Hester and Mary had very little in common besides being young and thrust into overwhelming motherhood, but they treasured up knowledge in their bosoms just the same.

That night her husband was out on business, as he often was. Hester slipped a cover over her nightdress and wandered the house, peeking in on the children and seeing that everything was set to rights. Of course it was. It always was. She then retraced her steps, seeing that everything was set slightly off. This picture, tilted just so. These papers pushed askew on the old wooden desk. This felt better. This felt more like home.

She took a candle and stepped outside. The cobblestone hurt her feet. She took a deep breath, snuffed the candle, and began to run.

The candle fell from her grip. Her loose hair bounced around her shoulders and elbows. The nightdress flapped like crow's wings and she finally felt herself free. She fled the street, turned down the back way and raced to the fields of grasses where she belonged.

The moon, being a woman and quite understanding of these things, lit her way graciously. Clouds parted to show the stars. Hester heard the panting of her breath and the slightly sinister sound of her sky-white feet passing through brush unknown. Here, she startled sleeping butterflies, which took to the air behind her. There, she tripped and fell, but clambered to her feet in a sea of fabric and dew-damp leaves. Her breath came in gasps, nearly sobs, but she ran and ran and ran. Away from something or toward, she wasn't sure, but what she did know for sure was that she had something to feel.

Fear.

Relief.

Desire.

Desire to shed her entrapments, desire to be free. Desire to be something other than a china doll with mechanical gears inside, grinding to starts and stops with elegant handwriting and a fine Sunday bonnet.

"You came," whispered the voice, and this time when she turned to look, he was there. A young man. Thin, with clothes whose lace rivaled that of her most opulent of dresses. He wore a mask pale as starlight, with holes cut for eyes and a tiny slit for a mouth. Hester felt as though she should be frightened, but she wasn't, not at all.

"I didn't mean to come," she said. "I simply ran."

"And here you are. As it was meant to be. "

"Who are you?" she asked, and although she couldn't see it, she felt that he was smiling under his mask.

"I am here for you. A gift from the universe, perhaps. Or maybe a punishment. But you are here, and I am here, and that isn't any coincidence."

There was truth in his words, a primordial conviction that thrummed through her veins as he spoke.

"I don't mind being unhappy," she told him. His body faded away in the shadows until only the mask could be seen in the moonlight. "Unhappiness is acceptable. But I don't want to be…"

"Imprisoned," he answered for her. She would have nodded, but it wasn't necessary. None of it was necessary. The stations and etiquettes and things typically required of her suddenly had no bearing at all.

"You want to hunt," he said, and this was true. "You want rain in your hair and blood on your lips."

"I suppose I want a lot of things."

"Then take them."

His hands were warm on her skin and his lips pressed against hers with the slim filter of the mask between them. She ran her hands through his hair and over the porcelain of his face.

"Will you ever take it off?"

"Perhaps."

"I'll wait."

The sun rose and Hester rose with it. Her lips were deliciously swollen and her nightgown and cover were askew in the most scandalous of ways. She felt more clear-eyed and lucid than she had been in years.

The way back to the house was far longer and more treacherous than the way out. But she smiled to herself and loosely linked her fingers with a tall, reedy man that nobody else could see.

It was strange having an imperceptible man around the house. He stood in corners while Hester brushed her hair. He leaned against doorjambs when she spoke to her husband. He sat quietly on the parlor couch while Hester and William argued.

"If you were here just a little bit more," she would say, and William would cut her off. It was an argument so well-worn that she could mouth the words alongside him. Sometimes the man in the porcelain mask *did* mouth along, and Hester had to put her hand to her lips to keep from laughing at the absurdity of it.

"Hester, my work is important and keeps you in the comforts you so well enjoy. It is necessary that I take these business trips. Why don't you busy yourself with the women's charity, or host a few more garden parties? After all, your standing in the community requires…"

His words tasted like soot and hemlock. They sounded like the unseemly shriek of carriage wheels and grimy harlots. She let them rain over her while she studied her white gloves. Not a speck of dirt on them. So pristine. So pure.

She caught her lover's gaze and blushed.

"What's this? You redden?" William said, and his voice softened. "I don't mean to speak so harshly, my dear. I only want you to be content and respectable. Are you not happy? Do you want for anything?"

"I want for nothing, my husband," she said, and he patted her on the head as he did his children.

"Will you try harder?" he asked.

Hester swallowed, and it hurt.

"Yes. I will try harder."

She performed her duties with a diligence that would have floored William had he been paying any attention. Each day more and more color fled from her face.

From her soul.

"Darling," her lover whispered, and when she turned to fully look at him, he saw that her blue eyes had gone nearly ice clear.

"Did you say something?" she asked.

"You're losing yourself."

"I'm afraid there isn't much to lose."

She took to painting reserved little landscapes on prim canvases up in the upstairs sunroom. Sea shores. Neat rows of breathless houses, lined up like soldiers or unhappy housewives.

Her lover didn't say a word, but brushed the wetness from her cheeks with his hand.

"At least I am painting, yes?"

He leaned over and kissed her trembling mouth.

"Shall I tell you a story?" he asked. He released her hair from its pins and began to speak, telling her of sunshine and suicides and other things of beauty.

"I wish you could tell me all the stories in the world," she said, and he smiled behind the mask.

"I can. Perhaps one day I will, my love."

Another year came and went. Hester did needlepoint and kept her knees primly together at all times. She spoke carefully in dulcet tones. Her heart turned its face to the wall and died. She feared her soul and body were not long to follow.

"Would you miss me if I were gone?" she asked William. Her hands twisted over themselves. Her eyes never left the carpet.

"What's that?" he asked. He was sitting at his desk, working on figures. Figures or bonds or letters or enchanted conversations with the stars, it didn't matter. Whatever he was working on took his full attention. As always.

"It doesn't matter," she said, and slipped away. For the first time in many, many moons, she crept into her old solace, the fields. She didn't run. She had not the energy. She walked. Staggered. At one point she dropped to hands and knees, crawling.

"How can I help you, lost little bird?"

Her lover had appeared beside her, his neutral mask lined with worry.

"I want to go home," she whispered. She continued pushing her way through the brush.

"Where is home, exactly?"

"I don't know," she said, and curled up into a little ball. Something chittered in the darkness. Something else hooted in reply.

"I don't know where home is," she said again, and covered her face with her hands.

"Shh, darling, my love. Don't cry."

Her lover sat beside her and caressed her hair, her face.

"Your home is with me," he said. "Wherever you are, that's where I want to be. Wherever I am, you should be there also. I love you. I've never told you this, yes, but it's true. I love you, my sweet little bird. You're with me. You are home."

She thought of her house, stricken of all color. She thought of William, who had stolen her very self away, piece by piece. She thought of their children, of their warm skin and big, bright ideas as fresh as the spring.

"You and the children are home," she slurred, eyes suddenly heavy. And then she was asleep.

She awoke with her head cushioned in her lover's lap. The sun shone in that gentle way that it has in early morning, before it remembers how horrid and loathsome humanity can be.

"Are you feeling better?" he asked.

She replied by lifting her mouth so he could kiss her. It was as if a first kiss, shy and searching and oh-so-wonderful.

"I meant it," he told her, his voice warm behind the cold mask. "I love you with everything I have."

"Thank you," she said.

There was more, and she meant to speak it, but the words made her shudder inside as though she had swallowed moths.

He kissed her again.

"You don't need to say anything more," he promised, and she knew he meant it.

He helped her breathe. Made her really feel that she could be enough for him, without the ropes of pearls and chains of gold. Never had finery felt so constraining. She realized now that's what it had always intended to be: leashes of silver and jewels.

"Your children are coming," he said, and Hester started at his words.

"Here?" she wondered, but the girl/boy children were already upon them.

"Mother. We thought you would be here. Are you well?"

Hester lay in the grasses, her fingers entwined with her lover who could not be seen. The children looked past him, although one seemed to notice a subtle glint of something like stone or porcelain.

"I'm fine, my darlings. I was simply restless last night. How did you know this is where I would be?"

The oldest child shrugged.

"Father often talks about how he found you running through the fields. You know, before. He says we should stay far away from here."

Hester sat up, her cheeks burning.

"Why is that?"

"He says it's unseemly."

Hester looked at her lover and he looked at her. She cupped each child's chin in her hand in turn.

"It is *not* unseemly. It's a place of beauty. Would you like to see?"

The children nodded and she took their hands in her own.

"Then come with me, my loves. See what draws me."

Flowers. Red ones. Blue. Butterflies with painted wings. Tiny frogs and crickets and the sound of the wind laughing in the greenery.

Vines in their hair. Bluebells in their eyes. The taste of nature in their lips, between their teeth.

They laughed. Oh, heavens, her children laughed. They played and rolled and their glee was as sweet as bells to her, as cold mountain water on parched roots.

"They, too, are wild things," she said to her lover, her king, and he kissed the tips of her fingers.

The sun finally swooned in the sky, and their bellies told them they had missed far too many meals that day. The walk home was one of sweetness. She had a child holding each hand. Her lover ghosted alongside them, humming something vaguely familiar but still altogether new.

Life was perfect. She was home.

And then, right before darkness fell, she really was home. Back to the stately house on the refined street, with her very dignified and righteously angry husband staring at her as though she were a filthy thing.

"Children. To your rooms."

"Father, but we haven't eaten supper and…"

"Go."

They had dandelion fluff in their ringlets and fear in their eyes. Wise children, they fled.

William turned to Hester.

"What have you done?"

His voice was hard and cold. It matched his eyes, the shiny pate of his head.

"Nothing, my dear. We were only in the field today."

"Never. Never again. You are never to take those children from this home."

"But darling, I only—"

"Do you not understand what you have done? How soiled they are? Why, after looking at them for only one instant, I could see the dirt ground into their cloth, the tears in their clothes."

"William, they are only children."

His eyes hurt her. The way he stared hurt her.

"They are my children. My children, Hester. You have borne me no children. These belong to me."

He said more, horrible things that would have shook her to her marrow had she heard, but she was incapable of that. She had lost all sense earlier, at what he had said about the children. Their children.

His children.

"And you are not to be near them, do you understand? You shan't influence them in any way. I'll see that the governess knows."

She blinked at him.

"Surely you don't….what did you say?"

He sighed and checked his watch.

"I believe I made myself perfectly clear."

"But William—"

"Go to bed, Hester."

He left. Turned sharply on his heel like a solider and walked into his study as if it were an armory. He shut the door. Locked it with a key.

Hester stood in the parlor, quite alone.

"I have the most magnificent of stories to tell you, my darling."

Her lover was so gifted at stories, telling her about fancies and things that lived just beyond her dreaming. She so wished she could tell the children. They would find such amusement in it. She missed them bitterly. The governess shepherded them away from her at every opportunity. She hadn't so much as spoken to them in several weeks.

"Yes?"

"This is a very special story. It is extraordinary."

"Will you tell me?"

"I would. But there is something you must know."

He spoke with gravity, and Hester turned to look at him. The smooth face of his mask betrayed nothing, and for the first time she was frightened.

"What must I know?"

His eyes, which nobody but Hester could see, were the clearest of blues, of greens, of browns, of yellows.

"It's a grand story, my darling, but I can only whisper it during the night before the sunrise. And the person I whisper it to must be my wife."

Hester's white skin, bleached even whiter after she stayed indoors at William's request, paled until the blood ran blue beneath it. Like paints. Like the colors she had given up in order to be an acceptable helpmate to her husband.

"But I cannot—"

He grabbed her arm then, the first time he had ever done so, and his lips moved oh-so quickly, oh-so passionately beneath the mask.

"I love you, my darling, do you understand that? I love you exactly as you are, as you were meant to be. I take nothing from you. Your freedom, your children, your desires. Can't you see it?"

She wanted to wrench her arm away but something inside her couldn't. If she was too rough, he would disappear. Or maybe part of her wanted to stay, to listen to what he was telling her. To ask him to say his words again more slowly, so she could close her eyes and let them cover her like the sea.

This made her pull her arm away quite firmly.

"I can't," she said, and the misery in her tone surprised her. She tried again, more regally.

"I'm sorry. I can't."

He stood there, her only joy, in his ruffles and frills and silly mask. He stood there, with his strange stories and songs and declarations of love. He stood there, and her heart beat too hard, too fast, and then it felt like it suddenly stopped.

"I understand. Of course. Forgive me, my lady," he said, and bowed.

Hester's dear lover that nobody else could see disappeared. She gasped, and then cried.

She had become just like everyone else. She couldn't see him, either.

"William! William!"

Hester raced into the spare room that had now become his. She pushed the door open and set her candle upon the table.

"William, I need to speak to you, urgently!"

He mumbled and snorted, then sat up in bed.

"Hester? What is it? Is it the children?"

She sat on the corner of his bed, pressing her hands tightly together as if in prayer.

"My dear William, I have done my very best for you all these years. You do know that, don't you?"

His brows pulled together in that way that made her cringe inside, but she continued on.

"I wear these clothes. I hold those vapid parties. I stay in our home and even when you took my paints away, and my meadows away—"

"It's the middle of the night."

"Even when you took my children away, I said nothing. Nothing! I have tried my very best to hold my tongue and be the wife you want me to be. Now I need to know, my darling husband, and I need you to tell me truthfully. Do you have anything in your heart for me?"

"Hester."

She grabbed at his hands, pulled them to her breast. She kissed his fingers fervently.

"Please, William. Please. If there is any feeling for me at all, even the tiniest bit, I need to know. I'm begging you."

He looked at her. He really looked. He took in her hair and the tears that ran down her face without shame. He saw her eyes and the wounded animal expression in them. Her fingernails, shaped and shined so carefully. Her night dress, mended so delicately.

"Of course, my love," he said, and she fell into his arms in such a way that he was embarrassed at first, and then merely stunned.

"Then I need you to do something for me," she whispered, and the tears made her voice sound hollow and strange. "Something to prove that I mean something to you. Do this one thing and I shall stay."

"Whatever you wish," he said, and held her fragile little bird bones tightly. "What is it that you need?"

She swallowed hard.

"Fetch me a flower from the fields. A red one. One that I can wear in my hair. Such a little thing, but it is so very important to me. Will you?"

"You want a flower?"

"A wildflower from the fields."

"And this will sate you?"

"Please."

William smiled at her, and she found herself smiling back. Hope is such a silly little thing.

"I shall fetch it tomorrow morning, my dear."

Hester nodded and slipped from the room, but she could not sleep. She found herself in the sunroom where she had put her paints and canvases away.

Her tidy little homes. Her squalid little landscapes. Her choked little seashores.

She threw the horrid paintings to the floor, one by one. Pastels and grays and sedate, starched things without any soul. She rifled through her paints until she found what she was looking for.

Reds.

Yellows.

Greens and blues and all of the colors of her lost lover's eyes.

She dipped the brush into the paints, but soon it was too little. Too small. Insignificant. She smeared the colors onto her hands, and gasped at their opulence. Jewels! Treasures! She swooped her hands across the walls, creating rainbows and day dreams and stories most magnificent. She stood on her tiptoes, climbed onto the stool, jumped as high and hard as she could to reach the ceiling. It was a dance. It was a military drill. She arched and stretched and crumpled and soon the walls and Hester and the room was one delirious kaleidoscope of everything that was right and beautiful and far too precious to exist in this world.

She spread out on the floor, staring at the art that spun around her like the universe on its kindest of days. She closed her eyes. She slumbered.

Light woke her. She blinked and rubbed her eyes with crimson and cobalt hands. Her mouth tasted of yellow.

William, she thought, and struggled to her feet. She hurried down the stairs and out the front door.

He was just returning home. His eyebrows rose when he saw her.

"Hester! What on earth?"

"Did you get it?" she asked, and pressed into him. He pulled away and examined his suit carefully.

She paid that no mind.

"Did you fetch my flower, dear husband? The red one for my hair?"

He took her in, her breathlessness, her outstretched, painted hands, and was filled with benevolence. Such a child beneath all of her womanly ways! Such a young thing with endearing enthusiasm!

"I have it, my child," he said. "Now close your eyes."

Hester did as he bid, biting her lip with anticipation. She felt something alight in her hair. A tear slid out from under her lashes, but she didn't bother to wipe the treacherous thing away.

"There," William said. "Now you look beautiful."

She opened her eyes. Reached up into her hair.

Felt something stiff and cold and sharp.

She pulled it out with trembling fingers.

"Just the thing for you," her husband said, beaming. "Quite expensive. The pearls are the largest I have seen, but it's such a lovely pin, and you wanted something for your hair. I'm sure it pleases you, my dear. I've seen few things finer."

She stared at the pin in her hand. She stared at her husband's pleased face. She put the pin in his hand and walked slowly into the house.

"Children," she said, and they pushed into her arms like warm puppies, like baby rabbits, like squirmy little wild things made of feathers and bones and fur.

"We've missed you, Mother," they sang.

"And I have missed you. Darlings, I would like you to meet someone. He is somebody very special. Will you say hello?"

"Hello, sir," they chorused, and her lover smiled.

"It is a pleasure to meet you," he said, and when he bowed, they giggled.

"He has the most magnificent story," Hester said, and her although her voice sounded a little different through the mask, the children could still understand her clearly. "It's a very special story for very special children. Would you like to hear it?"

"Oh, yes," the children squealed. One looked carefully at Hester's eyes, pinwheeling behind the cut-out holes in the porcelain, spinning like a color wheel of madness, but then the story began and the child was transfixed.

"This story," said the man, "is a fine story indeed."

"What is it called?" asked the youngest child.

"It is called 'The King in Yellow.' Your mother enjoyed this story, didn't you, my little bird?"

"Yes," Hester agreed. "It changes everything. Absolutely everything."

"Are you ready to hear it?"

The children nodded. Hester pulled them close around herself and kissed them through her mask.

"We're ready," she told him.

Her lover slowly removed his mask and began to speak.

IN THE QUAD OF PROJECT 327
BY CHESYA BURKE

The steady stream of three day old rain water trickled close enough for her to reach out and touch it, but she didn't for fear of catching something and needing another lockjaw shot. Although it hadn't rained in almost a week, she was in the basement of the three story schoolhouse and Shaka figured that was approximately how long it took the remnants of the previous storm to make its way from the hole in the rooftop, through the building and into that tiny little class room in the cellar. She absentmindedly touched the sight of the previous tetanus shot she'd gotten the year before when she'd cut opened her forearm on a rusty nail desperately holding together a long-past its prime wooden school desk. Danielle sat in the desk now, leaning to the side, just a bit, so as not to get caught by the nail that had been hammered downward by the janitor hoping to keep it from sticking anyone else. Sammy was cut on it last month.

In the front the new kid slid into his seat, no doubt hoping that the teacher wouldn't notice that he was late since his back was turned. The boy was tall, unusually so, but then Shaka herself was shorter than average, so most people were tall to her. Being just under five feet, the ninth grader didn't think she'd ever have the growth spurt that her mother had promised her that was sure to come. Instead, she'd resigned herself to looking up to people all her life—and them looking down on her. That was not a pleasant thought, but she accepted it like so many others in her life.

As the teacher turned to face the class, he didn't show any indication that he'd noticed the new kid had just arrived. That was good, Shaka thought. The new kid had confided in her that he had never been good in school and that he always seemed to get the teachers that were the least likely to work with him. Shaka had snorted at the thought. Was there any other kind of teacher? Mr. Jefferson—like the president, the man was quick to remind everyone—was worse than others, however. Most teachers there in Booker T. Washington High School were pretty apathetic (apathetic, that means that they just didn't care about the students). But Mr. Jefferson, he was different; he seemed to get off on making people feel bad about themselves. He was an ass. And Shaka didn't mind calling him an asshole either, because that's just how he acted most of the time, like a horse's ass. Teachers were like that. Sometimes they just wanted to be in control over children. They liked being the boss over them, liked ruling them as if the kids didn't matter.

Children to Gods, is how her brother, Richard, had always put it. Because, he had explained, that children were to teachers, as adults were to God. Insignificant. Meat and potatoes—end of the subject. Richard was okay, sometimes. Sometimes.

As Mr. Jefferson spoke to the class, the new kid—what was his name, again?—was slumped in his desk, naturally hoping that the short little man with the big mouth didn't call on him. It wouldn't work, Shaka reasoned. It never worked with Mr. Jefferson. Sometimes, sometimes apathy was better.

"Mr. White!" That was it, now she remembered, his name was Payden White. The white man smirked, laughing at the irony of the boy's name, Shaka was sure. "I see you're late. Can you afford that? You see, I've taken the liberty to look at your transfer papers, and I must say, that if you presume to take my class as seriously as you've taken your previous classes," he'd paused, smiled a bit, "then may I suggest something."

Payden didn't bother answering. What was the point?

"A respirator. Because, I'm as serious as a heart attack."

"Cute! Real funny," the boy had mumbled it, but evidently not well enough because the man had rushed toward him with such deliberate steps Shaka has wanted to jump out of her seat and run to protect the boy. She didn't though; she didn't want to get into trouble herself. She was a coward that way.

The man stood over Payden within seconds, breathing down his neck. "Something that this class isn't, is cute, Mr. White. Now if you were referring to my cute little trick for breaking down thermonuclear physics, then I can agree. But since, having read your transcript, I doubt you can comprehend that far, I'm going to assume that perhaps you're simply referring to my cute little ass"—he winked—"and then we may have something to talk about." Payden looked around, making eye contact with Shaka, no doubt unbelieving what was happening. None of the other students said anything, but they all sympathized with him. They had all been him. Jefferson probably didn't know anything about thermonuclear physics (whatever that was), this was an American History class, but, hey, it made him sound smarter than the rest of them. Made him feel superior.

The teacher stood there for a moment, just staring at the boy, "Yes, Mr. White, and were you talking about my ass?"

He shook his head.

"I can't hear you!" He shouted as if he were a soldier.

"No."

"Good, Mr. White." He seemed to get some kind of pleasure by calling Payden's name continuously. "Now we can get down to business. And don't worry, I'll take it slow for you, Mr. White."

Luckily they'd all gotten through the class unscathed and without the teacher calling on Payden again, but he had called out a few of the other students. Now a group of them stood outside Mr. Jefferson's door. "He's always like that, don't take it personal," Shad told him. She was shorter than him by more than a foot and at least three shades lighter.

"It doesn't matter." The boy didn't say anything else.

Shane walked up, put his arm around her. "What's up Z? What y'all doin' out here?"

"They call me Z, or Shaka Z sometimes. You know, as in Shaka Zulu." She was speaking to Payden, but never took her eyes off of Shane. "I've told them to stop doing that. I hate it."

"He was badass. Own it...."

Before he could finish, Payden was shoved really hard and fell to his knees in the middle of the group. Shaka bent down to help him up, but he pushed her away, probably embarrassed and angry.

"You hear me talkin' to ya, boy?" Tommy Noles stood over Payden, looking down on him. Shaka was sure that the boy was getting tired of having to look up to people terrorizing him; she knew she was getting tired of seeing it. Behind Tommy, other boys were egging him on, "Go on, Tommy!, he's a pussy, ain't he?, Kick his ass, Tommy-Boy!" but none of them made a move to join the fight or to help their friend. Payden stood to his feet slowly, not taking his eyes off Tommy. He was taller than Tommy but leaner. Shaka thought that the boy might just explode. His fist were balled up, his back straight.

"Answer me, boy." Only, the way he said it, it sounded like, Bo. They weren't in the country, no, in fact they were in a big city. Chicago. Where else could you get the excellent combination of run down schools, idiot teachers and pig slop for lunch?

Tommy grabbed Payden's shirt collar and pulled him closer to him. The two stood there for a moment, just staring at each other, in a sorta awkward dance pose. Shaka thought she saw Tommy deflate a bit as Payden didn't back down like most people did when they encountered him. Tommy wasn't a big guy, but he was mean and angry about everything. Most people just stayed away from him. He lived in the same building as she did, and she had heard things about Tommy's father who liked to kick the shit out of the boy at every opportunity he got. She supposed that made him mad as he was and as mean as the man was to him.

Now, Shaka reasoned that Payden wasn't really a fighter. But he had probably over the years, like most kids in inner city neighborhoods, managed a certain degree of self-preservation. One almost had to in that place.

So Payden unsquared his shoulders and spoke: "Okay, I see. I'm the new kid and you wanna fuck with me, right?" His voice was low and nervous. Everyone was quiet, waiting for what he would say next. He would have to choose his words carefully. "Well, I can most certainly tell you that I have been fucked with, and it will be no fun for you at all." Shaka closed her eyes, sighed, what the hell was that boy thinking, whatever his plan, this would not work. That sounded like a threat. Stop. Backup. Redo. As if reading her mind, Payden paused, regrouped. "I...I am a much better companion, you see."

Everyone seemed surprised by this, even Tommy himself, the other boys just stared at him figuring out what to do and say next. Shaka could, however, read people well, and she knew that Tommy was deciding whether to laugh or try to kick the shit out of Payden. You see Tommy was not one of those bullies who was all talk. He'd take his punches and gave more than a few any time he felt like it. He was always down for a fight. Then his face changed into a sneer and she knew the answer.

Just then Mr. Jefferson burst out of his door, "What in the hell are you kids doing out here?" He had the worst mouth that Shaka had ever heard on a teacher. "Surely none of you needs an extra hour with me after school. Now get to your next class."

Tommy looked at Payden and smiled again. He let go of his shirt, smoothed out the wrinkles as if his fingers were an iron, and then lightly smacked his cheek with his palm. Something else he must have seen on TV. "I'll catch up with you later." He walked away.

Some of the group still stood staring at Payden, Shaka by his side, until the crowd finally dispersed.

"Nice school, huh?"

Shaka didn't answer; he probably hadn't expected her to.

Every Saturday, Shaka and her brother scrounge up local kids to get a good game of baseball going in the quad of Project 327, where they lived. Really it was more like stick ball with a giant, hairy, round baseball-like thingy. They played in the yard just behind the housing complex. Although the grounds were usually unkempt and there were broken bottles and debris everywhere, it was secluded and quiet and there was little risk of breaking a window. Mostly because there were no real windows in the projects—just tiny, narrow, little slits of glass that allowed for the smallest bit of sunlight. It kept the days dark and the nights cold.

They stopped by to grab Payden who hadn't really gotten over the day before. Shaka coaxed him out of the house, promising him a fun time since he'd never played ball with them before. He eventually agreed to go, but only for a little while, because he wanted to be home when his mother got back from work. They had picked up a couple more kids on the way, and just as they had thought, there were even more kids playing around the quad who they could recruit into their makeshift game. By the time they got there, the other kids had already arrived.

Shaka and the others cleared off the field—it hadn't been used in a while, probably since they'd been here last—and picked teams. Shaka and Richard were the team captains. Nobody liked to play against them when they were on a team together. They were always the best players, and so to keep down confusion, they always split them up. As to be expected, Shaka hit the first home run. Sliding around the bases, she heard her team members screaming her name. "Run Z, girl, go!" She hated to admit it, but she was beginning to relate to the nickname, Z. It was different—unique—without her needing to have had to earn it at all.

"Well, well, well." The voice came from behind them. Shaka knew who it was before she even looked. Tommy. And his "gang."

His gang, consisted of who it usually did. Tommy, his brother, Bobby, Tony, Sammy, Robby, Larry and this time they had a girl with them, Louise Taylor. She went to their school too, and was in Shaka's grade. She was a real pain. Tommy hardly ever went anywhere without her now-a-days, as they were supposed to be an item. They were stuck to each other like with some kind of weird glue. Shaka wondered what in the world anyone would ever see in him, then she looked at Louise and realized that she was no real catch either, and that perhaps the two deserved each other. Shaka instantly felt terrible for thinking that about the girl and made a mental note about the type of people her grandmother told her that judge people by the way they look. They started with "w" and ended with "e."

"What you guys doin'?" Tommy, put his arm around Louise and pulled her close to him. He was trying to impress her. She smiled like a kid with a new big, stupid toy.

"Nothin. Just playin." Richard answered hoping to defuse the situation before it actually became a situation. Because with Tommy anything could become a situation.

"Playin baseball, huh? And nobody invited me? I think I feel some kinda way about that. What about you guys, you feel hurt for not being invited."

"Yeah," they all giggle, like a bunch of senseless hyenas.

"So, tell me, what in the hell are a bunch of faggots doing tryin to play ball anyway."

"We don't want any trouble." Richard was always the mediator; the big brother. Their momma had told him that if Shaka got hurt somehow, he might as well not come home either. She'd been kidding, but he took his big brother duty very seriously.

Tommy turned to look at Payden. "So I guess we still have unfinished business. Don't we?" The girl was smiling, clinging to Tommy's arm. Without giving him time to react, Tommy rushed Payden, grabbed him and pulled him closer so that they were face to face. Payden stood a full half a foot over Tommy, but he was stronger and had nothing to lose.

"Tommy!" Shaka screamed so loud she thought they'd hear her inside the buildings. The boy turned to look at her, caught by surprise at the power in her voice. She stood, four feet, eleven and a half inches tall, the stick thick enough to slam a baseball into the woods at her side, tapping her leg. "Baseball. We're playin baseball. Do you wanna join? If not, as I count, there are about half a dozen more of us, than there are of you. Now I'm not good at math, but I figure those odds aren't good for you."

He looked around. Unfortunately, most of the people in her group looked like they'd run at the hint of a fight. Tommy laughed. "You really think they're gonna fight for you?"

Darrius from downstairs screamed out, "We got your back, Z!"

"Maybe not all of them, but I will plant this bat into the side of your head. I can promise that. And I'm good. Never strike out." She was bluffing. Her knees were shaking so hard she hoped the boy wouldn't hear. "It'd just be easier to join the game, ya know. We ain't even gotta fight like that." People said she had a way about her, Shaka. She could usually talk the hot air out of pissed off folks. It had kept momma from using the belt on her more times than she could count.

Tommy let go of Payden and walked over to Shaka. He reached for her, but she resisted jerking away from him. Instead he took the bat and looked around. "So who's gonna try to pitch against this MVP?"

Tommy cracked the ball clear into the brush. Shaka chased it, though it was an obvious home run. She was just glad that bases weren't loaded and that Tommy hadn't used his skills with a bat to smack her skull in when she'd gotten too full of herself and threatened him. Thinking back on it, that could have gone terribly wrong.

She reached the spot where she thought the ball had landed, and bent down searching through the high grass to find it. She tripped and landed head first in the brush. As she stood up, her hands got caught in an old, dirty rag. She tried to get free, but the cloth was tangled around her fingers. She pulled it out of the dirt and realized that there was a small triangle box shaped thing wrapped within the dirty, black cloth.

"Come on Z! Where's the ball?" Shad called. Then right behind her, "Whoa, what's that?"

Several people had walked up behind her while she had struggled to get back to her feet. They all stared at her muddy find, like it was a forgotten gift left under the Christmas tree. She began to unwrap it, folding back one edge of the rag to reveal a sliver of faded yellow binding on a book. She quickly unwrapped it to reveal a tiny, faded yellow book. "What is it?" Richard had joined the crowd.

Shaka shook her head, then paused for a moment, her hand hovering over the yellow. There was something so intriguing about it. Who would bury this book all the way out here, in the middle of nowhere, among the nobodies, with little hope of it being found again? Maybe it was more than a mere book. She had all of these feelings and emotions and she didn't know why. Something inside her desperately wanted inside the pages of this thing that only moments before had not even mattered to her.

Without waiting, she reached out and laid her right hand on it. Just beneath her skin, she thought she felt her senses ripple and move like they were charged with electricity, so she moved her hand quickly away, afraid of what was happening.

"What's wrong with you?" her brother seemed concerned. He'd get in trouble if something, anything, happened to her, but really he was just the nervous sort.

"It's weird. It feels...weird. I don't know."

Not wanting her brother to stop her, she grabbed the book tighter, sending a wave of power through her body. She held on to the thin pages while her body began to shake and tremble so violently that she looked as if she was having a seizure. Suddenly a bright light ripped out of the book, through her finger tips and the force sent her soaring backward, landing against a tree.

Her brother, Richard, ran to her side helping her to her feet. "What the fuck...What the fuck... Shaka what happened?"

When she got to her feet, she realized that everyone was staring at her, speechless. She walked back over to the book. It lay on the ground, its pages opened to a page with a single line etched on the page: *Lost Carcosa*. She bent down to pick it up.

"No! Don't touch it. You saw what it did the first time." Richard was really afraid. She would have to cure him of this.

She ignored him, then picked it up, holding it with both hands this time. Whatever was inside this book was strong, and she felt it, overwhelming her, speaking to her senses, her very essence. She could sense hopelessness and vileness, but those things were not within the book itself, but pieces of it that men misinterpret. No, instead, this book offered any open mind possibilities unimaginable. It offered truth. And that seemed to be the thing that many men could not handle. She saw all of these things in her head, her mind swam with possibilities of new ideas and new knowledge.

She reached out for her brother, who took her hand reluctantly. "Come on! Everyone, grab on. Touch each other. Feel it!" One by one each of the members of their make shift baseball game, joined hands. Shaka closed her eyes, sending the images from her head into theirs. She spread the knowledge she had learned with them, while they shared dreams and imaginations that they had never thought possible.

As they shared thoughts and ideas, around them the grass beneath their feet brightened, the weeds which had long ago taken over began to die and flowers long dead quickly bloomed again. They lost all concept of time, as they shared the book, themselves and the great ideas. Each individual had separate thoughts, while the collective clung to the relevant ideas from each, leaving their individuality to prosper untouched. What they learned, she realized—they all realized—had not been previously unknown to them. Instead, it was the ability to be able to interpret lost histories and events and philosophies within their own lives. The power within them grew the dirty, trash riddled field into a vast, lush garden. Simply because one of them had imagined it and the others had allowed for the thought to prosper fully within their collect imaginary.

They were, they realized, because they deserved to be. And that, indeed, was a novel thought.

The collective reasoning of a group is very powerful. It can change things. Like the leaky roof of project buildings that haven't been fixed in three years. Or the boiler in building six, which threatened to explode every winter. Or turn dry vegetation into a community food garden. It can feed multitudes.

But sometimes that is not enough.

"We can't do this without you, you know that, don't you?" Shaka's brother was always the one that they sent to talk to her. Now that The Collective—that's what they called themselves—had studied how exactly their powers worked, they had realized that Shaka was somehow the catalyst. They needed her. But she needed them as well. They each had their own functions and hers was to lead them. She didn't really like it, but it got things done efficiently and effectively. He stopped in the middle of the side walk, held her hand.

"I don't know. We've never done anything like this. We help people. The roofs and the garden. That's what we do."

"I know...."

"We help people."

"This is helping! And he deserves it. You know that." His voice was louder than he meant it to be, but he wasn't yelling at her. He couldn't do that. But she could sense his emotions rising to the surface. He needed to control them better. Before the Collective, Shaka would have been able to read the expression on his face, and his body language to know how he felt. She had thought it was just one of those strange things she was able to do. But now she realized that she had had a gift. That gift had been heightened by the knowledge that the book had given them and now she could even know what he was thinking and feel what he felt. None of the others had the power she did.

He continued to hold her hand as they walked into school, but he didn't mention it gain.

In class, Payden slid into his usual seat in the front of the classroom. They didn't have assigned seats, but Mr. Jefferson forced him to sit there because he said the boy didn't need any distractions. Payden looked back at Shaka, holding her gaze. She wanted to turn away, but she didn't. She couldn't.

"Mr. White, I see again that you have forgotten that the important part of the class lays in the front." Payden straightened in his chair, angry.

"All right, class. Turn to page 223. Considering that Columbus Day is coming up next week, we're not going to focus on Christopher Columbus discovering America, which you have learned, but on…"

"That's not true." Shad had not originally been part of the collective, but they had bought her in recently. Her grandmother had been sick and the group had helped her to get over pneumonia.

"Who was that? What's not true?"

"Columbus was a murder and a rapist and you can't discover something someone already has."

"Stand up! You will not use my class to defile an American hero. Columbus was brave enough to set out to sea when everyone else thought the Earth was flat."

"That's not true either." Payden stood to his feet without being told. "By the 1400s no one thought the Earth was flat. Columbus was after riches. He wasn't a hero at all." The collective link was buzzing. Shaka could feel them all getting excited at the idea of proving Jefferson wrong in his own classroom. But more importantly, they needed to teach him in a way that he had never taught them. Her brother had tried to warn her that this needed to happen that very morning. Even collective members from other classes, such as Richard, had linked in, feeling and watching everything that was going on in that room. Offering their support.

Mr. Jefferson paused for a moment, speechless for seemingly the first time in his teaching career. Then the man moved toward Payden, stood before the younger man. "You presume to lecture me on history? Payden, whose mother could not spell her own son's name without sounding it out like a third grader, Pay…den. Whose best accomplishment in life is getting through the third grade after having failed it twice?"

The Collective line jerked in Shaka's head, sending a wave of pain through each of their bodies. Payden was holding tightly to the line, as he would a stress ball that he opened and closed in his hand. Instead he strangled the link between them, trying to maintain his composure. But Shaka herself had lost it, jumping to stand to her feet. The others followed her lead. She was angry. They all were. "You simple troglodyte! You try to teach us false history and lies, and now you want to punish Payden by saying mean things to hurt him."

"Troglodyte. A mighty big word, for such a small...."

"No!" She held out her two first fingers and her thumb, pointing only at him. "You will not speak again." As she spoke, the room rippled, their collective energy surrounding the man. As he tried to open his mouth, his lips sealed shut, then disappeared altogether, leaving an empty spot below the man's nose where his mouth had once been. "You have talked enough. We won't listen anymore."

The man put his hands over his missing mouth. The collective members all stood, staring at the man who had seemed to have so much power before. But now he simply looked like a pathetic man trying desperately to hold on to the little bit of power that he had in that classroom. They did not pity him, however. No, that was reserved for those who did not wield power the way this man always had. No, instead, they realized how insignificant he really was, how very small he was in a vast system of Mr. Jeffersons.

Shaka walked over the white man, placed her hand over his missing mouth. "Remember this moment. This is not a dream. Know us!"

༄

I awoke in my bed, not knowing where I was or remembering when I had laid down the night before. In fact, I didn't remember anything after class the prior day, or more importantly, anything past the odd dream I had just had of my students. Had I dreamed it all?

I touched my mouth absently, making sure my lips were exactly where they should have been and that they had not gone missing. Of course I was being ridiculous. Those students couldn't be trusted to tie their shoes, let along amass the brain power to do something so astonishing. But it had all seemed so real. So very real.

Maybe I was just uneasy, as my night's reading had made me anxious and discontented. I had been reading The King in Yellow and had had a nightmare. That was all.

Beside me my alarm went off, signaling the arrival of morning and another day at Booker T. Washington High School.

Thomas Jefferson Jr. was ready for it.

STONES, MAYBE
BY URSULA PFLUG

God knows what they farmed, Peter thought. Stones, maybe. And turned away from the winter fields towards the water and the marina office: a little brown painted clapboard house with a pitched roof and small casement windows, a screen door, one large and three little rooms inside. It always reminded Peter of the cabins at Camp Wawanesa. He'd go to camp for two weeks in August before the family came here all together, to stay at Myrtle's marina. Since he no longer used it as the office perhaps he should open a little sailing camp, with rows of bunk beds. The counselors could smoke up in the store room, looking out at the water, although, he thought, they usually did that in some locked room they'd swiped the keys to, a woods clearing, or beyond a place with a name like Cedar Point, on a scrubby, secluded little beach or island. Likewise where they went to have sex, discreetly, because getting caught meant getting fired. Although the kids always knew, he remembered, gossiping about things they were too young to understand. Had anyone known about Peter and Marti, either the other employees or any of the customers?

Probably.

The little house, situated as it was between the road and the boat launch, was intended to be the official entry point to the marina, containing in its large front room a solid brown desk and an equally solid oak swivel chair, the kind Peter remembered only the principal got at school when he was young enough to be impressed by principals. Now he was at an age where he could be one himself, figured it to be just another kind of job; not so different from sailing school really, just fewer water hazards. Better pay, though, and more regular. Peter went inside, sifting the dusty stillness. Nothing happened here, ever. Not since he and Marti used to come here to make love.

The old-timers understood when he told them why he came back. Because it was there, because his great-grandfather built the first version of the marina eighty years before, an eye on tourism as an upgrade from farming the stony unforthcoming fields. His parents and his brother, and even Aunt Myrtle no longer thought the old family farmstead on the water important, so why did he? Maybe because of that, because of them no longer wanting it. "Our family throws everything of value away," Peter had said, when his father had asked, perplexed; maybe one had to be eighty to understand a thing like that. Yet Peter understood, just as the seniors did. Was he so prematurely aged, inside, to believe something only very old people believed otherwise? "Someone has to stop it," he'd said stubbornly, and bought the land back from the stranger Aunt Myrtle had sold it to. The stranger had taken a loss, sold it to Peter for less than he'd paid Myrtle, who had inherited, along with Peter's father.

"I wanted nothing to do with it. It going for even less should've been a sign," his father had said, but Peter hadn't cared. He didn't want to be a doctor in Toronto like his brother Mark, who lived in a fancy condominium sixteen floors above Lake Ontario. He'd miss skipping stones from his private beach. What woman who wanted a family could resist this unkempt shoreline, these stony beaches? You'd look after toddlers here and not go stir-crazy, a stone's throw from the lake. But Marti was gone, a goner. And if Peter chose to sell, he'd take a loss too, and lose his shirt. And so he stayed, year after year.

Usually he didn't stay long, going back outside almost immediately to re-caulk the rental boats or back across the gravel road to the farmhouse to do his bookkeeping. He put the new computer on the main house's kitchen table when he upgraded, and not in the little office building at all. He told himself it was so he didn't have to heat two buildings. Most people who wanted him had learned to call at the house phone.

Peter remembered Myrtle telling him the office was spooky when she'd heard he was buying the place. They never saw one another much, although she only lived one township away. But she'd called him up, invited him to dinner when the news had broken of the sale going through. She looked good in her new blue sweater, better than she had when she'd run the marina, running around in old sneakers and an older anorak, her face drawn, always behind on the work and the bills. "The old people always said it was haunted," Myrtle said over salmon and white wine, "although I never saw or heard anything."

"It's not why you sold?" Peter asked.

"Oh no. It's a money sink; the farmhouse is log. It's never been re-chinked, because the repairs money always goes to the marina buildings across the road, it being the income generator. Ostensibly. And the barn's fallen down so bad no one will ever get it up again."

"Nobody's going to farm, Myrtle. Don't need the barn."

"But you already know all that, you already know we all think you're crazy to want it. Especially because you had to buy it, as me and your dad didn't."

"It's my childhood," Peter said, "and our family history." Myrtle had just rolled her eyes at his sentimentality. She had a gift shop in Buckhorn now. It didn't make any more money than the marina, but it was a lot less work. Like Peter, she'd never married or had kids. The marina required a man, and Myrtle'd had to hire them, although Peter had come and helped most summers when he was in college studying tourism, which was probably when he'd cemented his attachment. And then he'd bought it a few years later. Was it the second summer Marti came, or the third? He should be able to remember a thing like that.

All blonde and blue, like sun on water.

He hadn't thought anymore about the alleged ghost until the old-timers started stopping by. He'd laughed, shrugged, been too busy with the business end to listen to old people's tales of nameless fears. Horror meant, after all, wondering how to pay the mortgage on the property in the winter months when there was no income, hoping his summer savings from all those boat rentals to tourists would stretch till spring. But if the oldsters had been right about one thing perhaps they could be right about two, for today Peter didn't just feel the spiralling sense of dusty, empty mystery he'd gotten used to and learned to enjoy, but something new and a little menacing. The always present sense of mystery had acquired an extra tone, emanating, Peter was suddenly quite sure, from the kitchen he'd just left, more specifically from an institutionally painted green kitchen cupboard that he saw through the open door. But he didn't go into the kitchen, not yet, rather just glancing down the hall and through the door, at the cupboard, its door hanging ever so slightly ajar.

Making fun of himself, distancing his own fear, Peter went through the remaining rooms, looking at all the stuff the previous owners had left behind, which, in seven years he'd never brought himself to get rid of. It helped him think, he always told himself, when he was looking for a new angle on how to make a go of things. Objects from before, belonging to strangers, things that retained this alien sensibility of another life, someone's life beyond his own, unknowable, unreachable, yet here, made concrete by abandoned items: huge bags of pesticide, fertilizer; the previous owners grew corn and tomatoes to see to the cottage folk in addition to running the marina. Peter looked at the gargantuan, heavy bags leaning in a corner, too heavy to lift, really, even shove aside. What to do with the herbicides, the five-five-five? He knew he could unload them on local farmers who'd be glad for the stuff, but the thought of it running into the ditches bordering his own land, contaminating his own well water, the well water of his children-yet-to-come, elicited a profound distaste. He composted religiously, had a heap the size of a small shed. The neighbours were covetous, but Peter, who didn't grow a thing, was saving it for the wife.

The newly strange kitchen still called, and so he went back, if only to see there was nothing there. A sink, a hotplate, no refrigerator; he'd taken that up to the main house when the compressor on his own had fried. "Kitchen cupboards, panelling, click-handle latches that lock and pinch your fingers. Kitchen cupboards that have never belonged to a family, never been tamed by children. The moment suddenly framed and put in a late-night movie where it's difficult to breathe, or maybe like you're under water, you open that door. Your rational mind tells you there's no danger but your instincts tell you otherwise; you can feel your heart pounding, pumping adrenalin. You'd shut it except you've already started opening it, can't stop now. Somehow you have to complete the motion, as though, now, you are in one of those dreams where everything is hyper-real. Open the door. Hand goes in. Hmm. A paperback book." Late winter and he was talking to himself: suggestible, susceptible, cabin fever taking a wrong turn. He shut up, acutely aware that should anyone walk in on him, which no one would, not in a million years, they'd think him barmy. As if everyone didn't already, a little, just for buying the place.

But what about Marti? What would she think, if she chose this moment to return?

Peter took the book out of the cupboard. It was called *The King in Yellow*, and Peter remembered Marti reading it. She hadn't brought it with her; she'd found it here. It was strange, she said, like nothing else she'd ever read, but she couldn't stop—maybe he'd like to read it too? He hadn't given it another thought; every cottage on the lake was lined with musty paperbacks after all, but then she'd disppeared, leaving the book here and not in the shelf under the window with the one dollar used copies of Agatha Christie and Steven King and John Grisham.

What could it possibly mean? He turned it over and over, unable to let it go in spite of the fact it elicited a profound terror, a kind of childhood nightmare panic. His hand shaking, he at last replaced it gingerly, as though he'd been caught going through someone else's cupboards, which in a way he had; he couldn't remember ever cleaning them out in any methodical way. He glimpsed a few plates: green plastic, a tinfoil pie plate, some loose spoons. But it wasn't those objects which gave him the creeps, only the book. Being terrified of a book was even worse than talking to yourself; thankfully he had no audience unless he included the broken aluminum coffee percolators on the counter, the black-capped chickadees in the cedar outside the little window above the sink.

He left the room, bewildered. It was only a book. He could go back and get it, throw it into the middle of the lake, put it in the trash, use it for kindling in his wood stove. There were a million ways to dispose of it. But he didn't. On the one hand it was too ridiculous, and on the other, he was afraid to touch it again. They'd come and find him, dead of heart failure in the spring, his body frozen. It would be a balm to whoever discovered him; decomposition wouldn't have set in, or at least not much.

Peter sat down behind the heavy, scarred oak desk, made doodles of ducks and frogs on the unused memo pad, waiting for his hand to stop shaking, his heart to settle down. Because of a book. He thought of the warnings of gap-toothed, patched together oldsters dropping by the last few summers, never spending a penny, just wanting to yarn. They told him all the lake's old stories, stories he'd shared with his tourists. Probably some of them kept coming back because of it. Hearing the stories, they'd feel part of something.

And then inevitably just before the old guys left they'd ask some version of, "Have you felt it yet?" A knowing grin. "It gets everyone sooner or later; you've just held out longer than most." But Myrtle had never said anything about it getting her, although perhaps she'd been too embarrassed to admit it. Maybe for Myrtle it hadn't been the book but something else. The percolator parts, perhaps, or the tin spoons.

It had certainly gotten Peter, whatever it even was. He drew another duck, another frog. He'd forgotten how intrinsically inescapable fear could be, how impervious to the ministrations of the rational mind. He'd have to remember that when the children came. Night terrors came at age three or four. How did he know that? Had he really spent the winter skimming copies of "Today's Parent" he'd surreptitiously swiped from his GP's office?

He would've liked to leave, to walk down to the marsh bordering the lake west of the beach, say hello to the real frogs, following his usual spring patrol, but it was too early in the year; the spring peepers wouldn't be awake yet. Tiny dogwood-climbing frogs with suction cups for toes; in two months he'd wish he could shut them up, calling for a mate all through the night. And so, without frog songs to keep him company, it was once again back to the kitchen; at least his breathing was normal now. On the cracked and chipped counter there were three bent aluminum coffee percolators, but there wasn't one whole, usable one among them; while the coffee basket that was missing in one was there in another, of course it didn't fit.

For the hundredth time Peter played with the percolators. If he had a stem for the one with the coffee basket that fit, and a lid for it, instead of the twisted, non-fitting mess he held aloft, distastefully, between finger and thumb, he could make coffee, actually work down here instead of up at the house. And then if Marti snuck back through for old times' sake, he'd be there. She wouldn't come to the house, she'd come here, drawn to the bags of 5-5-5, where they'd done it, in great haste, before the boaters returned at sundown. And he'd talk to her, just as now, he'd already started talking to himself again, not even aware of it. "Hate to throw things away that will have a later use. I could buy cheap plastic for the kids when they're old enough to use sand toys, the kind of things I sell and then have to clean off the beach every fall, already split and faded. Truth is, these old metal percolators will be perfect; you can use the coffee baskets as sieves. These will last for years–they already have."

Of course, there was one small snag in this offspring fantasy; you had to have a mother first. And as far as women go, there hadn't really been anyone besides Marti. Not exactly mother material.

He was holding the book again, had removed it from its cupboard nest without even realizing it. He'd been right to be spooked by the mostly empty cupboards, to leave them alone. They were haunted, he was suddenly quite sure, by the demonic powers of this seemingly innocuous thing he was holding in his hand just now. He dropped it in a hurry, shaking again. Damn. He needed something to keep him from talking to himself, from thinking a cheap paperback book called *The King in Yellow* was a dimensional portal activated by human touch. As he was thinking now. He needed an extra little job for the winter, when the marina was closed, as now. And it would help with the more conventional panic over the bills. Never mind the market gardening; that would be the wife's thing.

He and Marti shouldn't have had sex on the 5-5-5 bags. If they had gone to the house, she'd have stayed. "In our family we throw everything of value away." Weren't those the words he'd used, to his own father? Get into hopeless debt buying back the marina, throw Marti away, as though the property wasn't useless without her. Wifeless. Kidless. Barren.

He'd thought she was that kind of girl, adventurous, finding odd locations a little thrill. And maybe she had; but sex in a store room is the kind you enjoy and then move on from. It was so stunningly clear; why hadn't he seen it before? "There's always a part of you that knows the truth, however hard you try to shut it up," Peter told the book sadly. Perhaps, he thought, it was the haunting that had value in this place, and not the stony beach, the blue still lake, the loons calling from between the piney islands. "We always throw everything of value away in our family," he whispered again. But not the marina, and not the book. He'd keep it forever now, treasure it for its moment of insight. He hadn't asked her to stay because she was a mess, even though he'd known by then he loved her.

In the storage room there was a wheeled, folded up cot: kept there for the nights you have a fight with the wife, Peter thought, patting the book in his jacket pocket, but really, he didn't know why the cot was there. He and Marti never had sex on the cot, in spite of it actually harbouring a remarkably mildew free mattress. "A bag of 5-5-5 doesn't have a mattress, it just emulates one. Sort of," Peter remarked.

"Since the cot is for cottagers too drunk to drive their boats back out to the islands after wandering back from the bar."

He'd never asked for anyone's keys, even the few times he should have. He'd been too intimidated to take keys away from drunks larger than himself, drunks deeply invested in their own competence. Pissed. Blasted. Wrecked. "Note descriptive words," Peter said, "They're very accurate." Every winter they were hauling frozen snowmobilers out of the lake. The sober frozen snowmobilers were often still slightly alive, at least alive enough to be rushed off to the county hospital. But the frozen dead ones had always, without exception, been pissed, blasted, wrecked. And never once a drunk dead female snowmobiler. Home with the youngsters they were, knitting and purling lavender worsted booties. Much too sensible to take the snowmobile out after consuming half a bottle of vodka, complete with exclamations about how well it made her drive. If a man would let anyone take his keys away, it would be his wife. Peter knew, he'd seen it: the largest, drunkest, most obstreperous man giving his keys to the teeny, tiny, soft spoken, completely sober wife, wailing toddler in tow. Name was Josie. Got the kid out of bed, wrapped him in a blanket, and drove like hell just so she could snag hubby at the boat launch where Peter let him keep his ancient Snow Cat, said, "Give me the keys." Why hadn't she let him crash through the ice? He just drank the money anyway. Josie had been one hell of a driver, Peter remembered, used to race when she was young, and drive in demolition derbies. If anyone could drive the icy back roads to the marina in the dead of night on bald tires, with a screaming baby in the car seat, Josie could. If she wanted to have a couple of beers and take the snowmobile out on the ice, Peter was pretty sure she'd handle it. But Josie never felt quite safe enough to leave the baby home with dad, go out alone on the lake at night, get some air in her hair. Daddy might drink half a bottle of vodka and drop the iron on the baby's head. And not enough money for sitters; besides, he'd be insulted, think she was out of her mind hiring someone when he was in the house.

Would Marti do any of those things? Not bloody likely. Marti, with her bravado and love of self-medication of all kinds, was, like the big, drunk, egotistical man in question, the type who'd tangle herself and the Snow Cat around an island pine. If it was sense that men were after when they looked for a wife, to compensate for their own lack of same, Marti would've been exactly the bad choice Peter had so often told himself she was.

Years younger, she'd been a summer employee. They'd had an affair, and Peter had surprised himself by falling in love. He'd wanted to know her then, had gotten to know her, too, much more than he'd ever known anyone. Had ever wanted to know.

It was March; soon time to open the marina. Or at least, start preparing to open it. Peter discovered he could care less. All the details of management and maintenance he used to obsess over, even enjoy, seemed as turbid today as the water coloured sky. "Even if I wanted to be like that again," Peter said, "I no longer know how. That part of me is a lost shirt, gone overboard from an outboard, sunk to the bottom. Or gone with Marti, more likely."

Marti's liquid body, made out of stars, arching over him on the floor of the store room, the stars falling out of her body, a dark sea, stars floating in it, five pointed stars he could pick up and stick up on the walls of the bedroom to entertain the children when they came: luminous, glow-in-the-dark stars. They jumped out of his hand, sat beside he and Marti on the bed, watched them make love approvingly. Smiled and told jokes to the lovers, in fact.

How terrifying it had been, the surrender required, the hard bitten edges of himself he'd have to give up to say, yes, I want this. Except that he hadn't. He'd pretended it wasn't real. And now he couldn't go back to sleep, no matter how much he wanted to. And he couldn't have Marti, either, because she was gone. A goner.

Faced with the unknown, there was only one thing to do. Ask it what it wanted, feed it. "What d'you want then?" he asked the book, "How do I get my real life back?"

Maybe she'd seen the stars too; he'd never actually thought of that. She'd played the reckless babe for him, lying beneath him on the stony shore of an uninhabited island, her skin smelling of pine woods and salt and wind in spite of the vodka they'd been putting away. Maybe it wasn't a choice; perhaps portals opened each time Marti made love, funnelling the lovers into more beautiful dimensions. And perhaps each and every one of her lovers, and he knew there had been quite a few, had closed his eyes to a beauty so much larger than he could fathom. I'd drink too much too, Peter thought, and remembered how, making love on their island, he'd briefly seen their future spread out before him, pretty and comforting as a star quilt. It was the last time, the time before she left without saying good-bye or even leaving a note. Leaving her few things behind. He'd thrown them away. Except for the book.

In his vision Marti had been leaving to go grocery shopping, Peter's list in hand, getting into her rusty little yellow car, her blonde hair tied in two long pigtails. She wore silver dream catcher earrings, a plaid car coat she'd made out of the same material as the worst couches in existence, a knee-length red and white striped skirt, black tights, black ankle boots, a black rolled-brim hat. Somehow, on Marti, this didn't look dreadful but fetching: a country punk chic that managed, impossibly, to be stylish as well as original. Smiling, sure of herself, as he'd never once seen her, she waved good-bye to Peter and Julian, who didn't squall at his mother's departure, solemnly sieving sand through a dented percolator coffee basket, knowing she'd be bringing home treats.

She reversed down the driveway, tires screeching, and Peter sat on the edge of the sandbox with Julian and played with percolator parts, until the real Marti interrupted, asking, "What are you thinking about?" And he hadn't told her, had run his fingers through her hair and smiled. Maybe she'd been afraid to tell him about the little stars, afraid he'd say she was crazy. It had never even occurred to Peter, how his silences might have hurt her.

He'd closed his eyes again and watched as future-Marti hung laundry, drove Julian to daycare, started tomatoes in flats to grow and sell to the island cottage folk. She invented cookie recipes from scratch, mainly successful, although there was one problematic experiment containing canned pineapple which exploded in the oven. When they put it outside the back door, even the usually indiscriminate stray dogs didn't touch it. Peter, who had taught himself how to cook over the years, perhaps also, like saving the aluminum percolator parts, in anticipation of the children, made most of the dinners.

He shuddered with longing. But what if it was her self destructiveness that he found seductive? The doomed Marti, the Marti who fucked everything in pants and then laughed at them. The one who was surprised as he was, to find herself loving Peter. The erstwhile coke head, the brilliant drunk? Maybe she didn't share his vision of their lovely possible future at all. Maybe that had been his job, yet another he'd neglected, like taking the keys away from Josie's husband himself, and growing tomatoes, and inviting Marti to stay in the house no matter what people said, and picking a smiling yellow five pointed star out of the crumpled sheet and putting it in her hand, saying, "Nothing like this has ever happened to me before."

Peter knew he'd never find her, not unless he gave something up, some preciously adhered to delusion or illusion, as much a part of him by now as his hair, which, truth to tell, was less a part of him than it used to be. For some reason this gave Peter hope. If he could lose his hair, perhaps he could lose his self-importance, his stubborn pride. Delusions could fall out each morning, come out in clumps in his comb. Marti had once said he looked cute balding, that he was lucky he had the right shape of skull for it. As she shared her peanut butter sandwich with him, told him the names of wild flowers he'd never learned.

LES FLEURS DU MAL
BY ALLYSON BIRD

Juliette. Mercury without wings. A time traveller—too. She stepped out of the black mirror. Her progress was slow and golden rose petals fell behind her where she walked. Dumas had the black tulip. She closed her eyes and the black held a hint of red—a tiny drop of blood seeping through the petals—near the base.

She wore a cloak. Feathers of peacock. Blue. Turquoise. Green. Ermine at the edge—cashmere lined. Over a black floor length gown. Too much she thought. A wave of her hand and the cloak disappeared leaving a small pendant around her neck—the eye of one peacock feather pressed almost into her pale skin. In Roman, Greek and Egyptian mythology the eye that sees all. It would not see the end of Juliette's life. There would be no natural end to that.

'To Paradise, the Arabs say,
Satan could never find the way
Until the peacock led him in.'

Dear Charles Leyland, educated at the Sorbonne in 1848, and then a captain at the barricades later on the RIGHT side. What a revolutionary. Was she related to all the revolutionaries? And his Italian witches. Aradia who walked amongst the down trodden and taught them to rise up against their masters.

Paris. July 1938. Fritz Henle would be here now taking his photographs, some in Montmartre, memories of a wonderful city before the occupation. The Woman and the God. Mademoiselle Niska. Housewives. All developed in the tiny bathroom by a small green light. Never used until Mme. Lazareff of The New York Times Magazine cried over them and published many in 1947. How could a city give up so easily? The Seinne would flow faster with the tears during the war, too.

Juliette's first destination—an old farmhouse in Avignon. Saint-Martin d'Ardeche where her friend was living at the moment. It was surrounded by chestnut trees—surreal statues of birds and horses in the garden. She would go and see Leonora. She would be here about now, too. Spring.

Leonora. Painting. Naked. A smear of red paint on her stomach where she had wiped her hand aggressively—forgetting the rag close by. She had been working from notes given to her by Juliette. A Dog and his Man. There would have to be a black bull, a not to be pitied writer with his head in his hands in a lonely garret with a cross on a wall, a larger than life woman with borrowed armour from Fini's paintings towering over him, a dog—well half dog half man—its head being the head of another writer licking the shoes of the other man, a devil playing a fiddle in the background, the requisite witches' broom, a pan of sausages nobody wanted to eat cooked by someone who had no culinary skills whatsoever.

The painting would be lost only to be discovered in 2015 in a second hand shop in New Zealand frequented by a writer of the weird who on reflection did the right thing—found the woman who had owned it for years not knowing the value, was the overseer of the sale of the now cherished work, and gave the money to the previous owner. That owner promptly gave her half back which was a good thing. It sold for $3 million N.Z. dollars. The Cradle also by Leonora, painted in 1948 was offered in a sale in 2014 for $1.5 to $2.5 million U.S. dollars. Juliette smiled again. I wonder how it ended up in New Zealand to be found. Naughty Juliette—she thought to herself.

'Ah—you. I wondered when you would turn up again,' said Leonora as she looked over her shoulder. She wasn't surprised.

'I said I would come back.'

'And you haven't changed a bit once more.'

Juliette shrugged and the peacock eye caught the light. Iridescent.

Leonora turned back to the canvas and stabbed with the paintbrush at the image of the dog with the man's head.

'Come with me.'

'No.'

'Why not?'

'I belong here.'

'You would not say that if you knew what was coming.'
Juliette wandered around the studio, and ignoring any paintings, was drawn to the bookshelves. She pulled one book in particular down from a shelf. She laid down on the chaises lounge, took off her shoes, and placed her feet on a red velvet cushion.

Leonora sighed. She always did when Juliette visited her. 'Which book?'

'Baudelaire.'

'You are obsessed with him.'

'Absorbed. Leonora. Absorbed.'

Juliette read from the book.

> *'Leonardo, dark, unfathomable mirror,*
> *In which charming angels, with sweet smiles*
> *Full of mystery, appear in the shadow*
> *Of the glaciers and pines that enclose their country.'*

She hesitated and smiled mischievously.

> *'Leonora, known to me,*
> *Who lies with devils, with wandering fingers*
> *Full of mischief, hidden in the dark*
> *In the depths of Carcosa. Gloom lit.'*

'I will be no muse.'

'But I will. Won't I.' A coy smile from Juliette. 'Remedios will use me. My armour—too. But she won't come with me to Carcosa either. None of you will. I don't understand it.'

'Have you ever contemplated the fact that I consider that if I'm with you, really with you, my madness will completely shut me down. Carcosa. Why would I live in a world created by someone else—it could turn out to be hell and I have enough of that already. I don't even know if you really exist.'

'And your world is created by?'

Silence from Leonora.

'Ask Remedios. She knows. If you don't come with me, well—you can't say I didn't give you the opportunity.'

Leonora looked puzzled but shook it off. 'If all the artists went what would be left here? Nothing. What would the women here have then?'

'So the very thing you paint about, freedom, you deny yourself?'

'This is my world Juliette—not yours. That is your reality now. Not mine. True enough we could paint other worlds into existence perhaps. One day. But this isn't your world now, Juliette. One day I won't be left out. The women will have a voice eventually. I'll be recognized one day.'

'Indeed Leonora but I thought I'd try to spare you the cost before that. Fini might...' Began Juliette.

'Enough! And I don't know if bringing me back anything from the future is a good thing.'

'Did you enjoy the book?' Asked Juliette.

'Yes.'

'Then it is a good thing.'

'In it are surely things I should not know?'

'It is fiction,' replied Juliette.

'But fiction is a product of the individual relating to the time they live in. Isn't that a sort of taboo – reading that?'

'I'm careful what I give you to read. Well reasonably so. It isn't like I've given you a biography of your life or anything.'

'You have one?'

A long look from Juliette. And a smile.

Leonora thought about the book. It was *The Master and Margarita* by Bulgakov. Published 1969.

'Fini read it. She got a lot out of it.' Juliette said quickly before Leonora could stop her. And another look this time one of—are you not interested in what I'm saying—came from her.

'Is that so. Then good for her.'

What Juliette didn't tell Leonora was that Bulgakov had read certain biographies, some time ago, and had access to the paintings by Leonora and Fini—also Remedios. He had his coven. Or rather Juliette's.

Leonora turned around, her brush full of yellow paint, and finally smiled. So did Juliette. Leonora stood above her and Juliette gently brushed her hand against the white thigh. Leonora knelt down, pulled the top of Juliette's black gown down below the breast, and painted the yellow sign upon it. Then she kissed her. They both laughed.

'Why are you really here?'

'I'm here early for a death. Not yours.' Juliette quickly changed the subject. 'The night we met Bulgakov. The Spring Ball at Spaso House.

Moscow. The baby bear the ambassador ordered along with the zebra finches and the mountain goats. And we led the goats into the dining room and they knocked over the tables with the black tulips on, and ate them.'

'We drank too much champagne, Juliette. Bulgakov thought it amusing but the U.S. ambassador didn't. He'd gone to a lot of trouble to outdo other ambassadors.'

'Anyone who goes to that much trouble to be outré deserves it.'

'Says she who has never gone over the top.'

'Name one time.'

'Just the one? Okay the party at the gallery—where you got so drunk you decided that the paintings of Manuel needed a little more to them than the artist wanted. That business with the paintings.'

Juliette laughed again. 'Ah. He'd insulted me once a very long time ago so I thought I'd do that. Not my greatest hour but funny at the time.'

'The bejowled little man. Arrogant. A misogynist and a Catholic to boot?'

Juliette nodded. Jealousy within groups of artists. She knew all too well about that. The Schadenfreude factor.

'You actually had the nerve to paint over the work. You couldn't decide whether to make it a goat or a donkey. Manuel had said that Pope Innocent VIII was right to instigate the persecution of witches—well the female ones. So you painted a donkey in every one of his paintings. In the one where a great poet is reading from a manuscript. The one with the cardinal in it—actually you did more in that one—didn't you—repainted the bottom half depicting the cardinal lifting his red cassock over his head. Didn't you? Then that other one—how did you get away with all that? Was that it? All of it?'

'There was poison in the ear.'

'Metaphorically speaking?'

'In reality.'

Leonora pulled back a smile. 'I wouldn't want to get on the wrong side of you. Aren't you afraid of the consequences of your actions?'

'They'd have to find me first.'

'There was another who offended you.'

'The other—mmmmm there was one who played Bottom in the Shakespeare play and when he tried to remove the head it wouldn't come off—everyone said the head looked so real.'

'What happened to him next?'

'Sideshow for a time then his real head was put back on. He still thought he was an ass though so he was committed to the Belmont Mental Institution.'

Juliette began to play with the silver charm bracelet on her left wrist.

'Any more additions to your bracelet?' Leonora enquired. 'You had added the donkey's head last time we met. What else have you from before my time? And it seems to have many more. Not all enemies I hope?'

'Indeed it has. And indeed not. I have the swan, the dog, the cardinal—the pretty red bird not the other.'

'Do you still have the one I found for you? The horse with wings?'

'Pegasus? I do.'

'Good. Don't lose it'

Juliette rose from the couch.

'Before you go—tell me you haven't met Shakespeare yet?'

Juliette raised one eyebrow. 'You know sometime in the future someone calls for his books to be removed from schools because they think he was gay?'

Leonora took on a serious tone. 'You tell me all this—you influence all that. I'm worried for the future.'

'You should be.'

'It is like being told a story—and the ending changes constantly. Also that if you can influence events there seems to be a protagonist who does too—to the world's detriment. Except I put you on the so called devil's side which could turn out for the best.'

'Religion again. Damn the Catholics? We're all damned.'

Juliette walked across to the window. The sun was setting. Against that beautiful sky one chestnut tree in particular reached its arms to heaven—its roots trying to pull away from hell.

'I have to go now.'

Leonora looked disappointed. 'So soon? No parties for us to go to this time?'

'Not this time but there will be another. I hope.'

Juliette crossed the room and looked at another painting. 'You've given the white horse wings now.'

The horse was centred on the canvas—about to fly. And there was the chestnut tree. Its leaves had fallen to the ground.

Leonora turned back to the painting she was working on. 'I've much more to do on this. But here is something again for you.' She pointed to the canvas. In the bottom left hand corner was the yellow sign.

How many times had Juliette been to see Leonora? This was perhaps the last time? She would try once more. For half an hour she tried to tell Leonora of the horror to come. Words continued to fail her. Leonora said no, quietly, again and again. Juliette finally gave up, and reached out to her friend, and held her gently in her arms. Juliette knew at that point Leonora would never leave—she had made her mind up. She would have to go on without her.

'Goodbye Leonora.'

'Until the next time, Juliette.' Leonora turned to the canvas— quickly painting over the one tear that had fallen upon the painting.

Juliette left but then sat under the chestnut tree and thought some more. The yellow. The Egyptians thought that it represented the eternal and that the gods were made of gold. In the Middle Ages the colour was associated with Judas Iscariot, and dissenters in The Renaissance were made to wear yellow. That would happen again but a yellow triangle would suffice. What did the yellow sign really mean to Leonora? It would change to the sunflower in Carrington's Eine Kleine Nachtmusik. If people looked for it—it was there in many works of symbolism. In all art. Van Gogh. It stood for hope now and again, too. But mostly for madness. Juliette was right by Charlotte's side when she wrote The Yellow Wallpaper.

Juliette found many people soulless. They had little kindness or no compassion within them. Except to appear so for self gain. All dried up and bitter. She liked artists because they gave some hope. And as for those called insane—she had as much time in the universe that there could be for them. She felt compassion for the isolated. In despair she would leave Carcosa now and again just to give them what little comfort she could. Now with no end in clear sight to her life she could try to do something—although she was limited in many ways. And she was not indestructible. Juliette would be there for some in the future but she would not be able to save many, perhaps. Or take them to Carcosa. She could try. But only HE could do that—or only when he let her. The King in Yellow would have the last word. And many times he said no. He had said no when she asked about Solveig. That had brought Juliette great sadness. He simply said Carcosa was not for her. Juliette loved actors. They put on masks and took them off. Most of the human race wore theirs all the time. Some of them she saw take them off now and again and she did not like that. Many were monsters underneath the glossy façade. Inhuman.

She remembered her childhood. Smells associated with people and other things. And then she remembered when the tobacconist also sold the most amazing vanilla ice cream. She hated the smell of cigars and tobacco but she would rush into his shop, thrust her money in Brindle's face, tell him what she wanted, and then hold her breath until she was blue. He would give her the prize and she would run out. There was the one time though when he paused and smiled, a sour smile—she had almost cried with frustration as she gulped for air.

With that last memory she left Avignon. She would never meet up with her friend in that place again.

The other business. Thought Juliette. Her memory was filled with the colour red, now. She could almost see the blood on the ground. When she closed her eyes she could hear the cries of the crowd and for one brief moment she felt a hand thrust her head towards the blade. She resisted, looked up and all she could see was a swan coming down to land on the Seine. There had almost been a terrible mistake, she thought. Place de la Concorde. Place de la Revolution—no—the first one.

When Juliette finally arrived at the Chateau she thought about why she had been sent. The woman lay in the Chateau de Nemoirs—within the Oratoire Romano Gothique to be precise. And the child—holding her dead mother's hand—guarded by the people who adored her. She would have enemies, though—many of them. It was too late for her mother to go to Carcosa. She had refused once and the king would never force her to go. But now it was time to think about the daughter.

The body was laid out in a cream gown ending at fine crimson slippers, and the face covered with a long silver veil decorated with a filigree of fine gold, twisted into the antique lace. Her brown hair cascaded over the edge of the white marble dais—the relief along the two longer sides showing twin moons and stars—and a strange city. She was surrounded by the black tulips. Her right hand enclosing one tulip cup as if to crush or caress it. The residents of the castle were seated against the walls. They formed a circle, except for where the old door was, and when Juliette looked up at the ceiling she saw golden stars swirling against a black sky. He'd sent that—that was all—and

Juliette. Those seated arose when Juliette entered the room, bowed, and then left her alone with the corpse and the child. The little princess wore a yellow veil. Face unseen. She had been named Fleur. And she had been looked after by the people who loved her but that would not be enough.

Juliette had many enemies, too. There was one in particular who hated poets, writers, and any artists who 'interpreted' the yellow sign—he would try to bring about their demise in some way. Silence them. Shut them down. She knew exactly where he was and Juliette had been told that he would not catch up with her just yet. She always lived on the edge. She thought of Salome and the red moon and the black cloud across it. The swans again. In Baudelaire. And how she had been back before her birth. Her fate. She was an artist, a messenger, and a muse. And she was nothing.

But Juliette had made another enemy. A new one. From a time when her good intentions had caused tragedy for another. The Red Queen had been thinking about Juliette and would find her the next time around.

As Juliette and Fleur made their way through the corridors the walls began to dim in colour as if one artist was shading them in. Juliette saw those who would suffer and the swastika everywhere—a symbol that would be reviled for centuries to come. The little girl did not look. She held Juliette's hand tightly and kept her eyes on her own golden slippers. Juliette held the child's head close to her black skirt and carried on. Then Juliette pressed a finger into the peacock eye at her throat and suddenly the voluminous cloak enveloped them both—as she did so Fleur looked ahead and thought she saw golden rose petals before them but what she could not see— were the petals of black tulips that shrivelled—and died behind them.

Fleur looked up at Juliette. 'When do I get to paint?'

Juliette's expression turned from that of concern to a broad smile. 'All in good time, sweetheart, all in good time.' With that she took the little girl by both hands and they entered the mirror together. For Juliette there was that liberation for the soul again.

As the Princess in Yellow stepped over the threshold she pulled the veil from her face, smiled— and looked up again at Juliette. For a moment Juliette faltered but regained her composure. At that moment a charm fell from her bracelet and landed on the stone floor. They left it behind.

WHILE THE BLACK STARS BURN

BY LUCY A. SNYDER

Caroline tucked an unruly strand of coarse brown hair up under her pink knit cap, shrugged the strap of her black violin case back into place over her shoulder, and hurried up the music building stairs. Her skin felt both uncomfortably greasy and itched dryly under her heavy winter clothes; it had been seven days since the water heater broke in her tiny efficiency and the landlord wasn't answering his phone. Quick, chilly rag-baths were all she could stand, and she felt so self-conscious about the state of her hair that she kept it hidden under a hat whenever possible. She hoped that her violin professor Dr. Harroe wouldn't make her take her cap off.

Her foot slipped on a spot of dried salt on the stairs and she grabbed the chilly brass banister with her left hand to keep from pitching forward. The sharp, cold jolt made the puckered scar in her palm sharply ache, and the old memory returned fast and unbidden:

"*Why aren't you practicing as I told you to?*"

Her father scowled down at her. He was still in his orchestra conducting clothes: a grey blazer and black turtleneck. His fingers clenched a tumbler of Scotch over ice.

"M-my hand started to hurt." She shrank back against the hallway wall, hoping that she hadn't sounded whiny, hoping her explanation would suffice and he'd just send her to bed.

The smell of alcohol and sweat fogged the air around him, and that meant almost anything could happen. He wasn't always cruel. Not even usually. But talking to him when he'd been drinking was like putting a penny in a machine that sometimes dispensed glossy gumballs but other times a dozen stinging arachnids would swarm from the chute instead. And there was no way to know which she'd get, sweets or scorpions.

"Hurt?" he thundered down at her. "Nonsense! I'll show you what hurts!"

He grabbed her arm and dragged her to the fireplace in the music room. She tried to pull away, pleading, promising to practice all night if he wanted her to. But he was completely impassive as he drew a long dark poker from the rack and shoved it into the hottest part of the fire. He frowned down at the iron as the flames licked the shaft, seemingly deaf to her frantic mantra of *Please, no, Papa, I'll be good I swear please.*

The iron heated quickly, and in a series of motions as artful as any he'd performed on the orchestral podium he pulled it from the fire with one hand, squeezed her forearm hard to force her fingers open with the other, and jabbed the glowing red tip of the poker into her exposed palm.

The pain was astonishing. A part of her knew she was shrieking and had fallen to her knees on the fine Persian carpet, but the rest of her felt as though she'd been hurled through space and time toward the roaring hearts of a thousand black stars, cosmic furnaces that would consume not just her flesh and bone but her very soul. They would destroy her so completely that no one would remember that she had ever lived. The stars swirled around her, judging her, and she knew they found her lacking. She was too small, unripe, and they cast her back toward Earth. It was the first time and last time she'd ever been glad to be a disappointment in the eyes of the universe.

Tears blurred her vision and through them her father looked strange, distorted. In that instant she was sure that she knelt at the feet of a monstrous stranger who was wearing her father's pallid face as a mask.

"Now, *that* hurts I expect," the stranger observed cheerfully as her flesh sizzled beneath the red iron. "And so I don't expect I shall hear you whining about practice again, will I? Now, stop your little dog howling this instant or I'll burn the other one, too!"

She willed herself to bite back her screams, and he finally let her go just as she passed out from the agony.

When she woke up on the couch, she discovered that her father had fetched some snow from the porch and pressed a grapefruit-sized ball of it into her palm to numb her burn. Icy water dripped down her wrist and soaked her sweater sleeve. The air was filled with the odor of burned meat. Hers. It made her feel even sicker, and for the rest of her life the smell of grilling steaks and chops would make her want to vomit.

Her father gazed down at her, sad and sober.

"I would never hurt you, you understand?" He gently brushed the hair out of her face. "If anyone has hurt you in this world, it was not I."

He bundled her into the back of his Cadillac and took her to see a physician friend of his. Caroline remembered sitting in a chair in the hallway with a handkerchief full of ice in her hand, weeping quietly from the pain while the two men spoke behind a closed door.

"Will her playing be affected?" her father asked.

"Christ, Dunric!" The physician sounded horrified. "Is that your only concern for your own daughter?"

"Of course not!" her father huffed. "Nonetheless, it *is* a concern. So, if you would be so kind as to offer your professional opinion on the matter?"

"She's got a third degree burn; her palm is roasted through like a lamb fillet. I can't see how she could have held on to a live coal so long of her own accord. Are you sure no one else could have been involved? Perhaps a resentful servant?"

"Quite sure," he replied. "My daughter has some...mental peculiarities she regrettably inherited from her mother. You know how unstable sopranos are! Her mother often had a kind of petit mal seizure; I believe some pyromania compelled the girl to take hold of the coal and then a fit prevented her from dropping it as a sensible child would."

"That is unfortunate." The physician sounded unconvinced, and for a brief moment hope swelled in Caroline's heart: perhaps he would challenge her father, investigate further, discover the truth. And then perhaps she'd be sent to live with her mother's people in Boston. She'd only met them once – they were bankers or shoemakers or something else rather dull but they seemed decent enough.

But it was not to be. The physician continued: "Her tendons and ligaments are almost certainly affected. She may need surgery to regain full mobility in her fingers, and I fear that her hand may be permanently drawn due to scarring."

"Well, she only needs to curl it 'round the neck of her instrument, after all."

It took two surgeries to repair the tendons in her hand, and all her father's colleagues marveled at how brave and determined she was in her physical therapy and practice sessions afterward. Her father glowed at the praises they heaped on her, and while he never said as much, something in his smile told her that, should she cease to be so pleasingly dedicated to the musical arts, there were things in his world worse than hot metal.

Caroline traced the lines of her scar with her thumb. The doctor's knife had given it a strange, symbolic look. Some people claimed it resembled a Chinese or Arabic character, although nobody could say which one.

She flexed her hand and shook her head to try to banish the memories. There was no point in dwelling on any of it. Her father was long gone. Five years after he burned her, he'd flown into a rage at a negative review in the newspaper. He drove off in his Alfa Romeo with a bottle of Glenfiddich. Caroline suspected he'd gone to see a ballerina in the next city who enjoyed being tied up and tormented. But he never arrived. He lost control of his car in the foggy hills and his car overturned in a drainage ditch that was hidden from the road. Pinned, he lived for three days while hungry rats gnawed away the exposed flesh of his face, eyes and tongue.

At his funeral, she'd briefly considered quitting music just to spite his memory ... but if she refused to be the Maestro's daughter, what was she? She knew nothing of gymnastics or any other sports, nor was she an exceptional student or a skilled painter. Her crabbed hand was nimble on a fingerboard but useful for little else. Worst of all, she knew—since she'd been repeatedly told so—that she was quite plain, good as a violinist but unremarkable as a woman. Her music was the only conceivable reason anyone would welcome her to a wedding. A thousand creditors had picked her father's estate as clean as the rodents had stripped his skull; if she abandoned the violin, what would she have left?

"Caroline, is that you?" Professor Harroe called after she knocked on the door to his office.

"Yes, sir."

"Do come in! I have a bit of a surprise for you today."

She suddenly felt apprehensive, but made herself smile at the professor as she opened the door and took her accustomed seat in the chair in front of his desk, which was stacked high with music theory papers, scores, and books. "What is it?"

He leaned back in his battered wooden swivel chair behind his desk and smiled at her in return. Her anxiety tightened; Harroe had been her music tutor since she was a teenager, and he almost never smiled, not at his colleagues' jokes nor at beautiful women nor at lovely music. She searched his face, trying to decipher his expression. He looked practically giddy, she finally decided, and it was a bit unsettling.

"Did you know that your father was working on a series of violin sonatas when he died?"

Her skin itched beneath her sweater. She rubbed at the scar again. "No, I did not."

"He was writing them for you, for when your playing would be mature enough to handle them. He told me he intended them to be a surprise for your 21st birthday. I think he realized his dalliance with drink might lead to disaster – as indeed it sadly did – so he arranged for his lawyer to send me the sonatas along with a formal request that I complete them in secret.

"I regret that I am not half the composer he was, but I am proud to say I have done as he asked. Six months late for your 21st, and for that I apologize, but at last his music is ready for you."

"I ... oh my. I really don't know what to say. That was very ... kind of you."

"I regret that kindness had nothing to do with it; as a composer I could not pass up the opportunity to co-author a work with the good Maestro. It was an extraordinary challenge, one that I am most pleased I was able to meet. I had to consult with ... certain experts to complete the work, and one is here today, ready to listen to you perform the first sonata. If you do well – and I am sure that you will! – I believe that he is prepared to offer you a musical patronage that will ensure that you're taken care of for the rest of your life."

Caroline felt simultaneously numb with surprise and overwhelmed by dread. Was this truly an opportunity to escape her slide into poverty? Few students in her position ever saw salvation arriving before they'd even graduated. She *had* to rise to the occasion. But knowing her father was behind it all made her want nothing more than to go back to her cramped, drafty apartment and hide under the covers.

Her lips moved for a moment before she could get any words out. "That's amazing, but I couldn't possibly perform a piece I haven't even seen —"

"Nonsense!" His tone left her no room for demurral or negotiation. "You are a fine sight-reader, and after all this music is made for you. You'll be splendid."

⁂

Feeling supremely self-conscious about her dowdy thriftstore clothes and the unfashionable knit cap over her unwashed hair, Caroline took a deep breath, got a better grip on her violin case, lifted her chin, and strode out onto the small, brightly-lit recital stage. Her footsteps echoed hollowly off the curved walls. The theatre was small, just thirty seats, and she could sense rather than clearly see someone sitting in the back row on the left side. Normally having just one listener would bolster her confidence, but today, the emptiness of the room seemed eerie. She bowed crisply toward the dark figure, and then took her seat in a spotlighted wooden folding chair. The music stand held a hand-written musical booklet made from old-fashioned parchment. Her eyes scanned the cover sheet:

Into the Hands of the Living God
An Etude in G Minor for Violin
Composed by Dunric Cage-Satin with Dr. Alexander Harroe

Caroline frowned at the title. Was this some sort of religious music? As far as she knew, her father had been an ardent atheist his entire life. Ah well. There was nothing to do but struggle through as best she could. At worst she'd perform miserably, lose her mysterious patron, and be exactly as penniless as she'd been when she woke up that morning. She opened her violin case, pulled her instrument and bow from the padded blue velvet cutouts, carefully ran her rosin puck across the horsehair, flipped the cover page over to expose the unfamiliar music, and prepared to play.

The notes bore a cold, complex intelligence, and the tonality reminded her a little of Benjamin Britten. But there was something else here, something she'd neither heard nor played before, but nothing bound in stanzas was beyond the capacity of her instrument or her skills. She gave herself over to craft and educated reflex and the stark black notes transubstantiated into soaring music as nerves drove muscle, keratin mastered steel, and reverberation shook maple and spruce.

The stage fell away, and she found herself standing upon a high, barren cliff above a huge lake with driving waves. The air had an unhealthy taint to it, and in the sky there hung a trio of strange, misshapen moons, and opposite the setting twin suns three black stars rose, their bright coronas gleaming through the streaked clouds.

When the dark starlight touched her palm, her scar exploded, a nova made flesh. She fell to her knees on the lichen-covered rocks, unable to even take a breath to scream as the old lines glowed with a transcendent darkness, hot as any stellar cataclysm.

She heard footsteps and the rustling of robes, and through her tears she saw a regal iron boot beneath an ochre hem embroidered with the tiny white bones of birds and mice.

"You'll do," the figure said in a voice that made her want to drive spikes into her own brain. "Yes, you'll do."

She felt the terrible lord touch her head, and it was like being impaled on a sword, and suddenly she was falling—

—Caroline gasped and the bow slipped and screeched across her strings. Blinking in fear and confusion, it took her a half second to realize she was still onstage, still performing ... or she had been until her mistake.

"I'm—I'm so, so sorry, I don't know what happened," she stammered, looking to her lone audience member in the back of the theatre. But all the seats were empty.

"It's quite all right." Professor Harroe hurried onstage from the wings, beaming. "You did wonderfully, just wonderfully."

"I ... I did?" She blinked at him in disbelief. "But ... I messed up, didn't I?"

"Oh, a mere sight-reading error ... I'm sure you'll play straight through to the end next time! And. Your new benefactor has requested that you perform tomorrow evening at the St. Barnabus Church on 5th Street. 6pm sharp; don't be late!"

"Oh. Yes. Okay." She set her violin down on her lap, and the pain in her hand made her look at her palm. Her scar had split open during the performance, and her sleeve was wet with her own blood.

When Caroline tried to sleep on her narrow bed, she fell almost immediately into a suite of nightmares. She was onstage again, and the notes of her father's sonata turned to tiny hungry spiders that swarmed over her arms and chewed through her eyes and into her brain. Predatory black stars wheeled around her as she tumbled helplessly through airless, frigid outer space. And then she was back in the strange land with the twin suns, but now she was a tiny mouse pinned to a flat rock, and a masked man in yellow robes told her how he would flay her alive and take her spine.

She awoke sweating and weeping at 3am, and in a moment of perfect clarity, she realized that she wanted no part of whatever was happening at St. Barnabus in 15 hours. There was not enough money in the world. She quickly dressed in her dowdy secondhand pants and sweater, threw a few belongings into an overnight bag and grabbed her violin case. The Greyhound station was just a mile walk from her apartment building, and there would be a bus going somewhere far away. Maybe she could go to Boston, find her mother's people and learn to make shoes or whatever it was that they did. Shoes were good. People needed shoes.

But when she reached the pitchy street and started striding toward the station, she realized that the city was darker than usual. Tall buildings whose penthouses normally glowed with habitation were entirely black. She scanned the sky: no stars or moon, nothing but a seeming void.

And then, she saw something like a tattered black handkerchief flutter onto a nearby tall streetlamp, blotting it out. She stood very still for a moment, then slowly turned, beholding the uncanny night. Tattered shadows flapped all around. She started running, the violin case banging against her hip. The tatters moved faster, swarming around her on all sides. Soon she was sprinting headlong down the street, across the bridge ...

... And realized the other side of the bridge was lost in the ragged blackness. No trace of light; it was as if that part of the world had ceased to exist, had been devoured by one of the stars from her nightmares.

She looked behind her. More utter darkness. The city was blotted out.

"I won't do it," she said, edging toward the bridge railing. She could hear the river rushing below. "*I won't.*"

The jagged darkness rapidly ate the bridge, surging toward her, and so she unslung her violin case and hurled her instrument over the edge into the murky water. The darkness came at her even faster, and she crouched down, covering her head with her arms—

—And found herself sitting in a metal folding chair in the nave of a strange church. In her hands was her old violin, the one she'd played as a child. Her father's sonata rested on the music stand before her, the notes black as the predatory stars.

"I won't," she whispered again, but she no longer ruled her own flesh. Her hands lifted her instrument to her shoulder and expertly drew the bow across the strings. The scabbed sign in her palm split open again, ruby blood spilling down her wrist, and she could see the marks starting to shine darkly as they had in the dream. Something planted in her long ago was seeking a way out.

Caroline found her eyes were still under her control, so she looked away from the music, looked out the window, hoping that blinding herself to the notes would stop the performance. But her hands and arms played on, her body swaying to keep time.

And there through the window she saw the glow of buildings on fire, and in the sky she saw a burning version of the symbol in her palm, and the air was rending, space and time separating, and as the firmament tore apart at the seams she could see the twin suns and black stars moving in from the world of her nightmares.

And she wanted to weep, but her body played on.

And the people in the city cried out in fear and madness, and still it played on.

And the winds from Carcosa blew the fires of apocalypse across the land, and still it played on.

OLD TSAH-HOV

BY ANYA MARTIN

Lights flash on, a door slams, I jerk awake. Footsteps approach, and through the bars, I see bent bodies, faces staring. She says the word enough that I know it to be his name—Archer. The adam shakes his head, adjusts his glasses. He wears a pricker-prodder white coat and on it a pin the color of the sun with six points like the one she used to wear.

I jump up and yell, lunge for the bars. I cannot help it. The pin makes me angry because it reminds me of her and how I am trapped in this place with no sun, but blinding white lights that hurt my eyes and how I am not with her, and most of all not in the city where I yearn to be with that longing so deep it aches inside my heart.

Archer and the woman, who has short red hair and a similar coat but no pin, pull back, stand up. They are not afraid of me which makes me yell louder.

"Let me out, you fuckers!"

The other prisoners start shouting now, too. Whenever one of us yells or screams or even whines, we all do. They cannot silence us.

The couple turns and walks away, out the first door, the one through which I was brought. The prisoners nearest to it talk loudly and happily when they leave and when they return. They think they won't be here for long, that their families will be coming to pick them up soon. Sometimes they don't come back and I assume their offenses were less than mine and that they have homes to go to.

The door at the other end, the one that slammed, is different—thicker, colder. Few pass through it but no one ever returns.

Once Archer and the woman are gone, we all begin to quiet, one by one. Saliva churns thickly in my mouth, but spitting does not help. I feel myself shaking not with cold but with a simmering rage that I cannot release. I glance at the full dish of food but am too angry to eat. The water, I cannot even look at, for in its reflection I see the King's eyes slitted and mocking.

I lay down again on the hard floor, curl into a ball and squeeze my eyes shut. I concentrate with all my might on the memory of her scent and her singing and imagine myself back in the city where the buildings and streets bore the same color as the sun, the city of yellow, the city of Gold.

I remembered the days when I ran with my brother and sister through the streets like they were just yesterday or a long, long time ago—never anything in-between. No one was faster than us. Our Ima had bade us be careful and avoid strangers. Sooner or later some thug would challenge us for a piece of food or pick a fight just because he did not like the way we smelled. Ima lectured us sternly that we were too young to win in a brawl, and every day she taught us a little more about how to disappear into a crowd of adams or fade into a shadow in a wall. She also warned us that most dangerous were the adams who were tall and could surprise you from behind with big thick sticks and stones. But we were young and like all the young, we believed ourselves indestructible.

Because I loved Ima and knew no other way, I listened and studied, but then one day I saw a fight between two adults, a rough-and-tumble ball of punches, kicks and bites. I was surprised at the victory of the smaller combatant—whose color was the same as mine, somewhere between the sun and the sand and the city. The only difference was that he had a short stump instead of a curled tail like my own—its absence likely a scar from some previous battle. His bigger foe, dark fur like the night, limped away, flesh torn and bloodied, while the winner feasted on the slab of smoked meat that must have inspired the struggle. My mouth watered at its delicious aroma, and I thought to myself if only I could learn how to punch and where to bite and claw, I would never have to worry about eating well again. That, and fighting looked like pure pleasure.

I stepped slowly towards the victor. At first, he raised his head and growled, but when I explained I had no interest in his spoils and complimented him on his combat skills, he calmed. He clearly enjoyed my admiration and began to consider my proposition that I would bring him food if he would teach me to fight. He told me his name was King of the Streets, and it suited him. He was the most impressive of my kind I ever met. Most of us just called each other by the way we looked and recognized each other for how we smelled. My brother was Big Eye, because one of his brown eyes was larger than the other. My sister was Straight Tail because her tail didn't curl like Ima's, mine and my brother's. And I was Lop Ear, because my left ear was crooked. But King, he earned his title in battle and the rest would either bow to him or give him a wide berth.

So my arrangement with King began. Every day while my brother and sister would siesta in an alley, I would sneak away and meet him. He taught me how to pick a fight, and soon I was not just scraping with others my age but some even older. From the beginning I was winning. King told me I had a natural talent. That he thought so made me happy.

The day that my life changed started like every other. While darkness still cloaked the city, the adams called from the sky in all directions. My sister would try to sing with them when she was younger, but Ima always hushed her—afraid to draw attention. We were just squatters among the big burlap sacks of rice, couscous and fava beans—so much more comfortable to lie among these than the cold hard stones of the alley where we were born. Ima had discovered the broken window on one of her explorations—the opening just wide enough for her to squeeze through. Then one day she never returned. Her scent ended by a wall of trash cans. We imagined an adam found her while foraging for food for us, and for once, she was not able to disappear. We searched all the streets we knew and even streets we had never wandered before, but we found no trace of her.

Once we heard the call, the three of us moved quickly. We needed to be outside before the adams who lived above the sacks were done spreading soft cloths on the ground and extending their forearms like we did when we wanted to communicate our desire to play.

We slipped out the window and into the alley. The first rays of the sun accented the yellow hue of the stones beneath our feet, like the first embers of a fire. We sniffed for signs of others who may have come in the night, and as soon as we caught even the faintest whiff, my brother and I lifted our legs and released our spray to declare this place was ours. After eight full moons, we were old enough that we could do that as adult males, not squat like our sister.

When we reached the market street, the scent of fresh bread baking tempted our noses. My brother and sister and I danced at the wonder of it, our stomachs yearning for its soft texture. After tasting the bread of the City of the Sun, no other food could ever fully satisfy—even raw meat, much less the bland hard dry pebbles in the bowl of my prison cell.

Shop doors opened, shutters lifted, canopies unfurled, and carts wheeled out onto the street. Soon adams would be everywhere, for this is how they hunted. They looked, then pointed, then exchanged wispy slips and metal pellets and took away their rewards. We needed to act quickly if we wanted to procure breakfast when eyes were still distracted with preparing for the day. Today, I didn't even have to snatch a loaf of bread from the cart. The adam let his son carry it out, but the boy's arms were not big enough to balance his haul and he dropped one. I grabbed it in my teeth before he could yell "Kelev Ra!" Then I ran back to the alley. I let my brother and sister each tear off a piece, but hid my own for King. My stomach ached with emptiness, but I couldn't arrive without payment and I'd found what he said to be true—one fights harder and better when hungry.

We wandered the streets, looking for other opportunities to scavenge and scored a few apples. As usual, I became restless for when the heat would become too much and my brother and sister would want to disappear back into the alleys to nap in the shade. My brother stretched himself against the wall, and my sister curled her back against mine. Once she was asleep, I gently eased away--not knowing it would be the last time we would sleep beside each other.

I found King waiting in the usual place on the edge of the square outside one of the adams' great houses of gathering. They had many such buildings in the yellow city, some with half-suns nestled egg-like in their roofs. I once tried to creep inside, but an adam quickly shooed me away, and one of the rocks he threw at me came close enough to convince me it wasn't worth the risk. King told me inside there wasn't any food—only crowds of adams shuffling for position in front of sparkly bright objects. I was impressed that he was able to get inside—but if there wasn't any food, what was the point?

I placed the bread at King's feet. He sniffed and ate it so fast I wondered if he even tasted the flavors. Then he announced it was time for me to advance my training. Today he was going to teach me how to steal from an adam. I told him I was already good at watching for when one dropped something or was distracted setting up his wares in the morning.

"You tasted the bread I brought you, wasn't it delicious? The best baker in the old town."

King turned up his nose and snarled. I jumped back, startled at the magnitude of his derision.

"Do you like meat?"

"Of course," I said.

"The adam never drops his best meat, does he?"

"No."

"And if he leaves it unattended, it's only for a moment and you have to move as fast as a cat."

I raised my jowl to reveal my teeth. I didn't like cats.

"Well, then, are you brave and are you hungry?"

"Yes."

"You don't have to be afraid of the adam if you strike faster than he can pick up a rock to throw at you."

King led me within sight of a butcher shop. In front was an adam dressed all in black and with a long mane of black fur hanging in front of his face. I stiffened, recognizing him as one who had yelled at me when I was simply standing across the street minding my own. But oh, the wonder of the meats that always hung outside his shop—some raw and others that had been smoked and seasoned! For me, raw was always the tastiest, but I would settle for either.

"I will run fast and bite his ankle," King said. "While he is distracted, you jump up and grab some meat. I'll let go, and you and I will run like the wind. By the time he has a chance to grab a rock, we'll be long disappeared up there."

King motioned with his nose towards an alley that led to another of the great gathering homes. I wasn't scared of fighting other dogs—I enjoyed that—but my mother's stories of how much the adams hated us dug deep into me, not to mention the times when I had narrowly escaped being hit by a rock. King was a formidable champion among our kind, but was even he taking on more than he could chew? Still, I was afraid of seeming a coward in front of King.

I stole another glance at the adam, who was now engaged with a customer—a female with long black hair in a light-colored dress that clung tightly to her body. The adam leaned in close to her, gesturing to various of the hanging meats. I assume he was describing them so she could select the one she wanted to eat, but his body language indicated he also enjoyed the way she looked.

"Are you ready?" King asked, not giving me a chance to object.

I wasn't but I scratched my paw on the stone to signal yes.

King shot forward. I charged after him.

When I reached the cart, King's teeth were embedded in the man's leg and the adam was screaming in pain. The woman had backed away, her hand over her mouth. I leaped up and sunk my teeth into a juicy raw slab. It gave way easily, but as my paws touched back to the ground, King let go, spun towards me and butted his head into my groin. The surprise assault from my teacher startled me, and I dropped the meat. King seized it up quickly from the ground and took off. The shock of his betrayal made me hesitate just long enough for the adam to pick up a rock.

I barely made it a few steps when it grazed the side of my hip and my legs slipped from beneath me, sliding me sideways onto hard stone. Several other adams shifted quickly out of my way as I hit the ground.

I scrambled to get back on my feet, but my leg hurt and my hip wouldn't cooperate so I had to just roll back down. I saw the adam bend to grab another rock. I growled but knew the adam had the advantage. Soon I would be gone to the place Ima went.

"Thief!!" shouted the adam, his cheeks flushed underneath his black beard.

But before he could hurl another weapon, I heard a loud shout.

"Isaac, no! Don't hurt the dog!"

The female with the long dark hair grabbed the adam's arm.

"But you saw what he did!" the adam protested. "He and his buddy stole one of my best beef shanks. Jerusalem would be better if all these mongrels were struck from our streets."

"Please," she said and waved him back. She turned towards me and then she crouched and stretched out her hand. I continued to growl. Again Ima's words came to me—never trust an adam.

"Sweet, sweet," she called to me.

The adam had backed away and was muttering irritably. Then she began to hum, her voice soft and soothing—the most beautiful sound I had ever heard. I stopped growling. Soon I was whimpering softly. She stroked my side. No adam had ever touched me, but her hand felt surprisingly nice. She scratched around my loppy ear. That felt especially good. I curled my front legs and rolled on my back. I don't know why I did that but I wanted her to rub my chest. She did, and it felt better than anything else I ever remembered.

She pointed to herself and said "Cassilda," repeating it three times slowly, lingering on every syllable. The pain in my leg had almost subsided, and with her help, I was able to stand. She took my head in her hands, placed her face close to mine, smiled and gazed in my eyes. If it had been anyone but her, I would have bitten, but I felt safe. I never wanted her to let go, to remove her face from mine.

Then she said: "Tsah-Hov." Again she said it three times, her eyes locked on my own. And I knew that was her name for me.

Isaac yelled again, and I suppose he was warning Cassilda about me—how our kind can't be trusted, how I would bite her. But I knew that I could never bite her.

She beckoned and I hesitated. I thought of my brother and my sister, and what they would think when they awoke, when like Ima, I just disappeared. I wondered if she had met her own Cassilda, but I knew that an Ima would never desert her children even for a Cassilda. Beyond the crowd in the entry to the alley, I saw King, glaring, the meat still in his mouth. I wondered if he was disappointed that I had found a savior.

I turned away from King and followed Cassilda. Sometimes she would pause and pet my head. I trailed her down the familiar market streets to the great wall, where I sat and waited while she did as the other adams did—slipped a leaf inside it, touched it, bowed her head, spoke.

When she returned to me, she said, "Good Tsah-Hov."

We continued out the giant gate—I had never traveled so far nor along such a wide street. In its center, giant mif'letzets rushed by us at speeds I could never run. I had seen such creatures before but never in such numbers. Finally we came to a building as tall as the gathering homes but so high that I could not see if its roof had a sun on top.

Cassilda held open the door then led me to a strange box. Inside it made a funny noise and shook slightly. The box opened and we emerged in a different place with many doors. She went to one of them and grabbed what looked like a paw. She twisted it and it opened into her home, my new home.

So that's how the adams used all the cloths that hung outside the shops, I thought. They spread them on the floor to make it soft and warm, not like the cold hard stone of the streets. She led me into a small room that smelled of food and placed a bowl of water on the floor. I drank it eagerly. Before then I never had so much water in one serving except perhaps when it collected in a pot after a rain.

Then Cassilda coaxed me into another room and lifted me into a pond of bubbly warm water. At first, I didn't like it, but she massaged me until I could almost faint with pleasure. Even Ima with her tongue had never washed all the street smells away from me. Cassilda rubbed me with more soft cloths, then blew hot wind from a paw she held in her hand.

When I was completely dry, she led me to where she slept and patted her hand on her bed. I leapt up onto a place softer than the cloths on the floor, soft beyond all imagining, so soft I jumped back down. But she tapped her hand again and I returned. She lay down beside me and I snuggled my back within her arms. Again she began to sing.

I had never understood what the adam had spoken before now, but I knew her words. Cassilda sang of the city, the city of the setting sun, the city of Gold, the city of Tsah-Hov. She sang of it as if it were my city, hers and mine and how we shared it with our tribes. Here it all began and here it would all end. The old city was lost but the lost has been found, and while we have our enemies, the city gives us strength and shall endure until a great King descends from the sky.

I saw a tear trail down her cheek. My eyes were full of tears, too. Until then I never knew that dogs could cry.

From then on I lived with Cassilda in her home above the streets, sleeping with her in her bed. During the day she would leave me, and sometimes I feared she would not return. But she always did, bringing bread and scraps of meat I did not have to steal. Before sleep, she sang to me the same song.

In the morning and evening, Cassilda took me for walks around her building. I marked my new kingdom zealously, but the only others of my kind I saw were clean like me, walking with adams. I had seen dogs with adams in the market before, but my brother, sister and I had laughed at them. She also took me to see the pricker-prodder for the first time. His house was full of many dogs and cats, some I saw and some I could just smell. Two adams had to hold me tightly when he pricked several sharp claws into my back. I wanted to bite him, and I wondered why Cassilda brought me here. But as soon as I saw her again, I forgave her.

Once a week she took me along when she shopped in the market. Sometimes I would see one like me who lived on the streets or a small pack. I sensed they were jealous of Cassilda and me. They knew I had found something special and different, even if they had no idea how it felt to lie on a soft cloth instead of cold stone or a bag of rice. I scanned the shadows for my brother and sister, but I never saw them. I only glimpsed King one time and he just turned away as if he pitied me. I dreamt of King nightly though, only now he wasn't giving me lessons. Instead we fought. Each time he appeared more bloody and scarred, but he still always won, admonishing me that my fighting skills had become soft from living with an adam.

Then came the day Cassilda brought Shmuel home. He had no fur on his head at all. When he visited, he would always pet me quickly on the head, and then he would ignore me for the rest of the evening. She laughed when he spoke, they'd sit and eat together, and after that they touched lips. Sometimes he stayed all night and I no longer fit on the bed. They made groans of pleasure and emanated mating smells. On those nights, I slept on the sofa in the living room. The cushions were softer than the bed, but I missed Cassilda. I wished Shmuel would stop coming.

Shmuel visited more and more often until one day he just stayed. Cassilda grew bigger in her belly, and I could smell the little adam growing inside. Shmuel started taking me on my morning and twilight walks, sometimes after dark if he came home late. He didn't talk or sing to me like Cassilda did. He just took me far enough to empty myself and then we returned home. I slept on the sofa every night now, King taunting me as we dream-battled about how I was afraid to challenge an adam.

The little male was born, and Cassilda called him Chanan. She seemed happy but always stressed. Though she no longer left every day, she had even less time for me, having to prepare his food and tend to him. Still, during the day she sang to both of us about the city, and while she sang, I did not feel replaced or alone.

Other days were not so nice. Chanan would cry and Shmuel would get a growl to his voice. One day he struck Cassilda. King's voice shouted in my head, and I yelled at Shmuel, started to lunge. I barely got close before he hit me hard on my head. I yelped and jumped back, growled more. I wanted to tear him apart, but I remembered what Ima said about adams being bigger and stronger, even if I had teeth and claws and despite King goading me in my head. I also knew Cassilda loved Shmuel like she loved me, so instead I retreated to a corner, where I lay down to stare at him. She cried and Chanan cried louder, and now Shmuel was soothing her, stroking her hair, putting his lips to her cheek. Later she crept out of bed to check on me, placed her hand on my brow. She couldn't sing because it would wake everyone in the house, but I could hear her voice.

Cassilda started taking Chanan for walks in a cart that she pushed. I danced when she indicated that I could come along. She gently calmed me, I suppose afraid I'd jump on the fragile baby, though she should know I would never harm him. She hummed to us as we walked down the old familiar path to the market, where she filled a bag with food from sundry vendors, and I filled my nose with all the old smells. I even thought I caught a whiff of King near the gathering house where we used to meet.

On the way back, a large clap seared into my ears and the ground shook with such anger that both Cassilda and I almost fell over. Adams screamed all around us and a cloud of dust enveloped us. Cassilda began to cough and run pushing the cart, Chanan crying at the top of his lungs. I sprinted after her. Everyone was running and yelling. When we finally got home, she locked the door quickly behind us, took Chanan in her arms and sang more loudly than I had ever heard her sing. I could hear both love and fear in her voice as she lamented that the city had enemies jealous of its beauty, enemies who also thought it holy. Even I knew that some adams didn't like others in the same way we didn't like the scent of all of our kind—and what had happened was rooted in an enmity so ancient that it might as well have always been.

Shmuel came home early. He held her like the old Shmuel had courted her. They talked for a long time in great seriousness. In the days that followed, I only walked with Shmuel and I saw the first signs that my life was about to change. Objects disappeared from shelves and closets, boxes and crates piled up in the living room, and King and I no longer fought in my dreams—he just raised his jowls and made a sound that I had never heard any of us make—laughter. Then one day adams came and took everything away.

Shmuel brought a large crate with bars like the cell I am in now. He placed a big beef-bone in my bowl, pushed it inside and called to me. The savory aroma enticed, but I didn't trust to enter a place so dark and narrow. Shmuel yelled at me, but Cassilda shushed him. When she stroked me and coaxed me, I couldn't deny her. Once I was inside, I heard a snapping noise behind me and began to whine.

Cassilda spoke to me through the bars, repeating my name "Tsah-hov," and from the gentle tone in her voice, I knew she did not want me to be afraid. I stopped calling out and lay down. I was more afraid than even when the adam was stoning me, but for her I would do anything.

The crate was shoved into one of the great street beasts, and then unloaded at a place full of terrible rattling noises and people yelling all around me. Next I was moved to a dark place with many cases reeking with the odor of adams. I felt a sensation like being lifted—as if the very ground was rising. I cried loudly in the near-dark but no one even shouted to silence me.

I finally fell asleep, and all I remembered of my dreams was Ima's stern warnings, and King opening his mouth to reveal too many sharp, pointy teeth. A heavy thud shook me awake, and I sensed I was on the ground again. Adams pulled the case out into the sunlight, but I knew I was no longer in the Gold City. Even the adams smelled different. They lifted me onto another mif'letzet. Then finally the creature stopped, its canopy lifted and I heard Cassilda excitedly calling my name.

"Tsah-Hov!"

She opened the bars and I jumped all over her in joy. She didn't scold me but hugged me. I could see Shmuel behind her holding Chanan, his sneer revealing he would have preferred to have left me. As Cassilda quieted me, I realized the ground beneath me felt like soft cloth under my paws.

And so I arrived at my new home, not a building with many homes but one place for just us with many rooms and stairs and what Cassilda called a "yard"—covered with the soft rugs in the back. I knew we must be faraway from the City because the only thing I recognized was the sun. This place was not the color of the sun, but different colors, colors that resembled shadows to me and for which I had no names.

At first I admit I was a little excited by my new home. Cassilda would take me and Chanan on long walks in his cart. The streets were smooth like a single stone, and I did not have to step carefully to protect my feet. The city of Gold had few trees, but trees were everywhere here, towering above. And the houses were big and separated from each other by yards. An adam family lived in each house and there was no market street. Cassilda and Shmuel would ride instead inside one of the mif'letzet and return with food. Sometimes they took me, and we would emerge to walk in different places, places even softer and filled with more trees. Or they took me to see another pricker-prodder, a female who tried to soothe me with a gentle voice and crunchy food, then stabbed me just the same. At night though Cassilda still sang the boy to sleep with the song of the City of Gold, and I would listen. She put on a mask of contentment, but I could sense we both were lost now. I still dreamed of King, but we did not fight and he was silent.

Many like me lived here, but unlike in the City, they came in more sizes, shapes, and colors. Their smells didn't tell many stories because they spent their nights in the houses with adams. Some would yell at me from their yards behind fences—and others would strain their leashes. I now had to wear a collar around my neck and walk on a rope like them. I hated both, but the others seemed not to mind, as if they accepted whatever the adams bade them do. Sometimes when Shmuel walked me, I would shout back and once when he took off my lead on a dirt path with lots of trees I even attacked a big prissy one of my kind whose long fur resembled a horse's mane and tale. When I walked with Cassilda however, I mastered an innocent stare that only seemed to infuriate my foes and make them shout louder at me.

At first the new soft place seemed to calm Shmuel's anger. But then he and Cassilda began to fight as never before—shouting and shouting. I swore to myself if he ever hit her again, I would rip him apart. One day he left and then he would only come sometimes to take the boy away for short periods of time. Those times when I was alone with Cassilda, I would crawl close to her and she would stroke my head. We both closed our eyes and were back in the City, the sun's rays painting all the buildings the color of my fur.

I was dreaming not of King but a happy memory of the streets and the scent of baking bread when a heavy knock jolted me awake. Cassilda rose and opened the door. Shmuel quivered with anger and wobbled unsteady on his feet, and even Chanan trembled in fear of his father. Cassilda shouted at him, yanking the boy away. He wiggled out of her grasp and ran towards the stairs, grabbing onto the railing and lingering as if torn between watching his parents and escaping to his bedroom.

I yelled at Shmuel to stay away from Cassilda, but she was consumed with the rage of an Ima afraid for her child and moved closer instead. His hand came up quickly and swatted her across the face. She fell back as he lunged again towards her, but tripped on one of my bones on the floor. I heard King shouting now loudly in my head, "Coward! Coward!" I pulled myself into position to leap while my foe's legs were still teetering.

Just as my paws left the ground, Chanan ran in front of Shmuel, shouting, "No, Tsah-Hov! No!"

It was too late for me to pull back my teeth which bit down hard now not on Shmuel's leg but on Chanan's cheek. The taste of his blood filled my mouth--both similar and different from the blood of my kind. The boy screamed, and something hard and wood descended on my head. I yelped and let go, my instincts cutting. But as I spun around to attack and grabbed the arm of my combatant, I saw it was Cassilda. I yelped again, let go and ran for the window, hurling myself against and out it. As it shattered, sharp blades cut my flesh like a thousand pricker-prodders. I dashed into the black night and to the back corner of the yard, scrambled into a hole under the fence through which I sometimes escaped to explore the neighborhood by myself. I had no place to go without Cassilda, so I crept to the front of the house and waited.

A giant mif'letzet covered in spinning lights charged into the driveway. It made a screeching noise which hurt my ears. Another smaller one followed with more lights and noise, and then another. Adams emptied out of them into the house, and soon they brought out Cassilda and Chanan. Her head was bowed and she clutched her arm. I called to her even though I knew she would grant no absolution. I had bitten her child. Ima would never have forgiven anyone who did that.

Cassilda lifted her head and looked at me. I could see tears flowing down her cheeks. Shmuel exited the house behind her. I shouted and raced towards him. At that moment I felt a tight noose lasso around my neck and a rough jerk backwards. Soon I was caged in the back of one of the mif'letzet and then I was here.

"Tsah-Hov," says Archer.

My eyes blink open when I hear my name, angry to hear anyone utter it but Cassilda. I growl and raise my lips to show my teeth.

Archer signals to another adam--a heavyset one who opens the cage. Then he lassoes the metal noose around my neck again. I lunge to attack but he wields his weapon with a skill I cannot evade and jumps back before I can snap my teeth. Oh, Ima, the adams have their ways to hurt. They have been doing it since the beginning of time.

The door to the Chamber stands open, and I enter, knowing I will never leave, never see Cassilda again. I wonder if she thinks of me, if she understands that I did what I did for her.

I no longer struggle, just allow the burly adam to lift me onto the cold smooth table.

I see Archer, the pricker-prodder, lift his claw and close my eyes. As its juice flows into me, I see the Yellow City. Cassilda stands before the great doors to the gathering home. She sings and opens her arms and I run to her, but when I reach the entrance, King awaits instead. His yellow fur is no longer drenched in blood but glows so bright and luminous I have to avert my eyes to avoid being blinded.

I turn to flee. But King springs and sinks his teeth into my neck, drags me in through the doors. Inside everything is shiny, just as King told me, with no roof, just open blue sky and not just one sun but two. Cassilda sings but I cannot see her. Adams are everywhere. King hurls me towards them. They yell "Kelev Ra!" in chorus and raise their arms so I can see the many, many rocks.

THE NEURASTHENIAC
BY SELENA CHAMBERS

The following excerpt is republished with permission from
The Surhistory Dossier, *catalogued by The Bas Bleu Sisterhood in 2014.*

Helen Heck (1937-1968) was a poet whose incomplete and fragmentary unpublished notebooks, collectively known as *The Neurastheniac,* garnered her a small underground following as a result of bootleg circulation, most notably during the Nineties' golden age of the punk zine. Heck became most notorious during this time when Boilerplate frontman Donald Lee made her last lines famous by quoting them in his suicide note, leading novelist Kathy Acker to write a small appreciation for *Vogue* magazine called "Lavender Sashed Wrists."

While she was a contemporary of William S. Burroughs and Sylvia Plath, and wrote of similar transgressive themes, she is considered a canonical nightmare and has been largely eschewed from any kind of academic or critical discussion for several reasons. First, *The Neurastheniac* is her only known work, and even then, exists only as a working draft. She never saw a byline during her lifetime, and there is no indication whether she intended the work to ever see publication. As a draft, it is raw and unstructured, and is at times completely in-cohesive and incomprehensible. It is because of this state that many critics dismiss it as an "Artaud-groupie playing in the Sanitarium" and often repudiate her accounting of factual events as pure fiction.

Even if it could be agreed that Heck was writing fiction, what kind of fiction is also debatable. Her work is highly confessional and lyrical, but her imagery titters over into high surrealism, and when her work falls out of its elevated strain for slang and simple language, it has the same spontaneous feel of a Beat novel.

While its literary significance remains in debate, her accounts of her Suicide Chambers trespassings are the only primary records known about the now demolished government building, making it a very important and rare historical document of a notoriously undocumented time, if in fact her account is true.

Staring Into The Suicide Scrye

Suicide is at the forefront of Heck's investigation and in the background of her life. The mid-ground was a struggle against the mental condition known then as neurasthenia and better understood today as bi-polar disorder. An only child born on a farm in lower Alabama, she came to New York City on a partial scholarship to Barnard College in 1955, and attempted suicide half way into her second semester citing constant disappointment in her surroundings, whether it was in Manhattan or back home, as too daunting to believe in a future. Having failed at death, she decided that Barnard was the better bet, and took advantage of the new policy allowing women access to Columbia courses. It is believed this is how she met the Van Dorens, who would provide tea and sympathy, encourage her writing, expose her to confessional poets like Robert Lowell, and introduce her to the Bohemian writers who hung around Washington Square Park.

With her southern accent, well-read wit, and sartorial eccentricities (she donned lavender sashes on both wrists to conceal her scars), Heck charmed the likes of Ginsberg and Burroughs, and while she felt a temporary affinity for their common interests in the occult, religion, mysticism, and mind expansion, a series of flings with other fellow intellectuals left her jaded and cold:

All the women here make poetry, while I write it like the men.
The women hate me and the men hate me and I hate myself.
The men who like me like me because they hate women and they can look at me and see themselves in a form they could fuck.
And so we all fuck and get fucked up and write and read and kill ourselves slowly by destroying our youth.
I can drink and shoot and snort and smoke all of them under the bed not because I want to die first but because I am the last to live.

☙

It always begins with the ribbons—
Yank and tug like they're shedding Clara's corset in the garden:
'Why ya wearin' those lavender Chanel cuffs, bowed around your bones?'
'Because suicide isn't lady-like.'
To prove me wrong, for they must always be right, they kiss and lick the scars as though their moment of drunken Don Juan charm is better than vitamin E.
The admiration only opens new wounds.
When life is an orgy, no one hears your moans. (22)

☙

An Existential Alchemy

What satisfaction Heck had came from her studies. At some point during this period, she found a copy of *The King in Yellow* in Columbia's library special collection, and began working on a thesis that focused upon the play's women Cassilda and Camilla. She theorized they were alchemical sisters and through several "*danse macabres*" knew how to traverse between the three worlds: the material, the after, and the imaginary: "It's an entire ether of the imagination and the collective conscious. It is there where Fates are made. The author of *King in Yellow* termed it Carcosa—if I had my way I'd call it Melpomene—and it is this dream-land the pallid Ladies reign, and it is over the entrance and exit to this existential twilight that they control."

From this connection, Heck theorized that the Queens in the mysterious occult play were of a secret alchemical sisterhood reigning over a realm that represented a mythical existence in-between the mind and the body. An existence she termed "the second act," and what we have termed the *surconcious*.

Her thesis was rejected as fiction and Heck ultimately flunked out of school and descended back into her depression:

Call me Helen—Call me
    Fuck-up and Failure—
Whose wasted vessel

Cracks ashore those
Nician barks of yore. (57)

She burned the original manuscript, and the theories that lied within are extracted from *The Neurastheniac* and seems to have either provided the foundation or delusion for the visions she would have during her Lethal Chambers experimentation.

The Winthrop Government Lethal Chambers

If the gatherings in Washington Square didn't provide Heck with intellectual stimulation, it did introduce her to the abandoned Lethal Chamber that was part of the controversial Winthrop program of the 1920s. Opened on the south side of Washington Square on April 13, 1920, the Death Chamber, as it would become called, opened its doors to any poor sod who wanted to off himself. It was also the prototype for future federal death chambers that were to be erected in every major city and eventually towns. However, the initiative never went beyond New York City and plans for the Chambers were kept confidential, especially when the Washington Square prototype was privatized in the 30s. Shortly thereafter, the program was considered ill-conceived and closed in 1949.

"They found that given the choice," Heck mused in 1958. "More and more people chose to die before they even could live. It was the only choice that did not lead to more hydra-like decision making." (70).

Because the ornate marble building was also part of President Winthrop's Haussmann-like redesign of the city, and was intended to rival the iconic Washington Square Park in its flora, fauna, and fountains, it was condemned to decay and rot, and the name was changed to conceal its original function to the Wether-Fieber Hotel, and the Beats who congregated in the Park referred to it as the Hades Hotel.

It was from them that Heck learned the facilities' legends and became fascinated by a place where "you checked in to never check out. How did they fend off the regrets that weakens one's resolve? People warned me that perhaps the place was booby-trapped. One big ole mine or marble maiden…. To enter into a building as beautiful as that, certainly the promise was to have a death of an exact pulchritude." (Ibid).

Heck began trespassing into the Chamber in spring of 1958, after failing from Barnard. Consequently, she began experimenting with opiates and other psychedelics, and would take an alchemical interest in mixing "cocktails" designed to "keep the mind elevated enough to find Melpomene. It's all fucking chemicals. It's all fucking alchemy. The mind has always been the philosopher's stone—the soul the e-o-l." (350). With each trespassing, interest in perfecting her cocktails increased. She became so enamored and convinced of her visions experienced in the Chamber, that she sought a "chemical change" that would allow her to sustain her residency in the dream-land.

"It was a challenge to the Fates," she wrote before her final vision, and it was one that she would lose.

Having spent a quarter of a century dabbling with self-destruction, Heck finally succeeded at taking her own life at 31 via one of her infamous opiate/psychedelic cocktails and a bullet to her temple. Her last rites, it seems, was to scrawl the now famous yagé-sipping bruja epitaph on every mirror, and shoot them one by one until the only reflection left in the room was her own.

Helen Heck is important to the Bas Bleu, even in fragments, for what may be her genuine exploration of the "surconcious." Whether or not the visions she experienced were in Carcosa or Melpomene is irrelevant—what is relevant is the mental map she explores, because it may guide us to the mental map within us all, and bring us that much closer to locating where the soul exists.

The following excerpts focus on Heck's exploration of the Chamber and the early visions that follow from her discovery of the execution machine. She never titled any of her fragments, and so all titles are editorial liberties made to convey a sense of time and development.

⚗

The First Trespassing

...was like a grand hotel, and explains the successful cover-up.
The Splitz-Carlton?
The Four Reasons?
The Callitoff-Hysteria?
Once you went up the bureaucratic stairs and passed Yvain's Fates, faces powdered white with bird shit, you entered Mrs. Havisham's lobby with:

- long mahogany tables full of molded and spoiled food rotting on tarnished silver platters.

- Empty chairs askew with broken legs and yellowed couches leered with broken springs.
- Floor to ceiling marble. Great corinthian columns as wide and tall as red oaks. The aortal lines running through the flesh-colored stone gives the walls a sense of circulation.
- One large bay window—my light source in this land of cut electricity.
- Frescos on the ceiling depicting some kind of afterbirth afterworld with three wet nurses delivering infants from cradle-graves and tossing them into the air like cherubs just learning to fly—narrative ruined by water damage.

Overlooking the lobby were the rooms. Doors ajar or unhinged. There had been a fire at the concierge desk:

- a cash register empty and charred—its gilding shining through the soot.
- Hooks in the wall for keys or hats.
- a leather-bound guest ledger half burned. A few pronoms still legible: Hank Mc——, Elizabeth Har——, Arthur C——, Meredith Jon——. Josephine Ch——. Lendell Beaureg——.

Behind the desk the drawers had been pulled out and also suffered torching.

Scattered on the floor are torched pamphlets advertising the special amenities of the establishment like:

"DIGNITY IN DEATH: Our PALLID MASK keeps one's countenance in place for a smooth, calm, and collected rendevouz with the Void."

On the front, a young woman with a Louise Brooks bob and a lavender tea gown wears a Louise Brooks mask—cool, collected, and glamorous. Her eyes are closed, and the mask's cupid's bow lips are painted in a boudoir smile.

"LET THERE BE NO GRIEF: Full-cremation package spares your loved ones from material disassociation and financial burden. Includes cremation, ash disposal at a location of your choosing, or thousands of urn options for familial delivery."

And it showed a Valentino looking ghost hugging what seemed to be his living family…

Up the grand staircase. Extravagant for just one floor. Counted the rooms—grew bored at 50.

Each room basically the same. It was bigger than any apartment in the city I had known, and definitely better furnished:

- Elegantly furnished and draped in what was once reassuring colors of cream, gold, and mauve with rosewood furniture.
- There was a sleigh bed and a fainting couch upholstered in mauve velvet, now matted and worn. It lounged next to a Victrola.
- Victrola ornate. The horn made of copper, now patinaed, and its cabinet carved in Art Deco geometries.
- Other flourishes of normality:
  - a vanity
  - an armoire
  - a personal lavatory with shower and bathtub.
  - a secretaire with unmarked stationary for any last thoughts.
  - a picked over book shelf—only had a copy left of Dickinson and Whitman.

I pocketed the Dickinson book and am taking notes on the stationary.

No windows, and in the waning light from the lobby, I tried to find the execution machine. No trap doors in the ceiling. Marble floor solid. I looked under the bed—nothing but monstrous dust bunnies.

Did the shower head produce gas? Or acid? Did someone come in the middle of the night and smother you with your extra down pillow? Room to room and more of the same—complete normality and not one sign of self-destruction.

Gave-up and started flipping through Dickinson. Music would be nice. Checked out the Victrola. Blew dust off the vinyl—Bessie Smith—and wiped it with my shirt to clear the grooves. Placed it on the neck and struggled with the crank on the side. Eventually wound the fucker up and I flipped the arm onto the vinyl. Surprised and relieved the needle wasn't dull. The Victrola's cabinet was also a lamp and radiated a warm white light into the room. This was alright.

I mocked fainting onto the mildew and dusty couch to read.

"Because I could not stop for death/He kindly stopped for me—."

I couldn't focus. A series of designs began to dance on the wall. I looked at the Victrola and saw that its lattice work body was a zoetrope and the art deco octagons, rectangles, and triangles foxtrot around me as Bessie Smith crooned:

"Noooobody knows you/when you're down and out/In my pocket not a one penny/and my friends, I haven't any."

Digging the vibe, I flipped through Dickinson and crooned along: "I'm noooooooobody, who are you?/Oh, well, honey, I'm noooobody too."

Turned my tickle box over on that one, and had to sit up and put my head between my knees to stop and catch my breath.

The song concluded and the room was full of white noise from the continued fornication of needle and vinyl that masked a mechanical whizzing sound coming from inside the horn. I stood up and took off the needle and heard the noise more. I looked inside the horn and saw something gleaming down its throat, and stepped back and tripped back onto the fainting couch as a mechanical arm began to extend out and in its tiny hand was a syringe containing a golden fluid. I watched as it reached its full extension towards the head of the couch, and the hand depressed the plunger and the gold liquid streamed and splattered. Had I been reclining, as I had been before I lost it, it would have pierced my carotid artery. The arm retracted back inside the horn, and the dancing designs slowed down and faded as the zoetrope extinguished.

In the next room, the Victrola had an extra dusty Rude Bloom record. Same ritual as before and watched as the zoetrope shined through the cabinet to illuminate the room. I closed my eyes and let the lights dance upon my eyelids. It was soporific, but once I heard the mechanical arm, I snapped to and watched it repeat the motions of its brother machine: extend, inject, withdraw. However, after years of no lubrication, the arm did not completely return inside the horn. Before I could look it over, the Victrola lost its steam and I was cast in darkness. Had to use up my matchbook to see how to get out of there.

It seemed elegant but monstrous. The noises it made were unsettling and I couldn't understand how anyone would complacently allow the thing to penetrate their neck like some kind of robotic vampire. Were they sedated already before hand?

The Third Trespassing

Sauntering through the lethal gardens—
Once you hop the tarnished gates—
The grounds are so vast and brown
Shades of their former monstrous elegance.
Solemn stroll. Sobering stroll. With each
Step you become intoxicated by your
Next to last oxygen gasp.

A glance at
The shimmering fountain—a gaze at the
Rusted fountain—around its base hovers
The Muses.

I have met the Fates—.
I have met the Muses—.
Don't be fooled by what you can take,
It's all a ploy in their ruses—.
Find yourself with their golden nooses.

You can see in my eyes the stars
                                     are gone.
You can see in my complexion the blood has stalled
                                     within its constricted highways.
You can see in my mouth the lost words
                                     caught in my teeth.

My dasein is perpetually weeping lactic acid
                                     from the exertion to live.
And yet,
        by some involuntary propulsion,

                    I move forward through the days and into
                            the weeks and into the months—
For how long?

Alone, alone, alone. Alone with all the wrong answers.

☙

~~what is death but the failure to live~~

~~the secret in living is failing to die~~

~~what is death but failing to live~~
~~what is life but failing to die~~

the secret to living is failing to die

☙

"I have a world inside of me I cannot see,"
Said the oyster to the sea.
"I have resolved to shuck that little world outside of me."

The Fifth Trespassing

I found a Pallid Mask and it is not as advertised. Neither the face of Louise Brooks nor any other human ideal. Made out of mercury with a silver arabesque around the brow and down the nose. An alchemical sign?

I reached into the Victrola and gently extracted the arm. I rigged a fresh vial of morphine into the hand, and returned it to its cave, hearing its hinges and springs lock into place.

Cranked, needle flipped, and Billie Holiday's "Gloomy Sunday" filled the room. I laid down on the couch and placed the mask over my face and closed my eyes as the lux ballet began. The cold mask was making all thought in my temples frigid and frozen.

An arctic serenity in the igloo-skull.

The flickering lights' somnolent effect seemed stronger. With each inhalation I felt my body relax. "Gloomy Sunday" faded out as the beating of my heart grew louder and louder in my ears. A white heat pierced behind my ear—shot through with smack-warmth, numbed body—I became nothing but ellipses….

…Hugging the trunk of a giant weeping willow tree, the sun sparkling through its matron-leaf curtain dazzles me awake like a junky Snow White.

A garter snake coils around my outstretched arm and constricts it, above the elbow, to show the veins in alabaster. A hummingbird alights on my fingers and darts to hover above my inner elbow. It stabs its beak into my vein, hovering and sucking. The snake hisses in rhythm to the bird's fluttering and my gasping.

Eden ecstasy.

When the hummingbird is through extracting, it flits to the willow curtain and falls dead as if it hit glass. The snake uncoiled itself and disappeared in a hole at the foot of the tree.

Liquid gold pours out of my veins, and I crawl over to the dead bird—stiff and straight like a syringe.

I pick it up and crawl back to the trunk—nestle back in to its exposed roots and stab the bird's beak back into the vein.

Perdition Pain.

Gold spilling around the bird's body as I squeeze it, crunching the bones until all it had taken was returned.

Tapped, I throw the feathered pulp down and the snake emerges to swallow it whole—then disappears again.

I feel fortified and can stand and walk.

I part the matron-leaf curtain and look out over:

Nordic latitudes pause the rising sun—
Dusk is frozen on the horizon—
Casting the sky in jewel tones of magenta, violet, and aquamarine.

The clouds reflect these tones,
mix them with brooding, ponderous, slate precipitation.

It is nothing but landscape—
which changes with the journey—
It is impossible to survey and map—
because it only exists at the end of our threads.

The Fifteenth Trespassing

Who are all these people with faces and names?

They were my friends, but they are not the same.
They are not the same.

They wear their last suits and gowns—tweed, silk, chiffon, satin—
worth more than all the money spent on their minds
worth more than all the money spent into their veins and arteries
worth more than all their lives combined, if life were ever capital
to trade.

They were my friends—they were my lovers—they were my family
These people with faces and names.
I recognized and unrecognized them
Their familiar faces wore unfamiliar expressions
Of last gasps—cardiac cancers, automobile crashes, undiscovered overdoses—
And faded beauties—Entropy, gluttony, jaundiced, flaccid Liver beauty spots.

These people with faces and names were erased
behind the masquerade of their own threads,
and looked out through porcelain hallows.
Each mask individualized by their individual demise
But made common by the same golden arabesque
that swept across the eyebrows and down the nose.
The secret code—the alchemical sign—that
Invites living specters to foxtrot at their own funeral.

They spin and twirl and jive
In their grandparents spats and stays
Around a grand table
That serves as throne and entertainment to
The two Sister-Queens—.
Whose corseted musculature

And golden-laced ligaments
And silk-skein tendons gorey gleam—.

Their visages veiled in gold masks
Socketed with third-eye diadems of lazuli and tiger eye.

Cassilda wears a halo-collar that crowns her
Head in the warm embrace of Helio's arms—
Golden rays inlaid with rubies and precious and imperial topaz.
Camilla mirrors her with Selene's serene beams—
Silver, sapphire and pearl.

They do not regard their subjects
They regard the marionettes on the table—
A makeshift stage for The Moira—The Fates—
marble life-sized puppets trapped in a pantomime
by the Sister-Queens' gaze—.

It's an interesting tableau.

Clotho

With bloodshot and puffy eyes,
Looks out a window with her hand
On the hip of her hourglass shape.
From her bosom and through her waist,
Falls infinite sand collecting at the foot of
Her petticoat. Her head tilts to consider
The long tapestry that is woven by Laisches
And stretches toward Atropos to cut.
Clotho guides them to the hemming and stitching.

Laiches

With fair hair that rolls
Around her head into
A chignon of yarn; Pinned

By countless knitting needles
Of myriad gauges.

A lock behind her ear curls to her cheek
And she takes from it strands to knit
Into the tapestry.

Around her lithe marble body,
A spider spins and spins and spins
Confining her body to her chair
Only her arms are free from the
Cobweb garb, and she can reach
And grab from a basket containing
All of the scrolls—each a timeline of
Our lives—moving from one life to another
Under her sister's direction,
Without missing a click.

Atropos

At the end of the tapestry, she sits cross-legged on the floor.
The murderer of men, her face is an open wound
From lacerations—the shark teeth tied
To the end of her matted hair—she shakes her head
like a gnashing rabid dog. Blood patina oozes from
damaged stone.

A string of black pearls chains her neck to the wall.
She wears a shawl made out of a fisherman's net—
Seashells, starfish, and rotting shrimp hang in the lapels—
Decayed brooches.

Ever ready in her hands are golden straight razors—
Once Clotho decides a life has ended,
She chops the thread with the velocity
Of a guillotine.

Atropos's arms flail at me.
She juts her knife at me—
    then at the projection on the wall.
The Sister-Queens' gazes go unwavered;
They take no notice of me.
I am just another reveler with a face and name.

I walk to the projection; grasp at the dust in the light.
The surface wavers and pools around my hand like
I had plunged it into a phosphorescent bay.
I felt minute pixilated threads stick to my phalanges
Like spider silk—.

In the projection, I saw myself—
A Helen who was not the fuck-up failure—
the windblown petals swirl around her face, catch in her hair;
their vibrancy against her raven hues appear as though her locks
Are wicks to blazing stars.

I look back to the Sister-Queens
And the incarcerated Moirai—

Clotho gestures to Laiches,
  who switches a thread between her fingers.
        The vision in the window changes.

Atropos juts her knife at me,
    then guillotines the tapestry.
She juts her knife at her sisters,
    and Laisches searches for another scroll.
The puppets regard me regarding them.
Atropos juts her knife at the Sister-Queens,
    and then runs her razor across her throat.

Cassilda gestures to Camilla,
Who explodes from her chair
To rush and push me out of the way,
To make wiping gestures over the image.
The threads shudder and settle into a scrye.

I see myself in my last frock
And last face.
Flowing from the right temple,
Ribbons of Pink and Crimson silk
Layered with Grey and Aubergine lace
Enshroud a shattered and cracked
Porcelain mask—
All part of a cocktail hat
Composed of Cockscomb.

My eyes stare out of carved lids
Kohl-rimmed and mascara-streamed.
My sculpted lips are swollen
And smeared—
Nose and cheeks rouged by blood specks.

I touch the ribbons and lace
And poke at the Cockscomb.
My reflection merely scratches her cheek
With a shiny little gun—

I reach out to my reflection
She reaches out to me and aims.

I caress my mask.
The Sister-Queens bicker.
Camilla grabs my arm:
"You, madam, should unmask."
I refuse.
"Indeed it's time."
I regard my nodding reflection—
Her porcelain lips now carved around the revolver's barrel.

"You can't help but look out of the mask you were given,"
I tell the Sister-Queens.
Cassilda orders Camilla to unmask me,—
I slap away her privileged stretching arms
And rip the mask off myself—
The revolver goes off—.

….
The small scenes open up broader landscapes until various worlds orbit around your eyes—
Its induced vertigo—
And you hesitate where your next step leads—
But you traverse—
You move on into Melpomene's weeping willow arms and wait.

For any minute now,
some soothsaying yagé-sipping bruja
will pass through this road-fork and clear the cursèd humors.

Or maybe she'll just walk by with a dismissive wave, laughing at the deer and snails in the sky.

DANCING THE MASK
BY ANN K. SCHWADER

Cee wakes to a flapping against her tower window, soft and heavy at once. Soft as feathers. Heavy as the coalescence of black stars above that lake she has danced beside so often, her bare footprints erased within moments by cloud-waves. It is an urgent sound: some message (or messenger?) sent for her alone.

She rises to investigate. Palest silk draperies flow around her body, transforming each step into dance. A response to whatever missive awaits the last of her Dynasty, sole survivor of the unspeakable masquerade and its final, fatal unmasking.

When she reaches the window, however, there is only a double sunrise staining her city with jaundiced light—

Double sunrise?

Still snarled in blankets, Cee struggles up from the back seat. A sheet of yellow paper flutters against her windshield.

The sound is barely audible in this empty church parking lot, yet it chills her. Someone put that paper under her wiper while she slept. Someone who might have tried something else—*done* something else—despite the door locks or the big hunting knife she has kept beside her all night.

And there are fresh dark smears on the windshield's glass.

Cracked glass. Cracked life.

Fully awake now, she feels the details flooding back. The rehearsal accident last winter that ended her ballet career. The surgeries and months of physical therapy her former company refused to cover. The increasingly desperate temp jobs that barely put ramen on the table, let alone a dent in the monolithic debt she'd long ago quit calculating.

Facing eviction last month, she'd headed for her boyfriend's place —only to discover he already had a new roommate.

Five years younger and two cup sizes larger.

The days and weeks since were a blur of couch-surfing. Yesterday evening, after yet another heart-to-heart with her most recent host on the topic of "moving on," she'd moved herself and her remaining possessions on to her Subaru. She'd considered a Motel 6, but the Episcopalians were closer. And God wouldn't care that her Visa didn't work any more.

Flap. Flutter. Flap.

Cee's fingers clench in her blankets. For an instant, she is back in the tower, awaiting that unknown message.

Then she is barefoot on cold asphalt, padding around to retrieve the yellow paper from under her wiper. She uses two fingers to avoid touching whatever nastiness glistens on the glass. Up close, it smells like something utterly, unimaginably dead.

At least the flyer itself is clean. Sliding back into her car, she relocks the doors before smoothing it out on her lap.

Nearly half the sheet is filled by one grainy black and white image. At first, she can't make out the subject – a spider? A skeletal bonsai? – but it finally resolves into a contorted figure wearing white body paint. As it crawls toward the camera, its face is a vision twisted by several emotions at once.

UNMASK THE DANCE OF DARKNESS

She blinks at the caption a few times before realizing she's seen it on the mall. She's been walking past this bit of urban flotsam for at least a week, giving it no more attention than any other concert or class or cause plastered on the lampposts.

Not much more, anyway. Dance is still a thorn in her soul. Any mention can send twinges down her damaged spine . . . start her feet flexing toward pointe even in street shoes—

Rubbing at the answering pain in one arch, she keeps reading.

There's something familiar about the photo, too: Asian avant-garde, maybe, with pallid paint standing in for kabuki makeup. Or a mask. If it's advertising a class, though, there's damn little information: no dates, no times. Just a storefront address a block off the mall, where at least half the shops are vacant.

Pay what you can, the ad continues. *Does zero work for you?* Cee starts to crumple the paper, then notices two questions penciled in at the bottom.

How do I learn this dance? You already have.
How soon will I be dancing? You already are.
The writing is as spidery as the flyer's blurred image, yet perfectly legible. There's something sketched underneath: not a signature; but not a doodle, either.

A symbol? A message?

Just staring at the graphite snarl hurts her eyes. Cee finally folds the paper up carefully and puts it in the back pocket of her jeans.

If nothing else, it's an option.

Her phone – her last link with the world of work and hope – hasn't pinged this morning, which means no temp assignment today. No check. And no idea whose couch she'll be surfing tonight, assuming she doesn't opt for the Episcopalians again. A part of her knows that would be a very bad idea.

Another remembers wandering alone through moon-washed streets, in the last days of the city when all masks had fallen –

Cee stiffens. *No.*

A few deep breaths later, reality in the form of car keys reasserts itself. What she needs right now is somewhere to clean up, somewhere safer to park, and then breakfast. One thing at a time.

And none of those things are the shadow now detaching itself from the deeper shadows of the church's entrance. A fading stain on the day's first light, it wavers in her rearview mirror and is gone.

The food truck across the street from the courthouse is faded pink and turquoise, a sad tacky echo of the Southwest. Its breakfast burritos, however, remain the best and cheapest on wheels. Cee joins the long line, trying not to notice lumps of blanket and sleeping bag under the shrubberies in this small urban park.

Before this morning, it would have been easier. Now these faceless ones might wear her face if she looks at them a moment too long. If she fails to see only masks. The people ahead of her all have their own masks firmly in place, anonymous in the gray early light.

Gray as cloud-waves –

Cee sucks in her breath sharply. Better to focus to the headlines spewing from the truck's little TV. These, at least, are not her crises. Not her luggage scattered amid corpses and scraps of fuselage, not her village obliterated in the name of faith. Not her friends unarmed against soldiers clearing free speech from the streets.

Not her world's mask of reason slipping more each day, revealing raw chaos beneath.

She cannot recall having this insight before. Yet it holds strange comfort: her life has stopped making sense because it never did make sense. Some pallid illusion only hid this truth for a little while. Then her body broke, followed swiftly by her plans, dreams, and love life—

"Next!"

"Bacon, hot. And a large coffee, cream and sugar." She hesitates. "Double sugar." Maximum calories for her money, because who knows when she'll eat next? Not the way she's used to thinking, but the guy in dingy whites just adds another spoonful to her cup before snapping on the lid.

Cee wraps her hands around it tightly. It's definitely autumn this morning, though most of the trees haven't turned yet. Only one sickly aspen . . . and something about its leaves echoes that dream she can't shake.

Inhaling steam from her too-hot, too-sweet coffee helps. She needs something solid in her stomach, though; green chile to burn through the thought-fog and ground her in this world.

When she gets to the truck's pickup window, she reaches out for her burrito eagerly.

Then nearly drops it as her fingers brush the worker's gloved hand. *What the hell?*

Cold sickness washes over her as she backs away, her hindbrain yammering. Only the watching eyes of other customers keep her from breaking into a run. Whatever she just touched – whatever filled out the flabby white latex—it wasn't flesh.

Not living flesh, anyhow.

Cee drowns that thought with a mouthful of coffee, barely noticing as it scalds her tongue. Heat is good. The fingers of her burrito hand carry a chill they won't shake for blocks, visceral memory of something boneless and liquid—

Her stomach nearly vetoes breakfast before fresh air wins out. After missing dinner last night, the burrito in its grease-splotched goldenrod wrapper just smells too good to ignore.

She's about to open one end with her teeth when she realizes the black scribble on that wrapper has nothing to do with Bacon, Hot.

As it did the last time she saw it—*when she received the Stranger's token in one trembling hand*—the snarl of lines makes her eyes burn. Cee squeezes them shut for a moment, wondering how many pallid suns will smear the sky when she opens them again. Or does it matter? Unable to answer, she settles for a mouthful of chile.

And feels her day's options contract to one.

༄

Set shadow-deep between two empty storefronts, the studio door is narrow and gray. It swings open at Cee's touch, revealing steep stairs illuminated only by sunlight. At the top of those stairs is a second door. A note has been taped to it, but it's impossible to read from this distance.

Shutting the door behind her feels dangerous. Final. She finds herself climbing before her mind or her eyes can adjust to the dimness.

Halfway up, the music begins. It is primal in its simplicity: hand drum and bone flute in a slow pulsing rhythm that both echoes and contradicts her own heart. Impossible to dance to. Yet somewhere beneath it lies the soft, irregular whisper of bare feet—

Cee pauses to wrench off her own flats. Her toes are ugly and misshapen, a dancer's first sacrifice. Each step after that jars her spine into memory: the leap, the missed catch, the awkward fall, the fracture. The unending twilight of recovery.

What can she possibly accomplish? Why has she come?

Her fingers are trembling by the time she pulls the note down. It crackles in her grasp like old parchment, and there are stains she does not care to examine. Four words in sepia ink spider across it.

You are already dancing.

The handwriting matches the flyer in her back pocket. The snarled lines beneath are the same as well, but Cee's eyes no longer slide away.

Before she can reach for the knob, the door swings inward.

The studio's windows are blacked out. Only a small constellation of spotlights illuminates the skeletal figure crawling and fluttering across its floor, draped in variegated yellow rags.

White body paint covers all visible skin, from face and palms to the soles of the twisted feet. The figure is ageless. Sexless. It does not move to the music so much as it is moved by it, a broken leaf in an uncertain wind.

Cee pulls the door shut behind her and settles on the floor to watch. Though the dancer does not acknowledge her presence, the dance itself changes. Spurred by a faster drum rhythm—a breathier wail from the flute—the dancer whirls and leaps, clawing up at the air with each landing.

The gesture lacks meaning, but the performer's pallid face is contorted with despair.

When the dance collapses into rags moments later, Cee is not surprised. Scrambling up as quickly as her own damaged body allows, she hurries to help . . . until one word from the fallen dancer stops the music at its unseen source. Stops her cold.

"Daughter."

It is a woman's voice, barely. Ancient. Desiccated. The merest exhalation of breath, yet its certainty makes her pull back her hand. There is truth here, but no truth of her world—

The Queen's gown is the color of candle flame. Rising to her throat, layered silk scallops flutter in the great hall's drafts, licking shadows across the pallor of her face. The porcelain stillness of her mask. It is a night for disguises, and Carcosa's court glories in them; none more brilliantly than its Dynasty.

At midnight—and only for a moment—all disguise will be surrendered. All truths revealed.

Yet on the twelfth stroke, there is one who does not unmask.

The Queen stares. Her entire court stares. This Stranger's appearance is grotesque past art or imagination, an affront to the night's festivity. Several courtiers have already complained of it.

The Queen points with her golden fan. "You are the last to abandon disguise, sir. We are all waiting upon you."

The great hall's clock ticks once. Twice. Thrice.

"I wear no mask."

There is a sharp, universal intake of breath. Then the glittering fan drops to the floor unnoticed, followed by the courtiers of Carcosa—and all its Dynasty, save two. Still echoing, the Stranger's words fall into a chasm splitting realities—

"Mother."

The fingers clutching her own are mere twigs, but Cee holds on tightly as she assists the other woman's rising. Step by hesitant step, they make their way across the studio, toward a long dressing table equipped with mirrors. The spotlights above them brighten as they approach.

Cee's companion averts her gaze. "This world cannot live without masks."

But there are no masks any more. Only cameras. Carried by unarmed heroes through war zones, perched above city intersections, shoved into pockets all over the planet, they are witnesses without discretion. Without pity.

Cee nods in hopeless agreement. "No world can."

"Ours did not."

The dressing table is a fine piece, marble-topped and honeycombed with strangely-labeled drawers—but its mirrors are hazed with cloud-waves. Cee helps the other woman to a stool before taking one herself.

"Hali." Frail fingers touch the glass, opening it into memory. "It took us both, after, when the city's streets filled with fallen masks. When the last stars shattered."

Cee stiffens. "Yes."

"We fell through into a place torn open by terrible light, and we lost each other. Lost ourselves." The saffron rags flutter with each breath. "I began the dance again there, and the people welcomed it; their broken island had known enough of light. They craved masks."

Another flutter. "And darkness."

So the dance was the mask, that pallid illusion drawn across the face of chaos. Cee is no student of history. She cannot trace its ebb and flow of madness through the decades since—yet she has *felt* it. Her muscles know the steps already, having danced them in dreams.

Beneath black stars, alone.

The other woman begins pulling out drawers in the dressing table. "It is time," she murmurs, selecting containers of crystal and alabaster, jade and lapis and porphyry. "I must abandon disguise at last."

Cee opens her hand for the first jar. "And I must learn it."

She pulls back her hair with a twist of fabric and begins as she is directed. The face paint goes on first, thick and silken as clotted cream. As it stiffens around her eyes – her mouth – she must give it full concentration, for the cloud-waves reflect nothing. This is the mask her world is lacking.

It cannot be less than perfect.

She proceeds to her throat and on to her shoulders, shrugging off her worn flannel shirt. There are fewer instructions, now, and those oddly garbled; though she dares not divide her attention to find out why.

The curious silver applicators are black with tarnish, and awkward in her grasp. The pale compound itself, however, feels perfectly fresh. Cool and pleasant against her skin, it carries a scent of lilies newly opened to a dual sunrise –

"Almost finished." Cee frowns. "Except for my costume."

When no reply comes, she glances over at last. The neighboring stool holds only torn fabric and dust, caught in a spotlight already fading.

As the hand drum begins its slow heart-pulse, Cee rises from her own stool. Kicking aside her discarded clothing, she takes up the yellow tatters and shakes them clean before draping them over her body. They flutter in a draft she hadn't noticed before.

Behind her, cloud-waves break against the mirror.

The last illumination in the studio is that constellation of spotlights. Five stars. She has danced their mystery before . . . on the moon-blanched sands bordering Hali . . . in the streets of lost Carcosa.

She must dance it again.

She has never stopped.

Crouching, stamping, shaking her shoulders to the bone flute's wail, Cee moves to the center and lifts her flawless Mask to her sister Hyades. The studio recedes around her into darkness. An ignorant world dreams on.

FAMILY
BY MAURA MCHUGH

Her call came, as it always did, at the yawn of morning, when the mind drunkenly staggers through the tatters of dreams into the awful glare of wakefulness.

The tune of Björk's 'Violently Happy' announced her.

"Do you know what time it is?" Oisín croaked, prone on the bed, phone misaligned against his face. His anger wasn't even awake. An indigo hue suffused his bedroom and familiar shapes bled into the walls.

Orla said something, her breath loud as if her mouth was mashed up against the receiver, her teeth clicking against plastic, but the rasps overwhelmed the quiet words.

"...he returns ... light fades..."

"What? Are you pissed?" He fiddled with the phone so it slid correctly into place over his ear.

She snapped into legibility. "I'm outside."

"For fuck's sake!" Irritation burned off the dregs of sleep.

"Can I come up?"

He fumed, knowing there was only one answer, but let his sister stew. He heard a car rumble past her in the street. One other mad person up and awake in Dublin.

She slid into a soft, American stoner accent with chameleon expertise. "Don't hit me with them negative waves so early in the morning."

A smile slipped past his resentment. For a moment he remembered her vividly as a girl in their cramped living room, her wild hair sticking out in tufts from under Mam's black bra lopsided on her head, enveloped in Dad's leather jacket, as she rolled around in her cardboard box 'tank' and quoted Oddball from *Kelly's Heroes*.

He sighed. "The bridge is still up."

"Put the kettle on."

༒

It was whistling when he opened the door to the apartment. Orla held up a litre of milk in one hand, and a package of digestives in the other as a peace offering. Her soaked hair clung to her face, and the bones of her skull seemed to press tight against her skin. In the dim hallway her eyes glinted amid deep shadow. Beads of water rolled off her battered leather satchel slung over her drenched trench coat, and splashed into a little pool on the floor.

"Christ's sake, Orla," he whispered, checking up and down the corridor to see if anyone was about, "did you swim here?"

She gave him a pouty sad face with puppy eyes.

"You'd get the Oscar for best seal impersonation, but you're a bit too rough to play the ingénue today." He opened the door wide to avoid her wet flounce into his apartment.

"That's not what my director tells me," she said, chin up, squelching past him with damp dignity.

"Yeah, but that's what's trending on Twitter. Hang your coat in the bathroom, but gimme your supplies first." He unburdened her and hurried to the kitchen.

"There are clean towels in the spare bedroom," he added, voice raised over the clink of china and the scraping of butter over toast.

She returned, a red towel twisted into a turban on her head, and wrapped in his favourite brocade dressing gown. Not for the first time, he was struck by her effortless way of drawing beauty about her in every circumstance.

He handed her a cup of tea.

"Hmm, milky perfection." She slurped, smacked her lips with comic vulgarity, and winked. "You'll make a lovely wife someday."

He snorted, then sipped his tea daintily with his little finger stuck outward like an exclamation point.

Orla picked up a slice of toast and wandered from the kitchen into the living room. Water sluiced down the two giant glass windows. Outside, dull light seeped through the low grey clouds, signalling the timid advance of morning. From their vantage point the car headlights of the very early commuters were hazy dots of light reflected in the slick roads either side of the River Liffey.

"Tea, toast, and cosy inside," she said, quietly, the expression on her face distant, as if she was looking through the veil of rain onto a different vista.

He finished their mother's mantra: "All's well, worries outside."

Instinctively he moved to her, and wrapped his free arm around her. She leaned hard into the hug, and he tightened his grip. Her skin smelled of sea foam.

A chill transferred from her into his bones. Her stillness alerted him. Tenderly, he spoke to the top of her head. "What's wrong?"

"I went back," she replied. "I saw him."

Orla sat in the passenger seat of the car, her boots up against the dashboard, her body curled defensively as she meandered through topics as varied as her dress disaster during her last trip to Cannes, and the intricacies of the Appalachian accent.

Oisín noticed the tightness of his grip on the steering wheel, and tried to loosen it. Ahead the motorway to the West of Ireland undulated across the patchwork of green fields in an almost direct path to the sinking sun, now a blinding orb in a clear blue sky. In his memory trips back to the West were uncomfortable bus jaunts down bad roads through gridlocked villages while whipped by torrential rain. He'd been a student then. The last time he'd taken this route it had been for his gran's funeral just before he graduated from art college. Obligation had forced him onto the bus that time, but the apocalyptic row with his grandfather afterwards had been justification never to return.

This smooth journey in clear weather seemed to want to prove everything had changed.

"What's he like now?" The words came out gruffly, he hated that he even wondered if the old bastard had decided to join the human race. He wanted to squash that tiny spark in him that yearned for some Hollywood breakthrough, which would launch a new relationship.

"Older."

He cast a withering glare at her, and noticed she was chewing the ends of her hair, an old childhood habit that always made him feel vaguely ill. Familiar words of censure rose up. He refused to say them. He was the big brother, but she was a grown woman. It was hard to unlearn rote expressions, but she had demanded freedom from his stewardship years ago, and he was determined to honour that even when he suspected she was incapable of responsibility.

"Calm down! He's ... shrunk. Remember how big he was when we were kids? He seemed to fill every room he was in. Now, he's smaller, white hair, and walks with a cane." She paused, and narrowed her eyes. "He's harmless."

"Pity he wasn't harmless when I was eleven." Oisín clenched his jaw.

Orla reached out and stroked his arm. He wanted to bat it, and her sympathy, away, but didn't.

"What prompted you to visit?"

"Lots of things. I've got a new part, and it's a bit gruelling." She hugged herself as if she was suddenly cold. "I needed to remember something ... comforting. I wanted to go back to the cottage, and to do that I had to see him."

Oisín remained silent under the onslaught of too many conflicting emotions.

She glanced over and judged his mood, before she continued. "After all, he's our only link to ..." Oisín guessed she wanted to say Dad, but was afraid that word would be too much for him on this reluctant journey. "... our childhood."

"What there was of it after Mam died," he said, barely able to get the words through his gritted teeth.

She loosened a long sigh. "But before that we had good times in the cottage with her. We were happy."

He nodded, curt. "Maybe. I was older. I noticed things you didn't after Dad left."

Orla removed her hand from his arm, and lifted a lock of her hair back up to her mouth.

He scowled, and she noticed. She dropped it, guilty.

She laughed suddenly, grinning. "Do you remember the plays we used to put on for Mam in the evenings? And the mad outfits she used to make for us from the likes of sheets, plastic bags, and egg cartons? She was a genius with a pair of scissors, cloth, and thread."

"I remember we couldn't afford a telly, and she had to distract two kids from hunger and a cold house."

She turned her face to the window, and he barely heard her mutter, "... his cloak, shredded, flapped around his vile visage..."

Oisín's foot hit the brake, instinctively.

"What?" His voice too loud.

Her face turned to him, dispassionate. "You remember. The play."

A fragment, shrouded, flitted across his mind, and associated with it: paralysing dread.

An exit loomed, and he wrenched the steering wheel towards it.

Orla clutched at the door handle, and the car in the lane beside them blared a warning.

He was still breathing hard when they pulled up to the petrol station.

"We're losing the light," she said, munching on a chip. Across the table Oisín nursed a large cup of coffee, and stared at it as if expecting answers to appear in its surface.

"Good. You're not the one driving into the sunset."

Nearby, inside a play area constructed around a large, custard-yellow plastic castle, a child wailed.

"Once we're off the straight roads it's a twisting drive. Are you sure you remember the way, in the dark?"

The cry escalated into a hysterical shriek. Oisín glanced over at the ugly structure, wondering where the parents were hiding. Huddled over tea and pastry, perhaps, wilfully ignoring their infant's tantrum, and preparing for the final push home in a car full of squabbling siblings.

The pitch of the child's scream notched upwards. "I'm the king!" he screeched, "Obey me!"

"Where the fuck are the parents?" Oisín wondered, frowning. The tables closest to the stronghold were deserted. He looked around, trying to spot the guilty party.

"Maybe they're tired," Orla replied staring out of the station's window across the fields at the setting sun. "Maybe they don't care."

The noise increased to a pitch Oisín did not think could be made by any human throat. He stood up, hands clamped over his ears. Orla didn't pay attention. Outside the sun dipped under the horizon.

"The light fades," she whispered.

In an instant, beyond the glass, darkness reigned.

The gaudy squat castle shuddered.

The eerie scream halted.

The ensuing silence held the ponderous weight of awful expectation.

Smiling, Orla drew a sign upon the glass, and cracks cobwebbed across its surface instantly.

"No!" he yelled, but the glass exploded inwards and the night invaded the room.

He dived to the floor, arms covering his face, but not before he saw a phosphorus glow spring up around the castle.

Then, in the booming voice of a victor: "Prepare for his return."

Oisín jolted awake, heart juddering, as Orla grabbed at the steering wheel. Before them the twin headlights of the car revealed a grassy verge. The car bounced over the soft ground. He pulled the wheel, hard, and the car skidded badly in mud, until it regained the road. He spotted a space by a gate to a field, and pulled in, gasping.

Orla panted beside him.

"Shit! I'm so sorry!" memory rushed back. They had left the station an hour ago and had been driving down quieter country roads ever since. "Micro sleep."

She punched him in the upper arm. "You nearly killed us!"

He turned to look at her face, so fearful, so precious to him.

"You've all I've left," he blurted out.

Orla placed her hand upon his cheek. It felt like a benediction. "I'm here. We're okay. Can you stay awake or do you want me to take over?"

He kicked open the car door and staggered upright. The wind ripped at his coat, and water from the hedgerow dashed into his face. His mind was so clear it felt cruel.

Orla sprang out of the car and came around so she stood in the wash of the lights, a spectral being.

He reached in and turned off the headlights. The night sky of his youth, awash with stars, crashed upon him. He grabbed the car door, dizzy from the majestic immensity.

"Were there so many back then?" he murmured.

Orla removed the keys from his frozen hand. "I'll drive the rest of the way."

He nodded, stumbled around the vehicle, and fell into the passenger seat, glad to be hidden from the dispassionate heavens.

He woke again, in darkness. His neck ached. Orla was gone. His first sight through the windscreen: the square outline of the white farmhouse gleaming in the dull starlight. Their hated home after their mother passed away. His stomach knotted in response.

No lights graced any of the windows.

A *cold welcome*, he thought, followed by, *same as usual.*

Oisín climbed out of the car in discordant movements, his body protesting his cramped, interrupted sleep. The mixed-up clean and nasty smells of a farm assaulted him and he wrinkled his nose in protest. The gravel crunched under his leather brogues, and he imagined the first comment his grandfather would make would be on how inappropriate they were. He stood before the blue door and braced himself for contempt and indifference, while reminding himself of his achievements and successes.

The door opened easily, and the stillness of an empty house greeted him. The long, dark hallway disappeared into a void where the kitchen lay.

"Hello?" he said, not too loud. "Orla? Fintan?" He'd begun calling his grandfather by his first name as an act of rebellion when Oisín was thirteen.

He didn't want to enter the house. It was the repository of bad memories and old hurts, and he felt they would consume him if he stepped over the threshold.

Instead, he leaned in and flipped the light switch just inside the door: nothing. Oisín turned it on and off several times before stopping. Now, he could smell a faint odour of mildew, and sense the coolness unique to a deserted home.

He turned away, shuffling his feet against the invasive chill, and buttoned his overcoat tight to his chin. As he moved he noticed the spark of light gleam between the hawthorn trees, up the *boreen* which lead to the cottage he had lived in for two years with his mother and Orla after their dad disappeared.

Oisín fished his mobile phone out of his pocket, and turned the flashlight app on. The bright LED was a tiny point of ease against the immensity of the blackness surrounding him. He gazed up at the sky bursting with stars, and wondered if each of the minute lights above him marked another being stumbling about, lost in a dreadful place.

We are alone, together, he thought, and there was a doubling effect. As if he had heard that phrase before, but said in his father's rich timbre.

A faint memory coalesced: his father in a chair tipped back in front of the fire at the cottage, reading through lines for his last play. Orla stood beside him, barely eight, and speaking the part of the opposite character. Then: his mother, raging, yanking the pages from Orla's hand.

"She's not speaking these unholy words, Miles!" she'd reprimanded.

And the mocking laughter in response. "You're never too young for great art, Ellie. And this will be my masterpiece. They will remember me forever after this is staged."

Bitterness blotted out the recollection, and Oisín hunched his shoulders against his father's egotism. Miles had always chased fame, and despite his talent—which everyone acknowledged, even critics who loved to disparage him—he had never found the right role, the right director, or the right theatre big enough to house it. There were always excuses and reasons for his failures. Until he abandoned them outright after his last play was stopped during its debut performance.

Oisín moved quickly along the grassy path, framed by rough, limestone walls, which led to the cottage. He was angry. Baffled at being left alone by his sister after taking this long voyage with her into their turbulent past, and most furious at himself for letting the shadows in his mind roil up so many emotions. He had never understood why Orla threw herself into a profession that required her to tap into the raw root of life's experiences, again and again. Sure, the results were luminous. Orla inhabited her characters on the screen in an exhilarating fashion, but he had also witnessed the cost she paid for her mercurial shape-shifting. He preferred to keep his emotional life under wraps, and guarded.

As he rounded the final bend before the whitewashed building his steps slowed. He had taken this road so many times before, every bump remained familiar. He wasn't sure if he knew the street he lived on for the past five years as well as this ramshackle path to his childhood home.

Welcoming light blazed from the windows. He'd expected the small house to be almost a ruin, since it had been dilapidated when they'd been forced to live there after being chased out of Dublin by debt collectors. Instead, it appeared renovated.

He approached the door, painted a bright red, and the top half of it swung open in the traditional style of meeting a passer-by.

"Surprise!" Orla said, leaning on the bottom half of the door. Inside Oisín could see a sympathetic restoration that harkened to the older period of the house while adding modern amenities.

"What on earth...?"

Orla unfastened the bottom half of the door and swung it open to admit him. Oisín walked in, confused. Before he knew it Orla had removed his coat and put a crystal tumbler containing whiskey into his hand.

With a cheeky grin she raised her glass and clinked it against his. "Oh yes, the irresponsible sister has grown up a little."

"You..." he glanced around. Traces of the past lingered, but the overall impression was of a new, tasteful history.

He sat down in a comfortable armchair by the crackling fire and downed a gulp of alcohol. Its fiery path down his throat woke him up.

"I've made money you know. Enough to pay someone to tidy this place up. A nice retreat for when I need to remember who I am."

"Why didn't you tell me?"

"Where's the drama in that Oisín?" She laughed, and sipped the whiskey. "If you could just see your face... I'm taking notes of that expression!"

He frowned, an unpleasant realisation surfacing. "Were you putting on a pretence in Dublin, to lure me down here for your big reveal?"

She stood up to stand by the fireplace, and drank a bit more, but he noticed the irritated swish in her step. Perhaps that was part of the spectacle. A weariness settled on him, mostly borne from the relief that the ugly scenes he'd anticipated had not materialised.

"So, where's Fintan?"

She arched an eyebrow. "I didn't think you'd be eager to meet the old devil again."

"Not exactly, but what's been going on here?"

"Fintan has been in a nursing home for a year. Great Aunt Nora contacted me. Everyone knew you didn't want to be bothered about him."

Protests crowded into Oisín's mouth, but he choked them back. He'd not contacted his grandfather in ten years, after all. What concerned him most was this disclosure exposed the gulf that lay between him and Orla. So much of daily life excluded from each other. All her travel, and his investment in his job. Their different social circles, and her growing fame. Their connections now seemed more fragile than he'd imagined.

A sadness at the rupture between them overwhelmed him. Once, they had been each other's only shelter against the world. He missed that conviction in her love.

"You're right," he admitted, defeated. "Is he okay?"

"Better cared for than we were by him." She winked and drained her glass.

Her glibness rankled, and yet he would have said the same an hour ago. The map of his universe had been altered, and it felt like he was scrambling to chart his bearings.

"I have another story to tell tonight," she declaimed, in a theatrical fashion. Dad had called it the *Getting the Punters' Attention* voice, and it was eerily reminiscent of him.

"I think I've had enough surprises for--"

She flicked a switch and the main lights extinguished, leaving a couple of candles and the fire as the only source of illumination. "I've engaged with a new collaboration. One of the most challenging of my career."

Oisín withheld his questions. He was now cast in the role of audience, not interrogator. If he wrecked the moment he would fuel resentment for years. It had been one of his earliest lessons: the show takes priority. He settled back and prepared for Orla's announcement of her next grand adventure.

"I've been approached by my first teacher, to take on a part in a play that has been banned from live performance in every country for years. We've assembled a cast in secret, conducted rehearsals, and we'll live-broadcast it over the Internet from here, in the outer lands crushed against the Atlantic Ocean." The shadows in the room flickered with the candlelight. Outside the wind rose. Oisín shifted, and glanced behind him, but there was only darkness. Yet, he felt as if he was part of a gathering witnessing a grave event.

Surely, he heard whispering?

Orla continued. "Soon everyone can marvel at the mysteries it divulges. All masks will be discarded, and our revels will reshape the world."

And she drew his symbol in the air.

It burned a dire mustard glow and hung there.

It would always remain, now it had been inscribed, even after its light had faded. And Oisín would never forget it. It lived in him now, stamped upon his cells, and all those he would ever pass on.

The building shook, but its foundations were set fast in ancient ways, and did not falter. It was forever marked as a way in for a receptive audience.

The atmosphere seemed denser, and Oisín struggled to breathe. Around him the shadows materialised into other forms and they leaned forward in anticipation to observe the first performance.

Everything vibrated to Orla's voice.

She held her hand out to Oisín, and before she spoke he felt the compulsion, and the love, pull him to her. "Tonight, we will have our first reading featuring a new performer."

He jerked upright, not in control of his limbs, terrified to see the assembly. A wave of applause coursed through him and spun him around.

Their expectation paralysed him more than their cruel faces.

Orla's tone turned exultant. "And, the oldest actor, the original. Our father who was before and who has returned. His guises are never false, but we rarely see him true."

She gestured to the left, and Oisín did not turn his head, for he knew once he looked upon that face, Oisín would be no more, there would only be the façade, and the performance inscribed upon his DNA that he would be compelled to act out.

The glowing sign vanished at the approach of its master. No longer necessary when its originator appeared.

Oisín heard the flapping of his tattered cloak, like the beating wings of crippled angels furious at their banishment.

Orla placed her hand upon Oisín's back, to guide him to face the artist.

The heat of his gaze removed all of Oisín's doubt.

Tears streamed down his cheek and he grasped his sister's hand. Family, reunited. Communion restored.

Together they spoke the opening words, and gladly unleashed the play.

PRO PATRIA!
BY NADIA BULKIN

"Colonial life with its senseless relationships and its psychopathic participants."

- Sutan Sjahrir, 1949

Joseph Garanga watched a small brown gecko crawl, belly to the wood, across the open window sill, and wondered why an institution that called itself the National University had installed neither window panes nor air conditioning. From the corner closest to the rotating fan, Adela read from a crumpled letter:

"Dear Most Honorable Professor G., I have seen under the bridge near the fish market, the words 'Garanga's Law: the Restitution of the Damned.' Professor G., do you truly think the damned can be redeemed? Consider the traitor Peter Sumit, who is running for parliamentary office. He may wrap himself in the flag, but the people know who he is and what he did during the war. Politely ask for your comment on this matter. Most Respectfully Yours, Tomas Touli."

When Joseph first heard about Garanga's Law, he had been flattered, thinking himself elevated to the same plane as Newton, as Fermi. And even after he understood that the people who had written this law were insane, because his countrymen couldn't drive through an intersection without inviting a head injury, Joseph still sang himself to sleep with thoughts of someday opening his copy of Foreign Affairs and reading, "*according to Garanga's Law, named after the preeminent political scientist Joseph Garanga, the ability of a former colony to meet expectations of a high-functioning state in the first five years of its independence directly corresponds to the former colony's ability to retain its functional independence.*"

Flores said, "Maybe it's a different Garanga. Maybe a cousin of yours that got famous." It was absurd. He told her so. His father was a goat farmer. The only other member of the family who had clawed out of the mud was his cousin Anton, a provincial-level government accountant who would never have a Law named after him. Only Joseph could carry their banner, and if Flores didn't marry soon, that banner would rot with him. He told her that too.

"Professor?"

"Just say that I don't comment on politics."

His graduate assistant gave him a look of accusation. He glowered right back. Yes, he was a frequent guest at the Palace—but he had been Michael's mentor, back when the National University was still Queen's Crossing University. And yes, he might include surly policy prescriptions in his papers, but that was simply a fulfillment of his responsibility as one of the nation's top social scientists. It was all he and his few competent colleagues could do to keep this newborn, fever-prone country from rolling off the bed and breaking its head open on the floor.

Adela was saved from further impoliteness by Robert Fileppo, who wandered in from the literature department. He looked very flush and very pleased, which was not unusual—coming from a family that had been mysteriously allowed to keep its tea plantation, Fileppo had never known the meaning of hardship. "Joseph, I am sorry to interrupt, but I must ask..." What was unusual was that Fileppo was rudely pointing several dainty aristocratic fingers directly at him, and grinning ear to ear. "Have you seen the yellow sign?"

"No, what does it say? Traffic closed again on Patriot Street?"

Fileppo's grin flickered, and after a pause during which he looked stuck as a propaganda reel in a humid jungle theater, Fileppo rushed to his desk and placed a book on top of the latest International Politics. "I cannot believe you haven't read this. Haven't you heard them yammering about it at the Polo Club? It's all about your subject, Joseph. Governance."

The book reminded Joseph of skin—leather-bound, sun-tanned pages, smell like someone who'd been cooped up in a dungeon for sixty years. *The King in Yellow* was stamped into the cover, in the colonists' language. "It sounds like a children's book," he said. There was no author, no publication information. Many colonial tomes wore such masks: naked except for their titles in huge block font. It was as if they thought titles alone—*Lord-Regent-Governor*—were enough to bring the locals to their knees. It had taken Joseph years to admit they were right.

Fileppo nodded, still grinning. "Read it immediately. It changes everything."

Joseph hated it already. "I doubt that."

"Professor, could I take a look?" Adela said. "After you're finished, of course."

Fileppo glanced awkwardly at Adela's dark skin and simple cotton. "It hasn't been translated," he said, and Joseph saw a hint of the real man, the pansy who bragged about wasting his money on imported wines, who would happily lounge on the backs of his people as long as he could keep his fantasy that a single colonist playmate might ever invite him to tea at the family chateau.

"I don't need it translated," Adela said, grimly.

"Adela's very well educated," Joseph added.

"I see," said Fileppo, and the strange velveteen curtain came down over his eyes again. The smile. "Good for you, dear."

Michael Dayamon sat wrapped in shadow behind a massive oak desk that had once belonged to the Regent of Concordia, signing edicts with the same focus that had consumed him during final exams. He had traded in the plain black cotton that he'd worn since he stumped for votes on the nation's first muddy campaign trail for a stiff white uniform that hung a bit too wide on his shoulders. Despite all its brass and brilliance, the uniform ate light. It always had.

Joseph had not seen that uniform for five years—not since Regent McMurphy walked out into the sun in that suit of blinding, funereal white on the final Colonial Day, to salute his guards and the Empire's flag for the last time. Joseph had been there, standing and grimacing with all the other prominent locals—doctors, lawyers, the occasional tortured artist—who had to be reminded every year that resistance was futile, and the Empire was their king. Michael would not have seen it; Michael had been leading three rebel battalions through the prickly eastern jungle, bleeding and sweating and running on fumes.

"You look like an emperor," Joseph told him now.

Michael glanced up—how deep the lines crinkling the boy's forehead had become! But he was President Dayamon now, not Commander, not War-Hero. *Don't become their everything,* Joseph warned, but Michael didn't know how to turn down responsibility. The people cried their love; he'd won in a landslide. "Professor," he said, standing out of habit. "It's good to see you."

"When the President calls, you answer the phone." Joseph groaned as he sank into a leather chair. It wasn't just the long walk through the National Palace's marble halls; it was the vertigo. Colonial architecture was drowned in mirrors and gold, totally unfit for a hot climate. He didn't know why they hadn't just blown up McMurphy's mansion, why they'd insisted on renaming it, *reclaiming* it. It had never been theirs to begin with. "How can I help you?"

"Professor, I greatly appreciated your guidance on nationalizing the imperial companies."

"It was the least I could do," said Joseph, but his heart was swelling. *An influential mentor to the nation's first democratically-elected president, Joseph Garanga is credited with spearheading Dayamon's effective and sophisticated nationalization policy.*

"I'd like your input on something else." Michael rifled through a paper stack until he found a book. Leather-bound. Sun-tanned. Joseph knew what was coming before it came. The damned thing was the talk of the town. He wanted to believe it was just another fetish of a culture-starved bourgeoisie—the year before, everyone went mad trying to secure tickets to the Bluebell Circus, which cancelled their only show when a grubby illiterate crowd swarmed their vehicles—but the way it had everyone bowing to a *foreign* king who wasn't even *real* truly crept under his skin. "The King in Yellow. I understand it's the new Machiavelli."

Joseph frowned. "Who told you that?"

"Willem the writer. You know he was educated in Rome." Joseph could not hold back a loud sigh. "I have on good intelligence that the top minds in the world's capitals are all studying this text. I had to use a dictionary, but I got through it." Michael grinned; foreign language had never been his forte, but he was smart enough to wing anything. "Have you read it, Professor?"

"No. And you should not be seduced by every flashy new idea that comes across the ocean. They do not have all the answers over there." It was tempting to think so. After three hundred years under the yoke it was of course tempting to say, *all hail the Empire, keeper of all that is wise and good!* "Besides, you cannot make this country your laboratory."

Michael chuckled. Before The King in Yellow docked at their ports, Joseph had never heard so much discomforting glee. Was it really so humorous, this *new* Machiavelli? "I remember. But Professor, this book has made me rethink our draft constitution. I know how terrible that must sound after all the work you and everyone else on the committee has put in."

A twinge of worry plucked Joseph's heart. They could not keep riding the interim "constitution" that had been cobbled together by a small group of half-crazed fighters, buccaneers, and librarians on the eve of revolution. They had frantically copied pieces of other constitutions, whether socialist or fascist or liberal-democratic, and ended up with something less like the noble eagle and more like the freakish cassowary: big feet, no arms, skull like a dinosaur.

"One of the many things The King in Yellow teaches is that as president, I embody the nation." Michael put his hand over his heart. His big bursting heart, the reason he was loved. He'd bleed for the country. He already had. "Those who threaten me, threaten the state. That means all these extra rules and provisions just give the imperialist counter-revolutionaries enough wiggle room to sow discord. I say we scrap the requirement for two-thirds parliamentary approval, give me final say over justices, remove the need for direct elections…"

For a moment Joseph could only stare. Where had he gone wrong? "Michael… there aren't any counter-revolutionaries, just politicians that disagree with you. And yes, some of them are very stupid, but you must let them grumble, if anything to ensure they don't launch a coup."

Michael leaned forward, eyes ablaze. Joseph sat back, startled, wondering if this Michael-in-the-trenches, except with paint running between his eyes. "You have heard talk of a coup?"

"No, no! You are the most beloved man in Concordia. Your approval rating is 85 percent."

"Then I should be able to guide this country in the right direction with no distractions."

"Michael, the constitution is not about you. Someday we may have a president who is not so well-informed." Michael stared blankly, as if the possibility of a different president was beyond his understanding—indeed, they had not written in term limits. Joseph suddenly remembered, with an odd feeling in his stomach, that he was speaking to the man who still commanded the soldiers' bullets, and instinctively lowered his chin. "With all due respect."

The President smiled at him—an earnest smile, not an inhuman one—the smile he'd seen in the lecture hall when the boy spoke of Rousseau and Locke. Michael the good student had argued for representation in the imperial Congress if such Congress was going to make decisions about Concordia's governance; he was jailed for that essay. This had to be a ridiculous mistake. "I'll take your opinion into account, Professor. Your guidance is very much appreciated." A heartbeat of polite silence, and then: "If you'll excuse me, I must run to a cabinet meeting."

"Oh, yes. Father of the country, you've got important work to do." Joseph heaved himself off the chair and made for the door, very aware of the ache in his joints and the hurry with which Michael was fastening his gold watch. With one hand on the cold door knob, Joseph glanced back at his former student. "Michael, I have to ask. Why are you wearing that uniform?"

Michael seemed to blush, but maybe it was a trick of the half-light. "You must make the people respond to you, Professor. They see this uniform and they understand 'power.' State power, I mean. See, I haven't forgotten everything."

He wanted to ask Michael what his parents thought of that, but remembered at the last moment that Michael's parents—like everyone's parents, it seemed—were dead. Father died building the railroad, mother died of an imported colonial fever, as he recalled. He heard Flores whispering, "Maybe we can all start over," and the thought of rebirth and amnesia, of the red sun taking the spilled blood down into the darkness, briefly coated his senses like syrup. It would never happen. As long as bureaucrats slept at their desks and ethno-religious fanatics banged at the gates, they would never be fully unchained. And sharks would come, smelling the blood. That was the entire point of his research. That was what Garanga's Law should have proclaimed.

༃

Joseph hated his commute. He hated the half-finished high-rises, silent charbroiled skeletons of other states' Leviathans. He hated the growing barrage of grim-faced boys in misfit helmets. He hated Michael's optimistic yellow billboards plastered with doll-like rice-gathering children. He hated the slogan *Onward to Victory*. Onward to nothing. Michael had cancelled constitutional reform. They were supposed to be climbing the developmentalist ladder, exporting toys and then televisions and then luxury cars – but Joseph felt in his marrow that they were on the wrong escalator. They would export t-shirts, cocaine, the occasional plague. And underneath, where the real economy still swirled with the micro-activity of bartered chickens and tin and cheapness, the taunt appeared in spray-painted Technicolor —*Garanga's Law: the Restitution of the Damned*. Enough soldiers to invade their neighbors, but nobody to scrub the walls of graffiti.

It was a long, lonely walk to his muggy little office in the back corner of the social sciences wing—closed door after closed door, peals of frightened laughter occasionally erupting from offices he thought were empty. Adela was outside his door, looking as if she'd been waiting all night. She did not even wait for him to finish fumbling with his key ring before mumbling, "I need to talk to you about that film. The one advocating transmigration into the east."

"The Fertile Heart." She was doing her doctoral research on colonial propaganda—arguing that colonist messaging had sunk into the national consciousness and could still be found in political statements today. A depressing, retrograde little topic, but he let her do it because he was afraid that she was right. She spent a lot of time in the library revving up the tick-tick-ticking of the National University's only film projector.

"There's a… something in it I can't explain. It looks like a man wearing a long yellow robe. He walks through the trees like he isn't using feet, behind the main action. He appears in locations… thousands of miles apart. When he's on screen, all you can do is watch him. And wait for him to notice you."

Joseph unlocked the room and opened the window. Two geckos immediately slithered in.

"You never see his face. But I know it's a warning. They're going to come back."

For him, for her, for everyone in Concordia, there was only one "*they*." Joseph walked to his desk; he had to at least feel the wood, even if it was fake, before he could rescue Adela from whatever insanity the library and the film and the ghosts of colonists past had afflicted.

"You must not be sleeping enough," he started, a bit uncertainly. "The Empire is fighting a war, a million miles away, it isn't interested in…"

"Yes, the war, that is why they will come, they need our resources, they will take us and put us in their war machines, they will feed us to their soldiers!"

"Adela!" The fear in her voice, as if *they* were standing in the hallway, banging on the door, saying *come out come out, your time is up* was enough to speed his own weakening heart.

She threw up her hands, lip trembling—he was afraid she was going to cry. "But what do you care if they come back? They won't be able to hurt you. You're a professor. You're educated. Not some throwaway peasant girl."

How old had Adela been when they declared independence – twenty or so? Not much older than Flores. A blast of trumpets shook the window and broke his thought-stream—not another military parade. Whatever battle hymn they were playing was unrecognizable as music, let alone the national anthem. It sounded like radio interference. The damned book about the yellow king, where was Fileppo's copy? He was going to burn it. "Adela, shut the window."

"I figured out what your law means, Professor. The Restitution of the Damned." He snapped his head up—since when was that madness *his* responsibility? "*They* are the damned. And they will have their restitution. They smell our blood." She let out a long, awful, undignified sob that made Joseph exceptionally nervous: he tried, very hard, not to dwell on the atrocities and humiliations their people had suffered, even if it meant shutting out memories of Flores' mother. It did no good. The only thing they could do was move… "We never stopped bleeding!"

The book wasn't there. The trumpets climbed to a crescendo – or were those gun shots? Cannons? What was Michael preparing that army for? Joseph covered his ears and shouted, "Would you shut that damned window!"

಄

The call came past midnight. It pulled Joseph out of a dream of stumbling through a blue-green jasmine-scented forest, fighting through undergrowth that rose mad and gnarled like bodies after a flood, because he was being chased by something hidden. Something that stalked, something that remembered. Something that wasn't fooled by their "progress." Michael was whispering: "You must come to the palace. There is something you need to see, Professor."

His silent house, filled with stiff makeshift altars to Flores' mother, shifted around him as Joseph dressed. He drove himself through a city that no longer slept, because eyes were watching all the time—from sewers, behind lamp posts, on the bloody side of sleeping faces. When the president calls, you don't say no. The interim constitution, that freakish cassowary, was gone. Michael said on his daily radio address that the nation had been freed from the tyranny of its confusion. His word was all that remained now.

The Palace was abuzz, maids and guards running around frantic and whispering as if preparing for a teatime state visit. Michael's wife, the pretty half-breed Isabella who always wore the latest colonial chic, stood biting a thumbnail at the end of a long mirrored hallway. Isabella grabbed at Joseph as he passed, whispering, "Have you seen the yellow sign?" He cast her off, disgusted. "Don't, don't. Don't look if you see it."

At the other end of the hallway, Joseph was holding a candle and moving at the command of a little woman in archaic village dress. "The left door," the woman would say, her closed eyelids trembling. Behind her, a younger man who had not bothered changing out of his rubber flip-flops was squeezing her shoulder. Entranced, Michael would move to his left, to a door that was closed. She would scream, "Now open it! Open it quickly!" and Michael would open the door to a dark meeting room, empty save for rattan furniture and dusty bookshelves. This continued for half an hour – Michael emptied china cabinets, shoved aside mahogany tables, dislodged enormous oily panoramas that imperial artists had painted of soft and pliant pre-industrial Concordia – until at last the woman collapsed. After the younger man fanned her back to life, she told Michael: "There is a ghost."

"I knew it," Michael said, grinning at Joseph. That clownish grin, so unbecoming on a head of state. Before that horrible *imperial* book, Michael had always seemed immune from all the little people's blistering nonsense about black magic and witch doctors. "I knew the palace was haunted. I always see it in the mirror. All blood and maggots behind the mask. It's probably that bastard McMurphy. I'm sure it disgusts him, knowing a dirty savage is sleeping in his bed."

Joseph had nothing to say. McMurphy had been spirited away to a secure imperial outpost days before they took Concordia—he was probably sipping tea in a chateau and mourning the sorrows of empire. But the little woman said, very seriously, "You inherited it from them. Like you inherited everything else. You take the palace, you take the ghost. You take the country, you take the ghost. You know."

"I don't want it," Michael said, rather childishly. "It's foul."

"But it wants you," she replied.

Michael wanted to know what should be done about the ghost; the psychic, renowned though she was for purging tree spirits and lifting accursed blindness, claimed there was nothing to be done. "But you are an idea man, Professor," Michael said, breathless and red-eyed. Joseph would have guessed he'd been drinking but he smelled only of moist, upturned earth. "I've kept up with your research. We all have. This is what you study. Getting rid of the Empire's ghosts. So tell me, guide me. I need a policy prescription."

Then he burst out laughing, or perhaps crying—it was so distressing to watch Michael, the President, the War-Hero, the top student of his class, blubbering like an asylum escapee that Joseph had to beg his leave.

On Patriot Street he nearly ran over several hoodlums running across the road. They carried cans of spray-paint, and when they looked at him from the sidewalk wide-eyed and empty as aerosols, he wondered if someone had exposed them to The King in Yellow. Had someone translated it into the mothertongue? Was it read to them? Then they grinned and started to spray the window of his car a sickly rippling yellow, shouting, "Garanga!"

He couldn't take the madness home with him. He drove to the university campus instead, where the night guards nodded him through without checking his ID, and circled round toward Building 2 to be with the geckos and the books that had been his guiding light, his reminder that no matter how terrible life became he was but a cog, a very small cog in God's most fascinating experiment of human civilization. As the library came up on his right he saw something dark run upon its roof, under the moon. The shock pounced into his right leg and forced him to stop, and he crawled over the gear shift to look up, expecting… what?

What he saw was a person, but he did not know until the person had jumped and died in front of him that it was Adela. He recognized her faux military jacket, though when he turned her over he no longer recognized her face. Just as some final trace of forward-looking hope for their future tumbled out of his heart, something physical tumbled from Adela's jacket. Something leather-bound and rotten, the corners of its pages curling like shed skin. He saw that she had marked it up violently as he flipped the pages, too quick to pick up words, thinking maybe he should allow himself a word or two or three thousand and join the madding crowd.

Maybe it wouldn't be so bad. Maybe he would finally understand the joke that up till now seemed only to be a tragedy.

When the president calls, you always have time.

Joseph did not need to drive through traffic to attend the president's Independence Day party. The streets were cleared, and Michael had insisted that as a special guest he be provided a car and driver and a Glock-toting bodyguard. At sundown the empty city was filled only with plastic bags and other imported black cars, tut-tut-tutting onto Patriot Street, converging upon the National Palace. An odd white spattering of flakes was falling in their midst—the driver turned on the windshield wipers. Joseph stuck his hand out the window, remembering Dante, thinking about hell—but it was not snow. It was paper. His bodyguard was laughing.

Anyone who was anyone had come to the party. Doctors, lawyers – even Willem the tortured writer, who was smiling yet looking as though he were about to scream – the old crowd from Colonial Days and Polo Clubs past. They did not seem worried about the black cars or the armed guards. They were all throwing their heads back, covering their eyes. "Oh Joseph, aren't you tired of worrying?" asked Robert Fileppo, drinking flat champagne from a chipped goblet. Thin, classical, *colonist* music was crumbling in bits and pieces out of some scratchy, distant record player. And there on the upper landing stood their savior: Michael in Regent McMurphy's white spirit-eating suit, weighed down with new medals for mythical honors.

Suddenly feeling faint, Joseph clambered up the stairs. Guards moved to knock him down, but Michael—good Michael, Michael who had read The Rights of Man, Michael who had cried at the parade on the first anniversary of Independence Day because he loved this baby country so—waved him through. "Professor," Michael said. "I have decided what to do. I think you would approve my plan. You always said we need a strong state, and I am the state, so…"

Joseph trembled. "You're reintroducing the Constitution? Letting Parliament return?"

"I am going to vanquish the ghost." A stone sank inside Joseph. "Poor Isabella, I think it killed her. It knocks on doors all night, leaves messages on the wall. The Restitution of the Damned. It speaks of *you*, Professor." Another stone—a damned concrete boulder. "It thinks it can hide but I will call it forward, and then we will see."

"See what?"

"See who controls the fate of Concordia. Us, or them. The King in Yellow tells us…"

"Damn that book, that book is an evil! It came from the old world, it probably came from *them*!" A coldness descended over Michael's features. Joseph frantically added, "The revolution is over. Michael, you finished it already. We were all there. You came rolling in with those tanks and that microphone and you gave your little speech about victory and liberty at last…" And he had been so proud. He had hugged Flores and said *he's done it*, and she said *we did it papa*. "We won. We are free. We just have to…"

Stop bleeding.

"The revolution is never over." Michael, no older than thirty-five, looked one hundred years old. "As long as there is Empire, they are always at our door." With his arms raised like a conductor—and oh, God, Joseph never got to see a live symphony performance, not Berlin nor Vienna—Michael swiveled toward the crowd, fingers curved just so. There was one final second, or so Joseph thought, when teacher and student made eye contact—when he last saw the earnest boy who had raised his hand on the first day of Political Theory and asked, "*What does the Empire want from us?*" He didn't know the solution to that riddle—whether domination or death, the answer couldn't be good.

"Citizens! It is time!" The party chatter died and Concordia's elites turned to look at the man that most of them had voted for. "Time to secure our eternal victory over slavery and subjugation. Time for us to rid ourselves of the ghost of Empire once and for all." Vigorous clapping from the esteemed guests, like automatons set to high-speed. No cheers, nothing so gauche. "Please. Please. You may not be aware, but there are traitors among us. Counter-revolutionaries. Those who would betray the victory of the state and send us back onto our hands and knees."

Michael swiveled his head and then pointed at the literature professor, the man who would be Kipling. "Robert Fileppo!" Fileppo —shocked or muted—blinked at him. "Do you love your country? Would you do anything for your fatherland?"

He gave Fileppo three seconds. Fileppo seemed on the verge of stammering something when Michael shouted: "Counter-revolutionary!"

The word, combined with the finger, was like a dog whistle. There was movement on the staircase and then a pop-pop-popping into Fileppo's body. The woman next to him, the wife of a minister, was suddenly speckled in blood. She jerked back, screaming, and then Michael shouted "Counter-revolutionary!" again and she jerked once more, far more violently this time. So Michael went, pointing at random faces in the crowd, and Michael's will—the state's will—was iron. In between executions Michael would stop and quiver, his voice warm and warbling like an animal about to be born, whispering: "I can see him! He moves through the crowd!"

Joseph's throat began to ache; he was screaming at Michael to stop. And so he was taken away, dragging his heels then losing his shoes, hollering, "Michael, what do you *want*?"

He never got that question answered, either. But he did get a cell in the old imperial prison that had once held pro-independence agitators. He could read their scribbles, carved into concrete: *Until Concordia is Free.* He could look out between the bars to barren flag-speared Revolutionary Field where enemies of the state—imperialist counter-revolutionaries—were taken to meet their maker. Sometimes when it rained, Joseph could see a yellow-robed figure gliding through the untamed trees on the other side of the electrified fence, staking this traumatized land for something that Joseph did not think was the Empire. The Empire was raging and splintering across the sea, eaten by its own light. Something older? Something truer. Something the Empire had dreamt into being. Something that would have its restitution.

HER BEGINNING IS HER END IS HER BEGINNING

BY E. CATHERINE TOBLER AND DAMIEN ANGELICA WALTERS

The Doorway:

Weary but not broken, Cassilda opens the door.
 Behind her, Carcosa fades. Crumbling towers of blackened iron fall into grey ash as twin suns are eclipsed by a singular burning orb in a sky so blue it hurts her eyes. Anticipation sits bright on her tongue; unease sharp in her belly.

The doorknob is ice beneath her steady palm. Did the door exist before she touched her hand to it, before the thought formed in her mind that there should be a door, a way out? (A way in.) Questions in a circle, questions without answers.

Cassilda opens the door; she is always opening the door.

The Scholar, Chapter I:

The used bookstore holds a single copy of the book. Fingers trembling, Cassilda slips it into her pocket. She feels no guilt taking the liar's truth; this is not a theft.

Behind the store, in an alley reeking of cat urine and littered with human detritus—a Chinese takeout container crawling with insects, a set of keys complete with car fob, scattered pages of the city's free newspaper—she begins to tear out the pages. First one by one; then several at a time. With each tear, there is a sensation of starlight dancing across her skin, and she feels the holes in the fabric of her self knitting back together.

The pages drift and spiral in the air. She stands in the center, arms outstretched. The reek of the alley fades, and in its place, she smells the sweetness of fruit, ripe on the vine and ready for picking, a hint of the sea in dense fog: scents of home.

A little like magic; a little like peace. This tether to what she knows to be true clears the rubble from her thoughts and the tension in her neck and shoulders.

The ink melts inward across the pages, running to the spine where it pools into a black hole. The paper breaks apart at the edge of this darkness, falling in, falling away, until there's nothing left but a ghost image of the Yellow Sign, the sigil, hanging in the air. Then that, too, vanishes.

The tether holding the true Carcosa fast to her heart breaks apart and she hunches forward, palms resting on her upper thighs, breathing hard, smelling only the stink of the alley. The destruction of the pages is merely a temporary balm, a salve; there are far too many holes for such a small act to fix. An ache inside her swells. Perhaps then, not a balm, but salt in the wound. A small cruelty.

Words written are not always true; nonetheless, once ink is committed to paper, once the pages are bound, there is power. If Cassilda could find every copy, she would consign the damnable lies to a bonfire the likes of Nero's fire in Rome. She was there, she has always been there, but the roads, though holding the same shape, bear new footprints as if the false words changed the weight of her steps. And why would they not? A body wrapped in lies is that of a body wrapped in disfigurement: forever altered, forever deformed.

She is a glass vessel filled with marbles and every turn of the page, every recitation of the story, every hint of belief, adds another sphere. She longs to tell the story, her *true* story, so as to tip the glass, emptying it of falsehood's weight.

I was a queen, she reminds herself, yet the lies strip the words of their meaning, strip the truth from her history. Her mouth twists. History, too, has changed. Carcosa was a city beyond compare, a city of riches. She remembers ancient rulers paying tribute, the healing waters of the lakes, the glimmer of the rising suns on the horizon. She remembers a king uncorrupted. She remembers…

No, she would not burn the book. She would burn the man and laugh as his flesh blackened and peeled. Her mouth twists into a feral smile, the wrong smile, but by now the feel has become familiar. Hated, but familiar.

I was a queen. But her fingers curve, the nails yearning to rake down her cheeks, pull her face into a scream.

"I was Queen," she says aloud, and the timbre of her voice does what her thoughts alone cannot, and her fingers uncurl.

She leaves the alley with sure steps. It's nearly time; the scholar is as ready as she can manage. She's taken her time—or as much time as she can risk—and she's chosen well. He's strong, capable, and he treats her as the queen she truly is, not as a by-blow of a faulty bloodline. This time, it will work.

First Woman's Fire:

Cassilda went back to the beginning, barefoot and brown as she followed a woman into a grass hut; the grasses brushed Cassilda's bare arms, whispered shaft against skin, and told the woman she was no longer alone. The woman turned and gasped, lifting a hand as if to ward off an ancient evil. Cassilda could not say the impulse was wrong. She paused in the doorway, then crossed the threshold. She would not reconsider. She could not.

"It must be so," Cassilda said.

The women shared no common language, but Cassilda watched the woman's shoulders slump in a kind of relief. The African night was warm and still around them, Cassilda appreciating the way the warmth never quite left the air, for Carcosa was ever cold.

The woman made no further protest as Cassilda crouched beside the low-burning fire with her. Smoke curled up through a hole in the shelter's cylindrical roof. The fire was a good sign, and so too the shelter; this woman was close enough to the beginning of humanity that Cassilda allowed herself to hope. It was a foolish thing, but moved in her chest like a heart should have. Before the season turned, this woman would leave this fertile place; she would cross the continent as those behind her would, and she would carry Cassilda's story with her.

For now, she spread out her catch with steady hands. The fish gleamed in the firelight as she began to clean them. Cassilda watched, strangely hesitant to touch the woman, to break the moment, but there was no cause for delay. As the woman gutted another fish, Cassilda covered the woman's hands with her own. Cassilda didn't have to speak to tell her; she let the story flow from her hands.

The woman—named Nuru by her joyous parents seventeen years before—had never seen a woman such as Cassilda. Cassilda did not let Nuru's thought distract her from the task at hand. She would not be charmed or swayed by the way Nuru thought she looked in the firelight, otherworldly (true) and like a goddess come from the heavens (patently false). Cassilda focused on the things she knew to be true, let them flow from her hands the way terror normally did, filled Nuru as though she were filling a vessel. Steady and sure, Cassilda worked, reassured by the ease she found in Nuru's expression; as if she were being fed after a long starvation, as if she had been given a key to understanding all things.

But here, when the dark of the African night was allowed to eclipse too much of Nuru's shining eyes, the vessel began to crack. Cassilda looked at their paired hands, smeared with fish guts and scale, Nuru's skin marked as they would all be marked, with the Yellow Sign so that Cassilda might know them, so she could—

Nuru's body refused.

Cassilda held her firm, refusing this time to give in. She tried to pull the woman back into the story she was sharing, the truths humanity needed to know, but Nuru rejected her. She bucked, sending fish skittering across the hut's dirt floor. Out into the night tumbled one fish until it came to a stop against a foot, a foot marked with the Yellow Sign. Now it was Cassilda who startled, who felt the eclipse of Carcosa's twin suns although there were nowhere near. The cold crept closer.

If one had come, so would another, Cassilda knew.

She released Nuru as if the woman was now wreathed in flames, but it was too late. The truth contained an inescapable madness and Nuru was pulled down, shredded into tatters as she vanished from this world and into Carcosa eternal. The Yellow Sign was the last to go, refusing its destruction to the end, clawing at the ground as if sentient, as if it meant to climb into Cassilda herself.

Cassilda fled the hut, from the other who had come, on feet that knew the way. She knew how to run, she knew how to evade, and when that marked body would have claimed her and dragged her back to Carcosa (into that shrieking girl she had been made), she opened another door. With her capable hands, Cassilda cut the air of this world and vanished into another.

Carcosa:

Cassilda could make a door of anything. Air, earth, water, starlight. She could cut into that which exists and turn it into that which should never be. She could move bricks and grass with equal ease; she could partition a pocket into This World and That World, and walk between. She marked the worlds as she did her people, with the Sign only she and they could see, could feel. Each rotted its way down to the marrow.

At the end of the world, the most extreme opposite point of the beginning she had rewritten, Cassilda emerged cold and tired. She should not have been either, and feared (was that the prickling sensation down her spine?) that she was growing weak, that she would not accomplish her task. This was nonsense raising its head—this was the King in tatters laughing at her from the shadows. She hushed him and walked into the world.

This world had been unmade. Cassilda paused for an uncertain moment, having not expected this—the end of the world did not always mean the end, after all. People found a way, life found a way, but here, the city in the distance rose in a cloud of ash, reminiscent of her last glimpse of Carcosa. Lifting her gaze to the sky, she confirmed there was but one sun, and though thick clouds occluded it, it was alone as was she. A gray plain stretched into a gray horizon, the city a smoldering gray lump in the center of it all.

Cassilda walked, toward the city so that she might see for herself. Had everyone gone? Had she so completely and successfully put things to rights that humanity had— Had consumed itself? Would that they were that clever; humanity always needed a nudge toward the edge.

But now, the city echoed with her steps even as she approached still barefoot. It was important to walk, to hold this form and feel the ground beneath her feet. How unlike Carcosa in every way: solid and sure though horrors had been visited upon it. Every intentional step told her she was no longer in Carcosa and her body rejoiced.

Still, that prickle moved down her spine, and she turned in a slow circle, looking for the King. For anyone who might be near. The gray plain behind her stood empty, dust slithering over her footprints to erase all trace, but when she neared the city and its broken, skeletal buildings, the dust proved less efficient in its work. Within the debris, she saw the footprints of others, and these she followed, intent on the path of prints that showed bare feet as her own.

Within the labyrinthine streets, a low wind swept the grime into the air, a long scoop up from the pavement and into the gray air, so that it might become more laden with the filth of a vanished people—the air saturated to the point where it would become dust itself, so that none might breathe. Cassilda took a deep breath and exhaled a wind of her own, to push the dust back, to clear the path of prints she followed.

In the distance, she spied a shadow, the worn-thin tail of a skirt flicking around the corner of a building. She did not call out, but ran, bare feet pressing into the prints that had come before. Even now she did not force herself beyond human limits; she kept to this body, enjoying the way the heart pumped, the way the muscles warmed despite the chill of the day. The ground beneath her feet was solid even now, her legs taking long bites as she closed the space between herself and the other.

Around the corner, Cassilda found the person within reach and without thinking, reached. There was no sense in hesitating, not when she had so many people to tell.

The world stuttered, the woman turned wearing Cassilda's own face. No masks here, and Cassilda had not worn one for longer than she could count. (She counted in her heart, every beat of that mortal thing inside of her telling her exactly how long it had been, exactly when the mask had last closed over her, carried her away, made her what she was only upon the cursed pages of that cursed book.) Her fingers closed into the tatters of the dress the other her wore, because to hold the shoulder beneath was to feel the hard line of bone beneath the taut skin. This other her stared at her with eyes that had seen too much, eyes that had endured this place. Eyes that, in the end, reflected the Yellow Sign.

"No."

They spoke the word together and Cassilda's knees buckled as the world seemed to tip out from under her, from under *them*. The idea that this woman—that *she*—had been left here, stranded, abandoned at the end of all things, was incomprehensible. Cassilda felt the weight of every Sign she had placed and held within her hands every single life she had bound. Every soul cried out that it had been for naught, that every step and every beginning led to this desolate place where Cassilda alone did roam. And how many times had it been this outcome—her mortal, traitor heart counted this too, so Cassilda did what she always did.

She turned away, opened a door in the ashen air of the world, and tried again.

Some Stranger's Hand:

She broke through a doorway; on the other side, Paris, France and an apartment on the rue Beautreillis. A man sat slouched in a chair, frowning over a notebook, a bottle of scotch by his side, a clutter of books on the floor. She moved closer; he blinked and offered a smile.

His hair was long and untidy, his blue eyes clouded dark and bleary with drink. His presence was both majestic and fragile and she went to him, her story liquid on her lips and ready to flow. But crouched at his side, she paused, for this man, this poet, held her gaze like no other. He was a king in his own right, a king of words and lizards, but not a King, not her King. Would that she could erase everything and make him so.

"'If the doors of perception were cleansed,'" he said. "'Every thing would appear to man as it is, infinite.' Aldous Huxley wrote that. Have you read him?"

She shook her head, suddenly afraid to speak.

"You should."

He laughed, took a drink from his bottle. "That's all we're trying to do, all of us, break through the doors of perception. See everything, see the other side."

"No," she said. "The other side is broken and crumbling and you, you are not of that world."

"We're *all* of that world eventually."

She grabbed his forearm. "No. Promise me you'll never try to go there." *He would be found by another woman; he would be cold and still and marked by this world and not the Sign. It was another wound within her, that she could not save everyone, everything.*

He smiled and took another drink as answer. She pressed a kiss to his hand and then his lips, tasting of his pain and his power. She shuffled through the books, wasn't surprised by what she found. She pressed it into his hand. "This is not the truth," she said and dared say no more.

He flipped through the pages, ripped one free, and tore it in half with his teeth. He chewed, chased it down with another pull from his bottle, offered the rest to her. The paper melted in her mouth, the lies drowning in her saliva and leaving a frisson of warmth behind. He tore another page and another and another, until nothing was left of the book but its binding. That, he tossed out an open window.

"Truth is man's creation," he said. "Real truth can't be written."

Her story danced across her tongue and she sensed, if spoken, the words would become his salvation as surely as they would become hers, but she refused to let them emerge. This man was already marked. She couldn't see a sign, but she felt the dark and terrible beauty of its presence. He was not meant for Carcosa, not meant for this world. She rose slowly, and he pressed her hands between his, flooding her body with the current of his intensity.

"Stay," he said. "Stay with me."

She stayed. For a little while, not long enough, but she stayed with him, breathing him in, breathing herself into him.

The Scholar, Chapter II:

She whispers the truth into the scholar's sleeping ears. He's drunk on whiskey and words, a deeper sleep than sleep alone, but she whispers nonetheless. Will his mind remember this when she repeats the tale? Because she will, she must.

My Queen, he calls her. His devotion will keep him faithful, will keep him anchored into this world, will allow him to hear the truth without the brand appearing on his skin. (And if not, the tattered part of her whispers. If not? There are doorways and other worlds. Always.)

The scholar, while greatly respected in his field, is not a man whose name is known by the greater world—not yet—but when he tells her tale, he will be believed. She has seen how this world works and knows that men like him—tall, commanding, self-possessed, and in positions of authority—are believed, often without question or complaint.

She checks his flesh for the Yellow Sign after these night-whispers, but it hasn't appeared yet. She nudges his shoulder, impatient to have it over and done, damn the Sign's possibility, damn everything, damn even the future of her beloved Carcosa. He mutters something unintelligible, doesn't wake.

She slips from the bed and stands at the window. The moon hangs heavy in the sky, and she closes her eyes, remembering the glint of two suns on the lakes. A sound breaks the night and she scans the darkness. Is someone waiting there, someone she once marked? Have they finally given up?

They will never give up, but neither will she.

"Wake up, damn you," she says, but he doesn't wake and she watches the moon and cuts half-circles in her palms. Inside, she feels the other Cassilda stir, the one created. That woman—mad, deluded creature that she is—wants to peel off this Cassilda's skin, to unmask, and take her place.

Will a day come when she forgets which is the fiction and which the truth? When she forgets the doorways that lead out and away? She tells herself that you can't forget who you are, who you're meant to be, but knows it isn't true because the King sits on his crumbling throne, ruling his damned lands. Lands that were once hers, lands he pursues her across and beyond.

She unclenches her fists. The wounds gape, revealing black stars before they close. She is strong, she has always been strong, but she's tired. Tired of running, of trying, of failing and falling apart. How many times will she have to tell her story before it erases the lies?

She glances at the man in his tousled sheets. The modicum of hope inside her rests heavy; best not to hold too tightly to such things. Still, she holds on.

His Explorer's Heart:

Cassilda entered through his explorer's heart. Among the materials of the world, she ranked hearts as easier than most. The muscle in motion was easily convinced to leap, to skip into stronger beat. Hearts of men had made her wary, but this man was unique, stripped of his manhood before he was ten. Most regarded him as having been made harmless through this action, but Cassilda knew otherwise. This man meant to explore the world—what was more dangerous than knowledge of the world?—and she meant for him to carry her Sign across all the waters, into all the lands. He was an admiral, but first he was a man who loved stories and knowledge and language. He called her Tianfei, celestial consort, and Cassilda could not say he was wrong.

In the lamplight of his work room, Zheng He's hands moved over the stone tablet he carved. History would say another had carved it, a servant, a slave, but Cassilda knew better than most the many ways in which recorded history could be mistaken. The motion of his hands across the stone drew her into a sense of calm she had never known. It was alien, this place in which she floated. Calm and assured as he carved the stone with three languages.

He made a list of offerings made to Allah and others, and between each character paused for Cassilda to tell more of her story. He wrote of gold and incense, of silks and jeweled banners; she spoke of fictions and betrayals. He wrote of lotus flowers and scented oils (Cassilda could almost feel them both on her fingertips and could see in his eyes the way he wished to spread his own fingers across her lips, her thighs; being a eunuch, he had come to take pleasure in the simplest of things, fingers partaking what the rest of his body could not.); she spoke of kings and their wordsmiths, and how her voice had been taken, silenced the way his own body had.

Within every line he carved, Cassilda poured the truth of her story, and the stone swallowed it as a sponge would water. Should any touch the stone, they would know, they would carry the truth of her beyond this lamp-lit room. Zheng He invoked the blessings of Hindu deities into the stone, for a peaceful world, and Cassilda whispered truths, that peace was never really peace—even the familiar was saturated with duplicity.

They carried the stone onto his ship and Cassilda bid him go without her, though in the end it was as if he had opened a door within her own heart, for when he asked her to join him upon the voyage, to witness the stone set upon a distant shore, she could not say no. For the first time, she was uncertain what it was that moved inside her; the need to see her word carried across the world, or the need to see *him* do it.

She had not marked him, did not *want* to mark him, but knew in the end she would. She shared his cabin the long journey through, this being his third across strange waters. She kneeled on the land where he placed the stone, and kissed its salty, carved edge, cautious of the way her truths threatened to overflow it. She did not want to leave it here, alone on the edge of a place she did not know. But she did leave, the story within the stone reaching for her even as the ship moved further away.

Cassilda made five more voyages with Zheng He, infusing stones every step of the way. Zheng He smiled at her, and she did not know if it was with amusement or love and only when they prepared to lower his dead body into the ocean waters did she realize that one could also be the other.

Before they came for him, Cassilda sat alone, having unwrapped the linens that covered his throat. She did not expose his face, for she could not bear to look at his handsome face—only the neck of him, so as to lay her hands on either side as she told him for a final time, her story. Her truth. She spoke soft, but loud enough the ship around them quaked, every timber threatening to burst as they understood at long last what they had carried. Cassilda pressed her body into his, warming his dead skin beneath the linen wrapping him. It did not matter, she told herself as the symbol flooded from her body and into his; none would see and he could not go mad, not now. Even so, when she looked upon her work and smoothed the linen back into place, she feared what she had done to this man. There was still no time to doubt, none, so she gave him up to his men and they in turn gave him up to the waters he had so loved. His people would make for him a tomb on dry land, but it would be forever empty.

Beneath the salted sea and over the course of long, long years, the linen binding Zheng He dissolved, water and beasts eating away at his flesh, at his heart. It was the heart that at last spilled the truths Cassilda had told, swallowed even in death. His heart vomited through the water a strange cascade of topaz light, a light that called to a fisherman in a small boat. A fisherman who rowed over, peered into the unearthly glowing water, and drowned.

The Scholar, Now as Then:

The doorway opened into an auditorium: low lighting, long rows of curving seats, a spotlight, a man at a podium. With the sensation of a hand clutching her wrist still dancing across her skin, Cassilda sank into the nearest empty seat. For the moment, she didn't care where she was, only that she was away.

(Breath on her neck, hand on her wrist, a smile of teeth and triumph, and the face, a face she knew—she always knew them, but it had been so long and her own surprise led to the pause that allowed the hand to grip—a face once filled with curiosity turned to rage and hate and worst of all, grim determination. There was something else, something even more horrible. Deep inside Nuru's eyes, Cassilda saw that the woman was not mindless, not stripped clean of her previous self, only masked with a new purpose she could not fight, and an apology hovered in the swirling depths, even as her hand tightened and began to pull. Had the others been the same? Had she not seen it or not wanted to see it and would the seeing change anything at all?)

"No," she whispered. No one paid her any attention; they were leaning ahead in their seats, listening, and the voice...she knew this speaker, this scholar, but he was gone. *Gone*. She'd watched him— Her fingers clenched on the seat's arms; her fingernails tore the fabric.

His voice, rich and melodic, drew her in now as it had drawn her in then. His words flowed—*and so we see then how the events of the changing world, and his discomfiture with those changes, influenced his fiction*—and Cassilda watched his mouth move, remembered the way he whispered, "My Queen." This was wrong, he shouldn't be here, she shouldn't be here, but his voice held her in place. Here, then, she could pretend she was sitting in the auditorium for the first time, listening to him, deciding, ignorant of the truth to come.

When he finished speaking and the auditorium cleared, she rose from her seat. On the other side of the room, another woman stood as well. The woman glanced over both shoulders, wary, hesitating, and Cassilda saw her own face, her own determination.

She pressed a hand over her mouth. Was this a trick? Had she fallen back into Carcosa, fallen to wander endlessly through the cobblestone streets, her mind caught in what was as the buildings fell to ruin beside her and the black stars shone their dark light on her skin?

Was she *this* Cassilda or *that* Cassilda?

She pinched her arm, breaking the thought's hold and answering her question. Loops of time, curving in, curving back. Doorways led; why shouldn't they sometimes lead back, but was she seeing a future changed—or changeable—or a fixed past?

The once-Cassilda and the man stood together and Cassilda heard their voices, saw the way he bent his head in acknowledgement, saw the intensity of his eyes. Saw the once-Cassilda place her hand on his forearm, gullible in her naivety. It hurt to see her face like that, to remember how in that moment she was so certain he was hers, certain everything would be different because he knew the power of the written word, knew and accepted and *feared* it.

"Wait," she shouted. The two continued speaking, yet there was a small flinch in the once-Cassilda's shoulders, almost imperceptible but Cassilda knew her body, knew the movements and the gestures.

Did she remember that, a strange thinning of the worlds between, and her own voice in the middle? She didn't remember, didn't *not* remember. This doorway was a mistake, a subtle torment, a way for the King to show her she'd never succeed, a way to torture her with her own failure, not her greatest failure—that belonged to the writer and would that she could go back to that moment and push him from the window, erase his lies before they fomented in his mind—but a failure that drove daggers into her heart.

But she did this for him, for her, for Carcosa, and she would make him remember what he'd forgotten.

She took several steps forward and pinched her arm again, savagely so, twisting the skin until a tattoo of raised blood appeared. Ahead, the once-Cassilda winced and rubbed her arm.

Was then now and now then? So many doorways, so many whens, so many men and women and words and inside, she was a circle of knots and nots.

The scholar's chin lifted, his gaze swept the auditorium, and his face, his eyes, were his own. Fool she might have become—fool, or blind—but she was not a fool in that moment, at least. He was nothing more than what he appeared to be: a chance.

Another pinch, another wince. Knots could be undone; circles, like words, could be erased, rewritten. She moved closer. She would break this when by giving him the truth now and all at once, giving him over to Carcosa and saving herself the false hope. Or she would drag the once-Cassilda elsewhen and save them both.

The walls of the auditorium began to shift, running as if a painted landscape doused with water or solvent, the colors smearing together. The air distorted, wavered, and the floor pulled her feet in, halting her steps and trapping her there. Below her, a doorway opened and she floated within the changing space, the sides too far away to touch. Time righting itself, ejecting her from this when. Already, glimmers of sun peeked through, and a wooden fence surrounding a village.

No, no, she had to at least warn her, to tell the once-Cassilda not to trust him. She threw back her head and raged at the ceiling, but only in her now did the sound emerge, a sound of despair and madness

(*We have all laid aside disguise but you.*) and she slipped deeper into the gaping doorway.

The once-Cassilda turned her face to the room; Cassilda reached out a hand, willing her to see. She opened her mouth to shout once more, but the doorway pulled and pulled and pulled. "Remember, you must remember," she cried, knowing that once-Cassilda would not.

Then she fell.

Guest, Writer, Chamber:

There had never been a time without doors.

Cassilda had never been confined by dungeon or moat, going where she would from the moment of her inception.

(Beginnings balanced on the edge of the known galaxy, a star condensing itself, splitting in two the way a cell would, twice but no more. Energy channeling downward, into one planetary body, into one *body* without flaw, the stars pressed black beneath eyes—her eyes, these too would become a doorway. Into Carcosa, that which she was named Before.)

The worlds—Carcosa and every single one beyond—were never not her playground, Cassilda moving between them as easily as mortals moved between rooms. A tap, tap, tapping upon a chamber door, the entrance of a raven—or was it? So many had been mistaken about her. The form she assumed rarely mattered, until the sundering, until all was rewritten and changed.

The Soul selects its own Society—
Then—shuts the Door—

A mortal woman named Emily had written those words—but so too words wherein she claimed to open *every* door, not knowing where dawn would come. Doors were problematic that way, whether open or shut; Cassilda had made them thus, long ago, and knew dawn for a lie.

She did not take a lover until the end—the *first* end, and she often wondered at every end yet to come, that if she had not stooped, if she had not allowed herself the need of such a thing, if all would have been preserved, nothing forsaken. But she had watched the mortals at play, had never wondered what it would be to take one of them, so had created her own plaything.

But such a creature—much as herself—once given form and function sought to reach beyond what it had arrived as; such a creature sought to be its own entity, no matter that pleasures of the flesh with one such as Cassilda were satisfying and rewarding both. Cassilda watched this creature surpass the plans she had for it, him. He strained at every limit, much the way she had (the way she would), until his fine and buttery robes ran down his body in tatters.

"Don't," Cassilda said.

"Must," he said, for if a thing were forbidden, he knew it to be twice as sweet.

He, like she, would not be confined, and she wondered—oh she wondered—if she had not made him, had not elevated him to her side, if all could have been avoided. For when he moved *beyond* her side, when he crowned himself King and his power washed like scalding water across the world of Carcosa, across Cassilda (which he now called her), she knew they had surpassed anything they had known before. They had been built for such things.

She let him go, knowing uncertainty for the first time, and watched this newborn King prowl through Carcosa and beyond. He took Earth for his lover then, reveling in humanity the way he once had her, and Cassilda, beneath the twin suns, stood alone as she had at the beginning of all things. She cut a door through the world and into another and emerged into a room she had not expected. An office, piled with books and papers, an office that held a man and only a man. Mortal, his beating heart calling to her in a way nothing had before. It was a song, her song, and she reached for it.

The man looked up, as if he had heard her, but he could not see her and would not unless she wished it. Cassilda held to the shadows and did not breathe, only watched him as he returned to his work. As his heart beat on. Cassilda closed her star-pressed eyes and let that heartbeat fill her, until she overflowed, until she believed again, but when she returned to beloved Carcosa, she found the new King not alone, but with a mortal man all his own, a man whose heart pounded fiercely as the King showed him the wonders of the city.

"It could not be," the man said.

"It was," the King said.

His tattered robes slid silent over the floor as he led the man deeper inside, to the place Cassilda stood, the door newly closed behind her. The King's eyes narrowed, but he did not ask, giving her only a slanted smile as the mortal man trembled in his wake.

"A guest," the King said.
But Cassilda knew otherwise.

The Scholar, Chapter III:

She refills the scholar's glass. Not enough whiskey to knock him out; enough to make him relaxed, pliable. They're sitting together on his sofa, the pillows set aside. She's taken the measure of his character in many ways: conversations, the silence between, sex. The latter to cement his devotion—a small subterfuge, yet one without malice—men can be easily led.

He has a sense of rightness about him; this she clings to. His words grow thick and she takes a deep breath, leans close.

"Can I tell you a story?" she asks, and even now, even after all this time, her voice still holds a quaver. Such a small thing, to tell a story; such a grave matter, to right a wrong.

"You can tell me anything. You know you're safe here, right? You're always safe with me."

She knows he wonders about this; he catches her peeking out the windows, darting glances over her shoulders. He's caught her standing in the doorway between the hall and his bedroom, running her hands along the frame, contemplating the solidity of the surface, the immutable nature of wood and nail and paint.

He thinks...what does he think? She's not asked, but she can guess. An abusive spouse, something mundane, but no less the terrible for it. She's traced wards on his skin, the shape of the Yellow Sign before it, too, was corrupted. She's hinted, heavily, spoken in circles (always circles), in ciphers, in small magicks of syllable and tongue. He listens, nodding all the while, but he keeps faith in the concrete, the real—as nearly all of this time do—although she's caught the light in his eyes, the wonder, and knows it won't take much to turn it into belief.

She keeps her voice low and starts at the true beginning. He raises his eyebrows once, twice, then his face stills as she pours her story into him. She wants to tell him everything—the rest of the words push, they shove, intent to be free, to have it done with, but she holds them back.

"And?" he says, when she pauses.

She takes his hands, holds them palm-up—the skin is bare, not even a shadow of the Yellow Sign.

"No more tonight," she says. "Please."

She lets go of his hand and looks away, knowing he will read this as unease and yes, part of her is uneasy, but part of her thrums with anticipation, and he touches her arm.

"I'm glad you told me this."

She pushes his glass into his hand and when he drains the contents, she fills it again. He dozes and she helps him to bed; when snores fill the room, she peels back the sheets. Uncurls his fingers and checks his palms again. Nothing there. She closes her eyes, touches fingertips to his temples, feeling for a shadow, a shade, of Carcosa, but there's nothing. She inspects the soles of his feet, the skin behind his ears, beneath his testicles, and everywhere in between.

Satisfied he is, as yet, unmarked, she rocks back on her heels, not ready to allow a declaration of victory, but unable to hold in a smile.

The Lost:

Cassilda spilled from the doorway, shading her eyes against the sun. All around her, trees and the smell of water and earth, birds and insects and leaves rustling in the breeze. No hum in the air of electricity or engines, no steady rush of car or bus or train. Not the very beginning, no, because she heard voices and the thud of tools against wood, but a beginning enough. A new world.

These people knew not of Carcosa save in snippets of dreams, in glimmers of sunlight on water, in the long shadows cast by fire, but she knew them. Oh, yes, Cassilda knew their kind. Children of men who took what they wanted from whoever they wanted. Who brought death and disease and destruction. Selfish and entitled, proclaiming themselves kings and gods, remaking the world in an image of their own design, never mind that the world was large enough to hold all designs and should hold them all, for who could say which was the greater? What mere human could hold such power? Their clocks held such a brief time, yet they insisted on owning the whole while she was relegated to the mindplace of forgotten things and broken queens.

She despised them, despised that she needed them, that they were responsible for this need. Pressing a hand to her chest, she stilled her thoughts and her rage. (Too much rage and was it her own or the false Cassilda's?) Filled herself with purpose instead and made her way to the tall fencing they'd built around their village. She inverted the air around her, shielding herself from view, as she sidestepped the man guarding the entrance.

Wooden houses sat around a central courtyard; some of the houses were being dismantled while belongings sat in bundles off to the side. Leaving then, leaving to spread their poison righteousness and their illnesses elsewhere. She would give them her story, let them carry that as well on their journey. She passed women cooking or mending torn clothing; children playing with wooden toys; men unmaking structures built not so long ago. The wail of a baby pierced the air, not long after, the faint strains of a lullaby. From the cut of their clothes, they were a simple people; from their eyes, she knew they'd tasted fear more than once. Perhaps this state of fear would serve her well, would make them strong enough to bear a little more without breaking.

A hand to her chest again. The false Cassilda rippled beneath her skin. Drawn to something in this place or these people or the sound of water touching the shore? No matter. She would be quick. She rounded the back corner of a house and there stood a man wiping sweat from his brow, an axe in his free hand and a pile of wood by his feet.

She let him see her, see her as she was meant to be seen, not the way others wanted. A true queen, the true Queen. His eyes widened, but before he could speak she grabbed his hands, brought her mouth close to his, and breathed her story into him. His back stiffened, his eyes rolled to white, and his body shook. She held him tight; no time for patience or caution. A thin line of spittle ran from one corner of his mouth.

If he was strong enough to carve a place in this world, he should be strong enough to hold her story. She poured the rest into him, watched it play across sclera in a tableaux of what was and what would be. (But inside her, the false Cassilda burned and hated and refused to acknowledge that her place was manufactured, manipulated—a monstrosity.)

His body jolted and a quavering moan escaped his lips. No, no, no. (The false Cassilda smiled.) The Yellow Sign bloomed to life on his forehead and opened, revealing a spray of black stars against a dark sky. Cassilda released his hands, shoved him away, as piece by piece, he tattered ("Shreds of paper, that's all you are," the false Cassilda said) and fell into the hole, fell into Carcosa. She smelled the sulfur of the tainted lakes, the stink of air gone wrong. When the last piece of the man disappeared, the Yellow Sign hung in the air, mocking, before it winked out of sight.

Cassilda balled her hands into fists, blinked away the sting of unexpected tears. She would take another and then another, down to the youngest babe, until one of them proved strong enough. She heard the laughter of the false Cassilda, heard her speak.

"Song of my soul, my voice is dead,
Die thou, unsung, as tears unshed
Shall dry and die in
Lost Carcosa."

Carcosa was not lost. It was *not*. And was it the voice of the false Cassilda reciting the words or her own? She didn't know, couldn't tell, and was the hand on her chest pressing in or pressing out?

A woman in a dress the color of drying mud stepped into view; her gaze moved from the axe and the wood to Cassilda and back again. Cassilda closed the distance between them with long strides, placed her hands on either side of her face, and shoved her story into the woman's open mouth. The woman shuddered, the Yellow Sign appeared on her cheek. Cassilda shrieked through a clenched jaw, didn't wait to see her descent into Carcosa.

All around her, the world turned grey. She was dimly aware of hands on skin, of Signs and holes. A baby crying. A child striking her with a stick, shouting, "Let go of my Mama, let go!" Black stars and screams and her story again and again and again.

The grey faded and she stood outside the fence, her chest aching, her shoulders heaving. Silence clung to the air. An unspeakable silence. She did not have to enter the village to know they were all gone, and while inside the false Cassilda was still and silent, she radiated a grim sense of satisfaction.

I did not do this, Cassilda told herself. *I did not.*

Even if the other had guided her hands, her hands had done the work. So be it, she thought. She would not shed tears for them; she would not allow herself the guilt and the sorrow. The burden of her failure was enough.

On a nearby tree, someone had carved a crude C into its trunk; the blade of the knife still embedded in the wood. Someone then, had thought to reveal the truth, had time enough for this? She grabbed the knife from the tree and plucked a word from the air, from the echo of a man's panicked shout, a man not knowing who or what had descended upon them in such fury: CROATOAN.

She carved the rest and let the knife fall, and then did what she'd done more times than she could count: she cut a doorway into the air and moved on.

Guest, Writer, Window:

He walked through the doorway and Cassilda followed, close enough to be mistaken for his shadow, and the young man, who wished so badly to make his mark upon the world, shuddered. Cassilda took pleasure in that, she couldn't not. He looked at her the way he might a serpent, something wild that he might not control no matter how he tried.

Be nice, the King cautioned her in the language they shared, but nice had long since fled and Cassilda did not care for this man—the one she had made, nor the one he had brought. Both were darkly handsome and compelling, but Cassilda felt certain she had made a grave error (impossible, her mind whispered, and yet).

The young man stood at the window, which might also be a doorway Cassilda knew (even now she ached to push him through, send him on), unable to tear his gaze from the strange skies outside. Cassilda watched him watching the sky, the way his eyes took everything in, the way he held his breath as if he were having to convince himself he was only dreaming.

"Strange is the night where black stars rise," he said as she watched the same black stars reflected in his eyes. "And strange moons circle through the skies," she murmured in return, and those moons, countless and colored in shades he had never seen before, seemed to rise by her command, heavy enough they might drop out of the stars altogether and roll to rest at her feet.

"But stranger still is lost Carcosa," he said, and before Cassilda could fly at him, push him through the window and send him into the depths of a Carcosa that was not lost

never lost—those people screaming in torment, her letter carved into a tree and the shriek of a child—

the King came to stand between them, guiding the young man effortlessly from her side, as if he knew—of course he knew, born of her mind and hands, surely he knew the worst things that simmered inside her. She stood rooted at the window, knowing this was the moment. The young man would ask about this world and the King would tell him and they—

song of my soul, my voice is dead—
Not yet, Cassilda thought.

She followed them, sitting nicely beside the young man, gifting him and the King a smile she had not worn in years. She allowed this smile to settle upon her face as easily would a mask. She was warm and not cold; she was living yet and never dead or silenced. The men talked and Cassilda slid her hand into that of the young man. He was unbelievably warm, to the point it almost hurt to touch him. So alive, filled with such hope despite the danger he found himself in. None had come back from this place, at least none sane.

When at last the young man looked at her, away from the glowing visage of the King, Cassilda held to her smile, allowing it to deepen. It was sweet there, a full bottom lip and a dimple because once, this young man had seen such a girl, a girl he longed to kiss; he wondered how his mouth might fit to her own, if she would dislike his mustache, and how her trembling hand might unfasten his high collar. Cassilda smiled this smile at him and felt the tremor of his hand in hers.

The hours did not matter then. Cassilda held him in her sway and believed he listened, believed even better that he understood. She plied him with fruits he had never tasted before, let him drink the wine of Carcosa, and he floated. Somewhere far away, midnight sounded from the misty spires in the fog-wrapped city, and still the young man listened, absorbed. Cassilda did not look upon the King all this time, feeling herself alone with the youth he had brought. Whatever the King had meant, Cassilda chased it away with the truth of this place, the truth that left the young man quaking and stuttering when dawn at last came. "Was it dawn at all?" he asked, as he finally slid his hand from Cassilda's. He looked upon the King as if startled to find another there; he too had forgotten. But upon looking at that face—proud and handsome even in tatters—the young man remembered. I wear no mask, he thought.

"Oh, but you will." With these words, Cassilda pushed him through, sending him back, away, out. In the silence that followed, she looked upon her King. She had not touched him in far too long, and did not now. It was his hand that reached for her, bony and trembling. How like an unsure young man, she thought, but allowed the touch. His fingers were a memory of the warmth that had been between them, but he did not seem to mind the chill. Cassilda felt nothing, until she saw the crackling fissures within her own skin, her own clothing. The longer his touch lingered, the more she began to fall apart the way he had fallen. She took a step back and looked upon his unmasked face, knowing there was no sense in trying to determine when they had gone wrong. Time was of little consequence in the end; the young man had come and the Carcosa Cassilda had known—had birthed— would soon be lost.

Little Attic Ghost:

Doorways did not always herald departures. This doorway was hidden and would hide those who needed to survive the cruelty of the outside world. Cassilda opened this doorway, behind a clever bookcase, and dared perch beside a young girl in an attic, writing in a small book. Cassilda slid her hands over those of the girl—her name was Anne—and meant to flood her with the story. But a more powerful story came from Anne herself, and Cassilda found herself drawn short. The girl's hands were cold, she longed to stretch herself tall in the sunlight, but hunched over her book, writing in a very precise hand. Cassilda could only listen as the words flooded from the girl.

A thing might be hidden away, the girl thought, but in the end, the truth would out. All would know. Truths could not be hidden forever and always. Darkness was not eternal. She would write and pray that one day—one day—all would know.

Cassilda looked at the girl's profile in the waning light of day; she was nothing more than any other human Cassilda had encountered, drawn with rough edges that were only sometimes pleasing. Nothing about this girl should have made her remarkable, to Cassilda least of all, yet still something stayed Cassilda's hand—

the shriek of a baby—the warm curve of its head in her own cold hand—there were trees, so many trees, and the people needed to go— needed to carry her word—

Was it possible? Cassilda took a breath. Teach me to wait, she silently implored the girl. Teach me.

My world is here between these walls, the girl thought and Cassilda wished her beyond the walls, but the world was terrible and would consume this girl, for girls were made to be consumed, devoured by everything greater than they were. But no. No. Cassilda refused the very idea.

She sat, still as she had never been, and did not think of black stars or golden robes worn to tatters. She did not think of the world falling ceaselessly through space, heedless of the people it carried along. She did not think of her own plight—nor the hollow ache it had carved inside of her. She waited and was still and listened to the breath of the girl.

This girl, Cassilda told herself, would stretch in the sun; this girl would feel the warmth of it sinking into her even as numbers were marked into her skin, no Yellow Sign this. The world was a horror (and so too Carcosa, though she loved it so) and would carry the girl away, into the ground at last, but the truth would be known.

Wait, Cassilda told herself.

The hours did not matter then, either, sitting quiet with the girl in the small attic. The hours did not yet matter.

The Scholar, Chapter IV:

She closes the doors in the scholar's apartment. Shutters the blinds, draws the curtains. He watches with his brows lifted in amusement but asks nothing. She'd have no answer to give if he did, for this containment is instinct alone. When the story is his to tell, he can shout it to the world without impediment or barrier. She will stand by his side, but not for long. She will make her last doorway and return to Carcosa. She will return *home*.

Sitting beside him on the sofa, she takes his face in her hands, memorizing the planes and hollows, tattooing the memory of his smile in her mind.

"And now?" he asks, when she takes her hands away.

"Now I tell you the rest. I tell you the truth." She picks up a copy of the book, fighting to keep a sneer from her mouth all the while. "And then you will know that this, this is falsehood." She opens a small door and the sound of metal grinding upon itself splits the quiet of the room. Unflinching, she shoves the book inside, locks the door tight behind it. His eyes are saucer-wide; his fingers clenched atop his thighs. She smiles, touches his cheek again.

"When I told you there were doorways and other worlds, I meant it for truth."

He swallows hard. "I see that."

"This is too large a tale for words alone," she says, her voice soft as she leans close, presses her forehead against his. "Close your eyes."

The tale spills from her mind in loops and circles and images—herself, proud and strong, the King in his rightful place by her side, his robe whole, his eyes holding court with sanity, the stars glittering on the waters of the lakes, the towers reaching into the sky, a flag twisting in the wind from the highest one, a flag of brightest white emblazoned with the true Yellow Sign.

He draws in a sharp breath; she pours in the rest of the story. All of it: the betrayal, the lies, the doorways, the faces. Shows him the towers, now crumbling; the flag, dirty and torn and discarded in a gutter of filth; the lakes, reeking of sulfur; the King, his face twisted, his eyes bright with the light of the mad and the damned. And last, she shows him the wretch wearing her face and name.

And then it's done, the last word melting between his lips like sugar. He sags back against the cushion, blinks rapidly. But he's still here. He's still here. He opens his mouth to speak; she holds up a hand and opens his shirt, running her fingers along his chest. Lifts his arms. Parts his hair to see the white of his scalp.

It worked. Finally, it worked. She covers her mouth with both hands to hold in a sob or a laugh or something between the two. He says nothing for a long time, then he exhales, long and low.

"My Queen," he says. "You deserve your rightful place."

The air crackles, the hairs on Cassilda's arms and the back of her neck rise. His eyes burn with a sickly yellow light. She scrambles off the sofa. Backs away. He stands, holds out a hand which she ignores. The Sign then, she missed the Yellow Sign, and Carcosa has claimed him for her own.

He shakes his head as if she spoke the words aloud. "No, my Queen. It is I who claimed Carcosa."

And he unmasks.

The sound of his tattered robes on the carpet is the rasp of sandpaper against stone. Shucked of its disguise, his face is pallid and drawn. "You cannot undo what was meant to be all along," he says. "Now it's time for you to return home. Accept your place."

"I will never accept such an abomination. Carcosa was never meant to be as it is now. It was never meant to be yours. *Never.*"

The word is acid on her tongue; the truth of his deception, even more so. He has never hidden the hideous truth of himself—and yet now, to deceive her, he has and she can hardly believe it. Her creation is monstrous indeed and even as he seeks to erase her, awe runs through her. Disgusting dichotomy.

He waves one hand, cuts a doorway in the air, and through that space, they come: Nuru, Zheng He, a motherless child whose name she still refuses to think upon, because a name gives a person power, and this child should not hold so much in its small, tender hands. All are branded with the Yellow Sign on their palms, madness in their eyes. She tries to run, but there are too many of them to outrace. They surround her, enfold her, grip her arms and her chin, her waist and her hips—how like lovers, she wishes, but this is not love, this is silencing. Their skin is ice, their eyes implacable. She will find neither mercy nor absolution here.

She turns to the King. "I will never stop."

He waves his hand again and the broken children of Carcosa pull her back, pull her down and down and down.

The Doorway, Everopening:

The door is heavy, banded with strips of iron. Is this a door back to the beginning? Is there even a beginning?

She wishes it were a rabbit hole—

(it had been, when they pulled her down, through dirt and roots, shrieking)

—a length of darkness she could plummet through until she falls hard against something solid, against something *true*. She wishes she had to shrink herself to move through the proper door, that *she* could be the change, instead of changing the world to open the door.

But it is only ever a door and she stands before it as she ever has. Carcosa thrums behind her, broken by a careless playwright who didn't know what fire he courted. Can she remake it? Can anything be remade? If she does not go, she will never know, and the unknowing is the worst part.

Worse than the silence?

This question rises in her from a voice not her own. She closes her eyes and listens. It is the voice of a young girl, who might be Anne, who might be her, who might be someone she has not yet met. If she met herself, would she know? (Hollow eyes, silent plea, come back, you must come back and try.)

You would know.

That voice. Cassilda exhales and the door in its frame creaks. She looks up at it, impossibly tall and narrow, but she has made this door. She will fit.

She can hear them coming.

Can feel their hooking fingers pulling at her skirts, her hair.

They will forever pull her down
She will forever rise.
Weary but not broken, Cassilda opens the door.

GRAVE-WORMS
BY MOLLY TANZER

The grey flannel suit might have looked masculine on the rack, or on another woman, but the close cut of the cloth, and the way the expensive fabric skimmed over the lines of her straight, slender figure was intensely, wholly feminine. If you saw her from behind, you might have thought she looked frail, or saint-like with her close-cropped hair—but when she turned, the determination that shone brightly from the grey eyes almost lost behind her long black lashes was anything but fragile.

Or innocent.

That evening, she had worn no earrings, little makeup, low heels; her charcoal blouse was without detail. Her only adornment was a wisp of a silk scarf knotted at her birdlike throat, grey as well, but suggesting to the viewer the idea of violet. She looked as though she had thoughtlessly thrown the outfit together—but really, she had dressed very, very carefully. She was meeting Roy Irving for dinner at Delmonico's, to discuss business, and other things.

Their first meeting had been a chance encounter at the mayor's fund-raising event, where they alone had objected to the statue the city wanted to erect in front of the courthouse, feeling it was far too abstract to represent something as absolute, as concrete as 'justice'. His determination had made her keen to see him a second time. After their spirited if whispered discussion about the utter inappropriateness of lions drinking with jackals she had asked him to dinner, surprising him… but he had agreed readily enough. She had seen his arousal when his pupils had dilated, darkening almost to invisibility the piercing ice blue of his irises.

He looked like that now. The Lobster Newberg and steak and talk of bottom lines had excited him, as had her declining champagne or the good house red in favor of a double Laphroaig with a bit of water.

"Scotch and steak," he had said. "You're a woman after my own heart, Ms. Calder."

"Docia," she said, not dropping his gaze. "If we're to be business associates, we should be on a first name basis. Don't you think?"

"At the very least."

If there had been any suggestiveness in his tone she would have instantly dismissed the possibility of whatever he might be suggesting, but the frankness of his desire stoked her own. She withdrew a cigarette from her silver case and lighted it off the candle at the center of the table.

"At the very least, *Roy*," she agreed, and exhaled another swaddling layer of grey.

Delmonico's was nearly empty that night, but though it was nine in the evening on a Friday, Docia was not surprised. A strange lethargy had claimed New York of late, slowly but undeniably. She did not know when it had begun, or when exactly she had noticed it, but *something* had changed. People, when they braved the streets, looked furtive, nervous, and hurried about their affairs without stopping to greet acquaintances in the street.

Docia Calder was not the kind of woman who believed in bogeymen, but just the same, it made her uneasy. The shift seemed sinister, though to believe that meant she must believe there was some intention or plan behind it all, and that she could not credit.

She and Roy lingered over their food, savoring it—though she could not help but notice it lacked the same flavor as she usually expected. Perhaps that meant *she* was the problem—even the scotch tasted less potent on her tongue. She decided to put it to the test, and order dessert. If there was one reliable thing in New York, it was Delmonico's Baked Alaska.

"Don't have it tonight," said the young waiter, almost rudely. He seemed bored.

Docia was astonished. "This is Delmonico's," she said, as if he might not be aware of where he was. "You always have Baked Alaska. It's your signature dessert."

"Sorry. Coffee?" he asked.

"No… just the check." The waiter slouched off without pressing the issue. "I've never seen anything like it," she mused. "Everyone here is usually so good. Do you think Delmonico's is going downhill… or is it something else?"

Roy shrugged. "Have you found the Yellow Sign?" he asked.

"Don't say that!"

He looked surprised by her outburst. "I'm very sorry," he said curiously.

"No, I'm sorry… I don't like that expression." These days, everyone said it, but it made her feel queer. "Where did it come from? Why did we begin saying it?" She shook her head. "What exactly does it mean?"

"I suppose I'm not really sure. I don't think anyone knows, really."

"It seems like… when I hear it, I feel like lying down… shutting the curtains, locking the door… going to sleep."

"Maybe we just need to get out of here."

The fresh air made her feel better. Though the streets were less busy than they should be, the city was still ablaze with light. Docia had matched Roy drink for drink at dinner, but it was only the sight of countless sparkling electric pinpoints against the dark heavens that made her feel drunk. She reeled, giddy. The sky was obscure, stars and moon invisible behind cloudbanks reflecting groundlight, and for a moment, Docia imagined the lights of the city were the stars; the skyscrapers, galaxies. But that was not the case—no human hand had made those stars and galaxies, but every I-beam, every sheet of glass, every brick and block and sheet of stone had been made with human hands out of strong materials and stronger human will.

She knew then that she shouldn't worry. Nothing could break the city's spirit. Nothing could make it lie down.

Lost in these thoughts, when she stepped down off the curb she stumbled—but he had her by the elbow, by the waist. She had not realized how tall he was, six feet at least, broad across the shoulders but narrow at the hip.

"Let me drive you home," he murmured, his square chin brushing her earlobe.

"Whose home?" she asked carelessly.

He threw his head back and laughed, a terrifying laugh, free and loud, the laugh of a living god… but she fell into his arms without any fear at all.

They met many times after that, but regardless of whether their encounters were in her office, or his bed, or her bed, or his office, she found them intensely arousing. Not that their lovemaking interfered with her ability to work; no, rather, her body's response to his presence heightened her awareness, fine-tuned her senses, made her mind sharper. She drove a harder bargain than she would have if they'd never once touched hands, lips, more. He treated her with humor and distain in equal measure, and she admired him for it, responded yet more eagerly when they were alone and his hand found her bottom with a sharp smack, or his lips her body with a bruising intensity that left her shuddering, satisfied, and yet wanting him more.

That, in particular, was the most natural thing in the world, this they agreed on. As captains of industry, they were neither of them ever satisfied with what they had. They wanted *more*, always more, be it profits, side-ventures, workers, productivity, or product. They desired.

"To desire is to live, and to live is to desire," she claimed, lying naked on his bed, the imprints of his belt still pink against the whiter flesh of her wrists, their mingled sweat stinging her bitten upper lip. He was standing naked at the window of his penthouse apartment, his prize-fighter's profile and taught muscular buttocks silvered by the lights of the city beyond. "To give up one is to give up the other."

"I have a desire," he said, turning to face her.

She propped herself up on her elbows. "Name it."

He walked to his bureau, and opening the top drawer, withdrew an envelope. He tossed it on the bed at her feet.

"An invitation," he said, as she withdrew two stiff, creamy squares of cardstock. "Two, actually… to a cocktail party."

"Delightful!"

"It's… being hosted by Fulvius Elbreth."

"The theatre critic?" she asked, resisting the impulse to cast the invitations away like poisonous snakes.

"The same."

"But Roy… don't you know what he is? What he stands for?" She shivered. "What he stands *against*?"

"Oh, I know. But Irving Properties, Inc. donated to the *Tribune*, and… well, no good deed goes unpunished. They're thanking all the donors with a party."

Suddenly cold, Docia got up to retrieve her Japanese silk robe from where it lay on the floor of his penthouse, crumpled, like a flower after a rainstorm. "Oh, Roy," she said, shrugging into it, "I don't know. The man is…"

"I know. Which is why I'm begging you not to make me go alone."

"Don't go at all!"

"You know I can't do that."

"Why not?" She stood with her legs straight and apart, as if braced to withstand some impact, chin defiantly thrust forward. "What is stopping you?"

"It's all part of being businessmen—forgive me, business*people*." He bowed. Ordinarily, she would have smiled, but the specter of Fulvius Elbreth had made her somber. "Sometimes we have to do things we don't want to do."

"But to be seen with Fulvius Elbreth! To lend him and his ideas credit with your presence! Don't you remember him, from the city council meeting? He was the most vocal advocate of that statue of 'Justice,' the one you and I agreed was a mockery of the very idea!"

"I remember, but—"

"Roy, the man once said, under the guise of reviewing *Hamlet*, that America would be better off as an imperial dynasty. Why? Because a king relies on his subjects, and thus feels beholden to them, will work to help them better themselves—but elected officials only rely on business*people*, who in turn rely on no one, and thus feel beholden to help no one but their bottom line." She shook her head, sending her tumbled locks tumbling in all directions. "A man who thinks a king's whimsical largesse—the returning of amorphous favors—is better for the world than someone like *me*? Someone who pays my workers a fair wage for the work they do—a wage meaning *money*, the best, most objective indicator of approval anyone can give another human? What sort of man cares for patronage over fairness? I cannot—no, I *will* not make small talk with someone who believes such… dangerous nonsense."

"Not even for me?"

She hesitated. She was not used to hesitating—to hesitate was to feel uncertainty, and she had always known what to do, and what was right, on both an instinctive level and a conscious one. It was right to be honest. To be forthright. To give her approval of only what should be approved. That Roy Irving, whom she had assumed shared her highest values, would ask her so casually to disavow them—and treat that disavowal as nothing, but a part of the cost of doing business… it troubled her, made her wonder if she had erred in agreeing to partner with this man, in any of the many ways that they had.

And yet, she felt her own will soften as he looked at her, his expression one of playful amusement. He was just a lover engaged in lover's banter…

"All right," she sighed.

"Think about it this way," he said, slipping his hand under the collar of her robe, to grasp the flesh beneath. "It's an opportunity to show Fulvius Elbreth that we're better than kings."

The city seemed yet darker the night of the party. The lights she could see from her office seemed fewer, dimmer. She gazed down at the city below, and shuddered, feeling a sense of unnamable dread. What, she wondered, did it mean? What might it foretell?

She shook her head. She might as well ask herself, *have you found the Yellow Sign?*

The answer would be the same.

Knowing she would not have time to go home, Docia had ordered her secretary to bring her dress to her office. With everything pressed and laid out, Docia mixed herself a Manhattan and began to change.

Usually, Docia's office was where she felt most comfortable, but that night, as she got herself ready, she turned on all the lights, feeling as if the darkness was leaking in around the windowpanes, reaching into her very heart. She found she wished she'd told Louise to fetch her anything other than a little black dress—Docia rarely wore color, even for the gayest occasions, but that night, her selection seemed dreary.

She had just fastened the clasp of her necklace when Roy knocked. Startled, she cried out, turning too quickly and knocking over the Manhattan. The crystal shattered into jagged stars as the burgundy fluid soaked into the rug. She swore, reaching for something to mop it all up.

"You alright?" Roy asked, finding her on her hands and knees.
"I spilled my drink when you knocked. I guess I'm a little on edge."
"Funny, you never seemed like the type to be frightened of a party," he teased, helping her to her feet and then helping her heavy black pea coat. Two princess seams running down the back, cinching the waist ever so slightly, were the garment's only concession to femininity. "How can a woman so comfortable in a boardroom be uncomfortable in a living room? We'll laugh about it later, you know."
"Of course. It's just… haven't you noticed? The city, I mean?"
It was the first time she had spoken to him about it. He looked at her strangely, and though the room was warm she felt a chill. He obviously had not noticed anything amiss.
Was it the city? Or was it her?
"It must just be the shorter days," she said, as lightly as she could.
He relaxed. "I know what you mean," he said. "I always feel a bit down in the autumn. But, a few bad drinks and some small talk with the moochers and the looters ought to cheer us up, don't you think? Come, let us go be despised by those who do less in a month than we do in a day. And then later," he whispered something in her ear that certainly gave her something to look forward to.

She needed it. The party was not fun. It was full of the sort of self-proclaimed intellectual she instinctively despised, women in heavy eyeliner with artistic pretensions and too many necklaces; men with moist, flabby lips and badly-cut double breasted suits. They spoke of politics and art as if they knew anything about either.

For as long as possible, Docia floated amongst these people, saying as little as possible and trying to listen less. Really, she was most concerned with avoiding Fulvius Elbreth. She knew him from his picture in the *Trib*, though in real life his chin was weaker. Unlike her, he was clearly in his element, enjoying everyone's company, listening to what they had to say and responding with his own delightfully pithy *bons mots*, as light and frothy as egg white on a Ramos Gin Fizz—and just as insubstantial.

She was refreshing her drink at the bar when she overheard the critic remark that abstraction was the only acceptable form of artistic expression in the modern age. In spite of herself, she ambled over, curious to hear what he had to say on the matter.

"Representational art is pure arrogance," he said to a group of vapid-looking men and women. "The act of representing a thing is to claim one knows a thing, and nothing is knowable. Only in abstraction can we truly show reality; only when we admit our own lack of rationality can we approach a subject with any real intelligence."

Docia was the only one not nodding her agreement. He noticed.

"You disagree?" His tone was lighthearted, but she could feel the insincerity behind it.

"I'm not sure I even understand what you mean," she said. "Plenty of things are knowable."

"Like what?"

She silently cursed herself for engaging with him. What had she been thinking? Her sole hope for the party had been to get away without being introduced to her host, and yet here she was.

"Like… this drink." She held it aloft. "It is bourbon. In a glass."

"But—forgive me—neither you, while beautiful, nor that bourbon, while tasty, are art." He smiled. She did not return the expression. "Now, if I were watching a play, and you appeared, bourbon in hand, and had this conversation with my character… why, how realistic it would be! Two individuals having a conversation at a party, how natural! How representational! But what would it mean?"

"It would mean we were having a conversation."

"Ah—but why? To what end? If we were having this conversation, but upon the stage, the audience would wonder what my motivation is for saying what I am saying—for beginning the conversation at all, really. They'd consider how what I wore, what I drank, and most especially what I said illuminated my character—and they would analyze how your reaction revealed your own. But, of course, all real people contain multitudes. No author can truly represent a person; that is why I say it is arrogant to pretend it is possible. But, an *abstraction*… that is a different matter. Through abstraction, we are able to nestle closer to the truth, for abstraction deals with ideas rather than realities."

"That's ridiculous," declared Docia, ignoring the snickers and titters of the group. "I'm sorry, but I can't share in your nihilism."

Elbreth snapped his fingers. "We've met before," he said. "I remember you, from that meeting with the mayor. You hated the new statue of Justice, claimed it was a travesty to erect anything other than a blind woman with scales and sword."

"Justice is blindfolded, for She is objective. Justice carries a sword, double-edged to represent reason and justice. Her scales show us that cases will be weighed. To replace those symbols with something else, something *lesser*, impugns everyone employed by the city, and does nothing to reassure suppliants who go there seeking fair treatment. That *thing* you endorsed doesn't say anything to anyone about what really goes on inside a courtroom!"

"I didn't realize there was really a goddess incarnate living at 60 Centre Street." Elbreth chuckled. "Or is it possible your darling Lady Justice is also... an abstraction?"

Docia stalked off, as embarrassed as she was furious. She was not accustomed to being verbally outfenced, especially by those who spoke glibly of their dislike of reason and their abandonment of rationality. He had known what she meant, but twisted her words to mean something else—the hallmark of the second-rater. A thing was what it was, and to claim otherwise was to deny reason and logic; or, in other words, the faculties that distinguished humans from animals—what gave mankind purpose, and for that matter, culture.

These thoughts comforted her, but she still needed some air, to get away from these people. Not seeing Roy anywhere in the crowd, she headed for the balcony. Another woman was out there, smoking a cigarette. Docia nodded politely, but otherwise ignored her as she stared down at the city below.

Was it just her imagination, or was it even dimmer than before she had entered Fulvius Elbreth's apartment? The stars were still masked by flat cloudbanks, invisible, obscure, far away. It occurred to her that she could not recall the last time she had seen them...

She sighed, leaning against the balcony. If only she'd been thinking faster, she would have suggested Elbreth come out with her, put his weight against the balustrade, testing its truth—it would hold, whether he believed it would, or not. And even if he personally felt an abstraction of a banister was more valuable, especially on the stage, Juliet would likely feel more secure with a railing designed by man, and forged of iron, between her and Romeo.

"Don't let them bother you."

"I beg your pardon?" Docia turned to face the small woman beside her. The first thing she noticed were the woman's eyes, huge and dark and expressive. As to what they expressed, it was intense determination, a single-mindedness of purpose Docia immediately admired. Her confident posture, sensible, side-parted bob and tailored suit gave Docia confidence that she was standing with someone who would not tolerate any nonsense.

"I said, don't let them bother you. They are beneath your notice." She had a clipped, aristocratic accent when she spoke. Docia couldn't identify it, but she thought it might be European. "Their goals are not yours."

"I suppose not."

"You are a businesswoman. A creator. Creators think." Her darkly-lipsticked mouth contorted around the butt of a half-smoked cigarette; she blew out smoke, and smiled. "They are independent, they follow their own reason to the end. Critics… they are not creators. They are destroyers. No—they are less than destroyers, for a destroyer must possess the will to destroy, which means possessing purpose. They—those in there, I mean—are mere grave-worms. They feast on that which is already dead."

Docia was a little uncomfortable with this bold speech. While she admired the woman's convictions, both the content and the way she delivered them, her familiarity was a little disturbing. She spoke as if she and Docia had been friends for a long time, whereas to the best of Docia's knowledge, she'd never seen the woman before in her life.

"Have we met?" asked Docia. "I'm sorry if I don't recall, but…"

"I know who you are—what you do. I know why you needed air after being in there, with those people. Would you like a cigarette?"

"I would *love* a cigarette," said Docia, and accepted one from the woman's pack. They were of a type she had never seen before, she didn't recognize the package, but upon inhaling the smoke Docia declared it was the most delicious cigarette she'd ever tasted.

"Yes," was the woman's only response, and finishing her own, she flicked the butt off the balcony. As it fluttered away in the breeze, the strangely yellow ember was the brightest light for miles.

"It seems darker, don't you think? The city, I mean," said Docia. For some reason, she felt this woman, strange though she was, would understand.

"Darker? Yes… it is." The woman turned to Docia, who felt as if she might drown in those starless pools. "Do you know why?"

"No…" Docia felt a queer prickling at the back of her neck. "Do you?"

"Me?" The woman laughed. "What's the fashionable expression? Have you found the Yellow Sign?"

Docia, perturbed, did not reply, turned back to the city. From behind her, the woman said, "Well, I must be off. Good night, sleep tight… and don't let the grave-worms bite…"

Docia whirled as she heard the door open, for she wished to ask the woman what brand of cigarette she had been smoking—but she had disappeared. To her displeasure, Fulvius Elbreth now stood where she should have been.

"Ms. Calder," he said, far more serious than he had been inside. "I owe you an apology. It was unkind of me to speak so freely, and in a group. I allowed my enthusiasm to override my manners. As a host, it was most unpardonable."

Docia was in no mood to be wooed by an apology, however well-phrased. After her conversation with the woman, she saw something distinctly wormlike about this Fulvius Elbreth.

"To my mind, your rudeness is far more pardonable than your views," she said evenly.

He stared at her, clearly at a loss for words. After a long moment, he laughed awkwardly. "Well… there's no accounting for taste, eh? But, I do admire your… passion for the arts, I suppose. It's too bad… I had rather hoped…" He hesitated, then turned to the door. "Perhaps I had better leave you be?"

His manner made her curious. "What had you hoped?"

"That you might accompany me to the theatre. Yes, I know you came here with that meathead Irving, I'm not asking you on a date. Just to come with me. There's a new play on Broadway, one that caused quite a scandal in Europe, where it was banned. A theatre-owner here invited the production, after hearing about it all, and well… at last the *Trib* feels I should go review it."

"At last?"

"The play has a rather dodgy reputation—a blinkered history, if you will. I had to convince my editor it was a good idea for me to go. But I did, in the end. I can be very persuasive."

"Beware that overconfidence. You haven't convinced me yet."

"No?"

"Why should you ask me?"

He shrugged. "Because taking a lady to the theatre seemed a gentlemanlike way of apologizing. Because you have opinions on art that intrigue me, even if I disagree with them, and discussing them over dinner seems pleasant."

"That's all?"

"That's all."

"Well… all right."

"Good!" Elbreth clapped his hands together. "I'll make dinner reservations. Thank you, Ms. Calder, you've made my night… by making me feel less of a cad. Tomorrow, then?"

"Yes, I'll… let's meet in front of your office, you're closer."

"Perfect."

"One more thing… who was that woman? Who was out here with me?"

Elbreth shrugged. "I couldn't say. I didn't see her."

He took his leave of her, and Docia finished her cigarette. It was really the best she'd ever had. Before she ground it out she looked at the butt, just to see if she could ascertain the brand. There was no name, just a strange, unrecognizable insignia, in yellow so bright it might have been painted on in real gold. Docia hesitated, then tapped out the remaining tobacco, pocketing the butt. She'd show it to the man at the drugstore to see if he could identify it. She was eager to find the brand so she could buy a pack of her own.

Roy was unimpressed to hear that Elbreth would be escorting Docia to the theatre. They had a stupid fight about it on their way home. He made it clear he disapproved of her being taken out by other men, even after she made it clear that there was nothing in the world less romantic to her mind than going out with Fulvius Elbreth. He was not reassured, and drove along in a petulant silence that made her yet again question the wisdom of their alliance. She had never yet slept with someone she did not hold in the highest regard. It was therefore something of a relief when his reply to her remark that jealousy was a sign of low self-regard was that it was likely better if they kept their relationship professional in future.

She thought of him one final time as she smoked a cigarette on her own balcony. It was like Roy—pleasant, but unsatisfying; not all it should be. She could enjoy neither as much as she would have liked, not after tasting the one the woman had given her; not after seeing Roy for what he was. She withdrew the stub from her pocket, gazed on the strange mark. She could not tell what it might be, not even under the brightest light of her apartment. The squiggles would not resolve themselves into anything meaningful. "An abstraction," she murmured, smiling. She traced the insignia with the tip of her finger. "What *are* you?"

Have you found the Yellow Sign?

The woman's voice came to her in that moment, her clipped, European accent, the strange, unanswerable question she had posed. Docia stopped smiling, tucked the butt away, and poured herself another drink. As she took it to bed, she looked at the phone. She wondered if Roy would call. She thought not—and indeed, he did not.

She had broken up with unworthy partners many times before. It was never fun, but it was also somewhat liberating. To remain in a relationship with someone she could not esteem would be to debase herself, a betrayal of her fundamental convictions. That was why she woke the next morning not feeling bleak and abandoned, but refreshed, renewed—and determined.

She made herself coffee, and after a hurried cup headed to the drugstore on the corner. There, she consulted with the owner on the matter of the strange cigarette stub. He inspected it, and declared he'd never seen one like it.

"Really?"

"I can try to find out, if you like… then again, perhaps I'd better not." He returned the butt to her, a curious expression his face. "Or maybe I should say… I'd rather not."

"Why? It's the finest I've ever had."

"Be that as it may. I don't know. You… keep that. Don't bring it in here again." He was getting oddly aggressive with her. "I don't want to look at it!"

"All right!" she exclaimed, and left, vowing to never shop there again.

The strangeness of the encounter cast a pall over Docia's day. Usually she disliked slow days at the office, but after her queer morning, she was grateful for the peace. She was troubled by everything she had to do, nothing sat right with her, and all the lights seemed too dim. She kept rubbing at her eyes, until her assistant pointed out how she'd smeared her mascara.

"Damn," she swore. "I'll have to re-do it before I go out tonight."

"Seeing Mr. Irving?"

Louise was an excellent secretary, so Docia didn't scold her for nosiness. "No, with Fulvius Elbreth, the theatre critic. He's taking me to some play that was banned in Europe. Probably has anti-Socialist sentiments or something that would offend the delicate sensibilities of those snooty soap-dodgers."

"Well, I hope you have a good time."

"I believe I shall," said Docia.

Even the lights of the Great White Way seemed dull and flickering beneath the clotted, starless sky when Docia arrived at the theatre, her arm threaded through Fulvius Elbreth's. She noticed, but was having too good a time to care. Elbreth treated her with respect and gentlemanly charm. To her delight, he had called ahead to ensure a booth would be waiting for him at his favorite Jewish deli.

"It's not fancy, but I just love a pastrami on rye after a show, and their cheese danishes are… well, they're just like Mama Elbreth never made," he said. "I hope that's all right."

"How's their corned beef?" she'd playfully replied.

"To die for."

"Sounds great."

"You're… full of surprises, Ms. Calder."

She realized she'd just passed a test of sorts, and was surprised to find she enjoyed his approval.

"So are you," she replied. "Or… perhaps I shouldn't assume. Perhaps their corned beef only an abstraction of a sandwich?"

He laughed. "See? You're making me question my convictions, for while very real, their corned beef sandwich is indeed a work of serious art."

They continued to chat as they picked their way to their seats. The theatre was already packed, and as Docia sat, she noticed they were all squinting at their playbills, or blinking in the light. So she wasn't the only one—Roy was just thick. But then again, Elbreth, who seemed a substantially sharper tack, seemed unaware of anything being amiss.

"Here we go," he said cheerfully, as the lights dimmed into darkness and the curtain rose. "Let's see what the governments of Europe think is too dangerous to be seen."

It wasn't an anti-Socialist play, as Docia had assumed. Nor was it blasphemous or seditious. At least, not in ways that she could openly identify. All she knew was it was the strangest hour and a half of her life, watching… whatever it was she was watching. There was poetry, there was action. Things occurred, and did not occur. It was more confounding than alarming. It reminded her a bit of *Antigone*, which she had also not quite understood, when she'd read it in school.

Her feelings were not shared. When the lights came up—as much as they did—Fulvius Elbreth looked pale, and sweat beaded his forehead.

"Forgive me," he said, when she remarked on his condition. "I fear I must... a rain check, if you will, on the deli? I do not feel I should stay for the second act. Something... something is wrong. I must go."

"Of course. I'm so sorry you're not feeling well... let me call you a cab."

The look he gave her was that of a man beholding a horror. "You're not leaving? You... want to stay?" he whispered. "Are you sure?"

"You are unwell," she said, alarmed by his behavior. "I'll see you home."

"I'm perfectly able to get myself away from here!" he exclaimed, and fled the theatre, not even bothering to collect his coat or hat.

Docia watched him, confounded—but the lights flickered. Eager to see the second act, she returned to her seat, alone.

Docia did not rise to get a drink or visit the powder room between the second and third acts, nor between the third and fourth. She remained in her seat, riveted, entranced. It was the most wonderful, terrible thing she had ever seen in her life. The most fascinating thing was, it was not an abstraction, as Elbreth had insisted theatre must be; what was occurring on stage was more real than anything Docia had experienced outside of the theatre. The truth of it resonated within her, as if the actors' words were mallets and her soul a tuning fork—she felt right, happier than she ever had, at work, in bed, eating delicious food, dressing for a meeting, any of the things she previously would have called pleasurable.

She could not say if she was alone in her sensations. The darkness of the theatre, and the troublingly insufficient light when at last the final act concluded and the curtain fell, made her feel as if she were alone in her seat, alone in the aisle heading toward the door, alone in the street when at last she emerged in the silent, pitch-black city. She looked up, and laughed. At last, the clouds had dispersed, and the night sky greeted her, the swirling constellations of black stars brighter than any artificial, earthly light, the moons—how many, she could not say—emanating a radiance undreamed. The foreign constellations did not disturb her; rather, she realized with a laugh that she had been lost her whole life, and had finally found her way.

The sound of a lighter drew Docia's attention from the vast and wondrous sky. The woman from the party was there, leaning alone against a streetlight, a cigarette burning in her stubby fingers. A trilby, worn low on her brow, shadowed her features, but it was unmistakably her. Oh, but she was a woman who could wear a suit—the drape of the wool crepe looked like a priest's vestments or royal robes of state, austere, somber, even awe-inspiring, but completely natural and lived-in.

"Did you like the play?" she asked. When she looked up, the yellow flash of her eye almost blinded Docia.

"I think so," she replied.

"You're not someone who appreciates uncertainties," said the woman. "Come, have a cigarette. We can talk about it."

She stuck another cigarette between her lips, lit it, and passed it over. Docia accepted it, inhaling deeply of the rich and fragrant tobacco. She knew without looking it was the same strange brand, with the strange symbol.

As she smoked, she found she did not want to speak. The silence was wonderful; the stillness felt right. Content, she took a long drag, and exhaling, noticed through the smoke the gold insignia was even brighter than the ember.

STRANGE IS THE NIGHT
BY S.P. MISKOWSKI

Rain cut diagonal streaks down the windows of offices and shops all over the city. Where the asphalt had been laid by cheap contractors puddles overflowed in the potholes, displacing gravel and slowing traffic to less than ten miles an hour. Occasionally a driver would lose patience with his timid compatriots and hit the gas pedal in a panic, only to be stranded without a lane at the next intersection.

By late afternoon, counter to the direction of the storm, dusk began to crawl over the hills and down to the bay. Darkness spread quickly to half a dozen residential neighborhoods where craftsman houses nestled between modular condos and homeowners competed for a view of urban greenery, although the parks were flooded for most of the winter and spring. There were so many more residents than the city planners ever expected. Street parking had become a vicious contest.

In his cubicle on the second floor of a converted warehouse on 12th Avenue, Pierce regarded the ceiling, listening. The storm continued with infinite patience. A growl of thunder overhead and Pierce imagined the ceiling cracking open, his oblong, cumbersome body drawn upward, sucked out of his ergonomic chair into the ebony sky. He regained composure with a measured pivot of the chair from left to right and from right to left, willing the dreadful weather away.

A photo occupied the center of his computer screen, a headshot of a young woman. Maybe nineteen, maybe twenty, she swayed and smiled uncertainly at the edges of his memory. Moon face; chestnut bob; an underlying fragrance, a mixture of honey and lemon zest.

"Plump," Pierce said to himself. "Not pleasantly, just plump, a fat kindergartner offering to share candy." Remembering irritated his sense of order.

He glanced at the open envelope and splayed invitation on his desk, an arrival in that morning's mail. Expensively engraved lettering, cream-colored paper with an elaborate seal. The wax had been shaped like a hieroglyph, probably a company logo, now broken in half. A stray bit of the saffron wax had dropped between the 'c' and the 'v' on his keyboard.

Ordinarily Pierce hated these attempts at wooing him with media kits. A week earlier a playwright had mailed him a rubber rodent in a nest of straw with a copy of her seventy-page monologue, *Memoir of a Rat King*. Pierce had tossed the package into the trash. He considered the same fate for the expensive invitation with its wax seal. But the oddly familiar words of the enclosed poem piqued his curiosity.

Song of my soul, my voice is dead…

He had read the lines before. No. Had he heard them spoken? The phrases kept teasing him. If he said them out loud he felt sleepy and warm.

The girl's photo, her insouciant grin, had occupied his computer screen when he'd returned from lunch. No one would own up to playing pranks on Pierce. The girl's face had annoyed him all afternoon. He recollected her scent but not her name. Her face was so much like all the others.

He clicked through several issues of the online edition, scanning his reviews from the previous spring and summer. When he spotted the word 'porcine,' he stopped.

Well, it was true, wasn't it? At least he hadn't called her 'fat.' People were so sensitive about everything these days. Who could keep up with the ever-shifting nomenclature?

When Pierce went to school, name-calling had been almost mandatory, certainly expected. Bullying was a required chapter in the adventure of growing up. So his father had reminded Pierce every time he limped home to bury his bruised face in a pillow. But he had toughened up, and that was the point.

No wonder the paper's interns acted like children. They were raised on faint praise and false promises, their education designed to accommodate weakness, delicate bones padded against injury, protected from the world for as long as possible. From pre-school to first job interview, no one ever told them the truth. Pierce could make them cry just by hiding their personalized coffee cups.

He had known the wrath of the sensitive all too well. He'd lost his chance at a coveted teaching assistant position at Berkeley over an ironic appropriation of the term 'pickaninny' in his graduate thesis. The department chair had made an example, rejecting his application, to the satisfaction--in some cases barely concealed glee--of everyone involved. In a final twist, the teaching assignment that would have assured his success went to the young Rhodes scholar who had accused him of racism.

The name listed in his review and the photo on his screen merged: Molly Mundy, roly-poly, round as a baby and just as free of guile. 'Porcine.'

If anything, Pierce had been kind. Molly Mundy had been one of those girls who drive up the coast from Beaverton or Pine Hollow, move in with a houseful of slovenly friends, acquire jobs waiting tables or babysitting, and spend every minute dashing between acting classes and auditions, eyes sparkling, lips parted, betraying a bottomless hunger Pierce found repugnant. Each girl a special snowflake, a thousand snowflakes every year, and despite dozens of fringe theatres and a few equity houses, the city couldn't support their fantasies. There was no film industry to speak of, no TV series, and very little commercial work, only theatre with its physical demands and non-existent pay.

Eventually all but a few of the snowflakes would drift back home to settle, in every sense. They would gain weight, fry their hair with henna streaks and home perms, and marry men they didn't love, men they wouldn't have glanced at when they'd thought of themselves as ingénues. They would birth another generation of unremarkable girls named Molly, who longed to be famous for some glittering accomplishment beyond their reach. Pierce clicked on the photo and dragged the moon-faced young woman to the trash.

All afternoon there had been lulls between the spells of icy rain. Again and again the storm subsided; then came another swell of clouds. In the evening, after rush hour, the dark streets grew sullen beneath the shivering damp.

"In short…" Pierce mumbled, hunched over his computer. His fingers arched and quivered above the keyboard. He was on deadline with another six hundred words to go.

"In *brief*…" Hurley corrected, sidling up to spy over one shoulder. Hurley's gag-inducing aftershave followed, a slowly evaporating shadow.

Pierce regained focus and nodded. Everyone knew Hurley was the worst editor-in-chief in the paper's history. He had attained the degree of incompetence and self-regard of which legends are constructed. He liked to stride around and sneak up on his writers, offering pearls and threatening extinction.

"In brief…" Pierce corrected the onscreen text. He continued, "Actors ought to use their well-trained bodies to *act*. They should not reveal their intellectual shortcomings like stained underwear at fundraising summits…"

"Good! Whip the losers into shape!"

Hurley clapped him on the shoulder and strode away in the direction of his office, the only one with a door. Editors and staff writers who had survived the last cut occupied cubicles with peeling walls ranged across one cavernous room. Underlings, mostly interns, divided their cubicles into smaller, shabbier units resembling rabbit hutches. The only remaining senior editor commanded a medium-size cubicle and worked at a lectern to give the illusion of more floor space. All labored under the shadow of the weekly paper's name, painted across the windows of the eastern wall. The paper occupied half of the second floor in a building that housed a healing arts studio, an herbal tea emporium, and a thrift shop.

"Corner of Zen and Mothballs," Pierce quipped whenever someone asked for the address.

He relaxed the muscles across his back as soon as Hurley walked away. He'd escaped torment this time. Hurley of the many backslaps also enjoyed impromptu wrestling matches and headlocks. He was a boy with an indestructible trust fund, a guy's guy who bragged about squandering his education and didn't believe in matching furniture. Behind that lone door lurked a monstrosity of post-modern decor shot through with an odor of moldering jockstraps.

A rumble of thunder brought Pierce to his senses. He typed. He forgot Hurley. Words raced across the screen.

Only two hundred words from his objective, Pierce was making excellent time when he noticed Ali Franco staring at him from her cubicle across the aisle.

"Problem, Ali?"

Instantly he regretted acknowledging her. The pause was negligible. She must have been biding her time, waiting for an invitation. She strolled the short distance to his desk and stood watching him type.

"Why the heck do you do it?" She asked.

Typically cryptic Ali Franco, with her intuition, her healing blog, her spirit guides and crystal skulls, or were they balls? In the evening she burned aromatherapy candles at her desk. They made the office stink of green tea and wax, and another note he couldn't identify, a spice he found irritating. Ali Franco, with all of her woo-woo (or was it voodoo? or hoodoo?) was unwittingly doomed.

Only a month earlier Pierce had conned Hurley into a drunken ramble across Capitol Hill. The idiot-in-chief confided; he was ditching Franco's column. She didn't know it yet. How about that for intuition? Pierce had to laugh. He was keeping quiet but it was killing him.

"When are you breaking the news?" Pierce had asked.

"Sometime next month." When he wasn't smirking Hurley puffed on a twenty-dollar cigar.

"When the moon is full and the wolfbane blooms at night?" Pierce asked.

They had laughed and laughed.

"What is the subject of your question, Ali?"

Even her name offended him, short for Alice, with the same number of syllables, and pronounced 'alley.' She had been here forever.

Pierce went on typing. His plan was to meet the word count, let it rest, and see a show. He would come in early next day, freshen things up, and hand over the week's reviews to the proofreader.

Ali Franco was wearing a shapeless gown of the 1970s, something his mother might have worn, a caftan or an afghan. Franco said she 'collected' them at flea markets and sometimes the thrift shop downstairs, information that made his skin crawl. Worse, she kept shifting the garment, folding and tucking and then resting in it like a Shar-Pei swaddled in flesh.

Franco said, "Seriously, my friend. Aren't you embarrassed to write like that, at your age?"

Pierce raised his eyebrows. "'Seriously?' Aren't you embarrassed to talk like that?"

She reeked of patchouli with an under-layer of something. Sweat? Ginger? It made him sneeze if she stood near him for too long.

"I write the way I write, Ali."

Pierce decided to skip the performance he'd planned to see. Instead he would give this new company his attention. The invitation was both pretentious and last minute. The upstarts had the nerve to offer a guest-only preview, basically a dress rehearsal at which the actors would undoubtedly stumble over their lines. It was taking place in a warehouse down the street on the very night the card was delivered to his office. Ridiculous. He would go. The resulting profile of their incompetence might do them good.

"You don't even like theatre any more, do you?"

Pierce swiveled in his chair to face Ali Franco. It was too much, the way she crept around challenging colleagues with her political stand against killing small things with big eyes, and her objection to microwaves and mammograms and some other 'm' thing. His chest burned with a desire to shout, "You're being fired, you hag! Good luck getting another job at your age!"

No. He would shake her hand when the time came. It would be worth the wait to see the expression on her face as she marched her box of trinkets and her pictures of kittens and her spell-books down the hall to the stairs.

"Why would you say that?" Pierce asked. "Of course I like theatre, when it's good. When it isn't good it's like watching someone cook and eat your intestines in front of you. Then having to write about it."

"There are ways to write about it, without doing damage."

"How would you know, Ali? Oh, sorry, I forgot. You wrote a couple of reviews back in the day, when it was just you and the publisher and the production manager keeping the lights on all night. You printed the paper yourselves and delivered it all over the city on your skateboards. What a time that must've been."

"U-haul truck, not skateboards. We put together a good paper," she said. "It was honest."

"Then why don't you like my reviews? I always tell the truth."

Pierce went back to work. Franco simply didn't understand his job. He couldn't give people a pat on the back if they were delusional. There were too many untalented artists treading the boards. Someone had to weed out the weak. Even if Pierce had overlooked their shortcomings, Hurley wouldn't stand for it. Hurley hated theatre, ranked it slightly above circus entertainment, the animal variety.

"Raise the bar on these fucking amateurs," he said, at least once a month. "If I'm going to keep a goddamn theatre section in this paper, it better be entertaining."

This is where Pierce always felt a pinch between his ribs. He had to steady himself. Any sign of fear and Hurley would chase him across the office, mocking his ungainly stride, knocking him to the floor, pinning him there and saying the one word that would destroy him. 'Fired.'

Sometimes Pierce woke in the morning, shivering with sweat, the word stomping through his head. He would lie in the pale dawn while the city cast jagged shadows across the art deco building where he had lived for twelve years. He would stare at his five hundred square feet of hardwood floors and fluted glass door knobs, and wonder if this studio would be the place where he would die someday, alone, shrouded in Irish linen.

A weekly gutting of theatrical ego granted Pierce two thousand words on pages forty-three and forty-four of the print edition. He wasn't about to let Ali Franco, or anyone else, interfere. Theatre magazines to which he'd once contributed lucrative features had gradually gone out of business. His day job was everything, financially speaking. Those two thousand words were all that separated Pierce from a world of illiterate bloggers, free-content hacks, and people who carried satchels containing sack lunches and the novels they were writing at the public library.

"You could get more people interested in seeing good work," Ali Franco said. "You could encourage artists to practice and mature."

He couldn't believe she was still standing in his cubicle. Staring at him. Resting her hands on her hips, Akimbo Ali.

"Dear woman," he said. "Everyone is interested in seeing good work. Most of the time, there isn't any. What I see on the stage doesn't please me. Since I have a degree in drama from one of the best universities in North America, I think it is safe to say that the work, rather than the critic, is—how do you say—'not good.'"

"You're jaded," she said. Beyond the eastern window the black sky grated against rooftops and chimneys. Clouds kept shifting, threatening more abuse. "Why don't you resign honorably, Pierce, while there's still time? You could write whatever you *feel*. Just follow your heart."

Franco's husband had given up a successful career in engineering and retired to a beachfront shop where he painted orcas on pieces of driftwood and sold them to tourists. Ever since he'd been commissioned by the mayor's office to create 'an original driftwood,' Franco had been urging all of her friends to quit their jobs and follow their hearts.

"My writing sells ads," Pierce said. "Keeping this section of the paper open. Without my acumen and dedication these artists wouldn't be properly reviewed. They would have only the enthusiasm of their friends, to gauge their competence. They would live and die without knowing if they have real talent."

As if waiting for this moment, Franco unfolded a scrap of paper. She read out loud, "'Astonishingly, in such a minor role, the porcine and barely audible Miss Mundy manages to ruin a production of Ibsen's best known play.'"

"I knew it!" Pierce said. "You left that photo on my computer, didn't you?"

Franco said nothing.

"I delivered a much needed antidote to an amateurish approach. They were a company of teenagers rehearsing in a garage. If an actor has talent and devotion to craft, he should make a commitment to a decent school."

"For thirty or forty thousand dollars?" Franco asked. "Whatever happened to learning the basics and practicing?"

Arguing was pointless. The woman had to go. The paper's intended demographic was twenty-five to forty. They didn't need herbal tea concoctions, holistic flu remedies, and comforting advice from mom.

"You're forty-six years old!" Franco shouted.

Pierce glanced up and down the row of cubicles. No one gophered; no one had the nerve.

"Forty-six," Franco repeated. "And writing like a middle-school boy with a grudge." She shook her head and walked away.

"Merciful fucking god," Pierce muttered.

🦂

By seven o'clock his text had been revised and set aside. Pierce left the office happy to know the next day would be easier than this one. He turned up his collar and ventured across the street.

The nearest café buzzed with fluorescent light, sweating condensation under white awning, a bright bowl of murmuring customers at every hour. Arrivals announced by a tinkling bell attached to the glass door. Pierce decided an espresso would give him the boost he needed to survive new work by an unknown troupe with nothing to recommend them except an oddly compelling invitation.

The twin suns sink behind the lake...

He felt so tired, sometimes, and unappreciated.

🦂

After the debacle of his thesis Pierce had wanted very badly to stage his work, to prove his talent. He knew he would starve in New York or L.A., so he retired to his father's house in the Pacific Northwest. Standards were so much lower there. He decided it would make a good launching pad for his plays. Eventually his success here would become so great, New York would come calling.

His father's house was an impressive rambler spread across a hill with a view of Lake Union. Pierce was granted a small room with a private bath in the basement. There he wrote fiercely, madly, in his pajamas and t-shirts, for six years. A housekeeper left his meals on a tray outside the door. On rare occasions he had the run of the upstairs while his father took his trophy wife and children on vacations to Europe and the Caribbean.

Pierce wrote constantly. He seldom attended plays written by his contemporaries, or joined them in debates about the lack of funding and support for new work. Two or three examples of local playwriting confirmed his suspicion that his talent far exceeded their pitiable attempts. Their writing was derivative at best, hackneyed at worst. It was inexplicable how they continued to be produced. There were days, weeks, when the hunger to feel the raw sweetness of success left him jaundiced, sick and exhausted, unable to crawl out of bed, unable to face anyone.

Every theatre company in town rejected his plays, calling them 'old fashioned' and 'over-written.' Each new coffee date with an A.D. left him shaking, fighting back tears. He couldn't bear to live this way, un-produced, insignificant, while so many people carried on perfectly well without knowing he existed. When he raised the idea of starting his own theatre with a substantial family loan his father disowned him, sent him packing with five hundred dollars and a bus pass. Pierce made the money last as long as possible, for the thought of menial labor made him swoon with nausea and panic.

This is when a former classmate, Gwen, appeared. Pounding one of her silk-gloved fists against his door at a fleabag motel on Aurora. Black suede pumps neatly sidestepping stray piles of underwear and newspapers. Pursing her lips at the sight of moldy pizza. Offering him a salary to write for a weekly paper.

"Because, darling, I'm moving back to New York where I fucking belong, and I promised my editor a decent replacement." And her first five choices had turned her down flat.

Pierce would inherit her readership. He could decide on the shows he wanted to cover and the artists he would profile. In short, he was to take over the theatre section, increase its popularity by any means necessary, and make it pay for itself. This was, she warned, a hard sell. Few artists could afford advertising. Theatre people needed discounts, special deals, and trades. They came begging for a mention, however harsh. Pierce said yes, yes, and his career (which would span three editors and five budget cuts) began the following day.

The thing he couldn't get over about the photo he'd seen was the young woman's skin. The image had been glowing with internal light. Pierce knew better.

'Porcine' had taxed him. He recalled how he had longed to write, 'pudgy' or 'bloated.'

Molly Mundy had come slouching into his cubicle on a Tuesday morning in the summer. She came bearing flyers and postcards—and a puppet, one she'd constructed for him, a puppet *of* him, with a blocky torso and a ghastly expression: tiny round mouth, raised eyebrows imploring, longing without hope. What kind of girl would craft such an awkward gift for a stranger?

She was no opalescent maiden or fairy lit from within. She was doughy and pockmarked. Her hair was uncombed, unwashed, a blunt cut ending at the jaw-line. Crunching bits of hard candy between unbleached yellow teeth. Her warmth was feral. Animal-like, she existed only in the moment, this infant who'd been coddled since birth. Her soft mouth was on a spree, munching a lemon drop and yammering about her boyfriend: a twenty-something prodigy from a family of writers and performers and the founder and A.D. of a theatre Pierce really ought to visit and consider reviewing if he wanted to find out what young people were doing all over the city in these tiny venues with no budget just building sets and sewing costumes and painting and rehearsing and selling tickets and really-really being alive in the way organic performance was meant to be instead of polished to the point of death...

"Tell you what," Pierce had interrupted. "Why don't I write a feature about your group? What is it called, again? Crude Motion?" He cringed inside. "Sounds like the sort of thing my editor-in-chief would love."

That same night Molly Mundy had come to visit Pierce at home. She came bearing more gifts, photos of company members in sophomoric poses in makeshift costumes on bare stages with poor lighting.

"Excellent," Pierce said. "These will help readers get a sense of who you are and what you do."

She had come wearing a gossamer dress, empire waist with satin trim and silk wings. Ridiculous and needy as a child, she lingered in the doorway to his studio with her hands clasped in front of her. Giggling at his poster of Hamlet in pajamas. Gulping his wine. ("It has a weird little aftertaste.") Breathlessly describing a 'radically re-imagined' production of Ibsen's most frequently produced play. ("So people can really see it, really for the first time.")

Pierce nodded and smiled. When the time was right, when her smile grew lazy and her words began to slur, he pulled Molly Mundy onto his lap and tugged her dress up around her waist. His eyes stayed with hers and she, fairy princess in love with her boy genius, let Pierce put his fingers inside her. The quick brightness in her eyes subsided. He shifted her weight and came without ever unbuttoning his trousers.

'Porcine.'

Two weeks later he had summed up her turn as an elderly housekeeper with one perfect adjective. He knew it was perfect because he never heard from Molly Mundy again. He hoped his assessment of her stage presence had driven the untalented girl back to the trailer park where she belonged.

The boy genius A.D. had fired off a predictable email questioning Pierce and his capacity to judge organic, ephemeral art. Pierce had run out of energy and patience. He replied, simply, "Eat me." Lowbrow yet effective, and the last time the company or its boy wonder had come to his attention.

※

He pushed open the door of the café. The place was teeming, thanks to the dreary weather. He was about to retreat when a woman in the far corner stood to clear her table. Pierce felt a pang of distress when he realized the woman was Ali Franco and she was crying.

Bastard, he thought. Hurley had done the deed after hours, fired his nemesis and said nothing, depriving Pierce of a pleasure he had anticipated for weeks.

Franco didn't speak, only scooted around him with her face averted and exited the café. He draped his jacket over the chair to reserve the table.

The bell attached to the front door jingled, announcing more customers, this time a couple of Goths in black capes. They regarded the saved spot with disdain. Pierce had broken another unstated rule of the city by claiming a table before placing his order. He sighed with boredom and wondered what else the night would bring.

※

The Tatters Performance Group was supposed to reside in an abandoned warehouse between Pine and Pike. One of the few not yet claimed by developers.

Pierce walked from one corner to the other and back. Two streetlights facing one another across an alley were broken, making it difficult to read the numbers painted on the curb. On his fourth attempt he noticed a small, rain-marked poster taped to a metal door.

TPG
presents
Strange is the Night

Of course! It came to him at last. Chambers' tantalizing mythos must be catnip to these people. When Pierce was in school Alfred Jarry had been all the rage. Now everyone was adapting Chambers' fiction, usually without understanding it. Pierce smiled. The quiver in his stomach might have been joy or indigestion. It would be fun to teach the Tatters Performance Group a lesson.

He pushed open the metal door. After a second the narrow lobby with its plush carpet and brass-plated ticket booth emerged from shadows. Behind the booth's window a dour woman, round-faced and bespectacled, stared out at Pierce.

He noticed a couple of things: Aside from two old women consulting their programs there were no patrons milling about, always a bad sign at these invitation-only events; and his feet were sinking into the dense mush of gold carpeting. He approached the woman in the booth and said, "I'm here to review…"

She cut him off with a ticket stub and a greeting devoid of mirth or expression. "Thank you for joining us tonight, sir. We appreciate your patronage."

Through the window she pushed a manila envelope with the word 'Media' printed in the same type as the sign on the front door. A glass of Pinot Grigio followed.

"Is the box office also the bar?" Pierce said.

"Only for special guests at special events, our finest private reserve," said the woman in the booth. "Complimentary, of course. Enjoy the show."

The carpet was so thick, so deep and spongy, Pierce had to lift his feet purposefully to make his way across the lobby. He felt as if he was goose-stepping but he had no choice. With each movement his feet sank heavily into the marshy substance.

"Strike one," he murmured.

He sipped the wine, found it deliciously bright and tart. The two old women stood nearby, heads inclined together. As he passed them Pierce noticed each wore a pencil skirt with a cashmere sweater set, one in blue and one in violet, with matching brooches, a glittering arc of diamonds forming the letter 'C'. He caught only stray threads of their conversation.

"There, you see, just as I said."

"Cam, there was never a doubt."

"Please."

"I only argued there was no *frisson* if no one identifies with the goddamn protagonist."

"Well, explain the effect of Kabuki, my dear."

"You're off topic. One identifies with a mask, a stereotype, if tradition prepares us for it. You're obfuscating my original point."

"Does it matter whether anyone takes the hero to heart?"

"Oh," said one of the women, eyeing the wine glass Pierce held. "I didn't know they had a liquor license."

He wandered away from the women. He drained his glass. He made a mental note to make a written note about the exceptionally good wine and its questionable legality.

A heavyset woman with chalky gray hair and orthopedic shoes stood next to a curtain separating the lobby from the seating area. She handed Pierce a program. The cover bore the same symbol as the invitation he'd received, a symbol he now recognized as pure fiction, part of the pre-show theatrics, like the two old women in the lobby.

He walked past the usher. She took the empty glass from his hand.

"No drinks in the auditorium," she warned.

Pierce caught a whiff of jonquil-scented powder, and a hint of urine. "Strike two," he said to himself as he entered the theatre.

He noted with dismay only five people occupying seats, scattered as widely as possible in the small space. Including himself and the women in the lobby, they would be an audience of eight, a dismal turnout worth mentioning in his review.

He fumbled his way to an aisle seat in semi-darkness. The scent of dust, decades of it, confirmed his suspicion that this theatre had been handed down from one acting company to another. Dust, as ubiquitous in theatre as the aroma of popcorn at movies, accrued, layer upon layer, over decades.

Nestled in a surprisingly cozy seat, Pierce studied what the usher had so arrogantly called an 'auditorium.' Forty-nine seats faced a thrust stage without a shred of scenery. In the failing light he opened the program and found it was merely a sheet of paper with the same text he had read on the front door. No cast list. No director was named.

He tore open the media envelope. No production shots, no press release, just another program and an out-of-focus photo. Pierce squinted but he could only make out a soft outline, a blob of light. He stuffed the programs and photo back into the envelope and took another look around.

A woman seated two rows ahead of Pierce glanced back over her shoulder. Before she turned away, quickly facing front again, he was struck by the amount of makeup she was wearing. The colors of her lips and eyes were too well defined, as if tattooed in place.

The feeble house lights blinked off and the room was consumed by darkness. There didn't appear to be an exit sign, a reckless violation of the fire code. A cold rush of night air swept from the back of the stage through the audience. Pierce chuckled. This neophyte company probably thought a tactile approach was revolutionary. Given the quirks and illegalities of the whole affair, his review would write itself. By opening night the building would be condemned.

Following this thought he was aware of a bright amber illumination descending from the flies. He marveled at delicate gold chains and pulleys, crisscrossing beams on a grid, a shimmy of rafters, and the ceiling skewing.

"Marmalade," he mumbled, tongue thumping the roof of his mouth.

Orange-yellow petals spilled from above, lazily looping in air, striking his face and blocking his vision. From the wings, offstage, something rumbled.

"How do you do?" Molly said. "Oh, no! We already met at your office, didn't we? Stupid me!"

His hand engulfed hers. Her skin was sticky, warm as candy on a summer sidewalk. Her laugh guttural, trapped in her throat, her left hand opening to reveal a bite-size lozenge.

"More lemon drops?" Pierce said. "No, thank you."

"Marmalade," she said. "So sweet and so tart! Please, try it."

He refused, disgusted by the offer of unwrapped candy from her bare hand. Later he was glad he'd turned it down, after the yellow gore came rushing from her mouth.

"Oh my god, I'm so sorry," she cried, and jumped from his lap. With one hand pulling her dress down into place, over her thighs, the other hand wiping vomit from her lips.

Pierce blotted the hardwood floor of his studio with a fistful of toilet paper snatched from the bathroom. Disgusting.

"It's this weather," she said. "So warm, and I've been working so many hours, and things have been crazy. Oh, please don't be mad. It isn't you!"

Apologizing to him, with the honey-scented moisture of her pussy still drying on his fingertips. Begging forgiveness for not swooning, for not coming in his hand, for instead vomiting on the floor. Asking him to visit the company, watch a rehearsal, join the actors for supper, get drunk with the A.D. and get to know what they were trying to do. Why were these vapid young people always trying to 'do' something? Everything had been done before they were born.

"Get out," he told her in the flat tone reserved for ingénues he had fucked. "Go."

Prompting the waterworks. Molly Mundy in her rumpled dress and bent wings, blubbering like a child reprimanded on the playground. All sputters and promises.

He had said yes, of course he would see their 'radical re-imagining,' of course, why not? It was his job to review the show. Don't give it another thought. Really.

And he had seen it. A typical disaster lightened by the young woman's bungled portrayal of an elderly housekeeper in powdered wig and clumsy shoes.

'Porcine.' If every person had one word by which they might be destroyed, 'porcine' had been Molly Mundy's word.

※

"Marmalade," Pierce mumbled and went silent. His eyes rolled. His tongue no longer knew how to function.

A substance as sticky as resin held him fast, facedown, petals smothering him. He knew saliva quivered on his lower lip but he had no strength to reach up and wipe it away. He groaned in the heat of a hundred lamps. Points of pain, sharp as pins, ran up and down his legs. Hot liquid spilled across his backside.

"That's enough honey. Turn him over," said a voice. "Let him see."

Pierce watched the pale yellow light spinning, arcing around him. When the smell registered he realized the arc was his vomit, an involuntary spasm. Hands pinched his pallid flesh, to hold and to cause damage, using his skin to roll him into position on his back. His vision was limited to a full-length mirror directly above, where he floated, bleeding and naked, smeared with honey, flower petals stuck to his hair and scattered down the length of his trembling body.

In a darkening pocket of his conscious mind he saw his next two thousand words spill across cheap paper, soaking it and disappearing. A blank sheet took its place and filled with a rush of words that sank and faded.

Fat fingers dug at his meaty shoulders, nails scraping bone, grasping for purchase, gripping, peeling. And somewhere in the wings, beyond this pale yellow light dancing over his naked corpus, Molly Mundy waited in her gossamer gown. Giggling. Patient. Hungry.

Author Biographies

ALLYSON BIRD. Once of England and now belonging to the Wairarapa, New Zealand, Allyson Bird thinks of herself as a new pioneer raising Dexter cattle, three goats and three chickens, on a farm below a mountain that looms over the valley.

Occasionally she is drawn to strange places and people and they are occasionally drawn to her. Her favourite playground, as a child and adult, used to be the village graveyard. Once she wondered what would happen if she took one of the green stones from a grave. She has been looking over her shoulder ever since but has never given it back. Now she is more likely to be found roaming the mountains and asking the Maori to tell her their stories.

She won the British Fantasy Society Award for her collection Bull Running for Girls in 2009 and The Bram Stoker Award for First Novel 2011.

This by Henrik Ibsen is never far from her mind.

> '*To live is to war with trolls*
> *In the holds of the heart and mind;*
> *To write is to hold*
> *Judgement Day over the self.*'

NADIA BULKIN writes scary stories about the scary world we live in. "Pro Patria" is inspired by her late father, Farchan Bulkin, an academic suppressed by Indonesia's Suharto regime. It is her first, but hopefully not her last, story about the Gordian knot that is post-colonial stress disorder. She lives in Washington DC, where she tends her garden of student debt sown by two political science degrees. For more, visit nadiabulkin@wordpress.com.

CHESYA BURKE Chesya Burke has written and published nearly a hundred fiction pieces and articles within the genres of science fiction, fantasy, noir and horror. Her story collection, Let's Play White, is being taught in universities around the country. In addition, Burke wrote several articles for the African American National Biography in 2008, and Burke's novel, THE STRANGE CRIMES OF LITTLE AFRICA, debuts later this fall. Poet Nikki Giovanni compared her writing to that of Octavia Butler and Toni Morrison.

Burke's thesis was on the comic book character Storm from the X-MEN, and her comic, Shiv, is scheduled to debut in 2016.

Burke is currently pursuing her PhD in English at University of Florida. She's Co-Chair of the Board of Directors of Charis Books and More, one of the oldest feminist book stores in the country.

SELENA "S. J." CHAMBERS's fiction and poetry has appeared in a variety of venues including *Mungbeing* magazine, *New Myths*, *Yankee Pot Roast*, and in anthologies such as the World Fantasy nominated *Thackery T. Lambshead's Cabinet Of Curiosities* (HarperCollins, 2011), *The New Gothic* (Stone Skin Press, 2013), *Steampunk World* (Alliteration Ink, 2014) and *The Starry Wisdom Library* (PS Publishing, 2014). She blogs irregularly at: www.selenachambers.wordpress.com; posts sparingly at: https://www.facebook.com/Twiggsnet; and hardly tweets at all @BasBleuZombie.

NICOLE CUSHING is a Shirley Jackson Award finalist and the author of the novel *Mr. Suicide*, the short story collection *The Mirrors*, and multiple stand-alone novellas. Her work has garnered praise from such diverse sources as Thomas Ligotti, *Famous Monsters of Filmland*, John Skipp, S.T. Joshi, Jack Ketchum, Poppy Z. Brite, Ray Garton, and *Ain't It Cool News*. In addition to her fiction writing, Nicole also writes nonfiction pieces for the U.K.-based horror film magazine *Scream*. A native of Maryland, she now lives with her husband in Indiana.

HELEN MARSHALL is a critically acclaimed Canadian author, editor, and medievalist. Her debut collection of short stories, *Hair Side, Flesh Side* won the 2013 British Fantasy Award for Best Newcomer. Her second collection, *Gifts for the One Who Comes After*, was released in September, 2014 and has been shortlisted for the Bram Stoker Award from the Horror Writers Association, the Aurora Award from the Canadian Science Fiction and Fantasy Association and the Shirley Jackson Award for outstanding achievement in the literature of psychological suspense, horror, and the dark fantastic. She lives in Oxford, England where she spends her time staring at old books. Unwisely. When you look into a book, who knows what might be looking back. She is also an Associate Lecturer at Manchester Metropolitan University.

ANYA MARTIN's first encounter with *The King in Yellow* was at about age 10 in a stack of paperbacks with weird-looking covers by authors such as Lovecraft, Peake and Tolkien, favorites of her book-collector father. Raised in a house with so many books it could have been a library, perhaps it was inevitable that she would abandon early ambitions to become a paleontologist or an actress for fiction and journalism. Her published works include: "The Prince of Lyghes" (*Cthulhu Fhtagn!*), "Sensoria" (*Giallo Fantastique*), "A Girl and Her Dog" (*Xnoybis #2*), the play Passage to the Dreamtime (*Dunhams Manor Press*), "Resonator Superstar!" (*Resonator: New Lovecraftian Tales From Beyond*), "The Toe" (*Feet*), "The Courage of the Lion Tamer" (*Daybreak*, Jetse DeVries' groundbreaking online sister publication to the Shine anthology of optimistic science fiction), and "Stuffed Bunny in Doll-Land," a dark comics fable with Spanish artist Mado Peña in *Womanthlogy: Heroic*.

In the realm of nonfiction, Anya has written more than 1,000 articles about spec-lit, film, music, comics, hauntings, weird poets, travel, health care and jumbo mortgages. She is the founder/bloggeress-in-chief of ATLRetro.com, a guide to Atlanta's grassroots thriving Retro revival. She has been lucky to have been loved by four dogs.

MAURA MCHUGH lives in Galway, Ireland and developed a love for myth, folklore, and horror fiction at an early age. Her short stories have appeared in publications such as *Fantasy, Black Static, Shroud Magazine, The Year's Best Dark Fantasy & Horror*, and *La Femme*, and her two collections—*Twisted Fairy Tales and Twisted Myths*—were published in the USA. She's written several award-nominated comic book series, including co-writing *Witchfinder* for Dark Horse Comics. Her story 'Bone Mother' is being adapted into a stop-motion animated short film by the Canadian Film Board. She's also a screenwriter, playwright, and a critic, and has served on the juries of international literary, comic book, and film awards.

Her web site is http://splinister.com and she tweets as @splinister.

S.P. MISKOWSKI's four-book series, the Skillute Cycle, is published by Omnium Gatherum. Two of the books were finalists for Shirley Jackson Awards. Her stories have appeared, or are forthcoming, in the magazines *Black Static, Supernatural Tales, Other Voices*, and *Identity The-*

ory, and in the anthologies *October Dreams II*, *Detritus*, *Little Visible Delight*, *The Hyde Hotel*, and *The Leaves of a Necronomicon*. She's the recipient of a Swarthout Award and two National Endowment for the Arts Fellowships.

URSULA PFLUG is the critically acclaimed author of the novels *Green Music* (Edge/Tesseract), *The Alphabet Stones* (Blue Denim), and the illustrated flash novel *Motion Sickness* (Inanna). Her story collections include After the Fires (Tightrope) and Harvesting the Moon (PS). Her edited anthologies include the CMHA fundraiser *They Have To Take You In* (Hidden Brook) and the forthcoming *Playground of Lost Toys* (Exile), co-edited with Colleen Anderson. She teaches creative writing workshops at Loyalist College, Trent University (with Derek Newman-Stille), The San Miguel Writers' Conference and elsewhere, and she co-organized the Cat Sass Reading Series. Her work has been produced for film, theatre, dance and installation, in projects funded by The Ontario Arts Council, The Canada Council for the Arts and The Laidlaw Foundation. Her award winning short stories and nonfiction pieces about books and art have been appearing for decades in Canada, the US and the UK, in genre and literary venues including Fantasy, Strange Horizons, PostScripts, Lightspeed, Lady Churchill's Rosebud Wristlet, NOW Magazine, Leviathan, Album Zutique, Mix Magazine, The Peterborough Examiner, and The New York Review of Science Fiction. Her short stories have also been taught in universities in Canada and India. Visit her at: ursulapflug.ca

JOSEPH S. PULVER, SR., is the author of the novels, *The Orphan Palace* and *Nightmare's Disciple*, and he has written many short stories that have appeared in magazines and anthologies, including "Weird Fiction Review", "Lovecraft eZine", Ellen Datlow's *Best Horror of the Year*, S. T. Joshi's *Black Wings* (I and III), *Book of Cthulhu*, *The Children of Old Leech*, *Year's Best Weird Fiction*. His highly–acclaimed short story collections, *Blood Will Have Its Season*, *SIN & ashes*, *Portraits of Ruin*, and *A House of Hollow Wounds*, were published by Hippocampus Press. Lovecraft eZine Press published his collection, *The King in Yellow Tales, vol. 1*. He edited *A Season in Carcosa* and the Bram Stoker nominated and Shirley Jackson Award winning *The Grimscribe's Puppets*. He has a new collection of weird fiction upcoming, *The Protocols of Ugliness*, edited by Jeffrey Thomas. Joe is currently editing several new anthologies, including *The Leaves of a Necronomicon* and *Born Under A Bad Sign*.

LYNDA E. RUCKER is an American writer born and raised in the American South and currently living in Dublin, Ireland. She has sold more than two dozen short stories to magazines and anthologies including *The Mammoth Book of Best New Horror*, *The Year's Best Dark Fantasy and Horror*, *The Best Horror of the Year*, *Black Static*, *F&SF*, *Shadows and Tall Trees*, *Postscripts* and *Nightmare Magazine*. She is a regular columnist for *Black Static*, and her first collection, *The Moon Will Look Strange*, was released in 2013 from Karōshi Books.

ANN K. SCHWADER's poetry and fiction have appeared in *Black Wings IV* (PS Publishing 2015), *Searchers After Horror* (Fedogan & Bremer 2014), *Dark Fusions* (PS Publishing 2013), *A Season in Carcosa* (Miskatonic River Press, 2012), *The Book of Cthulhu* and *The Book of Cthulhu II* (Night Shade Books, 2011 & 2012), and elsewhere. Her most recent poetry collection is *Dark Energies* (P'rea Press, 2015). She is an active member of both HWA and SFWA, and a 2010 Bram Stoker Award Finalist. Schwader lives and writes in Colorado.

LUCY A. SNYDER is a four-time Bram Stoker Award-winning writer and the author of the novels *Spellbent*, *Shotgun Sorceress*, *Switchblade Goddess*. She also authored the nonfiction book *Shooting Yourself in the Head For Fun and Profit: A Writer's Survival Guide* and the story collections *Soft Apocalypses*, *Orchid Carousals*, *Sparks and Shadows*, *Chimeric Machines*, and *Installing Linux on a Dead Badger*.

Her writing has been translated into French, Russian, and Japanese editions and has appeared in publications such as *Apex Magazine*, *Nightmare Magazine*, *Jamais Vu*, *Pseudopod*, *Strange Horizons*, *Weird Tales*, *Steampunk World*, *In the Court of the Yellow King*, *Shadows Over Main Street*, *Qualia Nous*, *The Library of the Dead*, and *Best Horror of the Year, Vol. 5*.

She lives in Columbus, Ohio and is a mentor in Seton Hill University's MFA program in Writing Popular Fiction. She also writes a column for *Horror World*. You can learn more about her at www.lucysnyder.com and you can follow her on Twitter at @LucyASnyder.

MOLLY TANZER'S writing has been nominated for the British Fantasy (Sydney J. Bounds) and Wonderland Book Award. She is the author of two novels: *Vermilion*, and the forthcoming *The Pleasure Merchant*, and two collections: *A Pretty Mouth*, a mosaic novel about the fictional, evil Calipash family, and *Rumbullion and Other Liminal Libations*, which pairs short stories with cocktails. She is also the editor of the forthcoming anthology *Swords v. Cthulhu*, and has authored many of her own Lovecraftian short stories. She lives in Boulder, Colorado with her husband and a very bad cat. Visit her at: http://mollytanzer.com

E. CATHERINE TOBLER first encountered The King in Yellow in a soggy library basement, where his tattered cloak spread to shelter them from the downpour of words in rain. They spent long hours together, wandering Carcosa until they had trouble telling one world from the other. When she returned to this world (did she?), she became the senior editor of Shimmer Magazine and a cupcake connoisseur. Her short fiction has been a finalist for the Theodore Sturgeon Memorial Award.

DAMIEN ANGELICA WALTERS' work has appeared or is forthcoming in various anthologies and magazines, including *The Year's Best Dark Fantasy & Horror 2015*, *Year's Best Weird Fiction: Volume One*, *The Mammoth Book of Cthulhu: New Lovecraftian Fiction*, *Nightmare*, *Black Static*, and *Apex*. "The Floating Girls: A Documentary," originally published in *Jamais Vu*, was nominated for the 2014 Bram Stoker Award for Superior Achievement in Short Fiction. *Sing Me Your Scars*, a collection of short fiction, is out now from Apex Publications, and *Paper Tigers*, a novel, is forthcoming from Dark House Press. You can follow her on Twitter @DamienAWalters or visit her website at http://damienangelicawalters.com.

MERCEDES M. YARDLEY wears stilettos, red lipstick, and poisonous flowers in her hair. She writes dark fantasy, horror, nonfiction, and poetry. Mercedes minored in Creative Writing and worked as a contributing editor for Shock Totem Magazine. She is the author of the short story collection *Beautiful Sorrows*, the novella *Apocalyptic Montessa and Nuclear Lulu: A Tale of Atomic Love* and her debut novel *Nameless: The Darkness Comes*, which is the first book in THE BONE ANGEL TRILOGY. Her latest book is titled *Pretty Little Dead Girls: A Novel of Murder and Whimsy* and was released in September of 2014. She often speaks at conferences and teaches workshops on several subjects, including personal branding and how to write a novel in stolen moments. Mercedes lives and works in Las Vegas. and you can reach her at www.mercedesyardley.com.